The Moon also Sets

PEAK Library

Fictional Works

Homing In – Marjorie Oludhe Macgoye
Secret Lives – Ngugi wa Thiong'o
Without a Conscience– Barbara Baumann
Matigari – Ngugi wa Thiong'o
Striving for the Wind – Meja Mwangi
Anthills of the Savannah – Chinua Achebe
Coming to Birth – Marjorie Oludhe Macgoye
No Longer at Ease – Chinua Achebe
A Grain of Wheat – Ngugi wa Thiong'o
Carcase for Hounds – Meja Mwangi
Weep Not Child – Ngugi wa Thiong'o
The Strange Bride – Grace Ogot
The River Between – Ngugi wa Thiong'o
Arrow of God – Chinua Achebe
A Man of the People – Chinua Achebe
Devil on the Cross – Ngugi wa Thiong'o
Land Without Thunder – Grace Ogot
White Teeth – Okot p'Bitek
Street Life – Marjorie Oludhe Macgoye
The Present Moment – Marjorie Oludhe Macgoye
The Promised Land – Grace Ogot
The Other Woman – Grace Ogot
The Herdsman Daughter – Bernard Chahilu
Hearthstones – Kekelwa Nyaywa
Chira – Marjorie Oludhe Macgoye
Of Man and Lion – Beatrice Erlwanger
My Heart on Trial – Genga Idowu
Kosiya Kifefe – Arthur Gakwandi
Return to Paradise – Yusuf Dawood
Takadini – Ben Hanson
The Last Plague – Meja Mwangi
The Missing Links– Tobias O. Otieno
Igereka and Other African Narratives – John Ruganda
The Moon also Sets – Osi Ogbu

Biographical Works

Detained – Ngugi wa Thiong'o
Not Yet Uhuru – Oginga Odinga
My Life as a Paraplegic – Esther Owuor
Never Say Die – Wanyiri Kihoro

The Moon also Sets

Osi Ogbu

EAST AFRICAN EDUCATIONAL PUBLISHERS
Nairobi • Kampala • Dar es Salaam

Published by
East African Educational Publishers Ltd.
Brick Court, Mpaka Road/Woodvale Grove
Westlands, P.O. Box 45314
Nairobi

East African Educational Publishers Ltd.
P.O. Box 11542, Kampala

Ujuzi Educational Publishers Ltd.
P.O. Box 31647, Kijito-Nyama
Dar es Salaam

First published 2002

ISBN 9966 25 151 0

Printed in Kenya by English Press Ltd.
Enterprise Road, P.O. Box 30127, Nairobi

Dedicated to Ogugua, my wife;
Adaora, my daughter; Uzoamaka, my mother,
and all the women of the world

Part I

A Widow's Might

CHAPTER ONE

She stood before the giant mirror in their living room, happy with her build and brain. Aloud, she wondered why she had not been admitted to any of Nigeria's universities.

Oby Onyia stood five feet seven inches tall. She was light-skinned, had a roundish face, long hair and a full chest. She had sat her school certificate examination two years back and attained a superior Grade II.

She had made two previous attempts to join university and failed each time. At 19, she was beginning to worry that she might miss admission yet again. Many of the new entrants had already received their letters of admission, and were busy shopping and readying themselves to travel to college. For two years, Oby had been an auxiliary teacher, a euphemism for an untrained teacher, and she saw no future for herself without a university degree. Some of her high school classmates were going into their third year of university.

"What is it?" she asked aloud. "I am qualified, better qualified than some of my colleagues who have received letters of admission," she sighed. "This thing is getting out of hand." Her thoughts were loud enough to reach her mother in her bedroom.

Oby's mother was counting money and working out how much she needed to buy stock at the following week's wholesale market for her shop at Eke in Isiakpu.

She thought Oby might have been talking to herself. They were alone in the house, having returned from the yam farm less than an hour earlier. When they got home, they had weeded all morning, nourishing the tubers for harvesting in a couple of months' time. Oby had gone straight to bathe.

Isiakpu could be very wet and cloudy in early September. Oby and her mother had taken advantage of the short dry spell to work on the farm.

Weeding was typically women's work in Isiakpu. There was a clear division of farm labour. If you had a large farm, you would ask your women neighbours to help you weed. No money changed hands but those who came to help were given food and drink.

Mama Oby had only a small farm, an acre of red soil. Tough weeds thrived on such soil. Yet your implements were the hoe and the hands.

She had put up a spirited fight against her brothers-in-law to get this land. In spite of the fact that she and her children were entitled to the land after her husband's death, her in-laws considered it an act of generosity on their part to allow her to keep it.

"Oby," she called. "Oby Obiageli."

"What is it, mama?" her tone sounded depressed. She knew she had been caught.

"So you still have ears?" said her mother as she came into the living room. "Who was that you were talking to?"

"Mama, it was Ego. She called in to say hello," Oby lied.

"Which Ego?"

"Ego Nwankwo ... From Amagu Village."

Mama Oby saw right through the lie.

"Where has she gone to? She couldn't even say hello to me?"

"She said that she was on an errand, and that she could not stay long." Oby's eyes barely met her mother's.

"I have told you that if you bring hypertension to yourself in this house you are going to bear the consequences alone. I cannot understand the problem with you children of these days. You dwell on one thing as if nothing else matters. Do you think going to university solves all problems? We have problems at every stage of our lives."

She was quiet for a moment, then spoke in a lower voice. "For us, women in Isiakpu, these problems are compounded by society. What you are going through now may be nothing compared to what you may face in the future."

She reached for her daughter's shoulder. "Let us pray about this admission thing ..." She chose her words carefully as she fully appreciated the value of a university education. She was equally anxious about her daughter but she did not want to show her anxiety.

"Mama, it is just that ..." Oby shook her head and rubbed at her eyes with her left hand.

"What is all this? I am your mother, Oby ... Is that not achievement enough?" She looked her daughter in the eyes. "Did I have to go to the university to be able to bring you up? Look, God has blessed you in many ways." Her hand swept the air in a geture that enveloped Oby's lovely figure and bearing.

"My daughter, let us see how things go." She added, "God's time is best," and moved to embrace Oby, the money she had been counting still in one hand.

She was struggling to conceal her emotions as she turned around and walked back to her room. Oby walked right behind her as if to remind her that they were in this together. That Oby's success was their success. But no one knew that better than her mother. She had to be a mother. And she also had to be a father.

"Mama," Oby began. "I know that God's time is best but events these days do not seem to follow any logic. The other day, Nkeiruka came here and told me that she had received her letter of admission."

"Which Nkeiruka?"

"The one you know. The daughter of Mrs Agbo of ..."

"I know her. I am simply surprised. That one whose bottom could not sit still on a chair for more than five minutes?"

"Yes, Mama. The one who always borrowed my homework when we were in high school."

"*Odiegwu*, life is full of irony," Mama Oby said. She started to count her money again.

"Even Ijeoma, that dunce, has completed one year at university. You can testify, Mama, that none of these girls was in my league when we were in high school. They could never see my back. Yet, I am now a school dropout. I have been an auxiliary teacher for two academic sessions, and if things go the way they appear to be going now, I will go into the third session. There is need to worry, Mama."

"My daughter, all these things are true, but I have told you countless times to let God's will be done. With Him, everything is possible."

At night, while Oby slept, her mother went over what they had discussed. She, too, was not happy. "What could be happening?" she kept asking herself. "This child used to be first or second in her class throughout high school. That she got Grade Two was a terrible disappointment. And now she cannot go to university. Is there some other way of gaining admission to university?"

Many things defy logic in this country, she thought. One is never sure when to queue and when to jump the queue. A lot depends on who you know and your standing in society. She remembered the words of a popular Nigerian musician who said there were those who owned society, and those who were messengers for society. "But what of those of us who are neither messengers nor owners of the society?" she said to herself. "At least a messenger will one day benefit from the master's magnanimity," she reasoned.

She had thought of contacting her brother in Onitsha for help. With money, he could unlock some doors, she thought. However, she reckoned that the situation was not desperate, and that with prayer, nothing was impossible. In any case, her brother, Amechi, was already doing a lot for her. He sent school fees regularly for his nephew, Amechi, who was named after him. He gave without expecting anything in return. His help was expected of a kinsman, but things were changing these days. Now money talked, and brother may not recognise sister. Uncle Amechi was different, but that did not mean that he should be saddled with every one of Mama Oby's problems. God's will be done.

Mama Oby, 40, was born Oyodo *nwa* Eze. She was baptised Abigail *nwa* Eze. When Papa Oby married her, she became Mrs Abigail Onyia. Mrs was a European appendage that came with Christianity. In Isiakpu tradition, women had carried their names to their husbands' home. But not any more. After the birth of her first child, Oby, she became simply Mama Oby. Since she did not care very much for either her first or Christian name, she encouraged the use of Mama Oby except, of course, on official documents where she remained Mrs Abigail Onyia. In Isiakpu, there was no greater joy for a woman than to be referred to as mother of her first child. For a woman, life was meaningless if you did not have a child. Society had no sympathy for a barren woman. Childlessness was not a matter of choice. Yet children born out of wedlock had no place in the society.

You had to be married and you had to have children. Even though barrenness was an act of God, the punishment for it was meted out by earthly men. The men of Isiakpu.

Mama Oby was a devout Christian and believed that nothing could happen without God's sanction. Her Catholic faith had helped her throughout the years of single parenthood. As an attractive young widow, she had endured many temptations, had had to fend off romantic advances from those who should have protected and helped her uphold her faith. In Isiakpu, being adult, female and single made you inconsenquential and, therefore, fair game for the hunters. A young widow belonged more or less to the same class. If she could not fend for herself, as was often the case, she would have to settle into an affair with a man. She had no mind of her own. All decisions affecting her life were made by someone else. Her full rights were only restored when she had adult sons. But by then, she would no longer be young.

Only sons could grant a widow status. Recognition in her husband's homestead was derived from the male offspring, the heir apparent. But things could not remain that way forever. Education, especially for one's daughter, was one way out. It could be the only way out, Mama Oby thought.

Oby's situation became even more worrisome as her mother recalled how Mama Ijeoma had boasted at one of their Christian Mothers' meetings that her daughter was the most intelligent girl in the village. Who was to question the wisdom behind her statement? After all, Ijeoma was going into second year as a History/Archaeology major at the University of Jos. As she rolled from one side of the bed to the other, her head swimming in rings of thought, the snores of Ikechukwu, the last of her children, reached her from the room across. He must be lying face up on his tiny bed, she thought. It was a small room with a double-decked bed for Amechi and Chika, her two other children, just enough room for Ikechukwu's bed.

"Ike, Ike," she called.

Ikechukwu was still snoring. She rolled out of bed and padded across to shake him gently.

"Ikechukwu."

"Ma," he said sleepily.

"Ike, turn this way and don't lie facing the ceiling again."

When she got back to bed, and was adjusting the pillow, the wall clock in the living room struck twelve. It was midnight, time for her to sleep. But sleep would not come. Her mind wandered back to the tribulations she had faced since her husband died eight years ago.

* * *

Mama Oby had always shielded her children from the difficult and sometimes infuriating experience of being a widow in Isiakpu. She had been living in the village since her husband's death at the advent of the Nigerian civil war. Just three months back, she had been confronted with one of those Isiakpu traditions. Early one morning, her husband's brothers summoned her to a meeting at Pa Okolo's homestead. Pa Okolo was the eldest of her brothers-in-law and was seven years older than his follower. When their father died, he held the family together with sheer hard work, determination and native intelligence.

All his children revered him, and called him Pa Okolo, short for Papa Okolo. It had become his name throughout Isiakpu. After him was Uncle Nebo, and then Papa Oby, and two other brothers, Uncle Eze and Uncle Ben. They had two sisters, Oyodo and Oyima who were married and lived in other villages.

Pa Okolo stood over six feet tall, lean but firmly built. He had prominent veins which were noticeable even from a distance. He cut an imposing figure and was a very intelligent man, hardworking, and knowledgeable on tradition and customs. He understood the politics of the village but restrained his participation to backing the winning horse. He gave the impression of being a straightforward man, but he calculated his gains properly before taking any side on an issue. He was well known in the village for his outspokenness. He had been denied admission to the select council of the elders of the town because he had made too many enemies, in part, because of his straight talk, and also because the late chief of Isiakpu was not particularly fond of him. He was still working on being recognised and admitted to this respected council and hoped that it would happen sooner than later.

He was a gifted orator who gesticulated as he spoke. It was once believed that his powerful and emotional speech once caused a serious misunderstanding between Isiakpu and another village, resulting in the death of a young man from the other village. Although not known for his generosity, he certainly knew when to give. He had three wives, the last and the most beautiful being just half his age. Rumour had it that he did not pay dowry for her and that the marriage was arranged to offset the many debts her father owed him.

When they all were assembled, Pa Okolo cleared his throat. He thanked them for responding to his summons. He thanked Mama Oby for being among the first to arrive despite the fact that she did not know what was to be discussed. He reminded them that, as was characteristic of him, he would go straight to the point.

Pa Okolo surveyed the room as if to make sure that all were seated in their right places. The room was littered with remnants of his chewing sticks: butts and spits, and at one corner was what could once have passed for a handkerchief but for its unsightly appearance and dirt from his slimy sneezes, the result of excessive intake of snuff. At the other end of the room hung a fly whisk which had seen many days on the farm and now had a permanent resting place on the wall as an artifact.

"It is not very common to see a toad running during the day," Pa Okolo said. "Usually, something is behind it. Mama Oby, we have all gathered here today because of you." He was gentle. "This issue does not require any delicacy since I am in charge of this family. Moreover, this should have been resolved earlier had it not been for the civil war."

His voice rose slowly. "The point is this: We want you to choose another husband." He stopped momentarily but deliberately.

"As you know, this is what the custom demands. It is also what I demand. After all, I am the custodian of custom in this family. All your husband's brothers are here. If you don't choose one among us, we shall choose for you. My brothers, is that not so?" He ended on an authoritative note as he adjusted his oversize coat and blanket, both of which he had received from Papa Oby as gifts during a trip to Kano. Oby's family had lived in Kano before moving to Isiakpu.

"It is so," the brothers chorused.

The brothers had met a week earlier and decided that if she did not pick one of them as a husband, they would ask Uncle Ben to marry her.

Uncle Ben was a loafer who had spent over 15 years moving from one Nigerian town to another with nothing to show for it. The family had contributed money – most of it from Pa Okolo – to bring him back home and to get a wife for him when it became obvious from the reports they were receiving that he had no means of surviving in the city. Because of his city tastes and ideas, adjusting to village life had been difficult. He was always smartly dressed in secondhand clothes but depended on his wife and relatives for his upkeep.

It was while in the city that he changed his name from Nwokenta to Benedict. Uncle Ben now took great exception to being called by his original name. Many, including children, who came to know of his distaste for his old name often teased him by calling him Nwokenta, which means a small man or a failure, from a safe distance.

Pa Okolo persuaded his brothers at the meeting that it was in their interests to off-load Uncle Ben onto Mama Oby since they figured that she had inherited their brother's wealth. Pa Okolo always saw the bigger picture. For him, if Uncle Ben married Mama Oby, he would cease to be the direct responsibility of the entire family. This arrangement would restore some honour to Uncle Ben and the family. Moreover, it would help to keep Mama Oby under the family's control. As usual, he never disclosed his full intentions to his brothers. Uncle Ben welcomed the idea wholeheartedly, and promised to teach Mama Oby a lesson if she did not toe the family line. At that meeting, Pa Okolo reminded him of the pain he had brought to the family.

"This is a big favour for you, Nwokenta," Pa Okolo said, calling him by his original name, to infuriate him. "If you fail again this time, we shall teach you a lesson you will never forget," Pa Okolo yelled as he stamped his feet.

"You have not told us what you did in those cities for all those years except roaming from one pub to another, watching naked women dance. I am sure you know that you are excess baggage to this family, and we cannot carry you forever." Pa Okolo was never interrupted. He was the only one in the family who could rain abuses on Uncle Ben and get away with it.

Mama Oby was full of emotion after she first learnt of the meeting's agenda, but she knew that now was not the time to speak her mind. This was one of those occasions when the pain of her husband's death brought her so much anguish. His early death had brought her untold humiliation. She rose suddenly, ready to speak, in a manner that would have been termed abusive, but she was quick to regain self-control. She knew that her husband's relations could make life very difficult for her if they wanted to. She knelt down in the traditional way of showing respect and thanked everyone present.

"My husbands, I am very touched by your concern for me and our children. I have always believed that I married into a reasonable and respectful family. Just like you, my husbands, I have learnt to speak my mind and to be direct, too." Her voice was shaky. "I know you, Pa Okolo, as fair-minded and considerate. Since I married into this family, I have come to rely on your wise judgement."

"Get to the point," Uncle Eze said impatiently.

"My husbands, what I am trying to say is that I have thought about this issue for long and concluded that I want to remain single and to concentrate on bringing up the children," Mama Oby had ended on a confident note.

There was murmuring around the room as confusion seized the gathering. Each person looked at the other, uncertain whose turn it was to speak.

Pa Okolo cleared his throat, and there was silence. "Well, Mama Oby, we have all heard you. You were certainly direct. You have just told us that none of us is eligible to be your husband. Thank you very much. We all thank you very much."

"I have not said anything of the sort," Mama Oby interjected.

"Shut up and let me finish," Pa Okolo thundered. "We are not deaf, and neither were we born yesterday."

10

"What is baffling is that while you want to keep busy raising our children, you have not kept your butt in one place."

He paused for effect. Nobody knew what he was talking about. He had never mentioned what he was about to say to any of his brothers. Which was not uncharacteristic of him. He enjoyed the use of surprise and liked to appear to have thrown the winning punch.

"What are you referring to?" Mama Oby asked, her voice shrill and faltering. She had first looked up at Pa Okolo but was forced to look down by his blazing eyes. She was losing her patience, but she realised that she was in a no-win situation.

Pa Okolo was getting visibly angry. "I said shut up and let me finish. I am aware that many of you who have lived in those rotten cities have lost respect for our tradition and the elders. Thank God that I am still in charge of this family. I will not allow any woman brought into this family to bring shame to it." His voice rose. "Never! God forbid." He was silent for a moment and then blurted out: "I have been watching your movements with that Reverend Father of your church. What is his name?"

"Damian," Uncle Ben volunteered.

"Those who have eyes in this village have also observed," Pa Okolo now spoke in a low, dangerous tone as if to imply that walls had ears, and one did not want to be overheard. His brothers stared at each other and started murmuring again. Mama Oby made the sign of the cross. She waited for the worst.

"You are not the only woman in this village who attends the Catholic church every Sunday, neither are you the only one who is a member of the so-called Christian Mothers Association. You are the leader of those women who have refused to cook for their children and husbands on Sundays because you are attending to the Father and his church affairs. How do you explain the fact that you are always glued to the front seat of the Father's car every Sunday and after every church meeting? Yet, you are 'busy raising our children'. How do you explain that, eh? Both of you have been seen giggling and joking as if you are teenage lovers. It is despicable that you should sometimes get the children involved in this immorality. We have chosen Uncle Ben for you. Do you hear me?"

Pa Okolo had exaggerated, and he knew it. He wanted to have effect, to counter Mama Oby's confident response to their marriage proposal.

She was extremely hurt by Pa Okolo's insinuations. She began to sob.

Then she stood up. She still had some energy to defend herself.

"These are lies and you know there is nothing between me and Father Damian. I have not done anything wrong."

Uncle Ben, who had been sitting quietly, dashed across the room in a gesture that showed clearly he was going to slap Mama Oby back into respect but was restrained.

"How dare you call Pa Okolo a liar?" he protested. "Are you crazy?"

It was perhaps a demonstration that he was capable of controlling this stubborn woman.

Under the surface of Mama Oby's placidity lay an indefatigable spirit. Her in-laws knew this. But they had to try and kill that inner spirit. They were not expected to give up. It was their social obligation not to give up.

"Teach her a lesson," Uncle Eze also added his voice to the disagreement.

Pa Okolo did not like to be defended, at any rate not by the likes of Uncle Ben. He reminded Uncle Ben that he liked to fight his own battles, and that if ever he needed his brainless skull or weak hands for defence, he would call him from his grave.

Notwithstanding her protestations and subsequent apology, Mama Oby was fined two white cockerels by her husband's brothers for being rude to Pa Okolo. The plan to teach her a lesson had just started. It was decided after Mama Oby left the meeting that Uncle Ben should follow up and do what he was supposed to do if he was truly a man. He now had the family's blessing and Pa Okolo's authority as its head.

By dragging Fr Damian's name into this affair, Pa Okolo had implied that for as long as Mama Oby wasn't noisy about her "singleness" they would let her be. She would be free to raise her children as she deemed fit and could continue with her petty trade. Most importantly, she would not be encumbered by the custom of *nkuchi* — wife-inheritance. But they had to extract other concessions from her. Now that she had announced her "singleness" at the same time as the concocted affair with Fr Damian had been revealed, the family had no choice but to move in and take possession of her.

Mama Oby was a devout Catholic. She was deeply offended by her in-laws dragging her parish priest's name in the mud. She prayed to God to forgive their heresy. She prayed to God to fortify her faith and not to allow whatever people thought or said to change her relationship with the church or Fr Damian. She had come to rely heavily on Fr Damian's counsel and valued his companionship without giving it any additional interpretation.

The attention Fr Damian lavished on her had not gone unnoticed by other members of the Christian Mothers Association. In Mama Ijeoma's heart, it provoked deep jealousy because she now saw herself as Mama Oby's rival. Like Mama Oby, Mama Ijeoma had lived in the city and returned to the village when her husband was prematurely retired from the civil service. Her husband was not respected among his peers in the village because it was believed he had no control over his wife. It was rumoured that his house was actually built by his wife who never hid the fact that she was in charge. She attended most functions alone, and generally behaved as though her husband was below her social status.

She was considered wealthy by Isiakpu standards but was not as physically well endowed as Mama Oby. Gossip in the village had it that she made her money by fooling around with wealthy contractors while they lived in the city. In spite of her average looks, she had a way of packaging what she had to make her very noticeable.

When Mama Oby came to live in the village after her husband's death, she met Mama Ijeoma at her first Christian Mothers meeting. Their exposure to the city had led them to have a common appreciation and disdain for certain things. It wasn't long, though, before they also discovered that they viewed life differently. Mama Oby was a modest woman who still clung to the memory of her husband's love long after his death. Mama Ijeoma, on the other hand, cared little about her husband but needed the social prestige associated with being married.

She had only two children, Ijeoma and David. After her second child, she was said to have told her husband that she did not have the energy for another pregnancy and that she did not want to lose her beauty on account of continuous child bearing.

Mama Ijeoma's insistence on directing the life of Mama Oby led to a further souring in their relationship. But Mama Oby's diplomacy kept the relationship alive even though she recognised that Mama Ijeoma had become very competitive and vicious.

Mama Oby was to later discover that it was Mama Ijeoma who had told Pa Okolo about Fr Damian. She had met him near the village market as Pa Okolo was rushing home to tend to his cows. She had greeted him and told him that she had something important to pass on to him. She had asked him whether he was aware of the relationship between Mama Oby and Fr Damian. She lied that the whole village knew about it and she was beginning to wonder whether the family would allow a woman brought from outside the village to spoil the name of such a great family. While acknowledging that it was none of her business, she asked Pa Okolo when he or one of his brothers would do what was expected of them traditionally. Or were they afraid of Mama Oby?

Pa Okolo thanked Mama Ijeoma and promised to keep the conversation between them confidential. Because he did not like Mama Ijeoma, he mentioned this encounter to his first wife who advised him to be cautious. It was through her that Mama Oby later learnt of this meeting with Mama Ijeoma.

* * *

In Isiakpu, it was difficult to forget the loss of Papa Oby. The memory of death lived on much longer than the memory of life that was purloined. As the memory slowly faded, the loss grew robust and alive. This was Isiakpu. Here, widows had no right. No say. You would never forget that your husband was no more.

Still, it could have been worse. In the olden days, when Mama Oby's grandfather died, somewhat prematurely, her grandmother was treated like a common criminal. She was accused of letting her husband die. For seven local weeks (28 days) after his death, she was kept in

14

isolation, clean-shaven and dressed in ugly black. She sat on a mat less than two square feet, on a bare floor with female relatives in attendance. They took turns sleeping and keeping vigil.

For seven weeks she had no bath and would only sneak out through a back door to relieve herself. Her sisters-in-law, the *umuada*, daughters of the family married elsewhere, looked at her and treated her as if she had killed their brother. In the family court, there was a silent agreement that she had. And she had to be punished for it. It was the *umuada* and her fellow women who meted out the retribution. Those meting out punishment behaved as if it could never happen to them. As the *umuada* mourned their brother they denigrated his wife for allowing him to die.

After seven weeks, smelly and all, Mama Oby's grandmother was led to the market place on a market day, carrying imaginary wares on her head. As she walked ahead of the procession, the *umuada,* walking right behind her chanted songs to mark the end of the initial phase of the mourning period. The songs suggested that the dead man's wife had partially atoned for her sins. At the market square she displayed the imaginary wares as market women poured scorn on her. She acted as both the buyer and seller. She was compelled to talk to herself as part of the ritual. The entire charade was designed as a deterrent to those who might be inclined to eliminate their husbands in order to enjoy their wealth. There always was an explanation for something. Premature death was not accepted in Isiakpu. It was either *juju* or the evil spirit of a man's wife or his jealous relative. For the rest of the year, the widow wore black and made no social outings.

Things were slightly different today. The one-year mourning period was still observed. Mama Oby had studiously observed it. The 28-day seclusion period had been shortened to a week and the bizarre market outing had been eliminated. Instead of donning black attire, some women chose to mourn in white. But a widow in Isiakpu whose husband died young, like Mama Oby's, still faced all kinds of problems. Things had not really changed. The more they seemed to have changed, the more they remained the same.

Mama Oby once told her eldest child the story of a fairly successful family from Isiakpu that lived in Lagos. One Saturday afternoon, husband and wife were relaxing alone in the house. Their three young children were out visiting a family friend. Without any visible signs of stress, the man had gone into the toilet. He overstayed. When his wife opened the door she found him slumped on the toilet seat, dead from a heart attack. She screamed so loudly that her neighbour rushed to their apartment.

The neighbour, herself a widow, had listened to the terrified wife's explanation and then advised her to wipe her tears first and sort out her husband's property. She was baffled at the suggestion. But the neighbour's voice was insistent. She was speaking from experience. She went around the house, looked into drawers and collected title deeds for the little property they had. The neighbour asked her own children to take the couple's only car to an unknown destination.

It sounds cruel that she was concerned about material things while her husband sat cold dead on a toilet seat. But she had to do what she had to do. It was sensible and practical under the circumstances. She had to protect herself and her children. When all was settled, she screamed again, a much louder scream. Many more neighbours came, and the death was announced.

True to expectations, the dead man's brothers arrived after a few days, and first attempted to secure their kin's property. The new widow feigned ignorance of the whereabouts of title deeds, car, everything. Her defence was that like most men, her late husband did not put her in the picture as far as his property was concerned. The car was probably with the mechanic and she did not know where. Like scavengers, the dead man's brothers combed the house while their brother lay in the mortuary. That was Isiakpu. A man's brothers and uncles had first claim to a man's assets, whether or not he had a wife and children. After all, it was his wife who prevented him, when he was alive, from helping them. The theft of a dead man's property often took place when the widow was mourning. Since the mourning lasted up to a year, she was trapped in a destitute's cloth.

If she dared to ask what was happening, she would be accused of being concerned about material things soon after her husband's demise. She would be condemned for lacking respect for the dead. It was *alu*. Sacrilege. She killed him, some would conclude. "How does someone go to the toilet alive and simply die there? Not possible." If a widow kept quiet, she and her young children would have nothing. Who would help the widow? Her relatives had no say in her husband's family. The only option was to keep quiet. If she kept quiet, she could, one year later, be at a bus stop waiting for a bus while her brother-in- law drove past in her family car.

"What of a legal will written by a husband to protect his family upon his death," Oby asked her mother.

"Legal will?" her mother asked. She knew what it was because she had heard other women discuss it. "A will in Isiakpu is a useless piece of paper," she went on. "If you take your husband's family to court, are you and your children going to live in the sky?"

"Maybe, one needs to go to court," Oby said. "What kind of a society is this? Who will protect the weak? Not the society, and not the courts?" Mama Oby only watched her daughter silently.

"The life of a woman in Isiakpu is doomed," Mama Oby said. "I am telling you all this to prepare you for what lies ahead."

"No mom, it will not happen in our time. Never!" Oby said with confidence.

"We hope not, my daughter. We pray not. That is why we want you, our daughters, to have as much education as we can give you. Maybe things will begin to change. We have been chained for far too long. A widow has no right in Isiakpu."

"Mom, it will change. It is not going to be easy. But I am optimistic. I am your daughter, remember?" Oby said.

Mama Oby had been spared the usual ordeal because of the circumstances of Papa Oby's death. None of Papa Oby's brothers could travel to Kano to ask all the nonsensical questions. The civil war was imminent, and travelling was risky. But Papa Oby had a house in Nsukka town, near Isiakpu. A friend, a Mr Okoye, acted as caretaker. When Pa Okolo sought to take it over after Papa Oby's death, it was a defiant Mr Okoye who refused and threatened him with dire consequences. Knowing Mama Oby and her stubbornness, Pa Okolo decided to let the matter rest.

CHAPTER TWO

Two weeks after Mama Oby's meeting with her brothers-in-law something happened that sent shivers down her spine.

It was a normal Saturday evening. The weather was cloudy and the sky dark. As Mama Oby was coming out of the usual Saturday Christian Mothers Association, she saw Fr Damian's cook standing by the door. Fr Damian wanted to see her. Since he had made many similar requests before, no one, least of all Mama Oby, saw anything unusual in it.

The parish priest lived in a colonial mansion that had two levels. It was sparsely furnished. On one wall was a three-dimensional picture of the Virgin Mary, praying, and on another side was a picture of her carrying Baby Jesus in a way that showed deep mother-child love. On the opposite side was an artist's impression of the apostles' last supper with Jesus, and a wall hanging with the inscription: "To fall into temptation is human but the courage to resist temptation is a gift from God."

Mama Oby was always in and out of this house in minutes and had never noticed these pictures. On this day, Fr Damian took a while coming down from his bedroom. When he finally did, he appeared in a most unusual attire for a parish priest who was expecting a female visitor. He wore a pair of shorts and a singlet that partly showed his chest and its scanty hair. He walked straight to her and hugged her, using his left elbow to rub against her firm breasts.

Mama Oby's unusually firm and full-sized breasts, the envy of most women in the village, had led to gossip and speculation that she did not breast feed any of her children. There was a certain uneasiness caused by the priest's strange behaviour, but Mama Oby dismissed it as the result of an evil thought. When she asked why Fr Damian had sent for her, however, he could not look her straight in the eye. He muttered something to the effect that he wanted to show her something upstairs.

Through the glass windows, Mama Oby could see the thick clouds that had enveloped the sky. It was going to rain. Still, there were streaks of sunlight. Perhaps it was only a passing cloud. But it was a cold windy day, and that made Fr Damian's attire completely out of place. Suddenly, Mama Oby noticed that the priest's houseboy was not in the house. As they went up the stairs, she stumbled and Fr Damian came to her rescue. This afforded him the opportunity to get close to her. She had never been this close to the priest and their sudden closeness discomfited her.

Fr Damian's bedroom had a huge bed, drapped in a brilliant white cover. There was a small table with a few books on it. Also on the table was a gas lantern that provided light whenever power went off, and a radio cassette player. There was only one chair in the room. Despite her protestations, the priest made Mama Oby sit on his bed. Her discomfort increased. A heavy wind blew and forced the bedroom door shut. Mama Oby began to feel like a caged animal.

"What was it you wanted to show me?"

"Oh, just ehm ... these," he muttered as he went for a collection of photo albums he had previously arranged on the floor. He seemed confused and extremely tense.

"Let me give you a little bit of my history," he said. "From my early childhood to date."

Mama Oby was not listening. Her eyes were on the door. She was hoping that a strong wind would force the door open and carry her out of the room as well. The cassette player was playing *What a Wonderful World* by Louis Armstrong. Unknown to her, it had been specially selected by Fr Damian.

I see trees are green red roses too,
I see them blue for me and you,
and I think to myself, what a wonderful world;
I see skies are blue, the clouds are white,
the brightless day and the dark of the night, and I
think to myself, what a wonderful world;
the colours of the rainbow, so pretty in the sky

are also on the faces of people going by,
I see friends shaking hands and saying how do you do,
they are really saying I love you,
and I think to myself, what a wonderful world.

He was acting child-like, sitting by her as they went through the photo album. So many things were going through his mind. He had planned this evening to the last detail but now the risks weighed heavily on him. It was getting too awkward for comfort and he could no longer postpone his plans. The many rehearsals he had had did not stop him from making a fool of himself.

He stood up, bent a little on the pretext that he was still explaining something from the pictures in the album, then suddenly grabbed Mama Oby and planted a kiss on her lips. His hands grabbed her left breast and squeezed it. She shoved him away so hard that he landed on his fours on the small table, then crashing with the books onto the floor. Mama Oby froze in shock. She closed her eyes for a moment, whispering a brief prayer. When she opened her eyes, she shook her head so vigorously as if to shake off a demon and reassure herself that it had all been a dream.

She got up, adjusted her dress and made for the door. She showed no emotion and did not say a word. Fr Damian was seated on the floor looking confused. When Mama Oby had walked out of the door, he quickly collected himself, made for the door in an effort to stop her. She looked back and the message in her eyes was clear. Fr Damian had to plead for forgiveness. He went down on his knees, saying the devil had been at work and had pushed him into doing what he had done. He liked her a lot and would not want anything to come between them. He was particularly concerned that no one should to know about the incident.

Mama Oby quickly descended the stairs, heading for home. She wasn't sure she had done anything to encourage what she had encountered. Whatever she had done for him was out of her devotion to the church. Fr Damian was younger than she, and should have shown her some respect, she thought. She had never taken any of the gossip she had heard about Reverend Fathers and women seriously.

The wind blew harder, the clouds thickened, and the sky darkened. Her steps faltered because she knew the implications of walking home then. It would raise suspicions. She paused and turned back to see the priest standing at his door, beckoning to her to come back. He had changed into his cassock but could not shout after Mama Oby for fear of attracting the neighbours' attention. As she turned to go back to Fr Damian's house, the first bolt of lightning cracked the sky. It was followed in quick succession by thunder. Then it started to rain.

It was a quiet ride back to Mama Oby's house, only occasionally punctuated by inaudible apologies from Fr Damian. The relationship between them was never the same again. But in keeping with her faith, Mama Oby did not tell anyone about the incident and it did not deter her from her regular Christian duties.

CHAPTER THREE

The following morning, Oby woke up – as she often did on most Sundays – at about six. She often started the day by preparing lunch for the family. Almost always it would be rice and *piri-piri* tomato-stew. Lunch was prepared early because when one left the house for nine o'clock Mass one would be sure to be back after 1 pm. No one was in a hurry on a Sunday. The Reverend Father's sermon, tinged with commentary on village politics and morality, could easily run into hours. And when you disagreed with him, you would never show it. He was God's own representative in Isiakpu and he commanded all the attention. The most bold members of the congregation could do was yawn intermittently and smile out of context. Even these signals were hard to read. They could be regarded as signs of a hangover from the previous night's carousal. The choice then seemed between toughing it out with a long sermon or being branded a drunkard on a Sunday morning.

The previous year, a city dweller who had returned to the village to see his parents walked out of the church while Fr Damian was delivering one of his long sermons. The priest did not find it funny. He sent the church wardens after him but they returned as they had left, alone.

The man was tall and fit. His parents were identified in church and given a dressing-down for raising their son badly. "It is a shame unto the family," Fr Damian intoned in anger and the congregation appeared to agree through their hisses and sighs. The young man later became the pride of Isiakpu when he made a generous donation at the annual bazaar of the Catholic Church.

Them say, money talks. And in the church money dey talk well well, sotee, it echoes.

Oby had one more chore this Sunday. She had to bathe Ikechukwu, the family's youngest member, and get him ready for church. It was a chore she had protested against over and over again. Ikechukwu had refused to grow up. And Mama Oby had a hand in it. Ike, as he was fondly called, was already seven years old. No Isiakpu boy of his age would be that dependent. At seven, he was expected to participate in farm work, to fetch water from the stream and to warm his own food. But with the encouragement of Mama Oby, Ike would do none of those things.

"This is my baby," Mama Oby would often say. "There will be no other baby after him. I will mother this one till I am tired of it. I am not tired yet. He is my husband and he deserves all our respect." This was not merely a last-born thing.

Mama Oby had been one month pregnant when Papa Oby died in the crisis in Kano city. Her entire life suddenly became a struggle. The pregnancy too was a struggle. There was the additional burden landed on her by her in-laws and the society. Speculation was rife that she was not expecting her husband's child. Everyone was counting the nine months from an imaginary conception date. But the pregnancy did not quite show until after four months. But they didn't care. They kept at it. Women counted the days. Men too. Even children got to know about it. It became a mathematical quiz and everyone had their guess. Some were certain she had committed an abomination. To get pregnant during the mandatory one-year mourning period for one's husband was an abomination, an *alu*. It was a custom Mama Oby was familiar with.

No harm would come to the man responsible for such a pregnancy. But woe betide the woman who allowed it to happen. And as always, women, aunts, sisters-in-law and grandmothers would be used to punish the "offender".

Her strong will notwithstanding, Mama Oby was worried. Not because she was not sure of the paternity of the unborn child but because any doubts about her child's paternity would weaken her standing in the community and her resolve to deal with the many problems that stood in her way as an Isiakpu widow. This child must not only be Papa Oby's but must also be seen to be his. The child had to be an Onyia beyond reasonable doubt. There were no paternity tests in Isiakpu. There was only one method of verification: seeing.

When Ikechukwu was born, many people – well-wishers and, gossips alike – rushed to see what he looked like. Barely a few days old, the child was obviously a spitting image of Papa Oby. Some rejoiced. Others left disappointed. Mama Oby was quick to name the child, Ikechukwu, the power of God. Again through His power, her enemies had been shamed. As Ike grew, his resemblance to his father became even more striking, not just in his physical features but also in his mannerisms. It was Mama Oby's husband reincarnated. She loved her husband dearly. Why not his reincarnation? No one, not even Oby, would wean him from her. Her child was her comfort.

Oby and Ike were ready for church but their mother was still in her room. There were only three of them in the house that Sunday. Amechi, Oby's immediate junior brother, along with her two younger sisters, Chika and Ngozi, had gone to Onitsha on holiday where Uncle Amechi Ude worked as a businessman. He owned six taxis, plying the ill-maintained Onitsha roads. The taxis were boldly inscribed with the word *Amechi* — roughly translating as "Who knows tomorrow?" One of them, poorly maintained and driven by Uncle Amechi's crazy cousin, had acquired a notoriety for breaking down halfway through a journey to the consternation of the passengers. They would insist on getting a full refund of their fare. After fiddling for a while with wires in the bonnet surrounded by angry passengers, the driver would point to the inscription on the car to prove he could not guarantee taking the passengers to their destination — as he could not foresee the future, only God could. He would often use this point to exploit people's belief in God and escape blame. Uncle Amechi had received numerous complaints about this driver but did not sack him or repossess the car because he was a relative. Once, however, the driver was confronted by heavily built men who found no amusement in his argument. Not only did he lose all his money, he went home with a broken jaw. While he was recuperating, Uncle Amechi repaired the vehicle and hired another driver.

24

The church was about two kilometres down the main road from Mama Oby's house. The road divided Isiapku Village into two. It was lined with *ukpaka* trees, the result of a colonial agroforestry programme. However, population pressure and the increased demand for fuelwood had seen a number of the trees felled. The fruit from the tree is a local delicacy which was becoming increasingly rare over the years.

It took Oby, her mother and Ike almost an hour to reach the church. They stopped often to exchange greetings with friends and neighbours. A traveller had to make allowance for this or he would offend people.

"Good morning, Mama Oby, and how did you sleep?" shouted a village woman from the back of her house as she walked to the road to greet them.

"Good morning. We slept well. And you?" Mama Oby had stopped to reply.

"And the little one?" She was referring to Ike.

The woman was prepared to go on but Oby intervened. "Mama, we are late and you still have time for these endless greetings."

The church was built from contributions of the Isiakpu Catholic community. It had been completed 15 years after the laying of the foundation stone. Construction work had been slow and painful but the community had persevered. The speed with which a church was built depended on the fund-raising skills of the various parish priests and their sincerity.

The building was, however, an imposing structure, a mini-cathedral that all Isiakpu people, Catholics, and non-Catholics were proud of.

"Mama," called Oby. "The Reverend Father is already at *krieeleson* and *christie-eleson*." They hurried into the church and settled down for prayer.

"Father," Oby prayed, "you have guided me throughout my life. For this, I thank you. But Father, the Almighty Father, this year's university admission exercise is almost over, and your child has not heard from any of the universities. You are my pillar. I still rely on you to sort this one out for me."

A few metres away, her mother was mouthing the same prayer.

"Our Lord, Jesus Christ," she prayed, "let thy will be done. I am confident that with you on our side, she must surely sail through this year's admission. For Lord, nothing is a mystery where you are concerned. Make me a worthy mother among my fellow women."

Fr Damian's sermon was on righteousness and the need to have faith in Jesus Christ. He was a powerful preacher, and a strong theologian who understood the Bible. His talents kept him in priesthood. As a seminarian and a parish priest, he had trained in psychological counselling for sexual indiscretion. And he was the darling of the archbishop. His personal indiscretion was not known by any member of his parish. But he was extremely effective as a priest. In fact, it was only after he had joined the parish that construction work on the church was completed. With the assistance of the archbishop, he had mobilised resources from Rome to supplement the community's commendable efforts.

After the service, everyone poured into the church compound, milling around and exchanging greetings, market information and gossip. Greeting friends and socialising took another hour or two. No one seemed to be in a hurry. Here, rumours were started and confirmed. The men slowly filtered away. They would meet at the palm-wine market. Most village meetings were organised on Sundays, and palm-wine drinking was a permanent feature.

Traders analysed the performance of the market the previous week. Specific indices had been developed to analyse market performance in and around Isiakpu. Though not as sophisticated as the New York Stock Exchange, the local markets were driven by certain fundamental rules which the village traders had tried to master. Advantage was dependent on one's ability to master these rules as well as access to reliable market intelligence.

The community specialised in commodity trading. Not unlike the sophisticated commodity trading of today, knowing what to buy and when to buy it was crucial to staying in business. Buying and storing when supply was high and selling at peak demand and low supply was part of the overall strategy. It did not always work out this way. If your analyses were wrong, your losses would be huge. This was not a guessing game. No one did well in the market without some training. At least six months of apprenticeship with the gurus.

Before the advent of Christianity and so-called modernity, information was exchanged over a keg of palm wine at the village square — the *otobo*. This was a piece of a commercial piece of land which was communally maintained. It had a common inheritance passed from one generation to another. Age groups took turns on a monthly rotation to sweep the grounds and maintain the one or two huts that served as meeting rooms or as the village's spiritual headquarters.

The *otobo* was central to the life of an Isiakpu man, woman or child. Morality, respect for the elders and other values were taught to children through folklore and role-play. At the *otobo*, mothers bonded and learnt the tricks of child rearing from one another. During the full moon, the *otobo* was transformed into a theatre. Drama, song and dance, wrestling and story-telling competitions were staged there. It was the place to discover and demonstrate talent. It was the place where the brightest in the village found expression in the brain-tasking village chess, the *eeche*. It was played by two people on a wooden board with 12 holes, six a side. Each hole was filled with four seeds. Success depended on mathematical skills together with the ability to strategise and anticipate an opponent's moves.

The *otobo* would host inter-community *eeche* games. Each village would select its best for a face-off in competitions. Yes, it was possible to cheat while playing this game but it could not be materially corrupted. There was nothing to win. No cash to be awarded. Success was recognised through other ways: honour, fame and respect. Cheating was severely penalised. A dozen or so spectators watched the two players and made sure there was no cheating. There was no need for a referee. One of the players would reach a dead end and surrender. *Eeche* may have contributed to the development of chess. Unfortunately, the game has lost its appeal. Lost with it are its recreational value and the ability to develop skills.

The church ground could never be an *otobo*. Each has a different role.

These days, anything tinged with tradition, including ceremonies and informal gatherings, is seen as anti-Christian and has to be sanctioned by the Reverend Father. Information exchange, like most other activities at the *otobo,* has lost its spontaneity. Protestants and Catholics do not mix freely and Christians and non-Christians can no longer interact even for their own benefit.

Still, Sunday is a special day in Isiakpu. It is a day for a special afternoon meal. Rice and tomato-stew is not had daily. For those who can afford, the meal is a Sunday treat. Making rice and tomato stew was a habit Mama Oby had picked from her mother. It was one meal that every family would rather eat alone. When she came back to the village from Kano, she did not understand why her house was always full on Sunday afternoons. Some mothers and their children would be at her door even before she had returned from church. They would linger around until she had served them with the rice and stew. It was served according to age or relationship to the family. Her children often complained about her generosity, arguing that it deprived them of their meal. The villagers often learnt of the meal under preparation from the aroma of frying onions and tomatoes in hot palm oil. Mama Oby, and now Oby, had to learn how to discourage the scroungers without offending public opinion.

Sunday in Isiakpu was indeed special in many ways. Most Christians dressed in their latest and best attire. Church wardens would fish out any woman whose head, or other body part, was not properly covered.

The church wardens were quite a breed. More Catholic than the Pope. In their overzealousness, they often misguided the parish priests sent to Isiakpu. They had little or no education, and were thus prone to misinterpret and misrepresent the spirit and letter of the Catholic doctrine.

Seeing the church wardens work reminded one of the half-educated colonial interpreters who exploited the ignorance of the villagers as well as that of the white district officers or court magistrates. With their limited vocabulary, they would confuse, misinterpret and misdirect questions and the demands of the colonial officers. There was a silent and sometimes spoken collusion between the interpreter and the

28

officers. While the villagers suffered, the colonial masters and their interpreters enjoyed the power and the booty of misinterpretation. The boots of their cars were often filled with foodstuffs, goats and chickens. "It is our people's way of saying thank you," the interpreter would explain. The people had been told to give what they had or go to jail.

Jail was something to be avoided at all costs. The few who had gone to jail came back so sick that they could not integrate back into the community. They often died soon after. The people of Isiakpu thrived on communal life. Isolation from the community was the greatest punishment you could mete out to any of them.

The church wardens at Isiakpu had become the colonial interpreters of today. They lent an idolatry slant to burial ceremonies, traditional family re-unions and such other communal activities and persuaded the Reverend Father to ban them or have them modified to suit the church. You could be excommunicated if found guilty of idolatry. No one wanted to be isolated. One would have to make several visits to the wardens and to the parish priest to plead one's case if one was caught transgressing. These visits were not made empty-handed. Gifts helped wardens and priests understand your point of view better and persuaded them to persuade one another to forgive you. The often educated parish priests would not want to rein in the wardens. What for? They enjoyed the power and the gifts in much the same way the DOs did.

The Catholics of Isiakpu had no hand in the selection of their priests. If a priest became unbearable, they simply prayed for him. All women had to wear head gear during service. It was one of those rules the church wardens would not compromise on. Failure to wear it was almost as serious as breaking one of the ten commandments. Hair, especially women's hair, was associated with strength, beauty and magical power. If a man died, his widow was expected to shave her head clean. The women of Isiakpu wore head-gears of assorted colours to church. If one took an aerial photograph of the church grounds after service, one would catch double-decked head-gears, apparently competing to be noticed. The women of Isiakpu looked splendid on

Sundays. Notwithstanding all their problems, their strength and unmatched beauty remained their distinguishing feature. Silently, they created the web that held society together and painstakingly straddled the modern and the old, the past and the future with unimpaired realism.

Mama Ijeoma spotted Mama Oby and walked up to her.

"Mama Oby," she called.

Mama Ijeoma was always dressed to kill — often in very loud, disordant colours. She considered herself the best dressed woman in the village and did not like what she saw as challenges from Mama Oby.

"Ah, Mama Ijeoma, good morning. How is your family?"

"We are all fine. We thank God for today."

"Nne," Mama Ijeoma continued, "this your head-tie is one in town. Where did you buy it from and for how much?"

"This is old stuff. Besides, who in this town can come close to you when it comes to fashion? Leave me alone with my poverty ... There are other important things to discuss."

"Don't be too serious," Mama Ijeoma said. She leaned closer to Mama Oby. "Has she heard anything?" Mama Ijeoma feigned great concern.

"Heard what?"

"I mean ... has she heard anything from the university?"

"She is yet to hear," Mama Oby said.

"God will assist," said Mama Ijeoma. She added, "I know someone who can help. He is a lecturer at the University of Nigeria. We can send Oby to him next week. She can use her charms to solicit his help. We should not stand in one place and watch events pass us by. As you know, a masquerade is not watched from one spot. If something defies a straight-forward solution, it cannot also defy other means."

Mama Ijeoma believed in going the whole hog to meet whatever objectives she had set for herself. She sensed a certain uneasiness in Mama Oby. "Are you listening to me or are you going to carry on with your straight-laced manners? It is up to you. But as I said before, you either move or get out of the way."

"I have heard what you said," Mama Oby said. "I will think it over, and get back to you by Wednesday. I thank you for offering to help. It was very considerate of you." Other women joined them and the subject naturally changed.

While her mother and Mama Ijeoma were chatting, Oby chatted with Isaac Eze, a fellow auxiliary teacher. A most unambitious man, he was so content with auxiliary teaching that he was asking Oby to stop worrying about university admission. He had taught for four years now and had no other plans. Had Oby been agreeable, he would have married her. But his advances were always rebuffed. In spite of this, he would seize every opportunity to bring up the subject, much to Oby's annoyance.

"So you are still hoping to leave us this year?" he said with a mocking smile.

"I am not just hoping, I will leave you people this year, by the grace of God."

"But I have heard that all universities have concluded all admissions, including the supplementary ones."

"Who told you that? And why are you so interested in this?" Oby said.

"Let's face it, Oby. You and I have a common destiny. We could make a nice couple. With our combined income, we could raise a decent family. We should forget the past and try again."

"You and who? I do not blame you ... God forbid, Mr Day-dreamer. Who wants to marry a man who has no ambition?"

"At this rate," said Eze, "by the time you complete your education, university graduates will be scrambling for our kind of jobs."

"Goodbye. And don't forget to send your trousers to the tailor. We can't afford to have a teacher who disgraces himself in public."

Oby walked towards her mother as Eze searched for the torn part of his trousers. Oby looked back and pointed at his open fly.

As they walked home, Mama Oby continued thinking of Mama Ijeoma's offer to assist but she did not think that it was wise to mention it to her daughter yet. Oby was desperate and might jump at it without understanding its full implications. She and her daughter could become the talk of the town. It would not be long before everyone in the village was told how Oby, the supposedly decent girl, had gone to bed with men in pursuit of a university admission. The veracity of this rumour would be irrelevant. Since Mama Ijeoma would have arranged the meeting, the rumour would be considered true.

Monday passed without event. The school was out on recess. Oby spent the day at home reading a novel by Agatha Christie while her mother went to the Eke market where she ran a small supermarket. By village standards, it was not that small. During the holidays, Oby helped her mother at the shop. She was highly respected in the village for her comportment and level-headedness. Her presence at her mother's shop exposed her to many amorous advances direct and indirect. Many men saw her as a potentially good wife and mother.

Many had gone to her maternal uncle, Uncle Amechi Ude, in Onitsha to solicit his help, and others had approached Pa Okolo who, although appreciative of the value of education, believed that marriage and education were not compatible. He thought that the value of a woman depreciated over time, irrespective of her education.

Oby always dismissed these advances because education was uppermost in her mind. Her mother had always stood by her and her prayer was that she should not disappoint her by say, becoming pregnant or by bringing home an outcast for a husband. If that happened, she would not be able to face Uncle Ude or Pa Okolo or worse still, Mama Ijeoma.

After dinner that evening, Mama Oby lay tossing restlessly on her bed. Her king-size bed was her only known luxury, and she occasionally shared it with Ike. When Papa Oby was alive, the bed suffered under the passionate use of the young couple. It now squeaked from the many years of service it had rendered. Alone, Mama Oby sometimes had flashbacks of those days, and would shiver feverishly at the memories of pleasure. On some of those lonely nights, she sobbed herself to sleep. But tonight, Mama Ijeoma's offer of help fenced off any such memories. She would not have given it a second thought but for the state of mind in which Oby was, and the girl's preoccupation with the matter. She still thought that it was a dangerous thing to do, but was tempted to broach it to her. She resolved to pray, and invited Oby, who was engrossed in the novel she was reading, to join her. That night, like on most other nights when the going was tough, she ended the prayer with the comforting words from the Bible. Tonight she read her favourite verse from Isaiah 40: 31:

"They that wait upon the Lord shall renew their strength;
They shall mount up with wings as eagles.
They shall run and not be weary.
They shall walk, but not faint."

All her children knew this verse, and Psalm 23, by heart. As they finished the prayer, they heard a knock on the door. It was about 9.30 pm. Anyone visiting so late had to have an important message. It was Oby who went to open the door.

"Good evening, Uncle Ben. Is everything all right?" Oby inquired as she stood aside, holding the door ajar.

"What sort of question is that?" the visitor yelled. "Are you all deaf? I have been knocking for the past 30 minutes," he lied.

Mama Oby approached the door, and pushed Oby aside. "Oh, Uncle Ben ... Is everything all right?" she asked gently.

"Why does a man have to answer a series of questions when he is visiting his own wife and children?" the man asked, striding past Oby and her mother into the living room. "I thought that you were Catholics? These days you people pray endlessly as if you were those Jehovah Witnesses who are expecting the world to end soon. I have been standing by the door for the past 30 minutes."

"Welcome," Mama Oby said. "But for you to come here this late at night, something must be amiss." Mama Oby went on, "We have finished dinner."

"A glass of cold water will do," the man replied.

He appeared tense and was sweating, although it was a cool night. Oby brought him a glass of water, which he gulped down. Then he asked for another. Mama Oby knew Uncle Ben had something to say. When Oby brought the second glass, her mother asked her to excuse them.

"Good night, Uncle Ben," Oby said. "And please do not keep my mother up for too long."

"Don't worry, my daughter. This is family business. Your mother and I are one," he said as his two hands clashed in the air as he tried to kill an imaginary mosquito.

Oby left the living room wondering what her mother could be discussing with her uncle, a man whose only achievement was his being recognised as a father of two. He had no idea what the children ate. She, like most members of the family, had no respect for him. On several occasions Uncle Ben had stopped Oby on her way home from school and after much adulation as to how great she was or how great her father was, begged for money. It did not matter in whose company he was, and he seemed able to time their meetings to coincide with that period of the month when Oby would have received her salary. Oby often obliged but later felt that it was never going to stop. Instead of giving her a break, Uncle Ben had become aggressive. On one occasion, Oby let her guard down and responded aggressively too. That was enough excuse to fine Mama Oby two cocks and a gallon of palm wine for not bringing Oby up well enough to respect her elders.

When Oby left the living room, Mama Oby asked again: "What is it that brought you so late? Is your wife all right?"

"No, eh! Em, I am sure you know why I am here. You know as our people often say that previous discussions between adults are usually concluded with a simple nod." He was looking at the floor.

It appeared that the two glasses of water had not helped. He was still sweating.

"I am not in the mood for proverbs this night. Please let me know what brings you here at this hour. It is already late and I have to be up very early tomorrow."

Mama Oby did not have to watch her words. It was not like talking to Pa Okolo. She could already guess why he had come but would never be sure with Uncle Ben. He was always borrowing money from one household to another.

"Well, since you do not want to understand, I am going to break the coconut with my head," Uncle Ben said as he sat up.

"Do what you have to do, fast. But remember that he who breaks the coconut with his head does not live to enjoy the coconut. So get it over with."

34

"I have come to do the necessary. I mean, eehm ..."

He sat down again and edged himself to that part of the seat closest to Mama Oby.

"Do what necessary? Please speak up."

"I have come to play with my wife as expected of me. I came because I thought that the kids would be asleep by now. It is the family's injunction that I have come to fulfil. My honour, and that of the family is at stake ... Do you understand?"

Mama Oby made a sign of the cross and closed her eyes. "God forgive them for they know not what they are doing," she said to herself.

She could not find the voice with which to respond. While she may have anticipated what could have prompted this visit, she only felt the full weight of it when the words were uttered. She stood up, went back to her room and put on a blouse and did her wrapper properly, afraid Uncle Ben could have lost his mind. When she returned to the room, she walked straight to the door and asked him to get out of the house.

"I do not think that you want to wake up Oby or any of our neighbours. Just get out before I shout that there is a thief in my house," Mama Oby spoke softly but firmly.

"Wait a minute, woman," Uncle Ben protested. "I am in my house. Do you know what you are doing?"

"If you do not get out now, I will scream and by daybreak, you will be very dead."

"Me? You cannot win this. Don't try to fight me. I may not have money, but I am still a man in this family. Nobody fights his or her family and wins. Nobody. And not a widow, in any case."

Uncle Ben was not noted for his courage. He murmured a few inaudible words and scampered out. As he left, Mama Oby could not hold her anger any longer.

"Foolish man, if you come back here again, I will circumcise you a second time. If you think that you have balls, do come back. Look at the skeleton that wants to sleep with his wife. Over my dead body. As skinny as he is, he should go and get tested for all those diseases before looking for a woman to sleep with. Ye-ye man."

At the end of her outburst, she seemed to realise that those were abominable things to say about one's brother-in-law. But she had no remorse. Uncle Ben had turned a knife in an old wound. When he had left, Mama Oby locked the door and looked with disgust at the spot where Uncle Ben had left a patch of sweat on the sofa. For a moment, she thought about the need to burn the sofa, and hissed long and hard to express her disdain. She went to her room. The full weight of the night's events hit her, and she began to cry. It was a difficult night. She looked up and saw her giant wedding picture hanging on the wall. She was only 20 when she married Papa Oby, and was hoping for a very happy and rewarding life with him. She reached for her Bible for the second time that night and read from Psalm 119:133-136:

> *Direct my steps by Your word,*
> *And let no iniquity have dominion over me.*
> *Redeem me from the oppression of man,*
> *That I may keep Your precepts.*
> *Make Your face shine upon Your servant,*
> *And teach me Your statutes.*
> *Rivers of water run down from my eyes,*
> *Because men do not keep Your laws."*

Oby was struggling to keep awake so that she could eavesdrop on the conversation between her mother and Uncle Ben. She did not hear much but sensed that it was not a very friendly chat. She knew how much her mother wanted to protect them and had, therefore, resisted the urge to come out when she heard her mother's voice rising. Oby had always felt grown up and thought that she should join hands with her mother to fight for their rights. She knew that if she had been a boy, the situation would have been significantly different. She knew that her younger brother had more rights in the family than she did.

She was a passenger in her own family. She could only acquire rights in her husband's home when and if she got married. Her mother's attitude on this frustrated her as well because by shielding her from these issues, she appeared to suggest that she was immature or that she subscribed to the tradition that excluded women from family matters because they did not belong there. She thought that since her mother valued her judgment, and often sought her advice, the answer must lie in the latter. These thoughts were going through her mind that night as she lay half-awake. When she finally got up, and went to her mother's room to find out what had transpired, she found her mother asleep with her Bible clutched close to her chest. She did not bring up the subject again.

CHAPTER FOUR

Amechi returned with his two sisters, Chika and Ngozi, the following Tuesday. Amechi had just completed his school certificate examinations and was waiting for the results. He was not as gifted in schoolwork as Oby, but it was difficult to say. He put in minimal effort to enable him progress from one class to the next. It was Oby's interest and advice that sustained him through secondary school.

He wanted to start a motor-parts apprenticeship soon after his primary school. He had seen their mother struggle to pay school fees and did not want to burden her any more. He had always felt that going into business and making money like his uncle in Onitsha would get them out of their financial difficulties. He had seen many other young men driving flashy cars in the town whenever he had gone to collect his school fees from Uncle Amechi.

Oby's argument, that he would become a better and more successful businessman if he had a university education, did not make much sense to him. His father was a successful businessman and Uncle Amechi was doing very well — and none of them had a post-primary education. But for her mother's persistence and Uncle Amechi's offer to pay his fees, he would have completed six years of apprenticeship.

As he awaited for his results, Oby, Mama Oby and Uncle Amechi prayed that he would do well. They still believed further education would be in his interest. That was what his father would have insisted on. He knew that it would be a miracle for him to make the grade for university admission, and was already planning for his apprenticeship. With a secondary school education he would now do three to four years instead of six.

In Isiakpu, like in most parts of Igboland, there was a unique apprenticeship scheme. It was designed to redistribute wealth from the rich to the poor. As one's business expanded and as one became prosperous, it became necessary to hire more hands to assist in the business. Rather than hire labour, a businessman would recruit apprentices who would provide "free" services. He would, in turn, train them in his line of business and provide them with the initial set-up capital. The master was not afraid of competition from his boys. Rather, a strong, almost filial loyalty developed over the years. Boys who had been settled by their trainers were also often used as retail outlets for the masters. Traditionally, there was a social contract, an understanding that this would happen. Master would settle his servant at the end of an agreed period. Now, formal agreements have replaced this social contract because trust has become increasingly rare.

The system had endured and Amechi was hoping to be part of it. The oil boom had encouraged many young men in Isiakpu and the surrounding towns and villages to go into business. Cheap imported agricultural commodities had made farming unattractive as a business. A new middle class was emerging, and the educated were hardly part of it. As the fortunes of the educated diminished, those of the young businessmen rose. This perception was, however, often wrong. Success in business was often exaggerated. A few successful businessmen was all boys like Amechi needed to see. They often failed to see those who did not succeed. Every apprentice visualised himself as a major importer and exporter, owning a fleet of flashy cars and houses in a short time. Who would deny Amechi this dream?

The family had just settled down to lunch at about midday on Wednesday when the officer in charge of the village postal agency rushed into the compound, envelope in hand.

"Where is Oby?" he asked. "I have brought you good news."

Oby had asked the officer to be on the lookout for any letters addressed to her.

"I am here," Oby said.

She rushed out to meet the postal agent who was extremely proud to be associated with what he thought must be good news. Oby opened the letter cautiously as she trembled. She knew some universities also sent letters of regret. Such a letter was known as an "obituary" by the youth who were anxious to gain university admission. Both the regret letters and obituaries, which were common in the Nigerian newspapers, all started in the same style. In the case of universities, the letters usually started: "We regret to inform you that your application ... was not successful," and the obituaries read, "With deep sorrow we regret to announce the death of ..."

Oby jumped into the air. She had been offered admission to the University of Embakassi to study sociology. Not her first choice. But right now, any course would do. That could be one of the reasons why her admission letter was coming that late, she applied to study English as her first choice. Sociology was her second.

"Mama, Mama," Oby called. "The admission has come. I am going to the University of Embakassi."

Mama Oby rushed out in great joy and embraced her daughter. She grabbed the mailman and hugged him as well. She was overwhelmed with joy. She knelt down and made the sign of the cross, thanking God for coming to their rescue.

"God," she said, "You have rescued me as you have always done before. You have silenced my enemies. They should go away in shame. God, thank you, Sir. You provide when no one is expecting."

Amechi was thrilled, too, but Ike, Ngozi and Chika did not fully understand what was going on. The excitement, the dancing and the noise attracted their neighbours who joined in the celebration as soon as they learnt of the news. While many did not fully appreciate what this meant for Oby and her mother, they were happy to rejoice at anything that made Mama Oby that excited. They had not seen her that way in a long time, and to many, she was simply a kind and generous woman. As each one of the women entered her compound she would ask them to join her in thanking God, and this was followed by a popular thanksgiving chorus which they sang.

"Mama Oby, what is happening here?" each of them had asked on arrival.

"God has performed wonders for my poor self. Who am I?" Mama Oby would say on each occasion, before going into the details of what had caused the celebration. Each one of them rushed to Oby, hugged her and praised her for having performed brilliantly.

"I am not surprised," one of the women said. "I have always

observed Oby's behaviour from the time she went to high school up till the time she became a Miss in the primary school. She has always behaved differently from other young educated girls in our village who pursue men like flies follow faeces."

"That is true," another said. "She is as reserved as her father was."

"A great man has begat a great daughter. The leopard has left its spots."

When the excitement had gone down, Mama Oby remembered the messenger.

"Oby, give the officer a chair to sit on. Officer, we are very sorry. Please excuse us. When God has been kind to you, you should praise Him fourfold."

"Yes, yes," the officer who was lost for words seemed to be nodding in agreement. "It is just that in my many years as a postal agent, I never imagined that a single letter could bring so much joy. We learn and experience new things every day, don't we?"

"Just praise the Lord for me. If I had another son today, I would name him Ejikeme — It-is-not-by-our-own-powers."

"No. No. It is by the power of God," the officer said.

He thought there was more than met the eye but did not know how to explain it. It was none of his business but Mama Oby's prayer got him thinking. He did not understand it. Nobody fully understood it.

"Please sit down, sir. What can we offer you?" Oby asked as she placed a seat behind the officer.

"Nothing really, nothing. I am only doing my job."

"No, you have to have something. What of a bottle of Star beer, sir?"

"Make it a big bottle of Guinness stout instead. I understand that it has certain medicinal value for older and weaker bones like mine."

"I have to check if it is available."

Oby was a little surprised at the sudden change of attitude.

"Check very well, my daughter. A great thing has happened to this home."

Oby did not find the Guinness but sent Amechi to a nearby kiosk to buy one. In the meantime, she came back to find out if the officer would have some food. Mama Oby was busy at the other end of the compound distributing biscuits to the women who had come to rejoice with her.

"Officer, I will get you the Guinness. But how about something to eat?"

"Don't worry about food. The only problem is that I have missed my lunch in all this commotion here."

Oby did not ask further. She had got the cue. The officer quickly settled down to a plate of rice and Guinness. He did not attempt to go back to his office after the food and drink. As he hobbled home, he was whistling a happy tune, and was saying to himself: "Today was better than yesterday. *Ikeme* is a good name for a son. It is indeed not by our own powers." He was thanking God for having placed this opportunity before him. It had been more than two months since he had taken a beer on account of the biting inflation, and the ever-increasing price of alcohol.

Late in the evening, when it became evident that there would be no more visitors, Mama Oby called her daughter to her room to discuss plans and work out the money needed. The euphoria over, the two had to face reality. Mama Oby knew she could send Oby to university but it would be a great sacrifice. A sacrifice she was willing to make. She would not want any of her children to feel the absence of their father. Oby fully appreciated the situation and was overly sympathetic.

Oby's admission had come late. By the time she reported, she would have missed the orientation period and some introductory lectures. There was no time to lose.

"Oby, a great thing has happened to this family. Let's not slight it. I thank you for placing me well above my mates. I don't know what would have become of us if I had taken some of the advice I was receiving on this admission thing." Her mind wandered off to Mama Ijeoma.

"We thank God, Ma. What suggestions are you referring to?"

"No, forget that. I called you so that we can start putting our heads together on what you need to buy, how much money you need to take with you and so on. I would like to throw a small send-off party for you as well."

42

"Mama, did I hear you well? A send-off what? Even if I am going to America, I would not want a send-off party. We need all the money we can get."

"My daughter, you don't understand. You are the first member of this family to go to university. This is more than going to America for me. Besides, I would be doing it the way your father would have done it if he had been alive. Except, of course, that he would have done it in a much bigger way."

"There is no point in arguing with you. I know how uncompromising you can be on some issues. But I have to be at the university as soon as possible. I am told lectures may have started already."

"When do you propose to leave?"

"This Saturday would be ideal. But it depends on the availability of money. We can only run at our pace."

"Run at our own pace? Lecturers will freeze and wait till you get there before they start teaching? We should aim for Saturday. I will send Amechi to your uncle in Onitsha tomorrow. I will give you some money for shopping tomorrow and we shall have the send-off party on Friday."

"I don't think I will be buying much, Mama. I don't even know as yet what one needs at university. It is not like going to high school. But Mama, where will the money come from?"

"We will manage. God drives away flies for a cow without a tail. We shall manage. Let it not bother you. I have just received some money from the caretaker of our house at Nsukka."

"But that is not even enough to pay school fees for Chika or to meet the expenses at home."

"I have told you not to worry. Everything is in God's hands."

"I believe in God too, but ... Mama."

"But what? Never you doubt the powers of God or He shall visit His wrath on you. Never! My only regret is that events such as this remind me of your father's absence. If he was here, you and I would only be preoccupied with the shopping list and the guest list for the Friday party. He was a kind and generous man. But as things stand now, we have to rely on the rent from the house at Nsukka and on our small savings."

"I thank God for your foresight and dedication, Mama. What would we have done?"

"Indeed, my daughter, where would we have gone to? Or who would we have relied on? My brother, perhaps? But he has his own problems, and his wife is a hard nut to crack. You are no longer a small girl. Since your father died, who among his relatives ever cared whether we ate or slept hungry? None of them has asked how I am coping with school fees. They believe that your father left me millions of naira to spend lavishly. They have been saying it behind my back without knowing that even walls have ears. But when it comes to making marriage proposals for you, they are quick to take you as their daughter and they will not hesitate to wake me up at three in the morning."

Oby had nothing to say. She had punctuated her mother's loud reminiscence with hisses in appreciation of all she was saying. It had been a long day, and she was also getting tired and sleepy. Her mother had inadvertently taken a route she now wanted to avoid. She had to let go sometimes if she was to avoid having a major breakdown.She suddenly realised what she was doing and asked Oby to go to bed.

Now alone, Oby's mother thought about how different life would have been if Papa Oby had been alive. Alfred Onyia, Papa Oby, as he was fondly referred to, died on the eve of the civil war. He had been living with his family in Kano, a historic and important commercial city in northern Nigeria. Oby was only ten when she last saw him. Her father had sent them home during the crisis that was to lead to the Nigerian civil war. As a strong nationalist, he was optimistic that nothing would happen to him, and that the crisis would be short. He also felt that he could rely on his many friends from the North to protect him if things got out of hand.

In spite of all the pleas from his wife and other relatives in the North that he go home with his family, Papa Oby did not budge. He believed that he had a right of residence in any part of Nigeria, and that the war-mongers were few and misguided. He was killed in the second massacre of the Igbos. His body was never found.

Papa Oby was a fairly successful businessman. He had built a

44

one-storey house in Kano, part of which he had rented out. He had also built an eight-room L-shaped house at Nsukka which was also rented out. After the civil war, the house in Kano was declared abandoned property and confiscated by Kano State. It was only through the intercession of their friends in Kano that Mama Oby was paid some compensation for the building. She spent a good part of the money performing befitting funeral rites for her husband. Part of the money was also used to see both Oby and Amechi through high school. The balance provided the initial capital for her business.

Mama Oby did not understand how one could abandon one's property in one's own country. The more she raised questions, the more complicated the answers became. Her friends told her that it was futile trying to question government decisions since the powers of the state were pervasive. But what of justice? She often wondered whether it was not the failure to address such injustices after the war that had led to the apparent lack of moral authority on the part of the government to keep Nigeria as one stable nation. It appeared to her that the Nigerian moral fibre was so decayed that the sins of the past were never treated seriously. We should not always forgive neither should we forget, she thought. Justice was an act of understanding, and not necessarily one of revenge. She prayed and hoped for Nigeria's salvation, believing that as long as her past remained unatoned for, it would continue to live with her people, and would continue to drag her people down.

CHAPTER FIVE

Amechi had set off for Onitsha very early in the morning. He caught the first bus from Nsukka. It was intended that he would give his uncle news of Oby's admission to university and return to Isiakpu the same day. By 11.00 am he was in Onitsha. As usual, instead of using the money for a taxi to his uncle's house, he walked the three kilometres to his uncle's house. It took him barely twenty minutes to get there. He was walking like someone possessed by some spirit.

"Ah ah, Amechi! Is everything okay?" his uncle asked in surprise. The boy had left his house only a few days before.

"Yes, sir. Good morning, sir?"

"What is 'yes, sir'? How is your mother and the kids? Has anything happened to the family?"

"No, sir."

"Now, it is 'no sir'! Which one is it?" he had interrupted his late mornin', meal and was eager for his nephew's news.

"My mother sent me to inform you that Oby has been admitted to university."

"That is very good news. So why didn't you say so instead of 'yes sir!' and 'no sir'! You kids can give someone high blood pressure."

"Yes, sir. Where is auntie?"

"She will soon be back. She went to visit a neighbour whose child is sick. What is wrong with Oby, why didn't she come herself?" his uncle inquired as he resumed eating *garri fufu* and *okro* soup.

"Mama told me that Oby is supposed to have reported to school a week ago. So she is very busy getting things ready. Mama wants me to inform you also that she is organising a small send-off party for Oby on Friday, and that you must attend. She said that you are the only one she can rely on."

"Don't mind your mother. Come and wash your hands and eat.

"But uncle, I am not hungry. Besides, I am supposed to go back to Isiakpu today to assist Oby and Mama."

"Stupid boy. Come and eat. You want to go back without eating ... And when you collapse on the way they would say that you were coming from whose house?"

"Yes, sir." He washed his hands and joined his uncle at the dining table.

"Well, all eyes will now be on you. If you do not follow your sister's footsteps, you will be declared a failure. It would not sound well that the daughter of A!fred Onyia went to university and his first son is a motor mechanic. I would be the last person to see that happen."

"I will not disappoint you, sir."

"You'd better not. My wife and I have already told you that we will pay for your education."

His wife walked in just as he was talking about money. She, too, was surprised to see Amechi. But since her nephew and her husband were busy eating and talking calmly, she knew it was not a bad thing that had brought him back.

"Auntie, good morning?"

"Amechi, good morning. Is everything okay?"

"Yes, ma."

"So, how is the child you went to see?" her husband inquired.

"He is fine. He had high fever."

"Amechi has come to inform us that Oby has been offered admission to university. Before you start asking why Oby is not here, I have also been informed that she is leaving on Saturday, and we have been invited to her send-off party on Friday. Amechi will go back as soon as he finishes eating."

"Oby the great! Why am I not surprised. She is a very brilliant and well-behaved girl. I hope that the university doesn't spoil her as it has spoilt so many highly educated women. I don't know whether there is something that they teach them there which makes men afraid of them. Many of them remain unmarried after university. But I trust Oby. She is very clever and well brought up.

"So we are going to Isiakpu on Friday?"

"Yes, by the grace of God. I have to be with my sister on this joyous occasion."

"Those of us without sisters, *nko*?"

"That is your problem. Amechi, eat quickly. You have to leave now if you are to get to Isiakpu in good time. I have to send you to your mom." He stood up and went to the bedroom.

Soon after, as he counted the money to send to Mama Oby, his wife walked in. She had already sensed what her husband was doing and had followed him to put a check on his generosity.

"How much are you planning to give her?" she asked innocently.

"One thousand naira."

"One thousand what? Even if she was going to America, we would not give her one thousand naira." She took the money and counted it herself. She divided it into two and gave him back five hundred naira.

"Is this enough?" he asked.

"If it is not enough, let others supplement. You are not supposed to cry more than the bereaved, otherwise they will think that you had a hand in the person's death. Remember you still owe me that gold-set we saw at the jewellery store, Mr Father Christmas."

Amechi left soon after, with the five hundred naira for his mother, and fifty naira for his transport.

"Ochendu, do you still want more food," Uncle Amechi's wife asked him. "I know that your ration has been reduced by the child."

Ochendu – one who protects life – was an unofficial traditional title given to Uncle Amechi by his fellow businessmen in Onitsha. He had done some of them big favours. His title was, however, not recognised in his village or town. Traditional titles were accorded a lot of respect if properly acquired. They were usually bestowed on important sons and, sometimes daughters, who had distinguished themselves in certain ways or contributed to the development of the town. Money now tended to determine who got a title.

Uncle Amechi's sycophants and admirers often addressed him as Ochendu. His wife used the title when she needed to extract a favour from him. But his sister, Mama Oby, detested the title because she believed that only God protected life.

"Eehe! What are you up to? I am satisfied."

Uncle Amechi loved *garri fufu* and *okro* soup. He disliked the cassava *fufu* because of the shame it brought him when he was a pupil in primary school. Uncle Amechi had often eaten cassava *fufu* in the morning before going to school. Oftentimes the *fufu* would be the left-over from the previous night's dinner. One day, he had suddenly come down with malaria and threw up in the classroom. His vomit had pellets of cassava *fufu* which filled the room with an awful stench. The teacher, who had been caught unawares by Uncle Amechi's sickness walked close to him and screamed: "Are these bullets or what? Cassava *fufu* for breakfast?" And the class roared in laughter. The teacher declared a ten-minute recess. After the incident, Uncle Amechi was nicknamed bullet, an alias he reluctantly accepted. He vowed , however, that if he grew up and took charge of his affairs, he would never allow cassava into his house. That decree still stands.

CHAPTER SIX

Oby's last week in Isiakpu was a very busy one: preparations before leaving for university, visits to friends and relatives. Everyone she visited had some advice to add to what she had already been told. Not everyone understood the importance of a university education for a woman. But they were all happy that Oby had maintained a sense of respect for tradition and avoided fooling around with men.

Many expressed fear that she was going to a place known for witchcraft. Knowing her mother's faith, many did not dare suggest that she seeks protection from their own medicine men. They knew what Mama Oby's answer would be: "Leave everything in the hands of God. It is not by our own power."

For Oby, the visits brought her face to face with the difficult life the villagers lived, especially the women. She knew she was lucky to be going to university and saw the challenges ahead as a badge of privilege. Oby knew that despite government rhetoric, fewer and fewer girls were gaining admission to the university. Her village was still asleep as far as female education was concerned.

The send-off party was well attended. The people of Isiakpu always looked for a chance to feast. Many women volunteered to help Mama Oby cook. Her protests that the occasion was a very small affair did not deter them from assembling at her home that Friday morning. Many turned up with three or four children who would no doubt have an opportunity to fight their apparent malnutrition at the party. Cooking, for her, was an art and the villagers attributed it to her city experience. But on this type of occasion, Mama Oby would prepare a special dish for select guests from the city like Uncle Amechi. Excluded from this category were those who appreciated good food but whose social circumstances had banished memories of its look and taste. There had to be a limit to egalitarianism, even for Mama Oby. Usually, special food was not served in full view of everyone to avoid bad belly aching from on-lookers.

Earlier that day, Amechi had gone to the neighbouring village to buy some of the quality palm wine for which it was noted. Pa Okolo also brought two gallons of palm wine in demonstration of his support. He never forgot that one day he would preside over Oby's dowry negotiations and wanted people to know that he had contributed his share for her upkeep. He left specific instructions that some of the "special palm wine" be kept for Uncle Amechi, who was expected from Onitsha. Pa Okolo did not want what he considered an act of generosity on his part to go unnoticed by important people.

By 3.00 pm, most of the guests were seated, and food and drinks were being served. People sat in small groups in the small village square close to Mama Oby's homestead. People sat according to their age, each closer to those he or she was familiar with. Oby was busy serving or directing others to serve guests. The children, many with rotund bellies and skinny legs, sat with their mothers, but had their eyes fixed on their fathers sitting close by. They ran between both parents, if both were present, depending on where the child thought there were better prospects of oiling one's hands and mouth.

Uncle Amechi arrived at 4.00 pm at the climax of the party. Behind him was his wife, who was dressed in a two-piece, white and blue george-waxed wrapper with a matching headgear that made her look much taller. He started off with the usual round of hand shaking. Many were struggling with their food and others were wiping their oily hands on their knees to greet with him. Soon, he realised the impossibility of trying to shake everyone's hand and walked to where Pa Okolo was. He saluted him and waved to the rest. Most of those who knew him responded by yelling "Ochendu". He waved some more to acknowledge his title. As he saluted Pa Okolo, the man drew him closer to himself and informed him that he should ask for something special that he had asked Mama Oby to keep for him.

"What is it?" Uncle Amechi wanted to know.

"Don't worry. You and I are strong in-laws, you know."

"You rub my back, and I will rub yours. It is our silent covenant.

You have been a giant in this house. Don't worry, just go inside. I will see you later."

Uncle Amechi and his wife were met by Mama Oby and Oby as they walked towards the house. Both Oby and her mother hugged them in turns.

"So you are going to university?" Uncle Amechi said.

"Yes, sir."

"Congratulations! Oby the great! So you will soon be an *Acada*."

"What is an *Acada*?" asked Oby.

"Rubbish! You don't know what *Acada* means?" Uncle Amechi was surprised. "You'd better leave this naivety behind in the village. Out there, it is dog eat dog, if you know what I mean. Neither your mom nor I will be around to watch out for you. You had better wisen up."

"My brother, join me in thanking God because it is not by our power," Mama Oby interjected. "If I tell you that I have not had sleepless nights because of this admission problem, I will be lying, " she continued. "If Oby fails, people are going to say that she failed because her father is not alive and that her mother is not capable of guiding her. I know so many mouths in this village that are wide open ready to utter such garbage. But God does not sleep."

"My sister, leave those things alone. It is the mouth that utters evil things that will utter good things as well. The world is full of pretenders. Please bring us food, we are famished."

Mama Oby had made special pounded yam and *okro* soup for her brother and his wife. Oby placed the food on a small wooden table before them. The table tilted a little. The food was heavy, but the floor was also uneven. As the plates slid, all hands went to the rescue. Oby went back into the kitchen and brought a small basin of water for her uncle and aunt to wash their hands. Mama Oby went to fetch Pa Okolo's special palm wine.

"This is for you from your special in-law," Mama Oby said, sipping the wine directly from the gourd and passing it on to Uncle Amechi.

"O ho! This is the special message Pa Okolo was referring to! At least he remembers ... He is a very clever man," said Uncle Amechi.

"Please eat," Mama Oby reminded him. "Your wife will soon finish the food while you are still praising Pa Okolo," she said in jest, then left them to attend to the other guests.

Just as Uncle Amechi finished washing his hands, one of his sycophants entered the room. It was Mathias Okeke, a distant cousin of Oby's. He was shell-shocked during the Nigerian civil war and knew how to exploit his handicap. He only heard what he wanted to hear. It is said that since partially losing his sense of hearing, his sense of smell had become sharper. He could smell a feast miles away. He was always found at village functions, usually uninvited. But that was besides the point. His philosophy was that man must wack — eat. Unlike most people who did not have any reasonable source of income in the village, he was robust but unkempt and dirty. He entertained people with his frequent use of big words, and infuriated others with exaggerations.

"Ochendu, so you have arrived?" Mathias asked.

"Yes, my brother. Since I am here, it means that I have arrived."

"Ha Ochendu, you mean that you crossed the Ninth Mile Corner and saw all those big shops filled with imported commodities ... the city that does not sleep ..."

"Is it possible to come to Isiakpu from Onitsha without coming through the Ninth Mile Corner? You and your questions!"

"Well, anything is possible for you tough city guys. I am flabbergasted. I have told you that you will be the only Ochendu for a very long time. For as long as I shall live."

As he said this he grabbed Uncle Amechi's right hand with his right, held it with the left and started rubbing it with his right palm (his own form of a superior handshake) while he counted: "Ochendu I, Ochendu II, Ochendu III .... Ochendu VI, Ochendu VII." He figured that the next Ochendu after Uncle Amechi would be the VIII and, going by his imaginary queue, that would take an uncountable number of years.

As he went through this routine with Uncle Amechi, some flakes of dirt fell off his hands into the *okro* soup below. As if this was not bad enough, when he had counted up to VII, he let out a noisy sneeze.

When Uncle Amechi's wife, who was watching the drama with utter disgust felt the sneeze, she covered the food in anger and took it away. All that sneeze and dirt in the same food? She had no stomach for this excessive sycophancy which her husband tolerated. As she took the food away, Uncle Amechi, who did not fully understand what was going on, was left agape. He had not eaten. Later, he settled down to a plate of rice because his wife had declared the pounded yam unfit for human consumption. When she left to take the food away, Uncle Amechi quickly pulled out a 50 - naira note and handed it to Mathias. He got the hint and disappeared, whistling his *Man must wack.*

"*Ewele*! (crook). Man must wack, indeed! I have been denied my pounded yam because of you. Rubbish! Go and wack your head."

The crowd had grown bigger. Mama Ijeoma and Fr Damian arrived together. He had found her on the way to Mama Oby's and offered her a ride in his car.

It was difficult not to notice Mama Ijeoma when she waltzed in. As usual, she was dressed flamboyantly in dazzling colours, her hips swung from left to right. She liked the effect walking in with Fr Damian would have on the crowd. Heads turned when she walked in with the priest, and many exchanged knowing glances. For a while there was a wave of murmuring.

Unlike most gatherings in Isiakpu, the evening was marked by little speech-making. Many had already spoken to Oby and offered their advice in private. But Pa Okolo never lost an opportunity to demonstrate that he was in charge of the family. Moreover, there were a few people in the audience who needed to hear how much he loved his younger brother's family.

Pa Okolo spoke quite intelligently in spite of the fact that he had drunk a good amount of palm wine, having had some before coming for the party. He cleared his throat three times and everybody knew that an elder wanted to address them.

"My people, you are all welcome," he started. "Please accept with honour whatever titles that may have been bestowed on you. Our elders taught us that a toad does not run in the daylight for nothing. We are gathered here today for something very important. I must say that

54

those of us who knew my late brother would not be surprised that great things are happening in his homestead. While he lived, he lived upright. He gave generously. I am sure that when he died, he had a smile on his face. He had principles and whatever he believed in, he fought for. It is the same principles that guided him until the end. I have come here not to bury my brother, because we have already given him a befitting funeral, but it is always important to appreciate and understand the source of water in a pumpkin leaf. If one does not know where rain started to drench him, he would not remember where he dried up. I want my daughter, Oby, to appreciate the foundation of this family and to emulate those qualities that endeared her father to many. It is my honest opinion that those positive attributes know no boundary. I have never been to university but I know that it is supposed to represent all that is good in our society. The University of Embakassi should not be different. But the society has also changed and we no longer know what to expect. However, a child who is well brought up, like she is, is usually known from the way she behaves. You can smell the rotten ones two miles away. We are sending you there to bring honour to this house and not shame.

"We are sending you to drink of white man's knowledge. When you drink, we drink, too. Knowledge is like the moon. It shines for all. But, I am not naive. A beautiful girl like you is surely going to find it difficult to escape evil and temptation. Please always bear in mind that you come from a respectable family. This should strengthen your resolve against temptation. We don't want to hear one day that our daughter is married somewhere and to somebody we don't know. Or that she has come home from university unable to explain what ballooned her stomach — as if she drank palm oil residue. (This drew laughter from the crowd). Yes, things happen these days. Children of these days have little respect for culture. Finally, let me call on God to protect and guide you as you sojourn alone to that far-away place. We have heard that there is witchcraft in Embakassi, but it will not get you. All you do will be protected by He that has protected this land and this family. We shall all live to assemble here for nice palm wine on the date of Oby's native wedding. As you all know, university or no university, there is nothing like a good husband. My people, we shall live. That's all I have for now."

The people thundered *Amio* (amen) and applauded the speaker.

When all the visitors had left, Mama Oby and her daughter sat together for a long time. It was Mama Oby's time to give her own advice. "You have to watch those wolves," she said. "Yes, those boys whose tongues are sweeter than sugar. By the time you know what they are up to, they will have taken what they want and you will regret."

"Mama, don't speak like that. I have a mind of my own. I have not been to university but I know a few things about men. Besides, university is not like other places. One must have respect and some integrity, Mama."

"I trust you, my daughter, but things are not always the way they seem. As for your teachers, always treat them as teachers. Try to avoid any close personal relationships. God will guide you as he always has, and you will come back to us in good health."

Oby began to cry. The thought of leaving her beloved mother, even temporarily, broke her heart.

"Mama, how are you going to cope with everything? I know what is going on in this family even as you try to protect us from them. When it is not Pa Okolo, it is Uncle Ben. I overheard the two of you the other day."

"Don't worry, my daughter. God does not sleep."

Her mother tried to console Oby but found herself shedding tears. Mother and daughter stood up at the same time, wiped their eyes with the ends of their wrappers and each went to her room. Neither of them sleep immediately.

Oby and her mother left the village early the following morning for the central bus station. She wanted to be at the university before sunset. It was situated in another state, and she estimated that she would take about eight hours by bus or five by a Peugeot 504 taxi cab. Young travellers preferred the taxi, but her mother and some friends had warned her against travelling by cab. The drivers appeared not to have any respect for human life, according to her mother, and they tended to fly rather than drive. Mama Oby took her daughter to the station to help her with the luggage and to be certain she travelled by bus. When Oby had purchased the ticket and was about to board the bus, she tried to avoid her mother's misty eyes, but Mama Oby called her back. One final ritual before she would let her go into this unknown place, unprotected.

"Bring your hand," she told her daughter. Oby had been part of this ritual many times before and would have been surprised if she escaped it this time. Her mother held her right hand and spat into it. She rubbed in the spittle gently as if to allow it to diffuse in the skin while she quietly invoked a prayer for protection. She was asking God and the spirit of her dead husband to take over as her daughter's mother.

"Only God protects life. God, I have not abandoned my motherly responsibilities to Oby, my daughter. I am only asking you and the spirit of Alfred Onyia to take over since I am now powerless. God will protect you, my daughter. Remember to read your Bible and write to me as soon as you get there."

Oby ran into the bus, choking back her tears. Tears ran down her mother's cheeks.

She stood there waving goodbye to her daughter as the bus pulled out of the station, then Mama Ijeoma appeared from nowhere.

"Eeh ya, so Oby is off to university at last. We thank God, Mama Oby. We are all very proud of you. All the women of Isiapku are very proud of you. Look at all the things you are able to achieve without a man behind you. Quite frankly, you deserve a chieftaincy title from this village. There are so many boneless spines, including my husband, who aspire to be chiefs simply because they have worthless balls between their two legs."

"Mama Ijeoma, what are you up to this morning?" She knew when to discount her ranting. She was, after all, a double-edged knife and could cut both ways. She chose not to join in her chorus.

"I have been running some errands this early morning. I will come home to tell you when I have tied all the loose ends on what could end in having our church split into two."

"What are you talking about?"

"Nothing. Let's discuss more important things."

"What could be more important?"

"I hope that you fortified your daughter as she entered a different world."

"Fortified? Only God fortifies."

"Holy Mother, don't be silly! I did not mean whether you went to see a witch doctor. If you did, I would not be surprised because of the stories about Embakassi. But that is none of my business."

"What is your business?"

"I hope that you have not sent your daughter away with bread and margarine and a couple of verses from the Bible, hoping for the best."

"What are you talking about?"

"I mean, did you give her any contraceptives or did you take her to see a doctor who could have prescribed some?"

"God forbid. My daughter is well brought up and I expect her to carry herself well. Why would I even have such thoughts?"

"Let's face it. You are still living in the dark ages. Despite all these years in the city, you are as naive as a raw villager. Let me be frank with you. I make sure that Ijeoma does not leave home without contraceptives. I don't want to hear stories. It is a different world out there. If you place everything on faith, don't come crying to me when the pot breaks and spills the water."

"Don't lose sleep over it. I will not come crying to you. I know how I have raised my daughter. What sort of Catholic are you, by the way?"

"Mother Teresa! You should ask Fr Damian what he uses."

Mama Ijeoma had turned to walk away.

"Your mouth will definitely put you in trouble. You need to wash it with a strong detergent."

She walked home wondering whether Mama Ijeoma and Fr Damian were having an affair. She kept wondering whether Mama Ijeoma had put out to the parish priest. You could never tell with Mama Ijeoma.

Part II

Searching for the Golden Fleece

CHAPTER SEVEN

It took the bus about eight and half hours to get to the university town of Embakassi. And in a few minutes' time, Oby was on campus. Although full of enthusiasm, she felt like a bird in a strange land. She stood at the taxi rank surrounded by her luggage, uncertain where to go from there. She didn't know whom to ask for directions. Yet many people milled around.

It was September 24 and registration of fresh students had begun two days earlier. She had arrived on the same day that students who had been referred in their final examinations the previous June were finishing their supplementary test papers. Pockets of students stood chatting. They all looked comfortable and familiar with the environment and she doubted that any of them was a new student. They must be students who had come for "by-elections", a term she had learnt back in the village referred to re-sitting examinations.

The campus was one of the second generation of Nigerian universities. It had been a college of arts and sciences, established to train middle-level manpower. It was converted into a university during the oil boom, and a lot of money had been spent on putting up new modern structures and landscaping the grounds. Except for the well-groomed gardens and the football pitch, the rest of the grounds were supposed to be tarmacked.

There was an imposing four-storey building still flashing with fresh paint, a Nigerian flag flapping from a pole at the top. A sign on it indicated that it was the new administration building. Oby did not know what the other buildings were for but was, for that moment, enjoying the scenery; happy to be part of it all. Beyond what the eye could see, from where Oby stood was the university "ghetto" with potholes on the road, dilapidated structures comprising the academic blocks and the laboratories.

As she continued looking around, she noticed a group of students who had been sitting under a mango tree dispersing. Suddenly, one of the students approached her. He obviously did not want his group to know what he was up to.

"Hi baby, can I help you?" he asked.

"Yes, sir," Oby said. "I am looking for the women's hostel."

"Which one?"

"I have no idea, I have just arrived, sir, and I have no idea where to go."

"Come along. I suppose you are one of our brand new students."

"Yes, sir," Oby said with the reverence due to a senior man.

He took the largest of Oby's boxes while she carried the two light ones. She was uncomfortable following the stranger. He was obviously straining himself for her sake.

"From what part of the country do you come?" he inquired.

"I am from East Central State," Oby obliged.

As they put distance between them and the taxi rank, Oby started feeling uncomfortable. She realised that the man was having problems with her huge box.

"Sir, let me help you with the big box."

"What do you mean by this 'sir, sir'?" the man retorted. "If it may interest you, I am only a student like yourself. Please, stop referring to me as 'sir'. Lesson number one: never refer to a fellow student as 'sir'. Looks can be very deceptive."

"I am sorry, I didn't mean to offend you."

"No problem. You are welcome to our *Acadaland*."

The student had a mature face though he was only twenty-two. He spotted a thick moustache and sideburns. He was tall and handsome. Judging by the man's appearance, he deserved the respect Oby was giving him.

Before long, they were at one of the women's hostels, the Mary Slessor Hall. This hostel was a beehive of activity in the evenings. All types of cars parked in front of it. The cars belonged to men from the town who came to see their girlfriends. It was usually quiet this time of the year, and no cars would be seen parked around the hostel. It would be a different place after two weeks when the older students returned. This should never have been the first choice hostel for a girl like Oby. But she had no prior warning. As she would later realise, many girls who considered themselves "senior" fought to be placed in this hostel. It was a hostel that would make a novice like Oby grow up faster than she otherwise would. There were two other smaller women's hostels, the Lady Asuquo Hall and the New Bethel, which was noted for its a large number of born-again women students. Men were uncomfortable visiting New Bethel. There were stories of men who had been dragged into prayer and fellowship sessions, kicking and protesting, when they went looking for their female friends there.

When they got to the porter's lodge, Oby's guide directed her to the porter on duty. He promised to see her sometime to find out how she was settling down, and left.

"Your letter of admission?" inquired the porter. She was huge in a matronly way, and wore a very stern look. She peered through her glasses as Oby fumbled in her handbag for her letter.

"Here it is, Ma."

"I am going to assign you to a room temporarily until you pay your fees and clear with the Registrar's Department. You can go to room 146. Some students are already there," she said as she scribbled into a long, tattered register which had obviously seen better days.

Oby found two girls, Ada and Fumi, who were to be her room-mates. They were friendly but drowsy on account of the sleepless nights they had spent preparing for "by-elections". It was a reasonably-sized room for three students. It had three beds separated by wardrobes and reading tables.

Oby was excited to be starting a new life. She lay on her bed, closed her eyes to pray, and went to sleep.

The following day, Oby was busy with orientation on the campus. She had already missed two days. Everything was new to her. Other activities other than church-related ones could be organised on Sundays. The orientation for the day was conducted by the university's security department. There had been a noted increase in crime at the university, including rape, and new students were particularly vulnerable. In their excitement on joining the university, new students were likely to have a false sense of security. They should not, they were told.

There were dos and don'ts. Girls were asked to always walk in pairs at night and to avoid dark alleys. All this sounded strange to Oby. On her first full day at the university, her image of the institution as the ideal place was being gradually demolished.

That evening, after the orientation, she walked past the spot where the taxi driver had dropped her off the previous day. Three men were seated under the same tree where the student who had helped her carry her box had come from. She looked at them long enough but did not recognise anyone. He saw her but did not wave or indicate to others that he had met her before.

He wanted them to freely assess the girl, as they often did many others from under the tree. They would be sizing up a girl who happened to be passing by, commenting on her appearance, her physique, comparing her to another and trying to find out who was "driving" her or was interested in "driving" her. It was a choice gossip spot because they could see everyone who passed by and be at a distance safe enough for them to say whatever they wanted without attracting attention.

"This must be one of the new students," Chike said.

"How did you know that?" asked Chris.

"I have an advanced male intuition," Chike said because he did not want his friends to know that he had met Oby the previous day. He wanted to hear what they thought of her.

"I think I saw her when she came in yesterday. Was she not the one surrounded by boxes and looking lost in front of the Administration Building?" Okoro asked.

"You tell us, Mr Memorex, since you seem able to rewind your brain so fast. What else?" Chike said in laughter.

"She has a good backyard, and nice legs," said Okoro. "I cannot see her face from here. But with make-up, the faces of most of them tend to shine. You cannot re-construct yam-tuber legs or mosquito legs or re-configure your backyard for sure, but you can always try with your face."

"Yes you can, at least the backyard part. They are doing it in America. But you can only reduce not increase its size," Chris added.

"God forbid! Are you crazy?" Chike interrupted. "Who in Africa wants a reduced backyard? African men are particular about this. When American doctors discover how to increase the size, they will have a ready market in Africa."

"Okoro, you left one important department," Chris said. "I am a chest man. I think that this girl has got it proportionately. Nobody wants to be rubbing bone against bone. She is a village beauty, bush meat, if you ask me. Look at the way she walks."

They laughed.

"I bet she will be eating her bread with fork and knife and drinking tea with a spoon. Bush meat to the power of two," Okoro interjected, causing more laughter.

"You have all had your say," Chike said. "Let me declare my interest. I am going to go after this girl come rain or shine. Haven't you heard that a cockerel that lands in a strange land walks with one leg up while it surveys the environment?"

"What? Are you sure?" Okoro asked.

"Experience! Experience! You cannot learn it at the university," Chike replied.

"Where is this coming from?" Chris was surprised at the certainty with which his friend spoke.

"Don't interrupt me, guys. Okoro was right. We saw this girl yesterday. For some reason, she was on my mind throughout the night. I have to be honest with you as my friends. I have already made preliminary contact with her."

"But when? How?" Chris and Okoro asked in unison.

"I have told you not to ask me how or such other questions. All I am saying is that I am interested in this girl, bush meat or no bush meat. I have already told you guys that a girl needs at least a semester to find her feet in this environment. Last year, you lost a very nice girl," he said looking at Chris, "because of your impatience and the fact that you wanted her to become sophisticated overnight. Look at that girl today. We never learn from experience."

"But you knew I wasn't really too keen on her. I was on a rebound from Ekaete, the Embakassi girl."

"Oh really, and you made us believe you were serious," said Chike.

"Give me a break, guys. You are right, Chike. I don't have patience. I have not come here to teach manners or to teach someone how to walk. As far as I am concerned these things tell me a lot about someone's upbringing. I am even willing to compromise on some aspects of her beauty, but not on mannerisms. Pure and simple. If others succeed where I have failed, good luck to them. I cherish your friendship so much that I don't want to be in the company of a girl who will irritate me."

"I will make sure that you swallow your words."

"You guys create your own headaches by insisting on university girls," Okoro told them. "As usual, I will resume my escapades at the nursing school when the new batch comes in. My girlfriend finished her training last year and left. I have no time for the romantic requirements of dating a university girl ... What are you really looking for? You will get all that and much more from trainee nurses. I will smuggle my bush meat into my room for the usual. If we feel like eating, we can always eat outside. I will not even bring her near the cafeteria. Am I going to eat manners? Besides, have you checked whether she is Igbo or not?"

"You are bush meat yourself, so shut up," Chike retorted.

"Well, if it has come to name-calling, let me remind you that we are not going to fight your fight when next we are told that a girl rejected you because of your big stuff, Mr B," Okoro quipped as both he and Chris laughed and ran off.

"Idiot. God punish you," Chike yelled as he ran after them.

Chris Onuora, Okoro Ohulo, and Chike Amaefuna had been friends since their first year at the University of Embakassi. They were all in their third year. Their friendship started when they realised they had a common hatred for their statistics lecturer. His teaching style, his epithets and humiliating language did not endear him to them. The three had planned a set of revenge incidents including puncturing the lecturer's car tyres, and rubbing glue onto his seat. But before they carried out their revenge, the plan leaked to the lecturer who confronted them with some evidence. Apparently, someone had overheard them discussing their plans and leaked them. He had settled the matter with them without referring it to higher authorities. Although statistics was not a favourite subject for any of them, they had put in extra effort to pass. Still, the three were referred, and had to come for "by-elections". They believed it was in retaliation for what they had planned to do to the lecturer. All three were Igbo. This had further cemented their relationship.

Chris, 20, was studying geography. His ambition was to be a commercial pilot. He thought that geography would be useful in understanding maps and reading compasses. He came from a very enlightened family. His father was a professor of business management at the University of Enugu, and his mother was a secondary school principal in the same town. He had been born in England while his father was pursuing his doctoral degree and his mother an MSc course in chemistry. His background gave him a polished look. He had a fine taste and dressed well. He was a moderate who did not hold rigidly to his views. He had two sisters, both studying medicine at the University of Enugu.

Okoro was also 20 and a business management major. His father was an illiterate, wealthy businessman in the commercial city of Aba. His father had two wives who did not see eye to eye. He ruled his household with an iron hand, and his authority could not be challenged. Okoro was one of eleven children whose upbringing was affected by the roughness of Aba and the intricate manoeuvres of a polygamous family around a domineering father. He was street-wise and intelligent, with a caustic sense of humour inherited directly from his father. His father wanted him to study business management in order to later take over his business. He had four other senior children, but they had not made it to university. The two senior girls, who were married, had obtained certificates in advanced education and worked as primary school teachers.

Chike, 23, was the unofficial leader of the group by virtue of his age and experience. Of all three, he was the only one who had lived alone without parental influence. When he finished his secondary school education, he did not immediately secure admission to university. He took up a temporary job as a secondary school teacher at Asaba, a town not far from Onitsha where his parents lived. He was with them for one year. His father had risen through the local government authority ranks to become an administrative officer. His mother was an ambitious trader who wielded a lot of clout both at home and among her peers. She had a misplaced ego, however, and tended to push her children to success at all costs. Chike was an economics major, but did not have any fixed career goals. He had seen a few successful economists and that was enough motivation for him. His mother approved of his choice, and was hoping that one day her son would join the ranks of arrogant bank managers who had shut their doors in her face so often.

CHAPTER EIGHT

Two weeks after Oby reported to college, most of the continuing students had returned to campus, and lectures had started in earnest. Oby's residence was now confirmed to be room 146, Mary Slessor Hall.

Lecturers spared no time in assigning heavy reading even though many students were still not in the mood for serious work. She had gone to the library many times after dinner to read, only to find a handful of students there. Some, to her dismay, had come to the library in pairs in search of privacy. Afraid of walking alone back to the hostel late, she always left the library early, only to get back to a noisy hall with girls prattling and boys streaming in and out of the rooms. She could not reconcile this to her strict high school boarding life. Not that she expected this place to be like high school, but she did not expect such an incredible amount of freedom.

That evening, she took a shower and put on a special dress and her best shoes, then went to the cafeteria. It was a Friday. She had already noticed that students from her hostel dressed up when going to the cafeteria as if they were going to church or to a wedding. She felt she should not join them blindly but nonetheless felt tempted to show off some of her own better attire.

Chris, Okoro and Chike had gone to the cafeteria earlier than usual. They had planned to see Okoro off to the nursing school to while away the evening. They were not badly dressed themselves.

Seated at their dinner tables, they saw Oby rise to go for tea. She was beautiful, elegantly dressed, and walked with graceful comportment. Okoro and Chris could not believe it was the same girl they had been analysing two weeks back. Chike had unsuccessfully tried to track Oby down. He had not waited to find out her room the day he took her to the Mary Slessor Hostel. Neither did he know her name or what she had come to study. He had been hoping for a chance encounter. And now it had come.

"I told you guys that this girl will go places if you are patient. Just two weeks, and see the transformation! I have not even taken the steering wheel yet ... Chris, you will pour hot tea on yourself if you continue staring at her like that. You boys must listen to an experienced hand," Chike crowed.

"You may have a winner here but we have to watch and see," Chris said. "At this rate, you will have very serious competition."

"What are you guys talking about?" Okoro remarked. "She does not even know that Chike exists."

"Folks, watch me. I am moving over to sit with her, and good luck at the nursing school as you search for your bush meat. And please, don't bid me farewell on your way out. I don't want her to know that I associate with people like you," Chike said as he turned to go to Oby's table.

"May I join you?" he said. She was sitting alone.

"Yes," she said. She was happy to see him again. "You have been lost." She also had been keen to meet him and had been searching for him. She had seen him once but did not know how to catch his attention.

"You remember me?"

"Of course! How can I forget all your help? Thanks again."

"Welcome. I have been looking for you without success since I did not get any of your particulars. Not even your name."

"I thought that you would find me because of my state of origin. That was the only thing you wanted to know when we first met."

"How funny! I tried but there were too many beautiful and shy girls from East Central State." Chike was enjoying her sense of humour. "Very soon, though, you will come to understand how important your state of origin and ethnicity are in this university."

"Yeah? At a university?"

"Ask me later and I will explain it to you. Well, my name is Chike Amaefuna and I am from East Central State. I am a third year economics student."

"Economics?" she could not conceal her laughter.

"Yes. What is wrong with economics?"

"We had an economics teacher in high school whose miserly behaviour was attributed to his having studied economics at university. It was said that he often measured the yam he gave his houseboy to cook and that he painstakingly noted what was left. He had not been able to marry because he always checked the opportunity cost of the dowry. The longer he waited, the more the dowry went up. In any case, who would have wanted to marry such a miserable person?" she laughed some more.

"Well I am sure you know better," Chike said. "Very soon you will take Econ 101 if you are not already taking it, and you will begin to have some idea of what economics is all about. Economists are among the most reckless spenders I know."

"You do not have to defend anything," she said. "I was only teasing you. That teacher was a test case. He was stingy and mean even to himself."

"Well, what is your name, etcetera?" Chike was now the nervous one. This was not the same girl who was calling him 'sir' on their way to the Mary Slessor Hall. She spoke very well, had an inner sophistication and composure. It could not have been these two weeks. Or was he seeing double? The reality was that Oby was shy and could hardly utter a word in the presence of her seniors. But among colleagues, she would be herself and quite humorous. She was still naive in many ways, though, but tried to cover up with a friendly demeanour. She had a very good high school education, and that made it easier for her to adapt to people and situations. Both learning and character were emphasised by the Reverend Sister, her school principal.

The first two weeks at university had also been significant. The near-absolute freedom on campus also implied independence, outspokenness and a sense of survival. There was a lot of peer pressure as well.

"I thought that you would never ask," she said. "I am Obiageli – Oby – Onyia. You asked also for etcetera. What are these?"

"Oh boy ... I mean ... Your department, your room number, etcetera."

"There you go again — etcetera. I am studying sociology and anthropology. What do you want to do with my room number, Mr Etcetera?"

"Well, it is standard practice here. How can one have dinner with a beautiful girl like you and not bother to find out how he would see her again to say thank you for the nice evening?" Chike knew he was stretching it a bit thin, and started laughing.

"What the heck! I am in Room 146. You know where you left me the other day."

"How have you been adjusting?"

"This is a very strange place: normal activities are scheduled on Sundays; the security of students is not guaranteed; lecturers are busy teaching but the students are not yet ready to study. The library is like a security zone: off limits. Each time I have gone in there, I have found it more of a lover's den than a reading hall. The hostel is very noisy. Where can one run to?" she sounded both worried and surprised.

"You've already got it. Very smart! How do you expect us to start reading now? We have not even finished the October-rush! Welcome to *Acadaland*."

"October what?"

"Never mind. I just made that up." Chike thought that it would not be in his best interests to explain what that meant, not now. They had now finished their food and were just chatting. And now Chike remembered his friends, Okoro and Chris, and looked in the direction where they had sat. They had long left.

"What did you expect before you came here?" Chike continued.

"I don't really know. But I was thinking of an ideal community commensurate with its status as an Ivory Tower. I don't want to jump to conclusions, but the university may not be different from the rest of society."

"It could be worse."

"Worse?"

"Well, it depends. Let's go for another cup of tea." Chike wanted another opportunity to size Oby up. He also wanted other students in the cafeteria to see them together. If he quickly identified with Oby, he could lessen the competition.

"There is one good thing for sure. There is a lot to eat here for the small amount we pay," Oby said as they sat down again.

"Oh yes, we think that we are paying too much. You know, because of competition, many of us from the East are not on any scholarships. But these guys from the North and the minorities are all enjoying double scholarships."

"How is that possible?"

"You will soon find out for yourself. You know there is this catchment thing. The North and the minorities are being encouraged to produce high-level manpower and they need lots of incentives to do so."

"Is that the same thing as quota? Someone once told me that that was why many of us were having difficulties gaining admission to university — we are required to have higher entry scores."

"I believe that they are designed to achieve the same goal. I honestly think that a little bit of it is necessary for peace and national integration. But if it is pushed too far, it can become counter-productive. Federal universities such as this should as much as possible strive for some regional balance without unduly sacrificing academic excellence or formulating policies that appear punitive to certain groups. On this scholarship thing, I think that there should be some sense of proportion. After all, this is one country. The current practice where every student from the North is enjoying two scholarships or allowances is discriminatory."

"I think you are exaggerating," Oby interrupted him. "I am hoping to get a scholarship next year. My mother cannot afford to pay school fees after this year."

"You think that I am exaggerating? Well, listen to this: The Embakassi boys here think that there should also be catchment in who is dating who on the campus!"

"I don't understand ... a quota system on inter-ethnic dating? No. I don't believe it!" Oby suddenly sat upright as if to make sure that she was hearing right. Her face could not hide the disgust she felt for what didn't seem to make sense.

"Well, welcome to *Acadaland.* Now you know why if you meet a

72

girl and you think you are remotely interested in her, the first thing you ask is where she comes from. Is it getting any clearer?"

"No. None of this makes sense." Oby was ready to go but wanted to hear more about this quota dating business.

"Sometime last year, around November ..." Chike checked his watch to see if they still had time for the full story. It was about 7.30 pm but it was Friday. "Yes, as I was saying, last year the Embakassi Students' Union had a meeting. When the agenda of the meeting was distributed, the first item on it was: 'The attitude of our girls towards our boys'. The president of the association indicated that Igbo boys, both here and outside the university, had taken all their girls and because of these Igbo boys their girls had become somewhat hostile to them. They were not going to sit and watch while they were made fools of. 'Nobody sits and watches when his house is being invaded,' the president said. 'Not if he calls himself a man.' As he went on, the girls walked out of the meeting. Initially, the boys tried to stop them from leaving and a few of them were ruffled. The boys called the girls all kinds of names — from sell-outs to prostitutes. They eventually let the girls go after realising that most of them came from very influential homes. However, they warned the girls of dire consequences if they continued to go out with Igbo boys. As it turned out, the consequences befell not the girls but the boys."

"Good for the girls! This is all very exciting. Tell me more," Oby could not believe what she was hearing.

"I thought you said this was nonsense?" Chike was confused but delighted at the acquaintance building between them.

"Something can be nonsensical but exciting. So what happened after the meeting?"

"Of course, their threat went unheeded. It was business as usual. Until one day, they beat up two Igbo boys who were playing with their girlfriends, ironically, in the freedom square. That same evening, they punctured the car tyres of another Igbo student. He had parked in front of your hostel. Chaos broke out when the student came out and took the law into his hands. He and two other students, one Igbo, and the other from Embakassi, spent a week in hospital. Since then, water don pass garri. You know that they outnumber us here, and they can even import hooligans from outside. It has not changed their dating habits – I mean for the Embakassi boys – but people are careful now, and they do not flaunt this type of relationship. Some people, like me, prefer to go with one of my own anyway, especially if it will prevent a few blows to my head, eyes or nose."

"And this is supposed to be a university?" Oby asked. "A ha! A good university for that matter. It is unbelievable that these things can happen here. One would expect that this would be an island of inter-ethnic harmony. If people who are supposedly being prepared for future leadership cannot even accommodate each other when little is at stake, what would happen if they had to decide who gets what slice of the national cake? This is disgraceful."

"Who told you little is at stake? Manhood, egos are all at stake, not to talk of the big backyards." Oby did not hear the last word as Chike had swallowed it in laughter.

"I mean fighting over girls, that's childish. People should concentrate on their studies. Is that not what we are all here for? Let's go. I have heard enough."

"My dear sister, you are too logical. There is very little room for logic here."

As they walked back to her hostel, Oby wanted to know what the authorities had done about the incident, and whether the students were still around.

"We have a very lousy VC — Prof Oluwole. That's all I can tell you. He addressed the students soon after the incident and promised to investigate it fully and take appropriate action. We haven't heard a thing since. Whenever he is addressing students, it is 'you are *de facto* this ... and *de jure* that ... and those acting *ultra vires* ...' I mean, some mumbo jumbo. It is difficult to understand half of the things he says. Students have changed his name to Ole-wole – thief has entered – because they think he is only concerned with lining his pocket. A wretched professor when he came here, he now has a new Mercedes. All the students involved in the incident are very much around."

As they approached Lady Asuquo Hall, a male student in a group of four saw them and shouted, "Mr B, take am easy this time oo. *Kubwa sana*." The group burst into laughter. Chike did not answer back, but he really wanted to tell the fellow, "God punish your mama." Any visible reaction on his part would call for a lot of explaining to Oby. Not this time. She would get to know what Mr B stood for at the appropriate time. Oby did not even know that the joke was directed at Chike.

The small parking lot in front of the Mary Slessor Hall was full, and some cars were parked on the grass lawn. This was the third Friday evening of the semester. Most students were now back. Just as they had come, most cars would vanish by about 11.00 pm, usually with an additional occupant. The students would be back on Sunday evening.

"What are all these cars doing here?" Oby asked. "Is this a car bazaar or what?"

"It is not a car bazaar. It is a slaughterhouse. Welcome to *Acadaland*."

"What do you mean by slaughterhouse? You seem very comfortable with odd stories and events." She was not amused.

"This is my third year here. This place has its own dynamics. Don't worry, you will soon get familiar with these terms, some of which are from foreign lands. I first picked up the term when I came to this university. It may be because women are valued like meat for consumption. I don't know. A lot of things happen here. Don't worry about it, you will get used to it."

"But the other two women's hostels we have just passed are not like this. Why did you bring me here on my first day?" Oby asked.

"You don't want to be anywhere else. This is where the action is. This place is for senior girls. You don't want to go through university without the university going through you. One day, you will thank me for bringing you here."

"Do I look like a senior girl — whatever senior means? This place is a mess. Some of the girls even smoke."

"You would not like to be with those born-again women in the New Bethel, either."

"Who told you that? I am born-again myself, for your information. Good night, Chike. It was nice talking to you."

"My pleasure. I will certainly come to see you soon."

Oby ran to her room as if fleeing from the scene in front of the hostel. As she turned to climb the stairs, she noticed the disgusting look on the porter's face, the one who was on duty the day she arrived. They all arrive innocent and naive, but turn into something else after a few months, the porter thought. She had seen it all. If only the men would leave them alone.

CHAPTER NINE

It was a relatively quiet afternoon. Oby and her roommates were taking a siesta in Room 146, Mary Slessor Hall. For Oby, it had been a tiring day. She had had lectures non-stop all morning. As soon as her head rested on the pillow, she had dozed off.

The commotion in her room later woke her up. When she opened her eyes, she saw two men, one holding and kissing Ada and the other talking to Fumi and touching her intimately. She flung the wardrobe open in an attempt to reach for something decent to put on. Visiting hours were still two hours away, and she was still in her dressing gown. But who obeyed the visiting hours? First year students, perhaps. But these men were in their final year. The two men had not noticed her when they burst into the room, and they had gone about their business without a word to her.

She got back to bed and tried to go back to sleep. But the excitement in the room continued.

Ben and Uche had become very close since they started dating Fumi and Ada. They had met the girls when they were in their first year, more than two years earlier. Uche was Fumi's lover while Ben was Ada's. Both men were going into their final year in geology. They had come back late to the university because they had had permission to work on their field project, an important part of their final year work. They had spent most of their long vacation at the Delta oil drilling sites working on two geological problems. They had planned it in such a way that they would be close to one another. Neither of them knew that Ada and Fumi had "by-elections". They were only getting to know about it now.

Uche's relationship with Fumi was not considered normal. She was Yoruba and he was Igbo. But Uche grew up in Lagos and spoke perfect Yoruba. Uche never experienced any major opposition from the Yoruba men on campus because they accepted him as one of them. But he was still called all sorts of names by a few who could not get out of their tribal cocoons. One of them had made serious overtures, trying to woo Fumi away from Uche without success. Both Uche and Fumi were above that, however. For them, their ethnicity was not a subject of discussion.

It was not the same with Fumi's parents. They had vehemently opposed the relationship at first and even threatened to stop paying her fees. For them it was not important that Uche was such a nice man. But Uche and Fumi had stood their ground. Fumi's parents had overcome their initial objections to the relationship and accepted Uche. It was an uphill task since Fumi was their only daughter whom they pampered a lot. Uche was serious-minded, and it was expected the two would get married as soon as they graduated.

Ben's relationship with Ada was not as strong. It was more or less a campus affair. Ada had grown most skeptical about men over the years, and she tended to treat them all like cash machines. This had reduced her relationships to cash-and-carry affairs. Ben liked her, though, and had stuck with her, on and off, for over two years — some sort of a miracle.

Tired as she was, Oby could not get back to sleep. She started reflecting on the weeks that had passed, her own expectations and the reality. Was it possible to reconcile all the counsel she had received at home with what went on at the university?

"My name is Uche. Welcome to our room." Oby was startled out her thoughts.

"And I am Ben, another of your roommates. Welcome." Both stretched their hands to shake Oby's.

"Thank you. Thank you very much. Nice meeting you both."

"Sorry, we woke you up. I am sure you understand," Uche apologised. "We have not seen these babes in the last couple of months."

"Well, very soon, she too will be keeping us awake," Ben added. "The October rush is already over and we are waiting for the results." There was laughter.

"Nobody will rush our sweetheart without our permission," Fumi said.

"Oh! You want to collect tax?" Ben asked.

"No. The usual gate-keeping fee. But we will increase the fee this time around. I am not sure of the stock of men we have in this campus these days."

"Tell me about it," Ada said. "You get a gift of cheap perfume from them, and they think that you should be eternally grateful. The unfortunate thing is that they forget so soon how it all started, the sweet nothings and the promises, the harassment."

"I agree," Fumi interjected. "But I think that women must look beyond the morning of love."

"What do you mean?" they all chorused.

"Well, you see, in the morning of love, everything moves smoothly. Few questions are asked, mistakes are overlooked, dangerous signs are ignored. Why not? It is the heart not the head that is in control. In the evening of love, familiarity sets in: lovers start taking each other for granted, a few wrinkles here and there, little things begin to irritate. Signs of yesterday become the reality of today. We have a special responsibility to make sure that our partners are those who can survive the evening of love." Laughter.

"But that shouldn't be a special responsibility of women," Ben cut into their laughter.

"Ben, we have a lot to lose if love goes sour," Ada said sarcastically.

Oby joined in the conversation. "My uncle has a proverb which captures the essence of what you have just said, Fumi. I don't know how to translate it into English."

"Try, we would like to hear it," Ben said as the rest nodded encouragement.

"Well, it goes like this: For an unwise farmer, the morning does not portend the need for water. In other words, the morning is so deceitful that a farmer who is setting out for the farm would not see the need to carry drinking water for the afternoon."

They laughed.

"Did you understand it?" Oby asked.

They all seemed to say they understood it clearly.

"When the sun hits him and the strains of the work sets in, he realises that he needed to carry water with him," Ben explained.

"We have two philosophers in this room now: Oby and Fumi. So guys, be very careful with us," Ada joked.

"Let's go men, these people don come with their wahala," Uche said while pulling Ben up off the bed.

"Don't worry, you guys are okay," Fumi said.

"Okay in what way? The only man who is okay is one who can provide satisfactorily. I no dey for free show. Make una go O jare,"said Ada.

Later that evening, Ada, Fumi and Oby came back to the subject of love and to the social activities at the university. They were as confused as Oby when they first came to the university three years back. Their different backgrounds certainly prepared them differently for what they would encounter. They had observed Oby for a while, and knew that some of the things she had already experienced at the university distressed her. Expectations always differed from reality here. You never quite understood it until you got there.

"One thing people have often talked about since I came here is October rush," Oby said. "What is it?"

"October rush?" Fumi and Ada chorused, laughing.

"Don't tell us that you have not been rushed yet?" Fumi said, still laughing. She threw herself on to the bed.

"It is simple," Ada started. "October is over. Most students come back in late September. Between then and the end of October, senior male students rush to get the first year female students who have just joined university."

"October is the decisive month. You either fail or succeed. You notice a flurry of activity," Fumi added.

"Is that what it means?"

"Yes, but we have not seen much activity as far as you are concerned," Fumi said. "Is there nobody rushing you?"

"I don't know what to call it but I have been rushed and crushed," Oby was using the term for the first time and enjoying it.

She had never seen her roommates this relaxed. She had always considered them as people who did not think of her. Uche and Ben had broken the ice, she thought. She could open up to them now.

"Tell us about it," Ada goaded.

"There is really nothing to tell," Oby said. "I am not interested. Academic work here can be overwhelming."

"Tell us about it. We have gone through it," Ada insisted.

"Really, I don't know," said Oby. "There is this guy I met on my first day here, sort of an overgrown baby. Good looking, though. He helped carry my things here and disappeared for a while. Then he showed up at my table in the cafeteria. We had a long and interesting conversation on what goes on here. But he has since changed gear. He talks about how much he likes me. He has memorised my class schedule. He appears from nowhere whenever I am coming out of class. If I am walking down to the cafeteria alone, he suddenly appears behind me. I feel like he is stalking me."

"But we have never seen him in this room. Maybe he is not adventurous," Fumi said.

"I don't know, but I gave him the impression that I am not interested, and that my room is off-limits."

"The adventurous ones do not obey any rules," Ada intoned.

"When do we get to see him?" Fumi asked.

"See him? For what? I am not in for that sort of thing."

"What sort of thing? Girl, you need to talk to us. Like I said, we have gone through it," Ada sounded wiser than she looked.

"Look at us," Fumi said. "Do we look like we came from an uncivilised world? Three years ago, we were all told what to do and what not to do before we arrived here. It took us less than a month to realise that this was a different world. It has its own rules. It was different. But it was the same. The same tyranny. The same treachery. Men were in charge — period. It was far from the ideal, but it was up to you to make your stay here enjoyable. You can opt to stick to your preconceived ideas but we can assure you that life will be very difficult."

This was becoming too serious for Oby's liking. She had come here not to make life difficult for herself but to prepare herself for that difficult future. But it looked like she must pass the test of true life in this place first. What options did she have? Or was everything predetermined?

"So what must one do?" Oby asked.

"For a start, drop all your preconceived ideas," Ada told her. "You must use all your survival tactics. For the most part, you are going to be on your own. Your parents cannot help you here. Not even lecturers can protect you. All those things that you were told at home on how to act or behave here do not work. After all, those who gave you that counsel have never seen the four walls of a university. Don't get me wrong. You have to learn to be firm and strong but flexible when necessary. It's up to you."

Fumi added, "Don't worry about all this serious stuff. It's fun to be here. Let's get to the interesting part. Who is this guy you were telling us about? What is he studying and what is his name?"

"He is a third year economics student."

"Economics?" they both asked with a touch of alarm.

"What is wrong with economics?" Oby asked, puzzled.

"No, it is just that we know a few guys with big mouths in that department," Fumi said. "They all seem to think that they will all graduate and become bank managers overnight."

"That's putting it mildly," Ada protested. "Some of them, especially in the third year, are most obnoxious. But there are nice guys there as well. By the way, we enjoy their parties. The Economics Association holds the best parties on the campus. They are often supported by the Bankers' Association in town. Now we may be able to get their invitations without difficulty."

The girls laughed.

"So what is his name?" Fumi asked again.

"Chike Amaefuna."

Both Ada and Fumi exchanged glances, trying to recollect the name. "We don't know him. But we might recognise him if we saw him."

"Don't worry, you may not be seeing him. At least not in this room."

"That is your problem," Ada put in. "You had better count your teeth with your tongue, Reverend Philosopher Oby."

"Ada, leave her alone. Experience is the best teacher," said Fumi.

Throughout the greater part of the evening, Oby thought over her conversation with Ada and Fumi. She was beginning to think that things were different here. There were lots of people on this campus but you could easily become lonely. At home, she would not think twice before rejecting a man's amorous advances, no matter how determined he was. Her mother would think she had lost her mind if she got seriously involved with a man. If the person wanted to marry her and she was inclined to getting married, that would be a different matter. Here, the rules were different. There was no mother to protect you. Your roommates, who were now your immediate family, told you to wisen up. Wisen up to what? Is that what Chike meant when he said that the university had to go through you? Was it possible to survive without playing by the rules?

That discussion on tribalism at the university also troubled her. Would the lecturers also discriminate against students in awarding marks, depending on where they came from? Would they apply the quota system in order to balance the distribution of grades among the different ethnic groups? She hoped that would not happen. What of academic excellence? Was that not rewarded? Nobody talked about academics with the same compulsion. What were the rules governing good grades? How could you study better in order to achieve academic excellence here? Would the university have gone through you if you were socially well rounded but failed to make a decent honours degree? How come the most important activity was given the least attention? Perhaps, it was taken for granted. If you failed, you packed your things and left. It was all very confusing. "It is up to you," was the advice from her roommates. Was it really up to her? Were her male counterparts faced with a similar dilemma? Or was this part of what her mother referred to as our burden — a women's burden?

CHAPTER TEN

A few blocks away from Oby's room, in Dr Akanu Ibiam Hall, Chike's friends sat on his bed after dinner. Not much was on the agenda. Campus gossip. Time to review their social life since the beginning of the semester.

Chike had been avoiding the subject because he did not have any good news to report. No scores yet. Plenty of barriers. Each time he thought he was winning Oby over, she turned round and made it look like they had met the previous day. She didn't know what he was talking about. He had found it difficult to understand what she wanted. But he was determined to win her come rain or shine. In fact, failure on his part spelt social disaster for him. He had invested a lot of time in chasing Oby.

"My brother, any good news?" Chris asked.

"Any good news from where?" Chike responded, acting surprised.

"I think that Chris meant for you to tell us when we can expect Oby to be part of our team," Okoro said. "In short, we want to know when she is coming to see you in your room — if you know what I mean," Okoro added his voice to the query.

"It is none of your business."

"None of our business?" Okoro protested. "Man, you are the head of the class, the pathfinder. If you fail, we will have failed. So don't give me this bullshit about the matter being none of our business."

"Watch your mouth! Someone else can lead the way. Who anointed me head of the class?"

"No, Okoro is right. We are in this together," Chris said. "Jokes aside. If you need our help, just say so. We expected this girl to be a walkover for you." Chris was serious.

"There you go again. Walkover! What makes you think she would be a walkover?"

"Well, in the first place, she cannot compare with the girl you got last year who later made a fool of herself," Okoro said.

"In what ways?" Chike asked.

"Well, I don't think she is as sophisticated. She is not ..."

"Stop right there," Chike interrupted Chris. "These comparisons do not make sense. They are superficial. You are judging a book by its cover. An inner sophistication belies Oby's outward appearance."

"That may be true," Okoro said. "But this semester will soon come to an end. You know how important it is for one to launch his new babe at our annual welcoming party, which is fast approaching. Especially so when you are the incoming president of the association. There is one thing my father told me: You are either winning or losing. It cannot be both ways."

"That is very true," Chris put in. "I don't expect this to drag on till then."

"Thanks for your concern guys. On a serious note, I am frustrated about this much more than any of you. But this girl is special. When you get to know her you will appreciate what I am saying. I want to believe that I have made some progress. I think that she is worth waiting for. You have forgotten that the patient dog eats the fattest bone."

"That is, if there is any bone left, not to talk of one with fat," said Okoro. "My father told me that all women are the same."

"That is crude," Chike protested. "Besides, Oby is not your average bush meat. You cannot do cash-and-carry with her."

Okoro laughed.

"Talking about bush meat, what are you guys up to with the nursing students?" Chike asked.

The evening Chike went over to Oby's table at the cafeteria, Chris and Okoro had gone to the Nursing Students' Hostel as they had arranged. The understanding was that Chris should accompany Okoro. Okoro acted like his father had taught him: like a squirrel who, while eating a ripe palm nut, uses his tail to colonise the unripe one. Since his girlfriend from the nursing school graduated the previous year, he had started to cultivate a new relationship during the previous semester.

Off campus, it was even more important to know where these girls came from. Okoro knew this only too well. He only talked to Igbo girls.

When they got to the girl's room, there were three other girls chatting with her. One of them fell irredeemably for Chris' gentlemanly demeanour and the remnants of his British accent. She was tall and beautiful. Chris could not resist her. Despite his reluctance to date outside the campus, he convinced himself that if anything worked out, he would of course make sure that the girl did not come anywhere near the university. Okoro had a tough time wooing his girlfriend. In fact, he only succeeded because the girl who fell for Chris put pressure on her. Okoro was riding on Chris' success. But he was not bothered. As far as he was concerned, the end justified the means.

"Well, you go first, Okoro, since you are the veteran of bush meat," Chris said, laughing.

"There is nothing new under the sun. As usual, I went, I saw and I conquered," Okoro said with some exaggeration, knowing that Chris was not the type to burst one's bubble. "I have smuggled her into my room a couple of times. It was very good, quite good. Her kicks and cries of passion simply drove me crazy. What else? I have gone out to dinner twice with her off the campus, and the last time I was in Aba, I bought her a number of things. I like her a lot and I, the son of my father, am actually considering inviting her to the annual welcome party. It has been good so far."

"Where were we when all this was happening?" Chike asked.

"Well, as you know, bush meat is not for public display. Besides, you have to consolidate your hold first before what belongs to you tempts others. She is quite domesticated."

"I see. It looks like you might fall in love with her?" Chike asked.

"Fall in love? What is that? What's love got to do with anything? My father told me that falling in love is a sign of foolishness and weakness on the part of a man and a clever way for a woman to milk a man dry."

"Oh boy! This crude mentality is in your blood," Chris said. "My experience has a twist to it," he said and started laughing uncontrollably.

86

"I don't think that it is fair for me to tell this story. This girl deserves her privacy. Moreover, I don't want this story repeated anywhere. I have my image to protect."

"Oh, so we have become people in the marketplace!" Chike said. "Tell us the story, O jare. You may have to worry about Okoro with his basket mouth because it may start leaking as soon as we leave here."

They had joined Chris in laughing without knowing how funny his story was.

"If you insist. You see, I took Ifeoma to this hotel where I had booked a room."

"You did what?" exclaimed Okoro. "How were you able to keep this from us?"

"Stop interrupting me or you will never hear this story. Nobody ever fully discloses the goings-on between him and his girlfriend. Not even to his best friends."

"Please get on with the story," Chike urged.

"As I was saying, I booked this room. We had lunch and later retired to the room. You can guess the rest. But at one point when I was making love to her, I asked her whether she was coming ... You know what I mean ... She opened her eyes, pushed me aside and asked me who was coming and if I was expecting someone else. In my confusion, I didn't answer. She suddenly jumped from the bed and ran into the bathroom. It took me a few minutes to realise that she had not understood my question. I calmed her down and explained things to her. She was embarrassed and apologised. But I had already lost the desire go on and we agreed to have another date. Afterwards, I was wondering how someone who seemed to be in emotional wonderland could still be so conscious."

Okoro and Chike were rolling on the floor with laughter.

Chris continued: "I told you guys that I am not cut out for this bush meat business." He was enjoying his own story.

"No. This is bush meat to the power of three. This will go into the Guinness Book of Records," said Okoro, panting after the laughter. "My father told me that if you are leading a goat to be slaughtered and suddenly that goat breaks wind but drops no turds, you should spare it.

It spells a bad omen. If you go ahead to slaughter the goat, your judgement will be in heaven." There was more laughter.

That night, Chike went over all that had transpired between him and Oby and strongly felt that things would work out fine. But when? He was racing against time. He picked up a paper from his table, and set out to compose a poem for Oby. He must bring all his talent to bear in his quest to get her. He went over the poem several times, changing several verses until he felt happy with the result.

Rules or no rules, he would take the poem to Oby's room.

CHAPTER ELEVEN

Chike's heart was pounding as he approached Room 146. He must really like this girl to be feeling this way. What if Oby became nasty because he had visited without permission or warning? It could ruin all his efforts. He was tempted to go back but felt that he had reached a point of no return. He was ready to face the consequences.

When he paused at the door, he could hear two girls speaking from inside. He knocked and both asked him in unison.

"Is Oby Onyia in this room?" he asked, nervously.

Before he had finished his enquiry, the two girls burst into laughter. They recognised Chike as Mr Big Stuff or Mr B. He was also popularly referred to as Mr Kubwa.

"I have a message for Oby," Chike said, riding over his embarrassment. He suspected that he had caused their giggling.

"What message? Are you Chike?" Ada asked.

"Yes, I am Chike. Why are you laughing?" The recognition of his name gave him courage. That meant that Oby had mentioned his name to them.

"You had better talk to us nicely or we will break the Nsugbe coconut, Mr B," Ada said as they broke into laughter again.

"Please, whatever it takes. My knees are on the floor." Chike realised that these girls knew him well when Ada referred to him as Mr B.

"Your knees are now on the floor but tomorrow when you get what you want it will be a different ball game," said Fumi.

"You had better start talking to us nicely," Ada said, blending seriousness with jest. "I don't mean just talking. This is a big one. In fact, it is so major, it would require a lot. Oby is our junior sister, and we are bound to protect her, especially from Mr Kubwa. There is no messing around here. When we sneeze, you should catch the cold immediately."

I know that. I know that you two can do or undo this relationship. I have told you, I am willing to pay the price."

"My brother, things are elephant. Did you say price?" It was Ada. "You've got the right word, baby. I like men who speak the same language as I do: there is no free lunch. If we must keep our mouths shut, it will cost you a bundle. We will start with a dinner at the Hotel Metropol, and finish the evening with a bottle of gin and lime. All imported, no local brew. We are not that cheap."

Fumi was giggling as Ada made her demands.

"You forgot to add an early invitation to the Economics party," Fumi added.

"It goes without saying. Who do you think will be the guests of honour at the reserved table?" Ada continued.

"That's fine. Thank you very much. What are your names?" Chike was no longer in doubt that they had discussed him. How did they know that he was an economics student? Well, if they knew that he was Mr B, they probably knew a lot more about him.

"Our names? What do you want to do with our names?" Ada retorted. "Are you trying to double-cross us, Mr Kubwa?" She was enjoying herself immensely. Ordinarily, you had to be at least a mile away to call Chike Mr B or Mr Kubwa.

"Don't mind her. I am Fumi and she is Ada. You don't know us?"

"You are senior girls, and ..."

"Senior what? So you came here to insult us? You had better leave before we change our minds," Ada said. "Senior, my foot! That's how they make you lose value."

"Thank you, ladies."

"There he goes again. In other words, you are saying that we are too old to be addressed as girls?" Ada teased.

When Chike left, Fumi and Ada exploded again in laughter and exchanged a high five. They had thoroughly enjoyed teasing him. It might be their only chance, and they knew it.

"*Ole! Omo buruku niyen* — that's a bad child," Fumi said. "How can we have Mr Kubwa as our roommate? Ada, you were very courageous," she went on.

"It can be fun when we have the upper hand. Guys can be a mess when they get what they want. Before then, they are willing to deny their mothers. Everything is yes, and yes ... until you give them your soul," said Ada.

"You are too hard on them. Some are nice. But on a serious note, what are we going to do? Are we going to tell Oby all we know?"

"Not really? We have a deal with him. He would be foolish not to come through on it."

"Are you going to hold him to the deal?" Fumi asked.

"Trust me! I will not spare that son-of-a-bitch."

"So, are we going to tell Oby or not?"

"Are you kidding? She will never hear it from my mouth as long as our understanding with Chike stands."

"But is it not our responsibility to protect Oby from the ordeal?

"Which ordeal?"

"From Mr Kubwa. This girl can be hurt if what we read in *The Bee* is correct."

"Fumi, everyone must bear his or her own cross. Besides, do you believe everything you read in *The Bee*?"

"Not everything. But the description was vivid — length, width and all. Everything ... all kinds of ugly statistics. *Omo yen Yadi gan ni o! Kini yen tobi o!*"

"Well then, she will undergo the baptism of fire from Mr Kubwa."

"These are the sort of men that give blacks a bad name in Europe and America ... spreading the myth that black men pack power between their legs."

"On the contrary, my sister. These are the type that make black men proud. White women do not want to date a black man whose manhood they would have to be searching for. At least that is what a white peace corps girl I met in my village told me sometime back. She said she had come to Africa in search of her own experience. It is not a myth. It is a reality. In my experience, I have seen men with dangerous weapons. Fumi, don't let me start."

"I thought that it was the act, not the instrument that was important."

"*Au contraire* again. No matter how well trained, a technician must have the right tools. Poor girl. How would you know? You have been stuck on Uche as if he was coated with sugar and honey. Girl, you are missing the spice of life."

"I am not missing a thing. Please leave Uche out of this. I want us to agree on what to tell Oby. You seem to hate this son of a b... and yet are not willing to help a sister. Don't you see any contradictions in that?"

"This is no time for philosophy. Each one must bear her own cross. I am still bearing mine. My mouth will not leak on this subject, full stop."

"I heard from Uche that Chike's version of what transpired that night was different from what we read in *The Bee*."

"What did you expect? There must be no less than three versions: there is the guy's version, the girl's version, and the version we read in *The Bee*. The truth must lie somewhere between the three. What version did you hear from Uche?" Ada asked.

"Well, the long and short of it is that the girl stormed out of Mr B's room after he refused to use a condom, not that he had an extraordinarily big organ."

"There you go! Can't you see the connection. He refuses to wear a condom because the manufacturers of condoms have not made any to fit him," Ada was laughing.

"Ada, that's a vicious thought."

"No. I am simply interpreting your version of the story."

"If that is the case, it makes it even more compelling for us to protect her," Fumi insisted.

"Let's change the subject, it is becoming boring. I don't want to play mother to anyone. Experience has taught me that one gets burnt easily if one is not careful with this sort of situation."

Fumi needed to persuade Ada that they should reach a mutually acceptable agreement on the subject. Ada was the social leader and adviser by virtue of her courage and experience, and she could impose sanctions if Fumi was seen to be going out of line. If Ada was determined that Oby should not be told what they knew about Chike, it would be so. Fumi seemed to be losing the battle.

Oby came back to her room after Ada and Fumi had left for an early dinner, on Ada's injunction.

She reached out for the envelope left conspicuously on her pillow. She did not recognise the writing on it, but was eager to find out who had written the note. It was a poem signed, Love, Chike. She dropped her books on her desk and fell into her bed to read the poem:

"Love is like a child;
naked in its innocence
intoxicating when it is care-free,
uninhibited in its flow
It must be embraced as
child embraces mother
cuddly, suckly and twosome;

one who gives, receives
knows neither boundary nor audience
from the flat river side of Onitsha
to the hilly valleys of Nsukka, it flows
the language is the same;

like a child, it might not make sense;
like a child needing attention;
touch, thirst, desire are time bound;
time is of the essence;

Now is the time!

She read this over and over again. Oby may not have had much experience in love, but she had read enough romantic novels. She had had romantic dreams that lacked expression because of her ignorance. Perhaps this was the time. Maybe Chike was the right one. He had been very persistent, yet gentle and respectful. His poem had touched a soft spot in her heart.

The following day, as had become usual, Chike was standing outside the lecture hall when Oby got out of the Sociology 101 class. It was difficult to notice anyone in particular since it was a huge class. Today was different. Oby wanted to see Chike and would have been disappointed if he had not shown up. She even allowed him to touch her in the presence of other people. She was warm and filled the brief moment with broad smiles. She acknowledged having read his poem, and expressed surprise at his talent.

Chike was content. He had good news to report to his friends, but would not do so yet. He had to be sure. Before they parted, they agreed to go to the beach the following Saturday, at Oby's prompting.

CHAPTER TWELVE

It was a bright Saturday afternoon. The sky was blue, with streaks of rainbow brushing the southern horizon.

Oby was dressed in a short-sleeved colourful white top, dotted with bold purple, and shorts. It had been a present from a man from her neighbouring village. He had been on holiday from the US and was looking for quick fun. He had presented the gift to her and had expected that she would warm up to him. After all he had just come from the United States and that, in his view, was enough to enchant any girl in the neighbourhood. Oby was visiting a girlfriend who happened to be related to the man. She was so cold to him that she never saw him again. He was obnoxious and had started with, "Hi baby, whaats up?"

Oby had pretended that the greeting was not for her. But, on second thoughts replied: "Nothing is up, everything is down."

"Man o man, you've got it in the right place if you know whar' I'm sayin'? How about you and me sweat it out together on Sar'day? You see waat am sayin'? T'will be lots of fun, direct from God's own country, man."

He moved closer to Oby and placed his hand on her lap. She politely picked it up and placed it on his lap. Oby was not enjoying this but her girlfriend who, in between cooking, was coming to check on them was. He later left Oby his hotel address. As if to further demonstrate his interest, he sent the clothes through Oby's friend before the proposed Saturday. Oby was curious about the hotel address. She later learnt that after two years in the United States, the man felt that his father's house was substandard quarters during his stay. His parents were very upset but they could do nothing to change him. Two years away from home and he now thought that only sub-humans would use the pit latrine. That was the last time Oby saw him. On her friend's insistence, she accepted the gift but never wore it until this day. What an irony — she was wearing it for someone else.

She looked good in it. She also wore a pair of brown sandals. Chike wore a pair of jeans, a T-shirt and a pair of sneakers he had bought at the Onitsha second-hand market. Of course he lied to his friends that a friend in America had sent the shoes to him. They still had a new rugged American look.

The beach was no longer crowded as it used to be. Apparently, there had been bad publicity showing how polluted it had become from the off-shore oil drilling. A local environment conservation group had mounted the publicity campaign to sensitise the people of Embakassi on the dangers of pollution. The demonstration had hardly begun than the protestors were dispersed by armed policemen. The government would not tolerate anything that might disrupt oil production, a key source of state revenue. Oil companies knew of the enormous power they wielded and the protection they had from the state. Pollution or no pollution, it would be business as usual.

Apart from the few people around, the only other hint that all was not well was a torn poster hanging from a tree deploring the activities of the oil companies.

As they walked hand in hand, traversing the length of the beach, the farthest thing from their minds was pollution and social consciousness. Oby wanted a romantic beginning to their relationship, in much the same way she had seen in the novels she had read. She wanted to trace the romantic footsteps of her major heroines.

Chike wanted to confirm that Oby was now his. The confirmation he was looking for was crucial in many ways, including the success of the Economics Department's presidential inauguration party. In a very important way for him, it would be a climax, and an opportunity to redeem his prestige, battered since the previous year. For Oby, it would be the start of a very long and romantic journey. She could not imagine its end.

Small shades made from raffia palm leaves dotted the beach. Oby was looking for a spot from where they could watch the receding waves and the sunset. When they had sat down, she leaned on his chest and could feel his heartbeat. For sure, it was faster than normal. Her heart, too, was racing.

Oby raised her head from Chike's chest and looked directly into his eyes.

"Chike, what did you see in me that gave you sleepless nights?" She said it as if in an effort to extract the truth.

"What I see is secondary. I feel something ... I know things about you that have made me a paper weight. I cannot believe it myself. I love you very much, Oby."

"Very interesting," she said sweetly. "Is that why your heart is beating so fast?" she asked.

"It's not just my heart, I am sweating even as we are lying on a cold sandy beach. You are a darling."

"What?"

"I have never felt this way before," he said. "Never!"

Oby was saying to herself that these were all very good answers. Chike had lived through a few relationships and knew all the right answers.

"How many girlfriends have you had before?"

"E ehm, one or two. Nothing serious."

"It is either one or two."

"Two. And, like I said ..."

"No need for that," she told him. "Your past is your past. I am only worried about now and the future."

"What sort of worry? Do I look like an absentee lover?"

"I am worried about your level of commitment. I am worried about tomorrow. I want to be able to trust you completely. If I give myself to you, what guarantee do I have that you will not hurt me?"

"I am the guarantee. My word. Oby, you are very special to me."

"Chike, I have dreams. I want to read until there are no other degrees to add. You are my first and I do not want a second or a third. I have made commitments to my mother and it is important for me to keep them. I cannot afford to disappoint her. I cannot afford to disappoint our family. Chike, I also like you very much but I am scared. I don't understand social life at the university. I need your help. I need your protection." Her voice was shaking and when Chike looked at her, he saw tears running down her cheeks.

"Please Oby, there is no need for this," he said wiping her tears with his T-shirt.

"Just hold me. Just hold me close to you," she said.

For a moment, everything was quiet. They both closed their eyes, clasped in each other's arms. Chike's hold was firm and comforting. He was well built and his embrace felt like getting a hug from a big teddy bear. They could feel the sun going to bed. They were totally lost in their world when they were suddenly woken up by the barking of a tiny, malnourished dog. It had been standing in front of their shade unnoticed. It was the size of a puppy but was a fully grown dog, stunted by lack of care. It looked as if it had been forced to feed on the polluted fish since food remnants from the beach visitors had become few and rare.

The barking startled them. Chike got up and chased the dog away. Oby remembered the biscuit and two small packets of Fanta she had packed. She brought out a biscuit, put it in her mouth and fed Chike from her mouth. The two lips had an electrifying touch when they met. Chike seized the opportunity to shower her with hot kisses. Oby moved and kicked with pleasure but he would not let go. When it was over, both were breathless, spent.

"Oh boy, that was the best there could be. Can I have some more?" he said after a while.

"Greedy. You are lucky you stole that. That was a mouthful. Did you want to kill me?"

"Nobody who saw you the first day you arrived at the campus would know you are so mature, so romantic. You certainly should never judge a book by its cover."

"Who said that I am romantic?" Again, she lay with her head buried in his chest.

"Look where we are, the romantic setting, your dress and demeanour. I am very lucky. I have a lot to learn from you. Yet this is your first?"

"I believe everything worth doing is worth doing well. Yes, this is my first, and hopefully my last. As I told you earlier, I do not believe in experiments. Not these days with all these things in the air. If you disappoint me, I will kill you. Don't move closer if you are not sure."

"Oby, there ain't no stopping now. No one has a whole elephant to himself and still pursues squirrels. Surrender your dreams to me and let me be in charge."

Chike was partly worried that this conversation was getting too serious for a first date. But today was not the day to express reservations. Not now, not soon. He needed to keep an open mind, but Oby appeared to have been setting the agenda right from the start.

"Do you want another one?" Oby asked. "You will get another short one if you catch me." She ran off in the direction opposite to the beach entrance. Chike was in hot pursuit. When Oby found a neat patch, she dropped on the ground allowing him to catch up with her. He seized her and pulled her towards him gently, enveloping her in his arms.

He kissed her gently, slowly, passionately. Twice, he tried to move his left fingers up her very erect and tantalising breasts, tapping them up her chest. He only stopped because he thought she would not approve of it. He also was trying to hide the bulge under his pants by frequently moving Oby from one side to the other. First, he thought that it would be rude for Oby to feel him. But more importantly, he would not have wanted her to know the size of his manhood. Not now. He did not believe it was unnecessarily big. But once bitten, as they say, twice shy. He still had flashes of what had happened the previous year.

Oby was totally cooperative. Perhaps because Chike was gentle and allowed a breather in between the kisses. Perhaps because she was beginning to trust him. They were totally oblivious to everything around them.

An almost naked man who frequented the beach saw them and walked towards them. He was encrusted with dirt and his hair had turned into dreadlocks. He was muttering to himself and laughing. As he laughed, he would hold his penis, leap into the air and laugh more loudly. His laughter brought Oby and Chike back to reality. He stopped a reasonable distance from the two as if to suggest that he didn't mean any harm. With both hands on his waist, a stern look on face and speaking in a deep voice, he began to rant:

"The truth is always bitter but only the truth shall set you free. Politicians are paid to tell lies. Judges are paid to cause miscarriages of justice. The policeman is paid to bully and steal from those he should protect. Mark, that is my name, is not paid, but he offers the truth free of charge. The truth is that no one knows tomorrow. Why do we insist something is white when it is black? God forbid! Mark, that is my name, is named after St Mark of the Bible, and he doesn't have to be paid to tell the truth. The truth put me in this condition. Look at your politicians. They speak from both sides of their mouths as if they have a hot piece of yam in them. The politicians have no principles. That is the truth. Outside government they criticise everything and everybody in government. Don't believe them. At night they are busy sending their resumés to the authorities for positions. Give them the responsibility of supervising the kitchen in a government house and they will defend the most indefensible of government actions. These include the educated ones who call themselves professors. Professors who profess lies. I call them quacks. What good medicine do you expect from a quack doctor? It is sad. I am really sorry for the young generation. Some politicians say the army must go. Others say the army must stay. It is a laughable bunch. Look at the army. Don't mind them. How can anyone who has never fired a shot in his lifetime become a general? A general of what? He cannot even defend his family against an armed thug. A knock on the door at night and he runs under his wife's bed. They claim to intervene in governance to fight corruption. That is not the truth. They are paid to lie. Not only do they institutionalise corruption, they give it baptismal names such as "settlement". Are you listening? Tell those khaki boys that is what I said. They should get back to the barracks as fast as their tiny legs and beer-bellies can carry them. Look around you, the filth around this beach is enough to go round, a basketfull, to everyone in Embakassi. This used to be a quiet, neat place. But everyone is shifting responsibility. The oil companies say it is the duty of government to clean up the mess and the government passes the buck back. What do you expect? The oil companies have "settled" the government or the government has "settled" the oil companies. It is a vicious circle, a merry-go-round with ominous consequences. Ha ha ha! What of the common man and woman who depend on this river for their livelihood? Tell me: what do you expect them to do? As for the two of you, the truth is that you are adding to the pollution of this beach. Not necessarily in a physical sense. For today begets tomorrow. This beach is my sanctuary, and only those who are willing to extol the truth are welcome here. Have you studied any philosophy? You have to in order to understand me, Mark, well. It seems like a full moon for both of you. But young girl, remember the moon also sets. That's all I will say for now. It is the gospel according to Saint Mark. You can quote me."

As he turned to leave, he suddenly made two giant strides forward. This startled Oby and Chike and the two drew back, not knowing what to expect next. Mark laughed; he was only confirming that they were attentive.

With both hands behind his back, he turned to look at his temporary hostages before saying: "You heard it from Mark, the moon also sets. Mark has seen it all, and nothing dazzles me any more."

He looked down at his penis as if to obtain its agreement, and then let out a high-pitched laugh.

Oby and Chike were transfixed, frightened throughout the monologue. They were surprised at the mad man's sensible utterances. Unknown to them, Mark had been a final year philosophy student at the University of Embakassi many years back. He had developed a "brain fag" and dropped out when he became uncontrollable. His family attributed his condition to witchcraft, and sought help from traditional medicinemen. Mark ran away from the medicineman who also felt that Mark's madness was beyond cure because he could not classify the condition. Others, including his classmates, said Mark had been witness to a heinous crime of passion. A local chief killed a girl who had spurned his advances. Mark had stumbled on the chief as he was trying to dispose of the body. Despite the chief's plea for Mark to seal his lips, he had said he would stand by the truth. The chief promised him that he would live to tell the truth, yes, but no one would believe him. It is believed that a powerful juju man sealed Mark's fate. No one could fully explain. Mark still lives to tell the truth but nobody believes him. He was up-to-date on virtually all the issues, especially politics, and would often be seen reading old newspapers.

When Oby and Chike got back to their shade to pick up their stuff, they looked to their left and saw the dog that they had chased away leading a band of equally malnourished dogs towards them. They sneaked out of the beach.

CHAPTER THIRTEEN

Pa Okolo was woken up by a loud knock on his door. It was 5.30 am. First, he thought he was dreaming but the knocks came persistently. He thought something serious had happened.

He had stayed awake till early that morning. It had been the turn of his youngest wife to put up in his house. Pa Okolo had grown so fond of her that he no longer adhered to the weekly schedule he had drawn for each of his wives to share his bed. Without explanation, he had instructed her to disregard the timetable.

His two other wives did not find this amusing but did not know how to redress the affront. His first wife was, however, compensated for the infringement in other ways. Pa Okolo recognised her contribution to his economic well being. The second wife, who lost her favourite status when a newcomer arrived, felt extremely frustrated and started long-distance trading. Rumour had it that she had adulterous affairs during her travels. She had also become fairly independent and relatively wealthy. If she got thinner, it was said that she had contracted some disease. When she gained weight, they said that the gods wanted to finish her once and for all by bloating her. She carried on, though, as if none of this bothered her.

As Pa Okolo struggled to tie his wrapper and find his torch, the knock came again.

"I hope they are not armed robbers," his wife muttered, half-awake.

"Armed robbers are not as bad as assassins. Those paid killers are no-nonsense people. They are not in this village yet, but who knows?" Pa Okolo said. "Where is my machete?"

"Machete? These people carry better guns than the police."

"Woman, let me hear ... Who is it?" Pa Okolo asked.

"It is Chief Ugwueze, the Igwe of Isiakpu, the Agaba Idu I of Isiapku."

"No, don't open that door," Pa Okolo's wife said as she sat up in bed. That is not the chief's voice."

"Pa Okolo, Chief Agaba Idu I, wants to see you. He is waiting in his car. I am his driver."

"The driver? Your name is Biaturus," Pa Okolo said as he moved closer to one of the two windows to peep through a crack. He couldn't see anything because it was still very dark.

"Yes, Bitrus, Pa Okolo."

"Please ask the chief to come. And you young woman, you have caused the chief to wait all this time because of your unnecessary fear. I have always wondered why I listen to you."

"Because of my wisdom," she whispered.

"What? Please shut the bedroom door and pretend that you are not here."

"Sorry, chief, for the delay. I did not hear the initial knock," Pa Okolo lied. "The Igwe shall live forever. Agaba Idu the first, I salute you," he continued as he bowed to greet the chief. He extended his hand for a warm handshake.

He looked around the room intensely, barely acknowledging the greetings, as if to be sure the place was safe for him and his mission. He wasn't particularly amused that he had been kept waiting.

Chief Ugwueze was a diminutive man, but what he lacked in size, he more than made up for in self-estimation. He liked to always be heard and seen, and took everything personally. He was said to be suffering from small man's syndrome. He had worked briefly as a junior immigration officer, made a lot of money from illegal aliens and companies that hired expatriates beyond the allocated government quota. He had gone into business and flew from one country to another, largely tying up his illigitimate business. When the last chief died, he took early retirement and temporarily moved to the village to vie for the position. Before the end of the mourning period, he had set his campaign in motion. Many were upset about this and felt that he was wasting his time. The chieftaincy would not be sold to the highest bidder. That was the message they sent him. He had a well organised campaign, oiled by his wealth and relative exposure.

The chieftaincy, through an age-old tradition, rotated between two families. When Chief Ugwueze came back to the village, he fought to change that. He argued that the system was undemocratic and that it tended to preclude those who would offer better leadership to the community. He lined behind him able members of the community who had one grudge or another against the system, including Pa Okolo, and promised to right the wrong's perpetrated against them once he became Igwe. The traditionalists fought back.

Chief Ugwueze's great grandfather was an *Osu* – an outcast – and was, therefore, a second-class citizen. His father had been sacrificed to the god of Isiakpu. This stigma had passed from one generation to another and could not be dispelled. Not even with sacks of money. No one in Isiakpu would want someone with a tainted lineage to be their traditional ruler. Yet, even though many in the village knew of Chief Ugwueze's lineage, not many could fight him openly. The chief on the other hand was aware of what his wealth could do.

When the matter of his lineage came up before the council of elders, a committee was set up at his instigation to investigate it. He had learnt over the years that it was easy to deal with committees. In his days in the city, he had seen the government set up one committee after another to investigate one thing or the other. They produced reports which hardly saw the light of day. Those that were published said exactly what the government wanted them to say.

Chief Ugwueze had no difficulty bribing the members of the committee who reported back that he was a free-born. His father, they said, was merely a servant to the god's high priest. He was never sacrificed to the god. He did not, therefore, meet the definition of an *osu*. Tradition had just been twisted. But everyone knew the truth, including the chief himself. But money turned facts into fiction. Those who could have fought it, like Pa Okolo, had their own agenda.

Ugwueze's chieftaincy divided the community because many believed money had decided the issue. He had tried to heal these divisions by aligning himself to traditionalists on most issues affecting the community. But by doing so, he gradually alienated those who had supported his candidacy, and his promise to right past wrongs remained just that: a promise. Pa Okolo was still waiting to be admitted to the council of elders, the Ozo.

"I understand, these are very different times: with armed robbers and paid assassins. Whatever they are called, one has to be very careful."

"But why should a common man like me worry?"

"Well, sometimes, they don't discriminate. We all have enemies, don't we? Even if you don't have enemies, there are people in this village who would not be happy that I visited you this morning."

"Agaba Idu, Chief, where would I get kolanut this early in the morning? I would have to fetch one of my wives. This must be a very important visit. A toad does not run in the afternoon for nothing."

"It does these days, and runs even at night — especially in those countries where toad meat is a delicacy."

The two men laughed.

"Sit down, Pa Okolo. Don't worry about kolanut. It is not always that I visit people very early in the morning. When I do, I bring along my own kolanut. Except that this time, it is a different kolanut."

The chief opened his briefcase and brought out a bottle of Vodka.

"Pa Okolo."

"Chief," he replied.

"This is a very special one. It is imported from Russia. Imported from the country that had sent people to the moon. Have you ever heard of Kruschev or Brezhnev? The two presidents who could have wiped out the whole world with their bombs, started the day with this drink."

"People have gone to the moon? Chief, you and your stories!"

"Of course, several times. Don't you remember Apollo?"

"Yes, the eye disease. My first wife had that ugly disease and for weeks I could not eat what she cooked. Her eyes were wet, red and constantly dripping mucus."

"The Apollo came after the visit to the moon. It was nature's way of warning us not to overstep our bounds."

"Apollo! I thought that it was short for Appolonia, the first woman

106

in this village to catch the dreaded eye disease. It is rumoured that she is always catching something."

"Do you know what this drink is called?"

"No, Chief."

"It is called Vodka."

"What does that mean?"

"Good question. In our language it means a drink that cannot be served to poor or useless people. To translate it more directly, it means that you cannot find this drink in an *akalogholi's* house. Do you know that this was what they drank on the moon?"

"Vodu-kaa. It has a very rich name."

"I will open it and give you a taste of it. Don't worry about glasses, we will use the cover of the bottle. It is so potent, you only need a few shots."

"Yes, it is potent indeed," Pa Okolo said as he gulped the second shot. The chief had one shot and handed the bottle over to Pa Okolo. "Vodu-kaa, seeing is believing. What a great drink!"

"This is for you to keep. But remember what I said: this drink can neither be served by a poor man nor to a poor man. It was sent to me from America by my son.

"Pa Okolo, this brings me to why I came this early in the morning. It is a subject of great importance, but which I am sure you would have no difficulty in handling."

"I am honoured by your trust."

"Pa Okolo, you and I go way back. When I wanted to be the chief of this town, I knew who my supporters were. You and I had a special covenant, an agreement that I would make it possible for you to become an *ichie*, a recognised elder of this land, and a member of my cabinet. But you know as well as I do that our enemies have been sabotaging our plans. These very powerful elders have not forgiven you for the sins of the past. But I am not going to give up."

"Chief Igwe! The goats of this land are not afraid to feed on the grass that is growing on my head. I don't blame them. Covenants are made and covenants are broken. But those who deny a child what is due to him shall be answerable not to the child but to their conscience.

They should always remember that the one who pursues the chicken falls, not the chicken."

Pa Okolo had his head bowed as he tapped his right foot on the floor. "I know that there is a more important reason why you are here today, chief."

"Why are you hurrying? If you finish licking your fingers, are you going to file them?" the chief said. "Well, as I was saying, our two families have been friends and I want to strengthen this friendship further. I am aware that this family has a beautiful, intelligent and well brought-up girl. She is a worthy ambassador for this family. When she went to university, I knew she had met all our requirements. I am speaking about Oby, your daughter."

"What about her?" Pa Okolo asked, for effect, as if he just woke up from sleep.

For a minute, he thought that the chief might want Oby for a second wife. Pa Okolo would have been incensed at that suggestion. The chief was older than Alfred Onyia, Oby's father.

"You remember my son who went to America about eight years ago? You know Ndubisi. He is now ripe for marriage and I know that no one else in this village will meet his requirements but Oby. I don't want him to marry an *oyibo* girl. Never! I will not live to have a daughter- in-law who does not fully appreciate our culture or is unable to speak our language. Who would become the next chief of this land if Ndubisi is lost with an *oyibo* woman?"

He paused for effect. The chief was, for the first time, revealing that he intended to have his son succeed him.

"In the last picture that he sent to his brother, we saw that there were a lot of *oyibo* – American – girls around him as if they were scrambling for him. Some were leaning on him, others holding his hands, while others appeared to be plastering his face with saliva. What sort of people are these? Women fighting over a man in the open. His brother told us that the picture was taken at a pick-nick. I told him that from what I could see, they were picking Ndubisi not Nick."

"What is a pick-nick, chief," Pa Okolo was somewhat bemused especially after the chief's hint on his succession. He also wanted to laugh but could not because for a long time he had never seen the chief this worried.

"Don't worry about that, Pa Okolo. It would take a whole day to explain. Pa Okolo, I must tell you that what we saw in that picture alarmed his mother and I. This is what we get for all the money we send to him. We decided that it was time we found a suitable wife for Ndubisi. You know that when a female dog is on heat it sends out a certain scent in the air that attracts male dogs. It can attract the right ones or it may attract even those with rabies — unless the owner acts to select a suitable mate. Ndubisi is ripe, and it is for us to act now or he will do something very foolish. When we both put our heads together, we searched throughout this village and beyond, and everything was pointing towards Oby, your daughter. This is why I am here this early in the morning."

"Thank you very much, chief. You have spoken very well. I feel very relieved. I didn't know what the nature of the matter was that had brought you here. Your visit is indeed a welcome one. I have heard what you have said. Who would not want to marry into the chief's home in order to partake in his wisdom? More so when we may be talking of being a future queen," Pa Okolo made the last statement sarcastically but wanted to let the chief know that he had heard his slip of tongue about Ndubisi succeeding him.

Continued Pa Okolo: "But I have to consult my family, and Mama Oby. As head of this family, I promise to meet your expectations. She is my daughter, and I shall decide."

"Needless to remind you, this would strengthen my arm and resolve in trying to bring you into the council of elders. No one can deny my in-law a place among the most respected in this village. By the way, as soon as I receive the signal, we shall initiate the necessary traditional marriage arrangements. We don't have to wait for the rascals."

"Igwe, leave that to me. You will hear from me shortly. I can only say that if I scratch your back, I expect you to scratch my back in return," Pa Okolo was saying this almost with a sense of *déja`vu*.

As the Igwe stood up to leave, he shook Pa Okolo's hand very warmly.

"Vodu-kaa. What a wizard of a drink!" Pa Okolo said. "My whole body is awake after only two shots." He led his guest to the door.

Throughout that day, he reflected on the chief's visit. At first he was unhappy that the chief had visited him only because he wanted something from him. He knew that the chief had not fought hard enough to have him admitted to the council of elders. Pa Okolo actually had information that Chief Ugwueze had postponed the discussions on the matter several times during the council's meeting. But he was willing to give him the benefit of doubt. If he became his in-law, the situation would indeed be different, and Pa Okolo could force him to put up or shut up. He knew how to manipulate events and people but had not been successful with the chief because he was a very slippery man.

CHAPTER FOURTEEN

Very early the next day, Pa Okolo knocked on Mama Oby's door. As far as he was concerned, he was bringing good tidings and if that meant losing a few hours of his sleep, so be it. He had not slept very well himself because he was not sure how Mama Oby would react. He had spent part of the night working and reworking the anticipated conversation. But he was angry with himself for not being totally in control. He knew Mama Oby would not be an easy nut to crack. But she would have to be crazy if she turned down the marriage proposal he personally viewed as unquestionably good to all in the family.

"Who is it?" Mama Oby asked, half asleep.

"It is Pa Okolo."

"Pa Okolo, my goodness! Is everything okay? It is barely 5 o'clock in the morning."

"Are you going to let me in or are we going to continue this question-and-answer song till all your neighbours wake up?"

"No, I am only trying to get myself together. I am sorry." Mama Oby was now at the door but had forgotten to pick up the keys. "Please don't be upset. I have to get the keys. I was in another land when I heard your knock."

"I hope that you slept well. I am sorry for coming unannounced and at this hour." He stood at the door inside the lounge for a moment not knowing exactly where to sit. He would have preferred sitting down directly opposite Mama Oby in order to look directly into her eyes as they spoke.

"Please, sit down," Mama Oby gestured towards a seat.

He sat on the chair with the full force of his weight, and the weak springs underneath the cushion gave way, making a squeaking noise. Were it not for his agility, he would have crashed to the floor. That in itself would have been a bad omen and a traditional appeasement from Mama Oby would be forthcoming. Pa Okolo was not amused as

111

he switched chairs, but he needed to be friendly to Mama Oby that morning.

"Sorry, Pa Okolo. I am very sorry. I hope that you were not hurt."

"No. That was nothing. Now that your chairs are falling apart, I hope that you are not encountering any difficulties that I need to know about. I don't have to repeat myself. Your problem is automatically my problem." He tried to be benign in his demeanor, in the hope that it would win Mama Oby over.

"Pa Okolo, all is well. We thank God for all His mercy."

She continued: "Pa Okolo, I don't want to be rude by asking you what has brought you into your own house. But I know that there must be something that brings you here this early."

"You are right, my wife," he said. "I have brought you good news. Great things happen in a great family. Do you remember the speech I made the day we had a send-off party for Oby? I reminded everyone that this is a great family and only great things happen here. All those who thought that the death of my brother, Papa Oby, would mark the end of great things in this family should dig a hole and bury their heads. There is a greater tomorrow. I also spoke to Oby, if you remember, about our expectations that she should marry well. As far as we are concerned, it is the Number One certificate for a woman. Every other thing is to embellish it: a good and respectable husband is Job Number One. There is no argument about this. Are you with me?"

"I am with you, sir. I am not supposed to interrupt you."

"God has buttered our bread. What everyone would be searching for has just been brought to our doorsteps. Just yesterday, about this time, our chief, Agaba Idu the First, our own Igwe, came to my house to ask for Oby's hand in marriage for his son, Ndubisi, who is in America. I was pleased that of all the families in Isiakpu and beyond, the chief considered us worthy giving our daughter to his son. It confirms my point that this is a great family. Mama Oby, are you still with me? You do not show any excitement ... your body is not moving."

"Pa Okolo, I am not jumping because it is too early in the day and I may wake up the children. Besides, I no longer know how to react to all these marriage proposals that come to Oby."

"This is different," the man said. "Can't you see? We are talking about the heir to the throne. Remember that we are talking about the chief's first son."

"So what did you tell *your* chief?" Mama Oby said as she wiped her face with one end of her wrapper.

"Well, I told the chief that I will bring the good news to you, and that between us we will decide and send word back to him. He is anxious. He fears that his son will soon marry an *oyibo* girl in America. I hear that those girls only eat in hotels and cannot cook any of our food. They even wear underpants in the public. God forbid!"

"But even if we were to make the decision," Mama Oby said "are we going to overlook so many things? No questions asked? We used to have a sense of value in this town and a lot of respect for our culture."

"Like what? You seem to know a lot more about these things than I do. What questions do you want us to ask?"

"You once told me that the chief's heritage had a comma, was not straight. You remember the thing about his great grandfather being an *osu*, an outcast," Mama Oby lowered her voice because of the weight of the subject. "How can we allow our daughter to marry into a family with a questionable heritage? Pa Okolo, let us not cover the dung with one hand and then eat with the other hand."

"That may be true. But this man has been made our chief, our Igwe. As far as I am concerned, we have erased that part of his family history."

"No, *mbaa*! I don't think so," she said. "There are things money can buy, there are others that it cannot. Money can buy you a chieftaincy but it cannot buy you a new heritage. You cannot hire the best surgeon and ask him to excise it as if it is some physical abnormality. It is not possible. You and I know that Chief Ugwueze could not have become chief of this town if men of principle were still around. How can we consign Oby and our grandchildren to such stigma that neither money nor fame can erase? I am surprised that you are excited about this marriage proposal — unless there is something I do not know." She sounded exasperated.

"Are you trying to insinuate something?" Pa Okolo asked, his voice rising.

"I am not suggesting anything, Pa Okolo. We are just having a conversation."

"I don't like the direction this conversation is taking. I gave the chief my word that we would work things out quickly and get back to him. I am equally surprised. Every Sunday you spend the whole day at church. You are one of the most respected church leaders in this village. I thought that this *osu* thing contradicted the preaching of Christianity: that we are all from one family. And how about loving thy neighbour as you would love thyself. Don't you see the contradiction?" Pa Okolo's prominent veins were straining against his skin as he got more agitated.

"Pa Okolo, I have seen contradictions in my short life within and outside the church. I believe that on judgment day, we shall be called individually to account for our actions here. This *osu* thing is not one in which I am willing to use my head to break the coconut. As you know, one who breaks the coconut with his head does not live to eat the coconut."

"So you are all hypocrites," Pa Okolo said, frustrated. He decided to become aggressive. "Mama Oby, I am warning you now. This is not a simple matter." He knew Mama Oby was right. But somehow he believed that it was better to be pragmatic in a matter of this nature. Being an in-law to the chief had potential for a lot of advantages.

"And this his son, Ndubisi," she told him, "are you trying to tell me that you have never heard the rumuor that he spent only one year at university in America and dropped out? He does not have any certificates. The chief is here claiming that he has this and that degree because of the number of years he has spent in America. In fact, we learnt that he now works in one of those pubs where women dance in the nude."

Mama Oby had heard the last bit from Mama Ijeoma but did not want to reveal the source of her information because that would imply that the information should be taken with a grain of salt. Even though this conversation was not going his way, Pa Okolo was trying to relate

114

the gossip about Ndubisi to the picture the chief had told him about. Perhaps, these are the girls who danced naked as he watched. No wonder the chief was suggesting that they were scantily dressed. So pick-nick is the English way of saying people are dancing naked? What a way to make a living!

"Mama Oby, that's rubbish," Pa Okolo said. "These things were all fabricated by the chief's enemy. I do not want us to be caught up in this. Many of those peddling this rumour would like to be in our shoes today. If this proposition goes today to Mama Ijeoma, your friend, she would jump at it. What do you care about his certificates? We are talking about a man who is going to inherit everything the chief has: wealth, connections, the throne."

"I don't know," Mama Oby said. "I am only saying that there are a lot of things to be examined. Besides, we would have to let Oby know about it and obtain her consent. She is a big girl now, and she may have her own plans."

"What? Obtain her consent! There you go again. Why are you always bent on taking a different course from the one I suggest even when it is for our mutual benefit. Why?" Pa Okolo was tapping his feet on the floor and adjusting his wrapper. "Listen to me. I am older than you are. I am wiser than you are. At my age we see things and pretend that we have not seen them. We know things and pretend that we have no clue. It comes from age and experience. It is only a young and naive man who discusses all he sees from the top of a palm tree. Think of yourself in old age. No husband and no capable in-law. Who is going to look after you. Don't think that these pennies and cents that you realise from your petty trading can pay for the children's education. The small house at Nsukka is not yielding much. Besides, it is collapsing and requires urgent repairs. I will not always be here to protect this family. Look at all my other brothers. Who are you going to rely upon? Tell me, who? When I die who is going to give me a good funeral and burial? It is in our interest that we have a very strong in-law. An in-law is like someone's brother or sister. Can't you see where I am coming from?"

"I can see. But I do not agree. God's providence is superior to that of man. The Lord is our shepherd. Put all trust in Him and you shall not want."

"It appears that I have been crying wolf and dancing with the deaf. God also helps those who help themselves. Now tell me what I should say to the chief."

"No, not me. You are the elder. You would know how to reply to him more politely than I could. I can't stand him."

"Mama Oby, I want you to watch what you say. You can insult me as much as you want, but please respect the chief of this town. Please! *I beg you.* Let's just say that I have wasted a whole morning and ruined a whole day. I have always believed that talking to a woman who wakes up alone every night does not often yield good results. I have been proven right again and again. If that good-for-nothing man called Ben had been doing his work, everything would make sense. Right now your actions are dictated by a clash of hormones. It is the worst thing that can happen to a woman."

Whenever Pa Okolo spoke at an occasion like this and discovered he was losing the argument, he became impertinent with such impetuousity you would think he was created to destroy. He knew that Mama Oby was right in raising all the issues she had brought up but he was more concerned about the possibility of being admitted the council of elders. As far as he was concerned, this took precedence over all other considerations.

"Mama Oby," he said. "Let's range principles against reality. Today, principles do not put food on the table. Besides, my brother, Papa Oby, told me something when he was still alive about Oby. I am sure you know what it is," he had lowered his voice.

"I have no idea."

"My brother told me that because you were living in Kano and you had the baby in an *oyibo* hospital, the usual ceremony surrounding the birth of the female child was not performed."

"Which ceremony?" Mama Oby asked with impatience.

"Why are you fond of interrogating me? You enjoy pricking between my teeth. I am telling you what my brother told me in confidence: that Oby was not circumcised. Is this news to you?"

116

"True. But what has that got to do with anything?"

"You are now exposing your naivety. If word gets out that she has not been cut, who in this village would want to marry her? She would be considered unwholesome. Can't you see the opportunity we have with the desperate chief and his uncultured son? Can't you see? You should open your eyes!"

"Pa Okolo, I am angry that you would refer to our daughter as unwholesome. She is going to be the first woman university graduate in this family. I think that you should open your eyes. Can't you see that times have changed? Who said that she has to marry from this village? There are lots of places in Nigeria and outside where such women are held in high regard."

"Never. There is no such place. Unless, of course, you are talking about those places where women run after men. If you have decided that she would marry a Japanese or a Chinese, the blood of my brother would not allow it. God forbid that I would receive dowry for my daughter from anyone whose language I do not understand."

"Those people do not know what dowry is," Mama Oby said with a certain amusement which infuriated Pa Okolo.

He stood up, folded his wrapper and walked out of the door, fuming. "Either Ben performs his work or I will drive him out of this town. I am receiving all these insults because he is good-for-nothing."

Mama Oby was visibly angry herself but not very surprised. As almost always when Pa Okolo went off on her, a storm of tears was gathering in her eyes but she struggled to control herself. "I will send the message to Oby," she said after him. "I will let you know when I hear from her."

She wasn't sure Pa Okolo had heard that. It didn't matter anyway. Mama Oby already knew what her daughter's answer would be. When she was home for the first mid-term break, she had discussed Chike with her and hinted that it was a very serious relationship. Oby wanted her mother to discourage anyone else from thinking that she was still available for a relationship. Her mother had concurred with her because she saw no point in debating the matter with her.

When she sat back in her chair, she could not hold back the tears any longer. They rolled down her face. She had decided to live alone for the sake of her children but at times like this, she wondered whether it was wise. She could have married another man long ago and left the village with the children if she had wanted. Many men had proposed to her but she had not given those suits any thought. Times like these wavered her resolve.

Part III

Is This Love?

CHAPTER FIFTEEN

Oby had just one examination paper left. The semester would come to an end in slightly over two weeks. It had been an exhausting first semester in which she tried her best to study and make time for Chike.

She had grown increasingly fond of him. She thought he was different; he had not pressurised her to do anything she did not want. In fact, she appeared to be in control of their relationship, and this pleased her a great deal.

She had also grown wiser and was beginning to reconcile herself to the fact that the university was not an island of peace and perfection. On the contrary, she had realised that this was where the unexpected sometimes happened. She had witnessed the activities of secret societies and heard awful tales of their nocturnal meetings; how they initiated members at night — usually at a cemetery with lots of human and animal blood involved. They had made so much noise one day that she thought the campus was at war. When it was all over, a few legs had been broken, a few heads required bandaging and three people had been hospitalised. Yet, the next day, most people went about their business as usual. Many people had seen enough of such acts of lawlessness and were apparently immune to them. For those who cared, their protests were muffled by their fears for their safety.

Response from the authorities was often muted and spasmodic. Perhaps they feared losing their exalted positions if those who put them there sensed negligence on their part and held them responsible for their inability to control the student body. The most favourite action was non-action, except for a terse statement from the Vice-Chancellor timidly asserting his authority. Most cult members, Oby was to later learn, were sons of the rich and the famous. She did not understand why they would choose this form of self-expression as if they were collectively maladjusted.

She had heard of girls being raped and, of amorous advances by lecturers. It was indeed a different world and there was no room for a child. One needed to be in charge of one's life, and whether one liked it or not, one could not be pristine for too long. There was a strong corrupting influence in the environment. She had found that this community was no more friendly to women than the larger society. Her mother's admonitions about the women's burden kept reverberating in her mind.

The Economics Department's gala night, the induction party and inauguration of Chike as president, had been fixed for the following Friday, exactly 10 days away, and one week to the end of the semester. Oby's last examination paper had been scheduled for early that morning.

Oby got ready to go to the cafeteria for dinner, certain that she was going to eat alone. Chike was fond of waiting for her on the way, suddenly appearing behind her or coming for her at the hostel. Today would be different. Chike and Okoro had gone to Aba. Chike had gone to buy a suit for the party while Okoro had gone home for money. Since she had finished most of her examination papers, she was more relaxed and, in spite of Chike's absence, decided to dress very well.

Chris was also on campus. He had thought of going to pick Oby up for dinner but refrained, fearing that it might generate unnecessary gossip. Chris had grown very fond of Oby and had begun to show it almost unconsciously. The two always took the same line on an issue. He would frequently touch or pinch her to emphasise a point. No one had given it any thought because their relationship was seen in the context of his friendship with Chike. The two had, in fact, never been alone before. He had quietly wished Oby was his girlfriend. He found her articulate and sophisticated, an impression contrary to what he held when he first saw her.

The more he met Oby, the more he wished Chike would vanish so he could take his place. But Chris was too much of a gentleman to make a move on his friend's girlfriend. Not even when he was sure he would treat Oby with greater respect and affection than Chike. But the risks far outweighed any chances of success. He knew that if Oby was truly who he thought she was, there was no way she would entertain a proposition from him. Besides, Chris was not a maverick.

Despite his many differences with Chike and Okoro, mostly in matters of style, he enjoyed their friendship. He had learnt a lot from Okoro's native intelligence and wisecracks, and relied on Chike's experience on the social front for occasional guidance.

That evening, Chris suddenly appeared from behind Oby as she was approaching the cafeteria and squeezed her shoulders with both hands. When Oby turned around ready to rain abuse on her accuser, the scowl on her face melted into a smile. No one else would dare do what Chris had done. Of course there are always pranksters. Chris leapt forward and then turned to face her. He was acting as if he was intoxicated.

"Baby, you've got it all in the right places and at the right sizes."

"Naughty boy," she said. "What are you looking at?

Oby liked him, even respected him. He was without doubt the most polished of Chike's friends. But she thought that there was a certain cockiness about him — almost a superiority complex. In sharp contrast, she saw Chike as humble and always willing to adapt.

The food queue was short and the two were served quickly. Although Oby got her food first, Chris was already ahead searching for a suitable table for them both. He wanted a corner table where they would talk in private. As he searched, two men left a corner table by coincidence. Oby got there first.

As they sat down to eat, Chris was somewhat uneasy and kept staring at Oby.

"A penny for your thoughts," Oby said to break the silence. "Why were you staring into the empty space?"

"It was not into empty space unless that is the way beautiful girls are described these days." He was trying to accentuate his British accent.

"Instead of dining with me, you are busy looking at women passing by. Thank you very much."

"There is none more beautiful to look at than you. I was admiring wetin my brother de chop. Chike is a very lucky man."

"Lucky! Who tell you say e don chop anything? Aa ha, is that what Chike said?"

"Don't get me wrong. You can chop in many ways — by looking, touching, even when the real chop still never materialise."

"So which one did Chike tell you guys e don chop?"

"We are not babies, any day that Chike chops the real thing we would all be having orgasm by association." Chris was laughing alone.

"What are you talking about? You mean, you guys just sit around discussing this sort of thing?"

"What sort of thing? Nothing is new under the sun. Do you mean you girls do not discuss such intimate stuff? Of course you do."

"I don't know and I wouldn't know. I certainly do not intend to discuss anything with anyone."

"Which means that you are ehm — you never chop before?"

"Is that not kind of personal?"

Chris did not think that such a discussion was off-limits. He wanted to pursue the subject further. "Chike is a very lucky man: bonuses upon bonuses. It is going to be a grand slam. I de envy am well well. I wonder whether it is going to be on a grass court, clay court or on synthetic grass."

"What are you talking about?" Oby was not a tennis fan and she wasn't sure she understood the metaphor. It didn't really matter.

"Never mind, I would surely know the result." Chris was laughing at Oby's obvious loss.

"I consider myself lucky to have him. He is a very considerate person. Very reasonable and understanding."

"I hope so for your sake," he said with a hint of doubt and sarcasm. "If you are lucky, what would you say he is? Luckier or luckiest? He must have been born on a Sunday. If I may put it the way I feel, I would say that he struck a gold mine. I hope he is serious."

"Well, thank you," she said. "He is as serious as anyone can be. I feel like I have known him for a very long time. And I do trust him."

"He is certainly very experienced. To be able to identify someone like you requires a bit of experience. The first day I saw you I thought that he was making a mistake. I wondered what he going to do with a village girl.

"You called me a village girl, you been-to! I don't blame you. What's wrong with being a village girl, anyway?" As she said this, she reached out and spanked his hand.

"Wait! Barely a few weeks later, I was eating my own words ... and imagining how happy I would have been if I had been the one who got you." Chris was trying to prevent his rice and plantain from spilling onto the table. It was not difficult at all to know which part of the table Chris ate from because the amount of food that fell there was always significant; half of it would have fallen off the fork because of his impatience, and the other half off the edge of his plate. It was a habit very unlike him.

"But you have a girlfriend, the student nurse. Chike told me that she is very pretty," Oby reached out to his plate and picked a piece of plantain in a gesture that non-verbally reciprocated his kind words.

"You two have been discussing me, I see! What else did he tell you?"

"Nothing. But there are so many beautiful girls on this campus as well. I was wondering why you had to go off the campus. Of course, love knows no boundary."

"You are lucky that Okoro is not here. He would have given you one or two lectures about love according to the wisdom of his father."

"Never mind that one. I have pity on whoever he will marry. He will be running home to consult his father every step of the way: 'Daddy, what do you think about this? Daddy, my wife wants us to change our bedsheet every Monday, is it okay?'He has to grow up. He needs to grow beyond his father's shadow. He is very funny, even though some of his jokes are caustic, raunchy and sexist." Both laughed. Chris could not believe that this was coming from Oby. She must be very perceptive.

"Okoro, the true son of his father. You have to give it to him. He is crude but real. He shoots straight. What you see is what you get — well, most times. His words make it easy for people to misunderstand him."

"But, how did the two of you get entangled with the nursing students?"

"It is a long story. I accompanied Okoro to see one of his prospective candidates – Cynthia – and her roommate, Ifeoma, fell for me. The rest, as they say, is history. I must say that I fell for the gap between her two front teeth. I read somewhere that women with a gap in the front teeth are exceptional lovers, if you know what I mean. I don't know whether it is a myth but I was curious." Oby silently sought a confirmation.

"Now, I can confirm that it is a myth." Chris giggled.

"I didn't know that you were this naughty," she said. She had never heard anything about a gap in the teeth before but was surprised that it did not come from Okoro. "Anyway, lucky you. When are we going to see her? You have never brought her around here. I hope that you are not playing games and toying with her emotions?"

"I don't know about that. It wasn't my idea in the first place. I am not really into this bush meat thing."

"I have heard you guys use this bush meat term several times. What does it mean?"

"If a babe is not domesticated or homegrown as a student in any of the universities, that babe is bush meat, caught in the wild, and she is not expected to have any manners. Do you get it?"

"No. So no university student can be considered as bush meat?"

"Never! The difference is clear. If she is from another university, she would be considered an import.

"So what do we call all these men that invade our campus from outside — night raiders or day hunters?"

"There are no such things."

"O yeah? So derogatory terms are only reserved for women?"

"Not really, they are called sugar daddies or resource persons." Chris had made up the last term and laughed at how appropriate it was. "They are indeed resource persons. Some of them are so ugly they are only as good as the resources they provide."

"Not really! Look at you. Even the name 'sugar daddy' implies that the old man provides the sugar. And now this new one, resource person, so he provides resources?"

"Well, don't they?"

"I see. I would think that the sugar is actually being provided by the young girl and not the good-for-nothing-daddy."

"Look, Oby! Why are you taking this out on me?"

"Because you are a man, and the world is so unfair to women. Our generation will teach you guys a lesson."

"I beg oo o."

Oby had developed a penchant for fighting women's causes whenever she could. Since her father's death, her mother's experience at the hands of her uncles had reinforced her belief that women should fight for more power and recognition. She did not understand how one should be made to plead for what was rightfully theirs just because one was a woman. Why were a woman's rights, including the rights to her own body, inferior to a man's wishes? She realised that some women, such as Mama Ijeoma and Ada, her roommate, preferred the status quo because it enabled them to use their womanhood to exploit men — or so they thought. It was confusing at times. Perhaps they did prefer the situation, perhaps their powerlessness manifested itself in their feeling a perverse sense of being in charge.

"No Chris, I didn't mean to be harsh to you. It is just that ...ehm ..."

"You don't have to explain. I understand. Your assertions turn me on. I do not like 'yes-women'. You should see how you glow when you are making a point you strongly believe in."

"Chris, you are something else. Do you really mean it?" Oby was bashful.

"Sure, my woman must have a high level of self confidence. That's why this bush meat thing is not for me."

"I thought that most men were threatened by self-assertive women?"

"No, not my genre."

"What of Chike?"

"I should ask you?"

"So far so good."

"That's good. That's really good," Chris said, nodding. He was uncertain on whether to probe further or not. "I have not been as lucky with campus girls. The one that I really liked and who equally liked me happens to have come from Embakassi. It is terrible. She was simply too much: beautiful, sophisticated and confident. We went out for only two weeks before the ugly incident of last year. Have you heard about it?"

"Yes, Chike told me about the crisis between Embakassi boys and the Igbo boys over Embakassi girls."

"Very ugly, wasn't it?"

"It is incomprehensible that such things should happen in a university. So what happened between the two of you?"

"We decided that we would be better off discontinuing the relationship since we would not want either of us to end up in hospital. Her very influential and well educated parents also got a hint of the relationship and started putting pressure on her. It was annoying. Since then, I have not met anyone quite like her. Well, of course eh ... until Chike brought you into our lives." Chris said this with an intense, piercing look at Oby. He wanted the message sent out loud and clear.

"What a shame!" Oby said with her head bowed to avoid the look.

It had started raining while they ate. Now, it stopped as suddenly as it had started. When they stepped out to walk back to their hostels, the ground was not very wet. It wasn't the rainy season after all. It had fallen in large droplets and sounded on the zinc roof like pellets of ice, creating the impression of a heavy downpour. It had, however, sent in cool, soothing fresh air, and turned the sky deep blue. Chris was humming the Louis Armstrong tune *When the Sky is Blue*.

Oby was lost in thought, and in a flash her mind went to her mother back in Isiakpu. She thought she was coping well at the university despite the challenges facing her. In a few weeks' time they would be sharing their experiences. Not that she expected her mother to offer much help any more; maturity and experience would make her mother know that Oby did not need to be protected any more.

Chris held her hand and she let him. They walked along a dirt road back to the hostels. The road was not busy. At this time of the semester, people took their time before going to the cafeteria. They came to a sandy patch of the road and she bent down to pick up the sand. There was a certain familiar aroma from it brought by the rain. She collected a handful and brought it closer to her nose.

"What are you doing?" Chris asked.

"Can't you smell something? Oh, I forgot that you are a been-to," Oby teased.

"Oh boy!"

"Excuse me, it is 'oh girl'! The aroma reminds me of my childhood days in Kano."

She picked up a fresh handful for Chris to smell. "Kano, as you know, can be very dry, and we used to have teasing downpours like the one we just had. We would play with the sand and even eat it."

"Eat!"

"I mean put it in our mouths and spit it out. Just for the aroma. Had you not been here, maybe I would have done the same."

"Well, I can close my eyes."

"By the way, I don't think that you would get this aroma everywhere. So don't expect this effect on your next trip to London. You English people expect universality in everything, *onye ocha nnia di oji* (white man with a black father)." She had run a few steps away from Chris as to tease him.

"Come back here, you village girl. I don't blame you."

They did not realise when they got to Oby's hostel. Suddenly, the evening had come to an end. For Chris, it was an evening of mixed emotions. He had accepted the fact that the status quo had to be respected unless, of course, Oby herself invited him to upset the balance. He very much wanted to plant a surprise kiss on her lips. But she had positioned herself in such a way that the kiss remained in the realm of his dreams. Not even a few minutes, awkward delay could change things. His hands dropped as suddenly as they went up her shoulders as the kiss landed on Oby''s cheek, and he whispered: "Can we do this again tomorrow?"

With a look that said it all, she waved goodbye to him and walked into the hostel a little confused but not making much of Chris' shenanigans.

CHAPTER SIXTEEN

Okoro and Chike returned from Aba the following day. With some money around, Okoro announced that he wanted to celebrate his birthday with the boys and their partners in two days' time.

The venue was the famous Hotel Metropol. Okoro arranged dinner for six and two rooms for Chris and himself. He planned to meet all expenses. Okoro could be generous when he so chose, and the good thing was that he did not expect anything in return. Well, not from the men.

He had earlier asked Chike whether he should also book a room for him and, with a sense of disappointment, he had declined the offer. Chike realised that it would be foolish to ask Oby to spend the night with him at the Hotel Metropol. He knew that the mere mention of it could ruin the forthcoming Economics gala night for him. It could even threaten their relationship. Okoro, of course, thought that he was a wimp who needed someone to kick his backside.

It wasn't his problem. But he thought that idolising a woman was a big mistake which, according to his father, was worse than being impotent. If you are impotent, you know that you cannot perform. But if you can perform and you are not performing, then you are dead meat. That was his father's impassioned way of explaining it, and Okoro had heard this several times from the man, usually after he had had a few bottles of beer. It had mattered little to him that the children were around.

Chike was worried, too, but did not want to follow anybody's lead on this one. He had his own plans. Right now, that plan dictated that he be averse to risk.

By the time Oby and Chike got to Hotel Metropol on that Saturday evening, Okoro, Chris, Ifeoma and Cynthia were already seated. This was Oby's second time at the Metropol.

Chike had brought Oby and her roommates to honour the deal he had struck with Ada in Room 146. Chike did not make that visit known to his friends and neither did he fully explain the real reasons behind it to Oby. He had simply told her that it would be normal to develop acquaintance with her roommates in an informal setting outside the campus. But Oby did not understand why Chike had spent all that money. Neither could she explain Ada's insatiable desire for the most expensive items on the menu. By the time they left the hotel that evening, Ada was drunk. She was barely able to get to their room. Fumi and Oby provided some disguised support in order not to attract the attention of other girls or worse still, *The Bee*. Unable to change clothes, she slept the whole night in what she had worn to the hotel. Fumi could not say much even though she knew about the deal. She kept exchanging glances with Oby in a way that expressed utter surprise at Ada's strange behaviour.

It was also a very rough evening for Chike. He had to deposit his gold watch with the hotel manager because he did not have enough money to clear the bills. He greatly valued the watch, sent to him by his uncle as a present from the United States. He got his watch back the next day after paying the balance with some of the money borrowed from Okoro.

"We thought that you guys were not going to show up," Chris said.

"Sorry guys, but if you are going out with the first lady, you have to have patience. Protocol has to be observed," Chike said.

Chris concurred. "You are right man."

"Which First Lady is this?" Cynthia asked, looking at Okoro for an answer. She was the talkative type and did not like anyone trying to upstage her.

"Ask Chike, he must be talking about his first lady," Okoro said disinterestedly.

"So, I am your First Lady, Okoro?"

"You guys are looking for trouble. If you are First Lady; who is the Second or Third Lady? Don't you realise that to rank presupposes that there are many?"

"True ... but ehm ..." Chris said.

130

"But ehm ... what? Guys, today is my birthday. Allow me please to set the agenda. Please!" Okoro said, rubbing both his hands in supplication. "I personally have a long evening ahead of me. Na first lady we go chop?" he continued.

"Well, first things first. Oby, this is Cynthia and this is Ifeoma, and you can use your tongue to count your teeth and know who is who," Chris said.

Oby stretched her hand to greet the two women.

"Nice meeting you two."

"We have heard a lot about you. Nice meeting you, too," Cynthia said. She was about to go on when Ifeoma nudged her and whispered. "BBC London, are you on short wave one or two?" She got the message and kept quiet.

Okoro looked meaningfully in the direction of the waiters and one of them appeared with a menu. It was a set menu but there was a choice of drinks. It was a cold beer for Chike and Chris, a big stout for Okoro, a small Guinness stout and coke each for Ifeoma and Cynthia. Oby stayed on Fanta. Her order generated some amusement.

"Fanta! Wetin that one go do for your body," Cynthia giggled. "How can you remain first lady if your body is always cold for your man?" Guinness is it!"

"Fanta works well with me," Oby maintained an arrogant calmness.

"I used to say so until I tried this combination. It is so natural," Ifeoma added softly.

"Engine oil," put in Okoro. "You've got to have it. It is like servicing a car without a dose of engine oil. My father calls it Onugbu because it is as bitter as Onugbu leaves. He said that it is medicinal, and I agree. I have never had a stomachache or any of those funny diseases since I don't know when." He gulped a mouthful.

"Okoro you should thank God for your good health," Oby said. "It is not Guinness Stout that has given you good health. You have it by the grace of God." She took a sip of Fanta.

Okoro, was still talking. "Leave those things alone. After all it is God who made it possible for stout to be produced. Thus in the final analysis it is still by the grace of God."

"If you were remotely right, Okoro, that drunken statistics professor, Professor Akambi, would not be suffering from diabetes," Chike reminded them.

"This guy drinks until he urinates in his pants. And he only drinks Guinness," Chris said. They laughed. "Yet he is so smart and sober the next day you would not believe it," he went on.

"Who is this guy? Do I know him? Is he married?" Oby asked.

"Married?" All the three men burst into laughter.

"He was divorced even before he was married," Chris said.

"He was married but he now specialises in under 18s," Okoro added. "His daughter graduated from our department last year."

"Well, that is an excellent lesson for those who want to warm their bodies," Oby said sarcastically. "You might heat it to the point where you either continue to give it Guinness to maintain the temperature or it explodes."

"Ride on, I couldn't agree more," Chris added.

"Yeh yeh man, useless man. You are always agreeing with women. I pity the wife wey you go marry. You would bore her to death: Yes ma. Yes madam ... Would that be all, madam ... Yeh, yeh. They should have left you to rot in that cold *oyibo* country." All laughed, entertained.

"Please Okoro, don't bring your acidic mouth near my man," Ifeoma said.

"Anyway, yours is better. You at least confirm that he is a man. Others are still doing hide and seek, catch and release, in constant search of what they have not lost."

This was an obvious reference to Chike and Oby, and everybody was still choking with laughter.

"Please let nobody provoke me, I want to have my food in peace. My father once told me that the only matter between a man and a woman should be settled sooner rather than later. Otherwise, one would soon find that what belongs to one is in a neighbour's house. Please! I know that you all want to hear it from my mouth. Not today. I am not going to be everybody's alibi and I don't want anyone to quote me. What else would someone be looking for at the bottom of a soup pot?

Tell me! Meat, nothing but meat. If they tell you that they are looking for something else, na lie. My father once told me that if you decide to ride a rocking horse it will keep you going but you get nowhere. Please everyone, please." Even those who were the subject of the joke were laughing.

Oby checked her watch as if to remind everyone that it was time to disperse. But they had enjoyed themselves so much that they had hardly noticed the hours pass by. Oby had planned to read that night after returning to the hostel.

Chike excused himself to go to the bathroom. Chris and Okoro decided to go with him. They were equally pressed. As soon as they left, Cynthia could not hold herself.

"Oby, is it true about the big stuff?"

"Which big stuff?" she asked, surprised.

"You know that Chike has an extra large dude."

Cynthia and Ifeoma burst out laughing.

"What are you talking about?"

"*Oyaa*, BBC! You and your big mouth," Ifeoma said. "You have to explain." She was enjoying herself thoroughly.

"Are you trying to tell us that you don't consider his manhood extra large? How accommodating! Even his fellow men are scared of him!" Cynthia was now direct and Oby got the message. She tried to laugh it off. "How would I know? I do not follow him to the bathroom."

"Don't tell us that both of you have never ... ehm ... seen each other nude?" Ifeoma asked innocently with incredulity.

"We take our relationship too seriously to be distracted by those kinds of things. Besides it is none of your business."

"So what is the problem? Are you scared of him?" Cynthia asked.

"Scared of him? No. As I said, it is none of your business."

"Take it easy. We are family. The left hand always knows what the right hand is doing. There is no point in trying to prove anything to us."

"Besides we are all women and we should bond." It was Ifeoma. "It doesn't really matter that you are at university. You never know ..." She trailed off. "My main problem is that I find this very difficult to comprehend. Are the two of you okay? What then do you do when you are alone together?"

She was earnestly looking for an explanation and she smiled, exposing the gap between her white teeth, waiting for an answer.

"Lots of things," was Oby's reply.

"I don't know about you," Cynthia told her. "But he cannot be happy that way. No way! You should not interpret the fact that a lizard is always nodding to mean that it is always in agreement with what's being said or that it is happy. Take it from me."

"Cynthi, Cynthi! Where did you get that one from?" Ifeoma said excitedly. "That is a serious proverb."

"I am the true daughter of my father."

"Well, let us have the unique statistics whenever the opportunity presents itself. We hope for your sake, sooner than later," Cynthia said as she and Ifeoma exchanged a high five and downed their drinks. The men walked in.

The women were almost choking on their drinks as the men took their seats.

They had taken much longer in the bathroom because Chris wanted to know where he could get a condom. Okoro thought such requirements were unnecessary.

"Do you know where one can get a raincoat?" Chris had asked. "I forgot to bring one along."

"What for?" Okoro had asked.

"What do you mean what for? You are asking that question in this day and age?"

"Yes, what for?" Okoro insisted.

"For my protection, you empty skull. Perhaps, your father gave you his own protection."

"So you don't trust the girl. You don't know how lucky you are. Brother been-to. You are probably this girl's second boyfriend."

"And so? What if she becomes pregnant?"

"Would you be the first man to make a girl pregnant? Big deal!"

"Hey guys, none of this concerns me but I would advise that whatever we do, we do it with utmost care so that no one gets hurt.

134

Okoro, I know that you have your ways but I support Chris on this one. Let's get out of here. We are keeping the ladies waiting."

"If you insist, you can order it on room service and put it on my bill. Better still, I will order it and send it over to you. If we still find the door open, we will deliver them. If not, ka Chineke mezie okwu. It would be an act of God. You know me, I don't beat about the bush. Shakara been-to!"

As Chike and Oby walked out of the hotel to wait for a taxi, both were hit by a strong stench from the open gutters. Hotel Metropol was located on the busy Kwame Nkrumah Avenue. The road was once the pride of the city. It was once smooth, wide and well lit at night. In the past people strolled along it leisurely on Sunday evenings to enjoy the fresh air. But, like everything else, it now lay in ruins. In the day, the clogged trenches brewed the concoction of filth and sin under the scorching sun as traders created a black market for foreign exchange, sold *suya* – roast meat – and second-hand clothes. At night, the unlit lamp posts stood silhouetted against the lantern light from the kiosks, the only refuge for prostitutes. It looked like a market for spirits, with everyone wearing masks. It was no place for a leisurely stroll. Certainly no street to name after an African idealist.

Oby wanted a taxi she and Chika could take alone so they could talk in privacy. But none came empty. Not these days. Not with the population in the city and the scarcity of taxis. They eventually settled for one with one passenger because Oby was becoming uncomfortable with the activities on the street and the stench was becoming unbearable as the sea breeze carried it to their noses.

The Peugeot 504 saloon was a moving tattered box. Nothing in the car was in its original shape. You could see the road through the floor of the car. If you chose to close your eyes, the squeaks, cries and noisy throbs of the car as it negotiated manholes and pot holes reminded you that you were riding in a distant cousin of a car. When Chike closed the door, the entire contraption rattled. The door handle was a string of fibrous wire. If you wanted to wind down the window, you had to obtain the miserable sole winder from the driver. When the taxi hit a bad pot hole, the engine would go off. In the absence of street lights, what would happen was almost inevitable. No key was required to start the taxi; the driver merely joined two wires and, with luck, the machine came back to life. If you waited for an apology from the driver, you would be wasting your time. He would be wishing he charged you four-fold for the pain you were inflicting on his precious vehicle. It required a great deal of ingenuity to keep the car running. If you worried about roadworthiness or pollution control, you had to be from another planet. It was not Chike's first time to ride in a dilapidated taxi but this experience was special, with Oby by his side.

The rough and bumpy ride back to the campus did not afford Oby an opportunity to have a smooth conversation with Chike. She tried as much as possible to use coded language in finding out what the conversation she had with Ifeoma and Cynthia was all about. She could not be explicit because of the additional passenger. She gave up because the squeaks and sudden bangs in and out of the pot holes kept cutting short her sentences. At some point, her only worry was that if she spoke, she would bite off her tongue.

When they got to the campus, Oby led the way to a concrete garden chair. It felt cold but they gradually warmed from the heat of their bodies close together. She was eager to ask her question and didn't give Chike a chance when he tried to suggest a different but more romantic location. She asked the question, somewhat more explicitly and tried to link it with other references she had heard people make when the two were walking around the campus. Mr K, Mr Big Stuff, etc.

She did not want him to feign ignorance, so she provided all the circumstantial evidence up front. Chike explained what had happened between him and his previous girlfriend, whom he described as suffering from pathological hysteria. He indicated that her reaction on the day *The Bee* carried a story on them had nothing to do with what was reported. She had wanted him to make love to her. But she had changed her mind at the last minute and dashed out of her room in a frenzy. Chike explained that the girl had come back several times asking for reconciliation. But he had had enough of her hysterical behaviour; one minute she was all loving, and the next minute she was screaming murder.

136

On a lighter note, he dared Oby to find out the truth for herself through a proper scientific investigation rather than rely on rumours. As he said this, he inched closer to her, and in one swift move grabbed her wrist and placed her palm between his legs. He felt a warm sensation as Oby wrestled free. Chike tried again, and this time Oby was more cooperative. She was lost as she felt his manhood pulsate and grow bigger and harder. She edged closer to him and buried her head in his chest.

She could hear his heart beat faster and faster. Chike was busy searching Oby's body erratically. His fingers were all over her, not knowing what to do or where to stop. He turned around and kissed her gently, passionately. He broke in between to tell her, "I love you, I love you baby." Oby struggled to reply, "I love you, too," but his mouth would not let off. When Chike's fingers landed on her breast and he fondled with it, Oby knew that things were getting out of hand.

A cricket buried in the grass nearby chirped so loudly it appeared to be warning the two lovers. Oby's eyes opened and she wrestled free from Chike. When she looked up, the sky was dull but a thick blue cloud revealed a passing storm. Here, unlike outside the Metropol, the air was fresh, clean.

It took him a few minutes to regain his composure.

"Did you feel anything big?" he asked. "I guess it is the wrong question since you don't feel it with your hands and against all these barriers." Chike breathed hard. He could feel the wetness in his pants.

"Do you mind?" Oby said. She did not feel like discussing her first intimate encounter with him. She was somewhat shy about it and quickly changed the subject.

"Now, I have seen what you guys mean by bush meat. Not that I agree with the term. But Cynthia is something else." Oby continued.

"What do you mean?" Chike asked absent-mindedly.

"She has no decorum at all. She is so raw."

"That's the way Okoro likes them. Money for hand, back for ground. You can't quarrel with success. As we speak they are in one of the rooms at the Metropol with the air-conditioner turned on full blast, enjoying each other. Sure thing: you can't quarrel with success."

"But ehm ... Ifeoma is decent. She is also beautiful. Don't you think so?" Oby asked without paying attention to Chike's telling remarks.

"Somewhat naive. But she is okay."

"Anyway, who knows what you men like?"

"Let's go and get some sleep, O'jare! Cow way no get tail, na God de drive am fly." Chike was not really up to this conversation. He was pleased with what had transpired between them but wondered for how long the teasing would continue.

For sure, he would have wanted to be where Chris and Okoro were: in a room at the Metropol with Oby in his arms. He did not see anything wrong with that: two consenting adults enjoying one another. His task would be to make it happen sooner rather than later. As Okoro said his father had told him once, he did not want what belonged to him to be found in another man's premises.

CHAPTER SEVENTEEN

Oby had just returned to her room from the bathroom when Chike knocked on her door. She had a towel wrapped around her, shower cap on her head. She had a dry skin and had learnt to apply body lotion with a little moisture on her body. She had one leg on her reading chair, and was slightly hidden by her standing wardrobe as she applied the lotion generously on her legs. The knock on the door took her by surprise.

Her mind was on that evening's event, and she was wondering how she would cope as a First Lady. She had not been expecting anyone that soon. Her two roommates were out, and were not expected to knock before coming in.

When she opened the door she saw Chike in a new navy blue striped suit, a matching tie, and a white breast handkerchief. He stood at the threshold with hands in his pockets.

It was the Economics gala night and Chike would be sworn in as President of the Economics Students' Association. Since the event was scheduled to start at 8.30 pm Oby was not expecting to be picked up until about 7.30 pm. It was now only 6.00 pm. Oby's two roommates, both of whom would undoubtedly attend the function, were not expected back at the hostel until 7.30 pm. But they would not be involved in the pre-dinner arrangements. They were, therefore, likely to come in just before dinner was served. As part of Ada's deal with Chike, a front row table would be reserved for them, irrespective of the time they showed up.

"I wasn't expecting you just now," she told him. "It is only 6.00 pm." Oby briskly walked back to where she would be partially hidden by the wardrobe. She knew that Chike's first act whenever they met was to draw her close to him and kiss her. But she felt exposed and did not want such a close encounter. Worse still, her towel might fall off and leave her naked. Chike would certainly have liked to see her naked, not to embarrass her but to make his objective much easier to achieve.He would of course not do anything that would ruin the evening.

"Yes, I know. I didn't want to take chances. Today is the D-day, and I didn't want to gamble. I wanted to be sure that you would be ready on time."

"Are you suggesting that I am always late?"

"No, sweetheart. You can afford to be late all the days of our lives, but not today."

"What are you going to be doing for the next one and a half hours?"

"Watching you dress delicately, put on each item of clothing. I came early so that I can watch everything from beginning to end. It is fascinating the number of articles a woman has to put on to be fully dressed. It would be my honour to assist wherever necessary."

"Thief!" she said. "If you don't shut up now, you will be going to the dinner alone." She threw a pillow at him.

"I beg oo. Anything you say, Madam."

"I have an idea. You have never seen my photo album, right?"

"Right. Let's see those old village boyfriends."

"You think that everyone is like you. You can't even count the number of girlfriends you have had, woman wrapper. Look at this, it will perhaps keep your eyes in their sockets, away from feeling me with your eyes." She handed him an old photo album stuffed with loose pictures.

As he went through the album, a picture fell on to his lap. He had initially not recognised anybody in the pictures except Oby but he now thought he recognised the Reverend Father. Oby explained that the picture showed her mother with Fr Damian.

"Small world," Chike said, his face lighting up. "This is indeed Fr Damian."

"You know him?"

"Do I know him? He has gained a little weight but I will never forget him. The rascal." Chike laughed, recalling an encounter he had had with Fr Damian.

"He was your family friend as well?"

"No. I knew him when I was teaching at Asaba. He was on his

last apostolic duties before ordination. I used to say that if Damian became ordained, rather than protest, I'd aspire to become a Pope," Chike's laughter rose. Oby knew that there was more to his laughter.

"There is something you are not saying," she said. "He is a very knowledgeable man and his mastery of the liturgy is not in doubt. He often animates the congregation with his sense of humour. Let me tell you, he comes highly recommended by the Bishop. Why are you laughing?" Oby was anxious to know what Chike knew about Fr Damian that she did not know.

"Did I say that he was ignorant? In fact, he knows a whole lot more perhaps than he should. Oby, we will be late if you don't hurry up."

"You will actually be going alone if you don't tell me what you know about Fr Damian," Oby threatened.

"Oby, please! There is nothing to tell. I was only saying that I would not go to confess my sins to him even if he was the only priest in town. Please, let's go."

"I think you are not taking me seriously."

"No, please. It is just that it is a long story. Besides, it is not my responsibility to report on anybody's past," Chike pleaded.

"Well, you heightened my curiosity," she said. " So let's get it over with."

"Fr Damian had problems with women when he was in Asaba and this was widely known. That's it. Can we go now?"

"No. From the look in your eyes, there is more."

"Oh boy, I hope that this is not going to be used against me," Chike said, making the sign of the cross. He went on. "One day, he came to my apartment unannounced with two sisters. I was grading some papers while listening to Osita Osadebe's *Makojo* on my small radio-cassette. As they walked in, dressed in their habits and all, he went and raised the volume of the cassette and they started dancing. We barely exchanged greetings. He drew and held one of the sisters so close to himself that you felt he would soon squeeze the breath out of her. For a minute, I thought that I was watching a movie. She was one of those sisters that you see and start thinking that she was wasted.

She was very pretty. The other nun, with an extra-ordinarily large bust, was initially dancing alone but she pulled me up, inviting me to fondle and caress her breasts, but I couldn't. My hands froze. Besides, I thought that I would be straining my poor hands and could develop arthritis if I were to effectively caress her. My eyes were fixed on the large bronze crucifix dangling from where she had placed my hands and I got very afraid. I quickly swung the crucifix unto her back and made a sign of the cross. She laughed heartily and held me so tightly close to her that I almost fainted. I kept hoping for a reprieve from the record but you know *Makojo* is a long one."

"I don't believe this," Oby said. "You enjoyed yourself with sisters. God will punish you." She did not believe what she was hearing about Fr Damian. She did not like it.

"Not me. She was soft and big and I was a reluctant partner. I was very frightened, by the way. I kept thinking that lightning would strike us dead. I kept asking God for forgiveness. I felt very bad that the Reverend Sisters dressed in their habits would put me in such a situation. I was equally angry at Damian.

"You mean Fr Damian?"

"Excuse me."

"What happened afterwards?"

"Well, before we knew it, Damian, I mean Fr Damian and company had sneaked into my bedroom while the other sister and I kept vigil over a few bottles of beer. The vigil was not without temptation. Apparently, Fr Damian had promised the two sisters a good time. Unfortunately, I had a severe case of frigidity."

"Are you sure?" she asked. "I don't trust you."

"I swear. I didn't do anything with her. I can't lie to you."

"This whole story is disgusting. How I wish you never told me,"

Oby did not like anything that challenged her faith. Not this sort of story about someone she held in such high regard. She would never let her mother know about it. If only she had known of her mother's encounter with Fr Damian!

"You asked for it. Please don't blame me. Oby! It is seven o'clock. We should be leaving in ten minutes' time. Oh, my God!"

CHAPTER EIGHTEEN

As they stepped into the new Social Science Auditorium, all eyes were on them. Chike was the man of the hour, and Oby was truly looking and walking like a First Lady.

He was very proud to have walked in hand in hand with her. She was elegantly dressed in a sleeveless dress, cut with a deep blue, tight-fitting velvet top that revealed much of her decolletage, and joined to a three-layer white acrylic material with large deep blue circular patterns. The dress had been bought by Chike, ready-made, during his last trip to Aba, for tonight's function. From the way it fitted her, it looked as if the dress had been tailored specially for her. Chike had used his eyes and intuition to decide on her size.

He acknowledged congratulatory messages as he made his way to the table he had reserved for Oby, himself, her roommates and their pals. None of them was there yet. He knew that when the function began, he and Oby would be invited to the high table. But it was more dignified to be invited to the high table than to proceed and take seats there unceremoniously. Chike appreciated the effect of the invitation and the ovation that would inevitably accompany it, especially knowing as he did that Chris was the master of ceremony.

Chris walked over to Chike and Oby. She was seated and Chike was standing trying to catch the attention of the head of the planning committee. He wanted to be sure that everything was in place, that the music and the DJ, the stand-by generator, the drinks and the food were ready. A very meticulous guy, Akpan Udo, had been chosen by Chike to head the planning committee. His organisational ability was recognised by everyone in the Economics Department. As he went over the details with Chike, Chris was busy pouring compliments on Oby, and stealing a few touches. He could never keep his hands to himself around her. Oby was particularly dashing this evening. He had not invited Ifeoma from the nursing school because he did not want to make their relationship public. By sheer coincidence, Ifeoma had to travel home, and this had made it easier for Cynthia, Okoro's girlfriend, to accept his invitation. Not that it would have stopped her but it would lessen the awkwardness.

"Everything is in place," Akpan said. "How many times am I going to tell you this?"

"I want to be sure that the generator is working. Was it tested?" Chike asked, still somewhat nervously and absent-minded. Nervous because he had to perform today, and absent-minded because his thoughts kept going back to how he planned to spend the entire evening with Oby.

"Have a glass of cold water and sit down for a few minutes. I think Chris should be starting the function in five minutes. Our guest of honour, the Chairperson of the Banking Society in Embakassi and her husband are already here," Akpan said before walking away.

"Over to you, Chris. Please call this meeting to order and start the function. We are already 30 minutes late." Chike downed a glass of cold water as advised.

As his eyes searched the hall for the guest of honour, Chike's eyes caught his ex-girlfriend moving around to exchange greetings.

She blew a kiss towards him. Chike froze, and for one minute thought whoever had invited her to the function a traitor out to humiliate him or cause trouble. This was not one of those parties on campus where you gate-crashed. The four security men at the door had strict instructions not to let in anyone without an invitation card. It was a dinner-dance and the organising committee had to be very strict.

Moreover, gate-crashers did not come to parties this early, Chike reasoned. Before Chike could make his way back to where Oby sat, Chris' voice brought the gathering to order, after a quick exchange with the guest of honour and her spouse.

Invitations to the high table over, the outgoing President of the Economics Association read a welcome address in which he catalogued the association's achievements during his tenure. Then dinner was served. Fumi, Ada, Uche and Ben walked in just then. Oby had begun to worry. But it was Ada's style to walk into any function at a time

144

when she would get everyone's full attention. She swung her hips from side to side, although she had little to swing. Oby felt a wave of embarrassment wash over her, and she sought to hide behind Chike.

The guest of honour's speech was short but its message was direct and clear. She deplored the absence of women in the banking profession and other economics-driven careers. The university had an economics student population of 125, of them only 12 women. She caused laughter when she said that if you looked around the hall that night, you would see a balance between men and women but that the balance was the result of imports and successful poaching from other departments by the sweet-tongued male economics students. During her tenure as president of the Banking Society in Embakassi, she promised to try to balance those numbers. She would hold further discussions with the head of the Economics Department, who was also present at the function, on some of her ideas.

Chike started his acceptance speech a little nervously. Soon after the initial formalities, his shaky voice firmed up with confidence. He gave an analogy of the experience he and Oby had had in the dilapidated taxi on their way from Hotel Metropol.

"Our economy reminds me of my recent encounter in a taxi that, out of charity, could be described as unroadworthy. Just like our economy has different sectors, this taxi had different parts. Just like our sectors, the different parts of this taxi had no relationship to one another as the original construct demanded. They were all partially glued together to make the weak and battered contraption. None supported the other. You were aware that the vehicle was moving but you were not sure when it would stop and, if it stopped, whether it would ever move again. It accelerated and jerked at the same time. When it suddenly stopped in the middle of the road, the driver simply connected two wires and it roared back to life as if nothing was wrong. But the fundamentals were wrong. The vehicle coughed and jerked as it struggled along. If this were a patient, no doctor would say "take three of these and call me in the morning". No, he or she would be a candidate for the intensive care unit. The driver obviously didn't care. He wanted to maximise his gains for the day. It did not matter to him that a little investment on this taxi would give it life and provide him with a better income, not to talk of the comfort of his passengers. When the taxi stalled he blamed the passengers for making impossible demands on his taxi. Yet, he sought the job and he was carrying passengers who had no choice."

"Look around you," Chike said. "Not one sector of this economy is working, from the agricultural sector to the manufacturing sector. Instead of integrating them, our policies create a wedge between them. Today, we liberalise because our gut feeling directs us to do so. Tomorrow we are quick to reverse these policies because our primitive instincts overpower us. Our forefathers consulted high priests and oracles whenever they wanted to undertake any serious activity or a major journey. Today, our leaders simply look up and down, scratch their heads and make profound policy pronouncements without any basis. It does not matter whether these will hurt our oil sector, the life-blood of the country. We are prepared to destroy the goose that lays the golden egg. Like the taxi driver, the leaders of this country are not prepared to invest in tomorrow. Like a roving bandit, the state plunders with reckless abandon. The resilience of the passengers of this ship should not be interpreted to mean the ship is not sinking. We are all stuck here because this is the only country we have. Many have indeed jumped ship. And the ship captain is encouraging more to jump out, the very good and skilful swimmers, thinking that it would lighten his burden. What folly!"

Applause and laughter punctuated Chike's speech. One person shouted, "Tell them!" Another said, "Speak on, brother!"

He paused for a glass of water and looked at Oby's radiant face. She was very proud of him.

"Fellow economists, bankers and advisers in the making, I have tried to give a sketch of where we are as a nation. A few lessons for us. Those who are trained to optimise should not optimise myopically by sacrificing long-term social goals for short-term selfish ones. If this ship, this nation, is to stay afloat and move at a pace that meets our needs, we must in our deeds and intent avoid opportunistic actions. Unlike the taxi driver, those who lead this nation must understand that putting bits and pieces of battered sectors together will not do. Our leaders must learn to procure, to process, to ponder before making policy pronouncements. There is no substitute to investment in infrastructure, in education, in health. There is no substitute to good governance and macro-economic stability. Ladies and gentlemen, it is our responsibility to insist on these minimum standards. Let's get busy. Thank you."

Chike received a standing ovation, and as each member of the high table walked over to congratulate him, Oby hugged him, and kissed him lightly on the lips. As Chike sat down, he once again caught sight of Margaret, Meg, his ex-girlfriend. She blew another kiss towards him. This time, both the kiss and the blowing lasted longer. Chike knew he had to do something fast or the evening could turn ugly. Meg was erratic and she could be worse after a couple of drinks. She could get aggressive. Her last statement to Chike had been, "I will never give you up to that low-class girl." This kept coming back to him.

Chike beckoned Okoro to the high table. When he came, he took him aside and whispered to him as they both looked in the direction of Meg. Okoro was simply nodding. When Chike returned to his seat, Oby wanted to know whether there was a problem.

"Is everything okay?"

"Oh yes, oh yeah! I just wanted him to take care of a little problem for me."

"I noticed that both of you were looking at a particular direction when you spoke."

"Yes, we have an important guest, I wanted Okoro to pay special attention to the fellow."

Seated at the same table with Meg was an economics student Okoro knew well — Jim Young from Rivers State. He was good looking and boisterous, and Meg wouldn't mind claiming him as a boyfriend even for tonight except that she had come to the function with her own set of motives.

Okoro took Chike's assignment seriously and quickly figured out how to handle Meg's presence. If his plans were to work out as fast as both men wanted, he would have to use Jim. He had to be very meticulous or Meg would explode the plan. Okoro's opportunity came when Jim went over to the bar to get drinks for Meg and himself.

Okoro crept up to him and briefed him about Chike's worry about Meg's presence and how Chike had asked him to handle the situation with Jim's assistance. Jim was flattered, and saw this as an opportunity to ingratiate himself with Chike, one of the big boys on campus. Chike had never paid any attention to him before. Jim was willing to do anything to be counted among the senior boys. The more dangerous the act, the better. After all, it was a mere coincidence that he had sat with Meg at the same table.

The plan was finalised and a new invitation card issued to Jim. He walked back to his table with the drinks, and began warming up to Meg. She just loved the attention. Just as the master of ceremony was asking the guest of honour and the new President to open the dance, Jim asked Meg to walk him over to a friend's car, purporting to have borrowed it for the weekend. He had to modify the plan a bit in order to suit the circumstances. The thought appealed to Meg who wanted an opportunity to walk out of the hall as everyone watched. The music aptly chosen was Osita Osadebe's slow and melodious *Osondi, Owendi* which translates into, while some are happy, others are envious.

As Jim and Meg walked out of the hall, Okoro followed them closely and only stopped to chat with the security men. He called the four security men, spoke quietly to them, and handed over to one of them an envelope containing some money. He gave instructions that they must not allow Meg back into the hall without an invitation card even if she shed blood. Okoro and the security men knew that all invitation cards were collected as guests entered the hall. Okoro returned to the hall to avoid attracting attention, and took up Cynthia to join the crowd on the floor. As they danced, Okoro edged towards Chike and Oby to reassure him that everything was under control. When their eyes met, he smiled at Chike and said "Congratulations, brother! Everything is under control."

"Thank you. Thank you very much," Chike said.

Jim and Meg walked hand in hand down the Auditorium Crescent as she stroked his back. He in turn pressed her to him. For a minute, it crosed Jim's mind not to go through with Okoro's plans. Meg attached little importance to flirtation. She enjoyed exciting men and dumping them as soon as they began to have other ideas. Flirting with Jim tonight served the overall objective of eliciting Chike's jealousy, or so she hoped. There were cars parked on both sides of the road and only a few spots were lit. Most of the street lights were not working. Ordinarily, it would have been a perfect place for a romantic stroll.

Meg was an attractive woman and that evening, her long dress with a low-cut neck clung to her body, revealing all of her cleavage. Jim would have wished that this was real but even if he wanted, he could not work against the plan hatched by Okoro. He had to pretend to be genuinely interested in Meg. But she was equally using him to camouflage her plans to confront Chike that evening.

As they walked down the road, Meg wore a murky smile on her face. He did not quite know how to interpret her happiness but was thinking of how he would pull off the assignment, hitch-free. If any of his actions gave anything away, he would be doomed. Jim chose a spot that was very dark and stopped suddenly as if he was fidgeting with his pockets. He stopped in the middle of the road and declared that what he had come to pick from the car was actually in his suit pocket. He apologised as they began walking back to the hall.

"Your invitation card, sir?" the security men asked Jim when he approached the gate first. "But we have just passed through here," Jim answered, feigning surprise.

"Our responsibility is not to allow anyone without an invitation card beyond this gate. We are only doing our job, sir! How are we supposed to recognise everyone who has passed through here tonight?"

"Your job! I wish you would take your real jobs more seriously!"

"Thank you, sir. You can go in now," the security men took Jim's invitation card from him.

Meg, with arms folded, was watching the whole drama with some irritation. It was getting chilly out here and her sleeveless evening dress offered no protection from the cold breeze.

"Your card, miss?" Meg tried to walk through the gate after Jim.

"We are together," Jim replied.

"We are sorry, sir. But your card says Mr Young only."

"She is my partner. Are you all crazy?"

"Your card no say so, sir. Others wey come together, their card say Mr and Mrs and some Mr and Miss. Even Miss and Miss, we de accept. We understand. We no be small boys. No be because you see us for uniform so. We dey see well well." The security men burst into laughter.

"What is this nonsense?" Meg was now furious.

"Madam, make you no vex. This Oga say make we do our job well, well. Na our job we dey do?" One of the security men said sarcastically.

"Jim, please do something. I am freezing."

"Okay, you wait here. I will teach these men a lesson," Jim said as he went into the hall.

"Please don't be long. Tell Chike that his security men are insulting me."

Mission accomplished, Jim reported to Okoro, who congratulated him and reassured him that his good deeds would not be forgotten. He warned him not to mention the matter to anyone, and that it would be best if he did not discuss it with Chike that night.

Ten minutes passed and neither Jim nor Chike had shown up at the gate. The wind was now blowing harder. Meg struggled to control the flapping of her dress, which had a long side slit. She had nothing else to say to the security men who were busy enjoying the beer sent to them and were relishing her anguish.

"Them de walk like them no dey shit. E don happen," one of the security men said.

"Osondi Owendi. When the wind blows, it exposes the nyash, inner behind of a fowl."

"The wind is blowing indeed," another said, choking with laughter.

Meg could not believe what was happening. If she tried to force her way through, she could be thoroughly disgraced by the security men. They now seemed drunk. She could not understand why Jim had not come back to let her in. It was him, after all, who asked her to escort him outside. It was like a nightmare. As she turned around to go back to the hostel, a sudden whirlwind forced her dress up even as she struggled to keep it in place. The security men burst into laughter once more.

She sobbed and cursed all the way to her hostel. "God will punish all of you. Useless illiterates. You will all die as security men."

Chike had two pint-sized bottles of whisky in his jacket, and he kept checking his pockets to make sure the contents did not pour out. When they took a break from the dance floor, Oby said she wanted a punch drink. She had had Fanta all evening. When he got the punch, he took a slight detour and emptied whisky from one of the small bottles into her drink. The only thing left on the programme was dance, and the dance floor was packed. Oby noticed that her drink had an unusual taste, that it in fact had alcohol but wanted to act grown-up. She was proud of Chike and thought that the only way of fending off girls who seemed to be after him was to act as sophisticated as them. A bit of alcohol would reduce her inhibitions, she reasoned.

"What was that?"

"Punch."

"Really, it has a certain unusual taste to it. Are you sure?"

"Yes, I am sure."

"Can I have some more then?" she said as she gulped down the drink.

Chike emptied the second bottle and brought back the same concoction. She wanted to gulp down the second glass when Chike intervened.

"Take it easy."

"Why?"

"Because ... eeh mm ... ehmm. You should just take it easy. Besides, I don't want to go back for more."

"Well, in that case, I will get some more myself."

"No, not that way. I mean ... ehm, just drink like a lady."

Oby was getting excited. Chike excused himself to go to the rest room. By the time he got back, Oby was on the dance floor, dancing alone. This came as a surprise to Chike who didn't know what to make of it. Were his plans working or was he going to be in bigger trouble, with the situation getting out of hand? His plan was to get her reasonably intoxicated but not drunk. This would reduce Oby's resistance to his advances. Chris was busy chatting with the other men when he noticed Oby dancing alone. He, too, thought Oby's behaviour unusual. He got to Oby a few minutes before Chike. She simply pulled him to herself and kissed him on the mouth.

He knew at that moment something was not right. When Chike arrived, she simply left Chris on the floor and fell into Chike's arms. But for Chike's agility, both of them would have crashed to the floor. Chike was still beaming with a smile not knowing that things were already out of hand. When the music stopped, Oby staggered to her seat. She put her face on the table and asked Chike to hold her hands. It was then that it dawned on him that he may be in trouble. But then, he did not appreciate how serious it was.

Chris observed all of this with discomfort.

"What did you give this girl?" Chris asked Chike after pulling him aside.

Chike told him.

"Which punch? Punch with what? You know that she has never had alcohol before?"

"How did you know that? And why are you interrogating me like CID people?"

"Better me than someone else. You have punched this girl out. This is no longer Oby." Chike looked in the direction of his girlfriend and realised that Chris might be right. It was a serious matter.

"Chris, you have to help me out," Chike said with visible anguish.

"Help you out? I thought that I was interrogating you?"

"Please, let's look for Okoro."

"Don't rush things. We should pretend that we are both dancing with her and then get her out of the hall before anyone else realises what is going on."

When they got out of the auditorium, it was so dark that one could not notice a thing. Chike went back to ask Akpan Udo to take full charge at the party. He requested Okoro to send Cynthia to his room and find them in Chike's room. Chike met Oby and Chris halfway to his hostel. Chris fully supported Oby as all she wanted to do was throw up. Chris asked her to persevere until they got to Chike's hostel. They almost carried her, an action that would have attracted a lot of attention. Chike's room was on the ground floor. It was easy, therefore, to escape notice. Moreover, it was some minutes to 3.00 am and few people were awake at that hour.

Oby was sweating profusely and her speech was barely audible. As they walked, she kept saying in between heavy, uncomfortable breathing, "My mummy, my mummy." When they got to the room, she indicated she wanted the fan on. She lay face down on the rug and, in a split second, threw up all over the rug and broke wind so explosively it startled both Chris and Chike. They could almost feel the weight of what Chike had done as they gazed at her motionless form in confusion. Oby had passed out. For the next couple of minutes both men did not know what to do.

"Let's take off her clothes so that she can get enough air," Chris suggested.

"I think that we should towel her with cold water."

"Are you going to towel her with her clothes on?"

Chike went to get the water and towel as Chris bent over to take off her dress.

"Do you mind? This is my girlfriend." In spite of the situation, Chike was struggling to protect her privacy and sense of dignity.

"By all means. But don't come crying to me." Chris tried to check her pulse and got hysterical.

"Stop Chike. We should take Oby to the clinic."

"Are you out of your mind? Take her to where?" Chike yelled.

"To the clinic. I think this may be more serious than we think. Have you ever heard of pulmonary aspiration?"

"Pulmonary what?"

"You see, she threw up and some of the vomit could block her airwaves, resulting in the shortness of breath, especially in her drunken state. Can't you see how she is breathing?"

Chris' mother had a nursing background and he had heard her use this term and discuss it with her friends.

"Going to the clinic is out of the question. What would we say happened?

"Exactly what happened. She had too much to drink and she passed out."

"I am not going to risk it."

"Risk what? But you are already risking her life."

"You are so childish," Chike yelled again as he moved from desk to desk searching frantically for a cigarette from the desk-drawers of one of his chain smoking roommates. He wanted something that would distract his attention and calm his nerves.

"Where did he keep his cigarettes?" Chike was speaking to himself.

"You are not going to smoke in this room. It will pollute the air and worsen her condition," Chris said as he sat down, frustrated by Chike's stubbornness. The sight of Oby lying almost naked and helpless made his eyes water. He did know whether to stay or leave. The room was quiet for a while as the two men, each deep in his own thoughts, waited for better or for worse. Chike was dysphoric and all kinds of thoughts were going through his mind. If Oby did not recover it would be the end of his university education. But he was optimistic that she could come to.

He had heard of people passing out but had never appreciated the severity of such incidents. He was genuinely frightened.

Both men were startled when the door opened and Okoro walked in.

"Holy Molly! Lord have mercy," Okoro cried out as he made the sign of the cross.

"Shhh, shhh," both Chris and Chike hissed in unison.

In their confusion, they had forgotten to lock the door. How lucky that it was Okoro who had walked in. It would have been a different story. Okoro stood with his mouth wide open, lost in his own conceit, gazing at Oby's naked body and unconsciously admiring what he was seeing totally in discord with the emotions of the moment.

His gaze was so intense he got dizzy. He muttered to himself, "This is foggy bottom."

"So what have you guys done?" he said when he recovered. He

154

took a few steps back and locked the door. He knew only too well the kind of scandal this kind of scene would cause if word of it got out. Chike had two other roommates who had been sent on temporary exile as part of his preparations for tonight. As things stood they could have their exile extended by another day.

No one answered him. Chris and Chike were mentally tired and confused.

"Guys, I want to know what you have done. Are you waiting for divine intervention? You should be on your knees praying."

"Shut up, Okoro," Chris muttered.

"What do you have in mind?" Chike knew that Okoro's street sense had saved him many times before.

"Well, I have seen this before. A worse situation, I must say. He slept all day. We thought he was dead."

"How was he revived?"

"They applied dry ground pepper to his nostrils. He sneezed and began to recover."

"Ground pepper? Are you out of your mind? I knew you would come up with one of your wacko ideas," Chris shuddered.

"It worked for them, so what is wrong with it?" Chike interjected.

"Well, go and look for pepper but count me out of such plans," Chris said furiously.

"Whoever counts on you when it matters?" Okoro said.

"You know, you should take partial responsibility for what is happening here."

"How?" Okoro was curious.

"Your cash-and-carry mentality can drive anyone crazy."

"You must be out of your mind."

"You have forgotten. The only matter between a man and a woman should be settled sooner rather than later, the gospel according to Pa Okoro."

"What has that got to do with anything? Look I don't have to take this from a scallywag like you."

"Hey guys, stop it. You are worsening my headache. I am responsible for whatever happened tonight."

When they were arguing, Oby shook her left leg and then moved her right arm and gave another loud blast of wind.

"Holy Moses!"

"*Ogbunigwe!*" Okoro exclaimed.

She still closed her eyes but it seemed she was gradually coming to. The room was lit with excitement. Chris and Chike moved her sideways and tried to clean her up as Okoro stole glances at her body.

"What are you staring at?" Chike asked.

"How did you see me?" Okoro asked. "Please concentrate on what you are doing."

"I will gouge your eyes out and you will forever remember this day but you will not be able to describe it."

"I don't have to have eyes to describe what I have seen. I can certainly verbalise it, foggy bottom." He swallowed the last two words.

Okoro and Chris left Chike's room at 4.30 am. It had seemed like a whole day. In order to avoid any further embarrassment, they agreed that Oby should not come to and find them there. When they left, Chike dried the floor with his old clothes and washed Oby's dress. He hung it behind one of the wardrobes. He did not expect Oby to wear such a ceremonial dress back to her hostel a day after the function. It would generate undue gossip. Oby would most likely go back in Chike's jeans and shirt.

For a while, Chike sat there trying to imagine all the possible outcomes. He was happy that the nightmare was over but he was not sure whether Oby would ever forgive him. He was angry with himself not only because of what he had done but because of his apparent weakness, succumbing to peer. He also hated himself for this impatience. If only he waited he would still have had it all. He was also angry because he might have lowered Oby's esteem before his friends. They had shared in her privacy; their emotions and secrets. He put his head in his hands and asked God for forgiveness. His eyes were red and tears flowed down his cheeks. He did not realise he could be heard. When he raised his head, Oby was staring at him. She knew something had happened to her but could not fully appreciate its magnitude. But she also did not like the sight of Chike sobbing like a child. She asked him to come and lie beside her.

"Are you all right?" Chike asked nervously.

"I am fine."

"You frightened me."

"But you wanted to kill me."

"Please forgive me. Please forgive me, Oby."

"Forgive you?"

"It was the work of the devil. You know that I love you."

"Get me a glass of cold water. Plain water, nothing more to it, and some aspirin."

She sat up, took the aspirin and went to the restroom with Chike providing the cover to make sure no one saw her. She had covered her hair with a hat and wore one of his shirts.

She slipped back to bed and again asked him to join her.

"What are you doing with all those clothes on," she said as Chike tried to get back into the bed.

"What did you say?" Chike asked, pretending that he had not heard her.

"I want you to remove all your clothes. You've already seen me naked."

"Not really."

"Don't argue with me. You almost killed me."

"Please forgive me," Chike was behaving like someone under a spell and Oby was enjoying her powers.

"Forgive you. I did not know you were a devil."

"Oby, forgive me, please."

"I said that you should take off everything."

"Sure?"

"Yes."

As he took off his underwear, Oby covered her face and began to laugh. She had a sudden burst of energy.

"Sure it's big! Sure it's big!"

He felt humiliated and wanted to put his underwear back on.

"I thought that you wanted forgiveness? Come and lie beside me if you want total forgiveness." Oby seemed to be acting out a part in one of the many romantic novels she had read. She wanted him to totally submit to her. She enjoyed being in control, and even after what she had gone through, she felt a sense of perverted happiness at the fact that she was directing affairs. Tonight was particularly important for her. But her actions seemed weird and humiliating to Chike. He had no choice but to join in the drama, not knowing where the plot would lead to. She acted as the audience and cheered on.

"So you planned to get me drunk in order to mess me up?"

He denied it.

"Not really, so what was it?"

"You see, ehmm ..."

"Shhh ...." Oby placed her finger on his lips and grabbed his penis from under the bed cover. Chike made a start. But Oby pushed him back. "Is this not what you wanted all along?"

"Not really."

"Then what did you want?"

"Ehmm, I want you but ..."

"Shhhh. You will get what you wanted." She gave his penis a few strokes. Chike's body boiled up. Oby had planned all along that she would lose her virginity to Chike on the gala night. As part of her plan, she had also thought that a little alcohol would reduce her inhibitions and ease the pain since it would be the first time for her. She had read something to that effect somewhere.

"Are you sure?" Chike asked nervously.

She did not answer him. She gave him a juicy wet kiss on his lips. "Be gentle with me. You know it is my first," Oby said.

Chike was experienced. He was soon in control, preparing Oby for the encounter. She was soon in another world. With her endurance and readiness, and his experience, it passed without much difficulty. As he fully entered her, Oby pulled up a pillow, the ultimate silencer, to gag herself. She chewed on it as he filled her up and went limp.

Except for a few red spots on the bedsheet, it would have been difficult to tell that it had been her first. They lay in each other's arms, with tears rolling down their cheeks.

She slept again and Chike slipped out of bed. With mixed emotions, he sat down to write a poem for Oby:

Lost in the Crowd

Lovely thoughts and evil plans
Driven by my emotions but controlled by the crowd.
As I succumbed to the echo,
I failed to realise that the path that leads to treasures
is often not well travelled.
It is not passion; it is greed, but it is also love.
Love with evil passion is like education without
morality.
Both are evil; both are destructive.

Shadows reflect reality; with light or darkness,
Your body radiates with gentle calmness;
Alluring, compelling and inviting.
Your "lifeless" naked body was my anguish; the
emptiness of my plans.
Faced with the loot as with an unseasoned criminal, I
trembled and fell.
The end did not have a beginning, and both the means
and the end were a carcass.
As dignified with clothes on as without;
Sorry that this reality had a sour taste to it;
As nature endowed you; so did it deny me appropriate
feeling;
My sense was gone, I could only cry.
Sorry my impatience, my impertinence, caused you
harm.
The dead are alive; with pain came pleasure and relief.
But it didn't have to be that way.
Your sanctuary, our sanctuary,
Broken into gently, was like removing the casing for

an old wine;
The content was a treasure: revealing the depth of
your warmth and inviolability; what a revelation.

It is now our melting pot; our bond.
A sacred treasure preserved and untapped;
Your wish has become my command.
How lucky I am; how ungrateful I was.
Forgive and forget.
For the broken seal is the seal of our friendship;
The many joys and pains are the glue to our love;
The grease to our roller-coaster.
Never again shall we look back and never again shall
we toast to others.
Time, place and speed shall be ours.
We shall be the masters of our destiny.
I am sorry. I sincerely love you.

Part IV

Tradition and Ambition

CHAPTER NINETEEN

Two days after Pa Okolo discussed the chief's marriage proposal with Mama Oby, he had not had the courage to face Chief Ugwueze, the Agaba Idu I of Isiakpu. The chief had sent his driver twice to ask Pa Okolo to see him. On both occasions, Pa Okolo had not been at home. He had not responded to the messages left for him.

He had thus far avoided any situation that might bring him face to face with the chief. During one close encounter, he hurriedly left a funeral through a back door when he saw the chief's car approaching. A very tactful man, Pa Okolo did it in such a way that it did not raise eyebrows. Anticipating that the chief would attend the function, Pa Okolo had announced on his arrival that he would not be staying long and would probably leave unceremoniously. He promised to explain everything later.

When Pa Okolo left a gathering, he often created a vacuum not because of his size: he was tall and not bulky. One would miss his wisecracks and humour. He had charisma and any conversation tended to revolve around him because he knew how to embellish stories. It was, therefore, difficult for him to leave the funeral the way he did without some people whispering, almost in his hearing, about his abrupt departure.

As he hurried away, he forgot his bottle of snuff which he had generously passed around for any interested person. His wives often accused him of being excessively generous to outsiders but tight-fisted to his own family. He could not help it; he cared about what outsiders thought of him and couldn't be bothered if his family thought that he was stingy. One could now understand why the delay in admitting him into the council of elders had been a source of great pain to him.

He ruled his family like a king, but he was an ordinary fellow in the eyes of those who mattered in the community. When one of the elders saw Pa Okolo's snuff bottle, he looked around to see who could catch up with him. He asked a young man to take it to him. "Young man, please run after Okolo with this bottle. He has forgotten it in his unexplained hasty exit." The man ran, calling Pa Okolo until he caught up with him. With such a twist of fate, Pa Okolo could not make a secret exit after all.

It was not easy for a man like Pa Okolo who wanted to be counted as one of the giants in the community to admit he was not in charge of his household. That his brother's widow could refuse to take orders from him.

He had tried to tame her by imposing Uncle Ben on her as husband but that had not worked. He had also tried persuasion and that had not worked either. He blamed the ineffectiveness of the first strategy on "useless Ben", as he often referred to him and on the fellow's inability to assert his authority.

Ben's inability "to perform" with regard to Mama Oby had reinforced his extremely low opinion of him. Pa Okolo now realised that he too could be accused of being unable to assert his authority because his diplomatic strategy had also failed. He spent sleepless nights thinking and vowed to do something about it. He had vowed that if Mama Oby did not accept peace, she must prepare for war; a war he knew she could not win because it would hit her hard where it hurt most. Besides, everyone would be scared of the wrath of the gods and no one would be on her side.

Early one morning, after yet another agonising night, Pa Okolo decided to speak to the chief. Perhaps, the chief would understand and suggest a different strategy. Two heads, after all, were better than one. For how long was he going to carry on this hide-and-seek game with the chief?

In the meantime, all discussions on his application for admission to the prestigious council of elders seemed to have been shelved. He had heard nothing of it, not even the usual rumours and half-truths that reached him from time to time. He knew that the chief had no good reason to bring up the matter now. From their last encounter, the chief had understood when Pa Okolo admonished that if he scratched his back the chief would return the gesture. The ball was squarely in Pa Okolo's court.

When Pa Okolo was ushered into chief Ugwueze's living room, he was sweating in the 5 am chill. This matter continued nagging him and, even before a servant, he could not pretend all was well. He felt denuded.

The chief's house was palatial in size and architecturally convoluted. Nothing simple appealed to him. His car had multiple colours and so did most things he wore.

It was said that he engaged many contractors to build different parts of the house because he did not want any one of them to have all the details of the house once completed. The principal architect had come from outside this part of Nigeria for the same reason. He did not want anyone from nearby to know how big the house was. Besides, he kept changing the design as the house was built. One of the reasons for this, according to village rumour, was that the house had to have escape routes which the chief planned to use if he fell foul of the law. His questionable activities in Lagos and his ill-gotten wealth would come home to haunt him sooner or later, many of his enemies reasoned.

No one knew exactly how many rooms the house had but they were certainly many. He had even forbidden members of his household from going into one wing of the house, his shrine as he called it. Those who claimed to be closer to him would never agree on the number of rooms. They ranged between twelve and sixteen. The chief, of course, relished this mystery and encouraged the debate. It suited him well and was part of his design and tactics of ruling by intimidation and mystery.

The house stood on a former forest, sacred land that belonged to the Ndu Nwa Agu clan of Isiakpu. It was respected as ancestral land, land with mystical powers. It housed the most respected shrine in the entire Isiakpu and the shrine was revered beyond the village. The clan relied on it for protection and prestige. Select male clan members could turn into lions. If anyone in Isiapku had doubts and expressed them publicly, the lion would visit his household leaving no doubt about its visit. It would usually come late in the night, kill one of his cows or goats, carry a big chunk of the animal away and roar as it left the compound. The next day, the victim would, without fail, visit elders of

Ndu Nwa Agu to retract his words and to offer an apology. It never was an empty apology. To restrain the likes of such people from careless talk about Ndu Nwa Agu, the elders would fine the transgressor four gallons of palm wine, several tubers of yam and a cock or a goat, depending on the mood of the eldest man from Ndu nwa Agu and depending on who the offender was. The fine would automatically double if the atonement was delayed. The offender also had to make a public proclamation of the power and mystery of Ndu Nwa Agu.

Always in attendance at such meetings held at the *otobo,* were senior daughters of the clan who would be chanting the praise of their father and protector, Agu the lion.

The women were often invited from their matrimonial homes to chant and sing praises to their forefathers and their protector, Agu, and to do a special Igbo dance, the *igbu owo.* It was not really a dance but a combination of majestic strides taken with show, vigour and arrogance in time with the songs.

They worked their hips in short, sideways movements as the men cheered. There was usually a lot to drink and, because these daughters had an important function to perform, the men were generous with the palm wine, a rare gesture. As they chanted, danced and ululated, some would go into a frenzy while others would cry out for joy. The drummers would beat on the special *okanga,* and the flutist pipe on the *oja,* as the men sung the praises of their daughters, the elderly women present.

"These are our mothers, the link between us and the future. They are the link between us and our past, our pride and our glory," someone would say. The flutist would play to this statement over and over. The women would be ululating, weaving and dancing, pounding the ground with their feet, occasionally stopping to gyrate their waists, their backsides clashing in the air and sending the men into wild cheering.

It was a source of pride for the women to have come from such a great clan, and they carried this pride to their husbands' homes. To be invited to these occasions, one had to have many grandchildren and be of exemplary behaviour. Childless women were excluded from the ceremony because it was believed that the gods gave children and if a woman was denied them, perhaps it meant she had not performed her role on earth. It would, therefore, be improper to include her in ceremonies that involved mediation with the gods. The clan elders had a way of investigating complaints against their daughters and, when they set out to punish anyone, the decision was arrived at by consensus. It did not matter whose daughter it was. The punishment was often to exclude the errant woman from the feasting and merry-making.

Senior daughters were invited because, at their age, they had ceased making the monthly trip to the moon and were considered spiritual. In the eyes of Isiapku people, the lives of the women had been fulfilled. They had earned a certain degree of respect and had a power connecting them to the spiritual world, the world of their ancestors. The men relied on them to plead their cases. No masquerade, no matter how potent, could beat or even threaten them as they would younger women. They had been masculinised. It was a ceremony that accorded women respect as senior members of a patriarchal society.

Besides, at their age they could spend nights out since all their children had left home and their husbands would have married younger wives. If a man could not afford a second wife, that was his problem.

There were benefits to their husbands, too. The women often took home food and meat, and the men felt protected by marrying from such a clan. The ceremonies were not only a source of spiritual healing for the women; they augmented the participants diets.

At the acme of the drumming and fluting, the lion would stride in majestically. It would first roar to signify its presence and then saunter into the *otobo* to greet the elders, stopping to acknowledge the presence of each one of them. Everyone would be chanting, *Nnam O, Nnam O:* "Our father, welcome," as it made its rounds. If it was supposed to discipline someone or to prove its existence to a sceptic, it would be briefed. Since it was a man-spirit in animal form, it often knew the mission beforehand. It simply walked away and got the job done. When it returned, the yelling, ululation and praise-singing would hit a new pitch. This time, it would have brought something for the supplicants to roast and munch on. It was from this great forest that it came and went as protector of the shrine.

The chief's great grandfather was condemned to serve the shrine of the Agu of Ndu Nwa Agu. A war captive, he was one of the male servants whose lives and those of their children and grandchildren were condemned to service at the shrine. They would always do the chief spirit's bidding. The chief's great grandfather was an *osu* and so would all his children and grandchildren. The family had a very small piece of land. His great grandfather had no farm; he had a lot to eat as he fed his children from the offering to the shrine and from the chief spirit's household.

The chief's father became a man in the latter part of the colonial period and the chief was born then. His father moved to another clan in Isiakpu, became a relatively well-to-do merchant, buying and selling palm kernel. In spite of this, he could not wipe off the stigma of being an outcast. No matter what he achieved, he was still an *osu*. He could not marry from his town and had to go to a neighbouring village to marry one of his kind.

It was said that at his instigation, a white man, an Assistant District Officer at that time, had come to clear the forest since it symbolised oppression for his likes. The Assistant District Officer, who thought that the lion story was a fetish concoction and a figment of the worshippers' imagination, did not come out of the forest alive. Since he had announced his visit in advance and dared the Ndu Nwa Agu clan, the lion was waiting for him when he arrived.

After the incident, the forest was left intact. No one was prepared to take the risk until the chief returned from Lagos and announced that he wanted to build a house there. He had no other piece of land, and no one was willing to sell him any. He was from Ndu Nwa Agu but he was an outcast, a second class citizen.

The chief had left the village for Lagos when he was sixteen. He had been a bright student but dropped out of secondary school in his final year soon after his father's death. He was very bitter and upset that his father, in spite of all he had achieved, had not been given a befitting funeral. In fact, when news got out that his family was planning a big ceremony, they were quickly warned that it would not be condoned. The death of an *osu* was not significant. This and other humiliations made him swear publicly that he would end the *osu* nonsense.

He was not taken seriously at the time, but unlike his father, he realised he needed an anonymous environment, a place where he would not be prejudged if his business was to prosper. Lagos was just ideal. He grew up in Lagos and married two wives who were not from his part of the country. Most Lagos women had no time to check the background of a prospective husband.

The chief was rich and that was all that mattered. In the olden days, he would have found it difficult to marry even in Lagos. No one in the village knew exactly what he did in Lagos but they knew that he was a businessman and that he had become very rich. In fact, hardly anyone knew him until he started seeking relevance at home. He wanted to regain his honour and that of his late father and great grandfather. He also knew that in Igboland wealth had no meaning unless it was felt in the village where you came from. As the Igbo say, *aku lue uno* .... It is only when wealth gets home that it is appreciated.

He understood well the changing values of the Igbo community since the civil war and the oil boom. Money spoke. Money ruled.

He knew that the people of Isiakpu had dignity even in the face of poverty and that values and traditions in the community had not died yet. But he also knew that this was a different historical epoch.

Men and women of honour were few and often very hungry. He started his incursion into the village with a campaign of generosity. He offered many scholarships to the sons and daughters of Isiakpu. He built a town hall, contributed generously to the building of a church. Through his initiative and influence, the government had brought piped water to the village. The different age-grade associations received his generous contributions. He still lived in Lagos but he was everywhere in the village. When he attended any functions, he left everyone in no doubt that he was well connected to people in high places. He always came in the company of different police commissioners, army officers or business associates from other parts of the country. It was not always a show of generosity; it also was a show of power and the sort of influence he would muster if challenged. As the Igbos would say, when something stands, something else will stand by it. He always had someone very powerful standing by him.

Wherever you went in the village, everyone talked about him. Some people spoke with trepidation and fear, others with contempt or cautious admiration. It was not easy to declare your love for him. There were die hard traditionalists who scoffed at whatever he did. *Ego Obala*, ill-gotten money, was the way they described his wealth. To them, he was still an *osu*, and a common one at that. Facts had to be separated from fiction. But such people were in the minority.

There were others who would go home and discuss him in their bedrooms, behind closed doors. Their dilemma was how to maintain the tradition and acknowledge his generous contributions to the village. Many suggested the tradition should be done away with but worried that money drove everything and changed their lives too fast for their liking. In a way, tradition and values were clashing with the pragmatism of modern life. And the clash was tearing the village asunder. Sometimes, it seemed as if everything was up for grabs, going to the highest bidder.

When the chief first floated the idea of clearing the forest because he wanted to build a house, the uproar was predictable. "*Tufia! Alu!* Sacrilegious! God forbid!"

"He is over-stepping his bounds," people would say.

"If he tried, his head would go with it," was the consensus.

"Even the white man with all his powerful juju could not do it," others said in reference to the Assistant District Officer who died trying to clear the forest. However, by the time the chief had made his late night or early morning rounds with his generous envelopes among the elders and the opinion leaders in the town, people were talking from both sides of their cheeks. The idea was no longer *alu*.

It was: "Well, if he thinks he can deal with the consequences, good luck to him."

Others, especially the new Catholic converts, felt that it was a sign of progress. "About time someone courageous dealt with this heathen tradition."

The daughters of Ndu Nwa Agu were not amused. None of them saw the envelope, of course. In any case, they were not likely to be as susceptible to bribery as the menfolk. The Ndu Nwa Agu ceremony, the lion dance, was the only occasion at which the community recognised their worth. They would not have been party to anything that would diminish this recognition.

Before he moved to cut down the forest, the chief brought in surveyors who lived in Nsukka town, but came from another part of the country. These would not be encumbered by the knowledge or fear of tradition in surveying the land. The chief also brought a squad of policemen not only to protect and intimidate the surveyors but also to intimidate the local people.

The land was large and it took the surveyors three days to complete their assignment. In less than a week, news filtered back to the village that one of the surveyors had died mysteriously and that another one was very ill and was receiving treatment from a very senior juju man from Enuguezike, some twenty-five kilometres away from Nsukka. The two were said to have been hallucinating and uttering gibberish.

Isiakpu was in the grip of rumour, confusion and fear. Those who had received envelopes were frightened. Even the Catholics who had been disrespectful to the gods that inhabited the forest were seen with their chaplets doing the rosary. None of them left home without it. By the time news reached Isiakpu that the second surveyor was dead, that the Enuguezike medicine man could not help him, people were certain that the gods had avenged the incursion into their territory. The envelope handlers, those who had eaten from the chief, could be seen sweating all the time — even early in the morning.

They were literally in hiding. People spoke in hushed tones. Those who had ordinary flu simply locked themselves out of sight lest everyone who saw them thought that they had eaten and would be the next victims.

The chief was scared, too, and hurriedly left for Lagos. Those who had received envelopes offered sacrifices to appease the gods. Many gave away the money in an unusual burst of generosity. Most of the benefactors were local juju men or sorcerers whom the eaters thought could offer them some protection. They were consulted in utmost secrecy. It was not a total loss, the families of the juju men suddenly started living on healthier diets, cooked from the cocks and goats

170

brought for sacrifice. When news of the second surveyor's death reached Isiakpu, die-hard traditionalists and the daughters of Ndu Nwa Agu rolled out their *okanga* and *oja*. They danced and sang praise to Agu and many imitated its presence.

"The deaths have reaffirmed the saying that no one should play with the tail of a lion whether dead or alive," they sang.

Agu, their father, was asleep but not dead, the women sang. The lion had ceased to appear for some time because the elders who held the *ofo*, the symbol of authority and justice, had been compromised. Many had also died prematurely. The forest was the last vestige of the Ndu Nwa Agu's prestige and mystery. That would also not stand for long. But this temporary reprieve consoled those who clung on to its past glory.

The chief monitored the situation from Lagos through the police commissioner in Enugu, the capital of the then East Central State. The first victim died at the Nsukka General Hospital and a postmortem was ordered. The second postmortem confirmed that they both had died from cerebral malaria, an uncommon form that was resistant to the therapy available. Those who died had ventured deep into the forest. The others were scared by its thickness. The chief had these facts but refused to share them with the villagers. On the one hand, he was not fully convinced that the deaths had nothing to do with the gods, and on the other, he wanted to destroy the myth and power of the forest and that of Ndu Nwa Agu. It would be the only way of demonstrating to the villagers that iron de bend iron and that there was a superior power.

After consultations with his friends in Lagos, the chief was led to two very powerful juju men in Ijebuode in south western Nigeria. The juju men were brothers and there was, therefore, no rivalry between them. Both were renowned and expensive because their services were much sought after. They had even been consulted in some neighbouring West African countries to cast out evil spirits. The chief brought the two brothers to Isiakpu. The event was spectacular: villagers watched as the two brothers performed their acts outside the forest before venturing in. They were offered two goats so huge you would have thought they were small cows. They also had live cocks for their work in pacifying the gods. As they chanted, the goats were hypnotised from then on and did as they were commanded. The goats would be asked to kneel down and they would obey.

The juju men drank gin, chewed kola nuts, and spat them on the goats. When the chanting and incantations reached a frenzied peak, the goats jumped ten feet high, fell to the ground, foamed at the mouth, jerked and died.

The villagers watched in utter bewilderment. Some were so frightened that they ran away. Others closed their eyes, making a sign of the cross as they walked away in utter disbelief. The juju men continued to chant. One could hear them mention the names of the chief, his father and that of the prominent Ndu Nwa Agu elders who had died. The people of Isiakpu did not understand Yoruba, but one could easily tell that they were invoking the spirits of the dead and singing their praise. In the land of spirits, there were no tribes or languages. African peoples were the same. You could invoke the spirits in any of their languages but not in English. The white man's language wasn't part of the lingua franca.

The juju men killed the cocks with their bare hands and sprinkled the blood on the goats. They collected all the animals, buried them at the entrance to the forest and circled the burial place three times. They dipped their hands into their bags, tiger skin bags, which hung from their shoulders, and took out what looked like short sticks with moulded ends. They were their pathfinders, their third and fourth eyes. One of them also brought out what looked like a dead white dove and placed it where they had buried the animals. Suddenly, like people who were totally possessed, the brothers ran into the forest, each in his direction, chanting. They would run, stop suddenly, change direction and stop again to dig the ground. The short sticks led the way, so it seemed. They picked up bits and pieces of juju that had been buried in the forest over the years. How they were able to know where they were buried was part of their craft, mystery and power.

As soon as they stepped out of the forest, the white dove staggered up, flapped its wings and flew away. The juju men threw their hands into the air in triumph as they danced and chanted with satisfied smiles. "*Okpari o! Okpari o !* It is finished, it is over".

The ancestors had accepted the offering. The spirit of the ancestors had given life back to the dove. If the dove had not flown, the ceremony would have had to be repeated another day with greater offerings. At the end of the day, they had declared the forest free and clean.

They were lavishly entertained by the chief before they left for home that evening. The jujumen of Ijebuode did not sleep outside their homes.

They liberated those who had been frightened by the death of the surveyors. The chaplets were no longer as visible as before and the brave men of Isiakpu could be seen beating their chests again. There was a general sigh of relief in the village. For a while, though, many people would not say much because no one was sure that this was the end of the story. The invisible but powerful hand of the protector of Ndu Nwa Agu could strike any time. But what they had seen during the performance by the juju men from Ijebuode convinced them that this was a superior power. If it were in the days of the forefathers of Ndu Nwa Agu, the jujumen from Ijebuode, like the white District Officer before them, would not have come out of the forest alive. Not one but several lions would have confronted them. If the elders of Ndu Nwa Agu had not been compromised, if they had not become envelope handlers, the dove wouldn't have flown. Never! Instead an ordinary dog would have been sent to devour it. Things were no longer the way they used to be.

The moon had set on the daughters of Ndu Nwa Agu. Their drums and flutes had been silenced by greed, modernity and corruption. There were no environmental groups to protect the forest and its sanctity. And even if there were, would they have withstood the chief's forces? When the Ndu Nwa Agu now beat their *okanga* and blew their *oja*, they would only do so with a sense of nostalgia. The dancing steps of their daughters, *igbu owo,* had also become timid and less assertive.

As the jujumen from Ijebuode had instructed, the bulldozers moved into the forest in twelve days after the cleansing rituals. In less than a week's time the forest was levelled. Iron had indeed bent iron. The chief's house was built in one year.

* * *

The living room into which Pa Okolo was ushered was very spacious. He had been there several times but something seemed different each time. One could say that it was lavishly furnished. But it was difficult to see the beauty because of lack of respect for colour, harmony and space. It was more like a dump, and one needed to manoeuvre around the many objects of different sizes and colours, the puffs, stools and chairs to find one's way in it.

The walls were plastered with pictures of the chief with all kinds of personalities he had met in Lagos. He was rich, and the living room reflected his flamboyancy and travels. The elders in the village loved it and recognised it as a sign of wealth.

One of the elders had aptly described it as a place where furniture and furnishings went into a riot. On one end of the room stood a high chair, well carved but excessively decorated with bronze and covered in part with different sizes and colours of quilt. This was the seat reserved for the chief. No mistake would be made about it. It was *Oche ndi eze,* the chair for the princely and kingly.

It was another twenty minutes before the chief appeared.

"O ho! Okolo, is it not too early? I hope that it is not something tragic? I came out because I was told that it was you. I have never known you for frivolous visits."

The chief walked over to him for the customary handshake, and walked back to his custodial chair. Pa Okolo was looking at the floor while tapping his right foot on the ground, an indication that the situation was very grave.

"Igwe, Chief, may you reign forever. I am very sorry. I know that it is very early. But it is difficult to see a toad running in the afternoon for nothing. If you look closely behind, something must be after it."

"Who is after you?"

"Igwe, I hope that your wife and children are asleep because this is not something to be discussed publicly," Pa Okolo was barely whispering.

"We are alone. Don't you know how big this house is? You can speak up."

"My brother's wife, Mama Oby, is after my head. That woman is evil. I said it from the day my brother brought her home to introduce her to us. I saw the way her eyes were flashing from one corner to another without blinking; even the way she stood said it all. I knew that if she was given a decent nose, she would snuff quite a bit of tobacco. How can a woman, one who was visiting her potential in-laws for the first time, behave as if she was already in charge of the house. I warned my brother then but it was too late. Besides, I could not convince the rest of the family who reasoned that she came from a good family. My father knew her parents very well."

"How is she after your head?"

"Chief, can't you see? This woman has been provoking me in all manner of ways. If I commit murder wouldn't you people come after my head? I have tried to be her friend to no avail. I have asked that useless brother of mine, Ben, to inherit her in order to provide her with some support but she will not have anything to do with him. I am simply going to teach her a lesson she will never forget. When I am finished with her, she will be running naked in the marketplace."

"Okolo, calm down and lower your voice. I thought that you did not want people to hear this conversation. It is very early in the morning, you know."

"Thank you, chief. But you know that when a man of my calibre is insulted by a woman, my own junior brother's widow, it is not a matter that I take lightly."

"Yes, yes. I understand, but eh emm ..."

"No, wait chief. Please don't be offended that I am cutting you short. I went to Mama Oby after you brought me the good news concerning your son and the good intentions for Oby and our family. I thought that she would jump at the offer and thank her God." Pa Okolo was again tapping his toes on the floor and shaking his head. "Not her, in her pretended calmness, she thanked me for the message, and basically told me to go to hell."

"What! She said that?"

"Not in those exact words. Chief, 'don't be silly' may not be an insult. But no one can tell a man of your type or my type: 'Don't be silly' and get away with it. You must size up a man before you tell him 'don't be silly'".

"What did she say?"

Chief, I cannot repeat half of what she said because even our gods would be after me for repeating her words. What is worse, she gave me a lecture on our history and customs. Chief, she is not in the hospital today because these are modern times. If it were in the days of my forefathers, she would have been declared missing and that would have been the end of the matter."

"Who does she want Oby to marry then?" The chief was most unhappy but was keeping a calm front.

"She opened the mouth with which she uses to eat yam and cassava to tell me that Oby can even marry a Japanese or any *oyibo* man if she likes."

"Well, Okolo, you know that I would personally consider it an insult that our proposal has been rejected by your family. There is not much I can do, but it has untold consequences. I am sure that you are aware."

"But chief, that is why I am here."

"I am surprised that a man of your standing who wants to be counted in the community cannot control a small girl, your junior brother's widow. I now agree with you, it is not something that you would want people to hear. But then Okolo, if my family is insulted, I think that the whole world would know why you could not be admitted into the council of elders. You were not man enough and we have evidence to prove it."

The chief was conscious of the effect his words would have on Pa Okolo.

"Chief, why are you talking like this? I have, eh mm ..."

"How do you want me to talk? I made up my mind to help you but you have not passed the first test. You know that any additional day that we waste my son gets closer to marrying an *oyibo* girl. This is very serious."

"But, chief ... You are a bright man, full of ideas. I came so that we could put our heads together and find a solution. We must sharpen our tools to be able to shoot a bird that has learnt to fly without perching."

"My friend, this problem is yours and the solution, therefore, must be yours."

"I know that, but I need your help. Do you want my knees on the floor?"

"That would not be necessary," he said, attempting to lower his voice. "All right. I will help with ideas. But before then, let me bring something that would wake up our brains."

The chief went into an inner room and came out with a half-empty bottle of vodka.

"You remember this?" the chief asked.

"Yes, Vodu-kaa. How can I forget? The one the Russians drink before going to the moon."

"You've got it. It sets the brain thinking. Why do you think that the Russians are so intelligent?"

"I have no idea."

"Well, you are looking at it." He poured some into a small glass and downed it. Then he poured some for Pa Okolo who also downed his measure and shook his body vigorously to help the drink have effect over it.

"Chief, this Vodu-kaa is something else. It works instantaneously. It is magic."

"Here is another one," the chief offered him a shot.

"Oh Lord, the second one is always better than the first."

The chief had his second shot, too, before closing his eyes. He went into a thoughtful pause. "Okolo, can you hear me?"

"Yes, chief. I am with you."

"I cannot get into a personal brawl with a woman in this village, a widow for that matter. It is not the sort of problem someone of my calibre should be called to solve. This is a matter not even for you but for the younger ones. Are you with me so far?"

"I am with you. Your words are full of meaning."

"We have fought bigger fights in Lagos. Even in foreign lands, in

Taiwan, Hong Kong, and London. Go to Lagos and ask them about me. We have fought lions with bare hands and won. You know that some of the *oyibo* people are like lions. We fought them and won. Those who did not accept defeat did not live to tell the story. Why do you think that I was called *Agbaraka,* the thunder?"

"Igwe, Igwe will reign forever."

"I have come home to bring peace to this land and to expose this community to the modern ways of life. You have been in darkness for too long. Let's just say that I have retired. My children and my grandchildren cannot finish the wealth I have accumulated in their lifetime no matter how extravagant they choose to be."

"You see, this woman has no sense," Pa Okolo said. "Chief, I told you that it was an honour for you to have come to us in the first instance. There is no sensible person who would leave a feast to join the poor and idealise. Look at me. If we become in-laws, are you going to allow me to be buried in shame when I die? Will she or her children lack for anything as long as you live? She has no common sense."

"What I am trying to tell you, my dear friend Okolo, is that I have seen it all. Have you ever been to Lagos? And have you ever heard of London?"

"What would take me there? My brother, Papa Oby, had proposed to take me to Kano before the civil war. You know what happened. He died. He was killed. You are my only other hope."

"Well, Lagos is a jungle. It is survival of the fittest. London is the white man's jungle, dog eat dog. I have been there. In Lagos, I have seen a man go to work and as soon as he sat on his office chair, puff up like a blown balloon, double in size and burst. Dead. I saw this with my own eyes. In London, I was having a drink in a local pub with some business associates when a man walked in and collapsed. Dead."

"Do white people also have juju?" Okolo asked, somewhat frightened by these stories.

"Okolo, what I am still trying to tell you is that I have seen it all. In Lagos I watched as the neck of a man who wanted to dupe us was twisted and he kicked like a fowl and died. I was there. When people went on business trips, they sometimes went with people's wives. Not ordinary wives, mind you. If the husband raised too many questions, he could be declared missing."

"*Tufia*! Lagos is not just a jungle, it is a sacrilegious land. *Alu*! How did you survive it all?"

"That's what I have been trying to tell you. Can't you count your teeth with your tongue? Life is not as simple and as straightforward as many of you think. Whatever you want in life, you have to fight for it. As we used to say in Lagos, you have to do the necessary. Look around you in this village and in the neighbouring villages. How many people can you count as being rich in the real sense of the word? I don't mean these two-for-three pence, rag-wearing traders whom you people consider rich. I mean someone who can match rich people from other communities. Apart from me, there is no one else. Have you asked yourself why?" the chief asked with calculated arrogance.

"Why, chief?"

"A good question ... It is because you people have clung to your values and traditions. If someone slapped you on one cheek, you would offer the other cheek for him to complete the humiliation. That's why. I am asking our people to wake up. Things are different today. The means of survival are different. We must grab our fair share of what is available. This is my message to you people and to the young ones in particular. Go to Lagos, find out what others are doing and do it. Don't tell me that it is immoral. Or that it is against what the Catholic Church says. I don't want to hear these excuses. I don't give a damn," the chief banged the table and startled Pa Okolo.

"On judgment day, we shall all go before God and provide the context for our actions and ask for forgiveness. God, who is a just God would forgive us," he said as he pulled out a handkerchief to wipe his face.

The chief seemed troubled. He had never had this sort of discussion with anyone in the village. In a way, he was making a confession, though not to anyone in particular. He also was sending a message as to how ruthless he could be. Pa Okolo was a perfect audience. He knew how to repeat what he had been told in confidence without violating confidentiality, especially now that he also needed the chief's help.

In this exuberant state of bravado, the chief failed to mention the contradictions that his life represented. He was rich, yes, but he was not free. He behaved and acted as if someone was always after him. His house had escape routes and he walked around with a gun. True, he may have accumulated enough wealth to last another generation but he was not happy. Right now, despite all he had, his power and all, his marriage proposal was being rejected by someone he considered inconsequential.

Each day, the chief wondered whether his past would return to haunt him. The occasional flashbacks captured his current struggles as he faced an environment that was not completely immersed in the trickery of modern life. However, he believed he was winning and had begun to re-mould the community. He had also kept his sanity because of his frequent trips to Lagos and close association with some of his business friends, many of whom had also become important traditional rulers elsewhere.

"But chief, the stories you have just told me of Lagos are frightening. How can you recommend that we send our children to that place to kill or be killed?"

"If that is what it takes, why not? Our fathers never chickened out of any war because someone would die. War is synonymous with death. If they did not fight, you and I would not even have this village."

"But that was war, chief. It was usually a just war. A war fought for a particular purpose."

"This is the modern warfare. The context is business. There is no land to be fought over. And who told you that it was always a just war? It was always a war over resources: land, water, people. The powerful always wanted to take from the weak, sometimes out of necessity but often out of greed. Did you invite the colonial *oyibo* people when they came here to teach you how to live?"

"Chief, your words have meaning but, eh mmm ..."

"But what? Send those children out. One will die but two others will survive. My father used to say that it is not a basket full of children that counts; it is what they are worth. A tree can certainly make a forest if that tree is a giant tree with its branches spreading all over. If Isiakpu had three people like me, we could swallow the rest of the surrounding villages."

"But chief, come back home. Retreat. *Haba!* I am telling you to soft pedal. I was born before you. I may not have gone to Lagos but I have some God-given intelligence. Everything comes with a price. There is always a cost. Are you with me?"

"Go on," the chief said, his head bowed.

"Yes, this village may be backward and all of that but we cherish our values, our traditions, our spirit of sharing. There is a feeling of contentment here. We may be materially poor but we are spiritually wealthy."

"Did you say spiritually wealthy?" the chief cut in. "Is this not the same village that classified some people as *osu*, as perpetual second class citizens. If someone like me did not come along to quash the silly belief like you would squash an empty can of beer, wouldn't we still be singing the same ugly songs our forefathers sang? Tell me about your spiritual richness."

One could feel the chief's anguish as he squeezed tight his fist to demonstrate how he squeezed life out of the *osu* belief.

"Chief, that is not what I mean. Let's not get into this sensitive area, I beg you. I was only saying that we have a certain standard of conduct in this community, a certain morality that we cherish. It is only in this village that it is taboo for anyone to invite the police to settle a quarrel. We have our own judicial system which you now preside over. I would want us to make progress, yes, but I don't want us to make the sort of progress that will come back to haunt us. It is true times have changed, we are also changing, maybe not as fast. There are a lot of people from this town who are now going to university, thanks in part to you. We are even sending women to university including Oby, my daughter. What of trust? In this village, we may not have money but our word is our bond. It is worth more than a million naira. It is not something you can buy. If you said that you are from Isiakpu, people had confidence in you, trust in you. If you are saying that all this is not worth anything and that the only thing that counts is money, well, what can I say?"

"Okolo, don't be naive. All those virtues are good in the books. But I can assure you that it is not worth much any more. It reminds me of a professor who went to his community's fund raising event in Owerri and pledged moral support while young boys, his son's age, donated thousands of naira. One semiliterate man who was not sure what moral support meant wanted to know its monetary value. 'Ladies and gentlemen, my people said that he who asks never gets lost. You know that my education is limited. Please, what is the monetary equivalent of moral support?' Everyone started laughing. The professor was forcibly carried out of the venue by the youth."

Pa Okolo found this funny but unbelievable.

"Chief, you are making this up. Was he really carried out of the function? Was this man a professor? The type that teaches at the University of Nigeria at Nsukka?"

"Yes, my friend. Would I lie to you? I am telling you that money is the only language that people understand today. By the way, I am no longer looking up to your generation to understand my language. It is too late for your generation, even if the spirit is willing. I am sure that the younger ones would understand me better. I know this because I have seen a few promising young men in this community."

"Chief, I think that you are right. I am having my final dance. I just don't want any headaches in my evening. That is why this Mama Oby's obstinacy has to be dealt with squarely. So, please chief, let's wrap up our discussion on what to do with her next. Your household will soon be waking up."

"What else is there to wrap up? I have told you that if you want something badly you have to fight for it. If you want to turn the other cheek, that is up to you. As you said, just remember that everything has a cost."

"But what concrete actions do you propose?" Pa Okolo asked.

"Okolo, you are not a small boy. Find out what makes your brother's wife tick and hit her where it hurts. I cannot get involved in this matter directly because she could become my son's mother-in-law."

"I know what makes her tick. She thinks that she is too beautiful for this village because her breasts are still standing." The two men laughed.

"Please be serious. *Oyibo* people can now make a woman's breasts stand even when she is sixty years old."

"There you go again with one of those your fairy stories. How can they work against nature? You give this *oyibo* people too much credit." Pa Okolo sounded unconvinced.

"Don't worry about it. You don't know that someone who has lived all his life in this village is like a blind man. On a serious note, if I was not the chief of this town and I was not proposing that Oby be part of this family, I would have made Mama Oby part of my entourage during my next business trip to Accra, Ghana. By the time I would have finished with her, it would be a different story."

"Chief, it might still be a good idea. After all she has refused to be inherited and I don't think that there is any man around her. I used to see that priest, Fr Damian, with her but not any more. I think that he may have found better fortunes with Mama Ijeoma."

Pa Okolo said this with a subdued giggle, not wanting to appear as a gossip. The chief smiled sarcastically as if to suggest that there was something Okolo did not know. Indeed there was. When both Mama Ijeoma and the chief were in Lagos, she went to him for a favour. This was before he became chief of Isiakpu. One thing led to another and they had a one-time affair. Both realised that it was a serious mistake and kept it to themselves.

"Is there something else that makes Mama Oby tick?" the chief asked, still amused at the suggestion that Mama Ijeoma and the Catholic priest might be involved. He knew Mama Ijeoma well and knew that she didn't care about the appearance of things. But sometimes only perception was important. It might be the only basis for passing judgement. She was not wayward but her actions, her mannerisms, could easily be misinterpreted.

"Yes, chief. She has a small provision store. You know that little store by the Eke market. She has more supplies these days than before."

"Well, there you go. You can organise to teach her a little lesson. If you hit someone's economic power they listen even when you may have to rehabilitate them later. Your useless Ben can be useful here. Don't quote me. I can always deny that I had this conversation with you. Your word would be worthless against mine."

"Chief, why are you talking like that?"

"Because I don't engage in small boys' fights."

"I am not a baby," said Pa Okolo with some indignation.

"In the meantime, I will try and see if I could also use Mama Ijeoma. I will send word to her that we are interested in her daughter for my son. Of course it will be a farce. I know that she will jump at the proposal. Her Lagos spirit would be driving her. No one goes to a place where he will eat on the floor if he has a choice of going to a place where he is guaranteed to eat at table, a golden table for that matter. Once this message is sent out, I am hoping that Mama Oby will hear of it before long. I am trying to arouse Mama Oby's jealousy and perhaps force a change of heart. In Lagos, we called this a combination strategy or a mixed bag — 'kill me quick' combined with 'kill me softly'," he chuckled.

"Chief, thank you. Those are good ideas. This Lagos is something else. It teaches you a lot of things. If Mama Oby thinks that she can prevent my admission into the council of elders of Isiakpu she should think again. Not me, Okolo, a one-time commander of the armed forces of this village."

As he stood up to go, the chief realised that he had not offered Okolo the customary kola nut.

"Please wait Okolo. I forgot the kola nut."

"Don't worry chief, we had the Vodu-kaa."

"Vodka is not kola nut." He reached into a clay pot seated on one of the shelves and brought out a big kola nut.

"Okolo, take this. There is no point in trying to break it. When the kola reaches home, it would explain itself. It would be evident that this kola nut came from a great home."

"Thank you very much. Igwee! Igwee! Agaba Idu the First. The one and only Agaba Idu."

184

"I know that the vodka I gave you last time is finished."

"You are right. It was irresistible. Even my youngest wife has noticed that something gives me extra strength at night. She doesn't know what it is but she loves it."

Both men laughed.

"Well, you can take home this half bottle. As I said before, this drink is not for everyone. But give your youngest wife a shot and see what she would do to you that night." They laughed some more.

"Igwe, never! She would kill me," Pa Okolo said with a childlike shyness. "That woman is *enwu* honey. The more you lick, the more you want. And you know that sweet things kill slowly. I cannot cope as things stand."

"Oh Okolo, it is said that when an old lady hears a familiar tune, she remembers her youth and her dancing shoes," said the chief as he stood up to see Pa Okolo off.

"These bones are very weak as you can see. You know that the village she comes from has a reputation. She plays certain tricks with my body and I often feel like I am drowning. I lose control completely. At that point, I could even sell all my land to her for nothing."

"So she is that good? Okolo, I didn't know that you were this bad," the chief said as they both continued to laugh.

"She is good but I have often wondered where she learnt these tricks. *Enwu*! Hallelujah! I want to die in peace. She tends to get carried away with our local gin. With Vodu-kaa, the drink that brought Appolonia or is it Apollo to Isiakpu? You people would be singing my requiem sooner than I care for. Thank you very much, Igwe. Thank you. Igwe shall reign forever."

A happy and energised Pa Okolo left the chief with a murky smile on his face.

Pa Okolo was not sure how to translate the chief's suggestions on what action he needed to take against Mama Oby. What was he supposed to do? What did the chief mean by hitting her hard where it hurt? He didn't want to ask the chief to be specific, because he didn't want to appear naive. "Maybe that useless Ben might know," he reasoned. He is young and had also lived in the city before coming back to the village.

He was likely to understand the chief's language. But then, in the eyes of Pa Okolo, Uncle Ben was a very un-enterprising man. He could not be relied upon in any matter. But Pa Okolo had no choice. Whatever would have to be done, he felt, was going to be Uncle Ben's responsibility. A man his age should not be caught with his hands deep in a neighbour's pot of soup. He, therefore, decided to stop by Uncle Ben's house on his way home.

"Where is your useless husband?" Pa Okolo said as Uncle Ben's wife met him at the door.

"Good morning, sir. Is everything okay?"

"Just ask him to come and meet me outside," Pa Okolo said, ignoring the greetings.

"Ah aah, *Nnanyi,* Pa Okolo. You are visiting us this early. I hope that everything is okay?" Uncle Ben said.

"Useless man. You call this very early? Serious farmers are half way done in the field by now. Palm wine tappers have finished their morning rounds and are only now preparing to go to the market. Only lazy and good-for-nothing people like you think that it is still very early."

There was hardly any encounter between the two that did not start with Pa Okolo chiding Uncle Ben in a most virulent language. However, if someone outside the family tried to use Uncle Ben's supposedly irresponsible behaviour to get at the family, Pa Okolo defended him fully. This was the relationship that existed between them, and Uncle Ben had learnt to live with the insults.

"Is anything the matter this morning? Won't you even come inside?" Uncle Ben said without reacting to the familiar tirade.

"Come inside where? When have you ever seen me entering little huts? A hut that was built by your wife for that matter!"

It was not a little hut by village standards. It had two decent bedrooms and a small living room. Originally constructed with a mud wall, it had been plastered with cement. The cement had been sold to Uncle Ben's wife by someone from the neighbouring Amankwo Village who had allegedly stolen it from a relative constructing a house.

The house was roofed with old corrugated iron sheets. That rainy season, the sheets had not only revealed holes that had threatened to turn the house into a dam whenever there was a downpour, but holes big enough to illuminate the house when there was a full moon.

"Let me go and get kola nut then," Uncle Ben said. He turned around to walk back into his house.

"Stand where you are. Something serious brings me here. For once in your life, I hope you will perform. Go and close your door. This is a matter that not even your wife should know about." Pa Okolo walked away from the house and Uncle Ben followed.

Once out of earshot of those in the house, Pa Okolo gave Uncle Ben the brief. It constituted of a little background to the problem including all the insults and humiliations that he and the members of the family had endured over the years because of Mama Oby's behaviour. He did not tell him about the marriage proposal, neither did he mention the fact that the matter hindered his admission to the prestigious council of elders. Pa Okolo made it sound like everything was being done in the interests of the family's honour and, in particular, to redeem Uncle Ben.

As he spoke, he eye-balled his brother with the intensity of a psychological prop. He would equally have detected any weaknesses likely to hamper delivery. When he was through with outlining the broad strategy, he asked Uncle Ben to give him his own assessment of the problem. Uncle Ben had understood what needed to be done but did not see how it would be executed. Pa Okolo cautioned him to be extremely careful.

"An old man like me cannot be caught with my hands soiled in a neighbour's pot of soup. Never! But that does not mean that if the soup is presented by a younger one, he would not eat. He would eat and ask questions later, if at all. A word is enough for the wise."

He made a quick turn and began to walk away like an army commander who had just finished giving instructions to his battalion and did not want any questions or follow-up reactions.

"Wait, Pa Okolo. Wait." Uncle Ben waved towards him.

"Yes, what is it again?"

"Nothing serious. Just ehm ... Pa Okolo, can't you spare a tot of what you have in that bottle? It is especially good this early in the morning." Uncle Ben had been eyeing the bottle which Pa Okolo held firmly under his armpit.

"Give you what? Is that why you stopped me? You must be mad. This is not a drink for poor and useless men like you. In any case, do you know what it is?"

"Of course! It is vodka."

"A ha! No wonder you went to Lagos and instead of bringing back prosperity like the chief, you brought back misery and a sack of tattered clothes. No wonder!"

"Pa Okolo, why are you raising your voice? What wrong have I done now?"

"You don't know, Mr Clueless? You are asking me to help you finish yourself. Look at you, incompetent and lazy."

"There you go again," said Uncle Ben, head bowed.

"If I give you a shot of Vodu-kaa, the drink of the great Russians, I know what to expect. When the Russians drink it, they fly to the moon. As for you, with one shot you will dive into *enwu*, sex is that palatable: the more you lick, the more you want. But it can destroy you equally. It looks like your wife has it in abundance. As for you, you are like a bee. With a shot of Vodu-kaa, you would be at it all day, and that useless wife of yours will never go to the market to fend for the two of you. She does not seem capable of saying 'no' because she is always hot. Look at her waist: She is Mrs Ever-ready. Her waist is expanding and yours is shrinking."

"Please, leave my wife out of this. She hasn't done anything to you. She is a very decent woman." Uncle Ben did not want Pa Okolo's acidic mouth to deliver uncomplimentary remarks about his wife.

"I see, she is a decent woman. Of course! You should be ashamed of yourself. In the end, we still do not have the children to show for all your monkey business. I am yet to discover what you are good at." Pa Okolo walked away, thoroughly satisfied that Uncle Ben had been sufficiently provoked to prove himself.

Uncle Ben stood there for a minute watching Pa Okolo's back recede on the meandering footpath that led to his house. As the man walked, he struggled to use one hand to fend off dew from the overgrown grass that crossed the path and to adjust his wrapper whenever it fell out of position. His other hand held firmly to the vodka bottle.

For another two minutes or so, Uncle Ben mulled over the nature of the task before him. A brilliant thought flashed through his mind and he was so excited he wanted to run to Pa Okolo's house to explain the details. No. He retreated. He wanted to surprise him and to use this task to debunk, once and for all, some of these good-for-nothing epitaphs.

He wanted to prove to Pa Okolo and to everyone else that he was a courageous and intelligent man. Nothing would give him greater pleasure than to prove it using Mama Oby. She had contributed to his humiliation.

CHAPTER TWENTY

Oby was home in Isiakpu for the long vacation after completing her first academic year at the University of Embakassi.

She had spent the first night of her holidays narrating her university experience to her mother, and catching up on what had happened at Isiakpu in her absence. Her mother sat in rapt attention as Oby took her on a tour of her life in the past year. She spoke generally, but the revelations were striking and worrisome for her mother.

The year had been full of new experiences; it had completely initiated Oby into the university world, the real world. It had seen her fall in love and suffer for it. She had learnt very quickly that love was not all about happiness; that it had heartaches, disappointments, and was sometimes full of lies. She had also discovered that relationships were not always about love. In this arena, there was no level playing ground. One person must give more than the other. In most cases, the woman always gave more. At the university, you were expected to be free and in control. But you were also expected to respond to the stimuli of the environment, an environment that was not always friendly; one that mimicked the trickery and chauvinism of the real world.

At the University of Embakassi, spirituality was not about Christianity. It was more about a deep philosophical and social orientation, and there were various shades, from the Christian right to the sea dogs. This was a place where there was great pressure to conform, but also where oddity and weirdness were admired and rewarded. The learning was not over, by any means, Oby confessed.

The year past had been an eye-opener, and the exposure had matured her into a woman. She hoped that her mother would appreciate this change and relate with her woman to woman. Oby was ready to go on and on, but her mother was impatient with the generalities and wanted specific experiences relating to her life.

"What of the boys? You talked about the pain of falling in love. Is there something that you are not telling me?"

"No, mom," she said. I have told you before about Chike and some of his friends like Chris and Okoro. Have you forgotten?"

"No, I have not forgotten. But then you did not talk about love. Besides, I want to hear more. You have always wanted to talk adult to adult. This is your chance."

"Well, what can I say? He is cute, tall, intelligent and generous."

"But he is also a brute?"

"Mom!" Oby was wondering where this came from.

"Well, I am only reading your face. I am still your mom, remember?"

"Everyone has their faults. Our relationship is not perfect but it is very good. The only problem I have with him is that even though he is a leader in his own right, he seems unable to withstand the pressure of the crowd. He realises it and he is working on it."

"What I hear is you making excuses for him, and this could hurt you in future. Lesson Number One is not to excuse your partner's bad behaviour, a man who is not in control of his emotions, who dances to the crowd is dangerous. If he is easily influenced, you have to be very careful. If his friends are doing it today, tomorrow it could be his father or his mother. If your father was not his own man, he would never have married me. Your Uncle, Pa Okolo, did not like me from day one, but your father's mind was made up. Thank God that your grandfather supported us."

"What did Pa Okolo have to do with it?"

"He is your father's eldest brother and as such had some influence. Haven't you seen how he has been trying to boss us around?"

"Well, Chike and I are very far from where you and Dad were. We are not talking marriage at all."

"That may be true but it is always good to keep these things in mind. You never know. In any relationship, however, your man should be in charge of his actions. Sometimes, the pretext of not being in control is an excuse for doing whatever he wants. You just have to be clever and watch his every move."

"Mom, the problem with the university is that you really have no senior sister or mom to confide in or seek advice from. They will advise you all right but warn you that you should be in charge of your actions, and that the responsibility is yours. It is very confusing."

"They are right in a way. After all, they are still children in spite of the fact that they may be older than you are or that they have been there before you. Your weapon is really your common sense and the strength of your up-bringing. There are certain things that I would swear you would never do because of the way I brought you up. It is as simple as that."

"Like what?" Oby was laughing because she remembered what her roommate had said to her once: 'Those who give advice, and who have all the expectations have never seen the four walls of a university.'"

"There are so many examples ... eehm which ..."

"Just give me one example," Oby insisted.

"For instance, I have heard some of your age mates discuss abortion almost lightheartedly. But I would swear that if you were pregnant you would never contemplate it. Not my daughter, God forbid."

"But mom, who is talking about pregnancy. You seem to be walking faster than your shadow." Oby was getting somewhat shy about this subject.

"No. I am not saying that you are going to be pregnant tomorrow. But we use discussions such as this to learn and re-affirm our own values. I am only saying that I would expect you to have the baby if you were to find yourself in such a situation. I could raise the baby if you didn't have the time, that's all I am saying."

"But have you considered the fact that by deciding to have the baby, I might be jeopardising my future and that of all those who ultimately depend on me, including that child?" Oby's voice rang out abruptly.

"God forbid, Oby. Please ask God for forgiveness for even trying to rationalise such a thing."

"I am not trying to rationalise anything. I am simply giving you the other side of the argument."

"My daughter, there are things that do not have the other side of the argument. Abortion is a sin against God and against humanity. It is not a matter of when and under what conditions."

192

"Mom, please have an open mind. It should depend on the circumstances."

"What circumstances? What are you talking about," Mama Oby, with eyes aglow, was getting agitated. "That is why young people like you should not engage in sex unless you are married. Otherwise, you should be ready for the consequences. Pure and simple."

"It's not that simple, mom."

"Oh my God! Oby, what has happened to you?"

"Mom, we are discussing adult to adult remember?"

"Yes, but I am getting very worried. What has happened to you?" asked Mama Oby again.

"Nothing, mom. What do you think of family planning?"

"You do family planning when you have a family, not when you have none."

"No. I am talking about, you know ... using something to prevent pregnancy. You know, planned parenthood."

"Prevent pregnancy? The only way to prevent pregnancy is not to have sex. It was what we were taught when we were growing up and it remains true even today. Just don't do it. You plan parenthood when you are ready to be a parent. It is that simple. Oby, are you saying that you are ... thinking of doing it? My God!" Mama Oby covered her face with her two palms.

"Mom. Please! We are just discussing. Let's not get emotional about this. There is nothing to worry about yet."

"Oh, my God! Emotional? If you can't talk to me, who else can you talk to?"

"How can I talk to you when you are not open to any meaningful discussion? For you the answer is always simple. Everything is simple and straightforward. But you are not the one at the university. You are not the one feeling all the pressure. The virtues of your time have become the vices of our age. Who cares whether you are a virgin or not? In fact, most boys deplore the fact that you don't have any prior experience."

Her mother's voice pitched suddenly. "Oby, please stop. What is happening to you?"

"I am not going to stop," she said. "During your time, you saw nothing and heard nothing. This is the age of information. Important as the home training is, there are now a lot more ways of getting information. All of this constitutes additional pressure. You can get it from the novels, and we were encouraged to read a lot in high school. If you know how much information we are bombarded with from television, you would not treat certain discussions as if they were off-limits."

Mama Oby could not believe how much her daughter had changed. Just one year at the university and she was now a woman with all kinds of ideas. Some of Oby's ideas she could not comprehend. Was this what university was all about? Was this why so many university graduates remained unmarried? she wondered.

She shuddered to think that her word counted for much less than before. It was no longer gospel. She stood up and went for a cup of water as if to allow Oby's new found wisdom to sink in.

"It is not that I don't understand," Mama Oby started. "It is just that things tend to move too fast for me. I cannot say much. I know my daughter. I trust my daughter and I know that as a good Catholic, you will use your God-given wisdom to avoid temptation and to make good judgment. What else can I say?" She said this with resignation in her voice. She reached out for her daughter's hand to reassure her.

"Mom, this is no longer the age of innocence," the younger woman said. "The innocent is actually held hostage because her options are limited. Don't get me wrong. I still have my moral standards. There are no-go areas for me irrespective of the circumstances. I don't believe that we should shift and juggle our ethical standards depending on the circumstances. I am only saying that the standards of your time may have changed and that you should open up and discuss them."

Oby's voice and her stuttered words bespoke the emotional nature of the subject. For a moment, her eyes misted as if gathering a storm of tears. She tried to wipe her eyes with her left palm but her nose had started running as well. She simply bowed her head to hide it all from her mother. These issues were not simple and she knew as much. But she expected her mother to show some understanding.

"I did not mean to doubt you one bit, but ..."

"That is not my point," Oby interrupted. "Mom, when you speak the way you do, you are simply giving voice to your experience, the experience of your generation. For you, the answers are known before even the questions are posed. But we have to match experience with reality. The force of moral logic is not sufficient to eventually reconcile the gap between your experience and our reality. As if that is not enough, this reality is complex, confusing and sometimes contradictory. You cannot take anything for granted. If you do, you are likely to be swept by a flood."

Tears were rolling down Oby's eyes by the time she uttered the last word. She knew that she did not have answers to her reality, but she also knew that her mother was the wrong person to help her discover it.

"I am sorry, Oby, if it looks like I am not showing sufficient understanding. I get what you are saying but ... I am simply not comfortable with discussing some of these issues. Just remember that the world is not fair to women and that in whatever we do, we should realise that those who set the rules have different expectations for women." Mama Oby stood up, stretched both hands to her daughter. She ran into her arms like a little girl.

The two women hugged and held each other firmly. For some two minutes, each was lost in her own thoughts but they were united by what both realised was their common destiny.

"The burden of women. I got you."

"Yes, my daughter. I am glad that we can agree. The truth is that I am scared. Two weeks ago, I had a dream in which something terrible happened to you on account of this abortion issue. I was very scared. I woke up but could not go to my shop the whole day." Mama Oby reached for the cup of water from the table and drank from it. She sat down and gazed at her daughter in amazement. She could not believe how much Oby had changed.

"No, mom. You should trust your daughter. I cannot do anything to harm myself or to bring shame to you. I am not that stupid. Let's leave this subject."

"I trust you, my daughter. I trust you. I get confused, too, sometimes and, like you, I have no one in this village to run to for advice. Values in Isiakpu are changing faster than you can imagine. Nothing is sacred any more."

"Mom, what has been happening in Isiakpu?"

Oby was eager to change the conversation.

"A lot, my dear, a lot." She did not know where to begin.

"There is nothing to cheer up about," said the mother. "Right now we have a major crisis in our church." Mama Oby had a strong sense of regret in her voice. It hurt her to discuss the church and the priest in a way that did not put them in good light.

"Crisis? What crisis?" Oby asked with considerable surprise. She could tell from her mother's facial expressions that she was disgusted with whatever it was.

"It is a long story," she muttered, not sure where to begin.

Oby invited her mother to start from wherever she wanted. "I am on holiday." At least I hope I am.

"This is one of those things you would want to wish away," Mama Oby said. "But when you are dealing with people who want to play God and you are caught in a dance with the deaf, your steps would not be in harmony with the music. That is the situation we are in."

Oby was becoming impatient with her mother's circumlocution. "Who are 'we' and what are you talking about?"

"All the Catholics from Ishi-ugwu have been excommunicated by Fr Damian," Mama Oby said tiredly. She was genuinely tired of discussing this despite the fact that it touched on her faith. Oby, however, needed to know.

"During the short two-week vacation in April you mentioned that a problem was brewing in the church," Oby said. "You talked about Mama Ijeoma and Fr Damian. I don't remember exactly what it was. Is it the same problem?"

Her mother said it was. She had forgotten having mentioned it to Oby. Mama Oby said as she sat up: "I told you about Obeta, Obeta Nwaeze from Ulo ni Ishi-ugwu. His house is not that far from Mama Ijeoma's. He walks with a limp from a childhood sickness. It must be polio. You know him, he has this ugly habit of grinding his teeth, which many attribute to his wickedness."

Oby said she knew him. "He is very short. To me, he doesn't look particularly happy with anybody's achievements."

Mama Oby was surprised that Oby knew the man that well.

"Obeta was accused of poisoning his brother's son when he returned from Lagos last Christmas. The boy had been doing business in Lagos. Ezekiel Nwaeze died just before Christmas. All investigations seemed to point at Obeta. According to tradition, since none of his family members are Christians, he was asked to swear before the *alusi,* the Owushi of Isiakpu. On the appointed date, he simply disappeared from his house. The next day, Fr Damian brought him home and declared that he was a full member of the Christian Association of Ishi-ugwu and as such all the Christians from Isiakpu should make sure that no harm came to him. Mama Ijeoma was charged with the responsibility of reporting any Catholic who disobeyed Fr Damian's instructions."

"Interesting," Oby said, and asked what had caused the crisis.

"Well, according to tradition, if you are accused of poisoning someone, you would have to swear an oath by the *alusi* if you believe in traditional religion or swear by the Bible if you are a Christian. If you don't, the village will ostracise you. It is as simple as that.

"You would be prohibited from interacting with anyone anywhere. The practice has been around since your grandfather's time. Now Fr Damian wants to split the entire community because he is behaving as if he doesn't understand our custom, as if he flew in from Ireland yesterday. As a Reverend Father, you must study and understand the customs of the people you minister to, otherwise you alienate them. I know that he understands everything; he is just trying to be mischievous. And he has found a willing ally in Mama Ijeoma."

Oby was very attentive. But she still did not understand how Fr Damian and Mama Ijeoma had precipitated a crisis in the church.

Said her mother: "The village elders ostracised Obeta Nwaeze according to the custom and tradition. And the enforcement of the decree is carried out irrespective of whether you are a Christian or a traditional believer. No one in Ishi-ugwu was supposed to make contact with Obeta.

"Now, Fr Damian, having received Obeta as a Christian, insisted that we should ignore the decree and that, as Christians, we had no business obeying orders from 'heathens'. But this is one village and this community stands together on matters like this. We cannot split it because one group happens to be Christian and another traditional. I am a faithful Catholic but I cannot, in good conscience, participate in what would split this community. Even the Bible says that we should give to Caesar what is due to him and to God what is His. We should have found a way of resolving the crisis without Fr Damian asking us to disobey our elders on such an important matter."

Mama Oby paused for a moment before proceeding. "What is more, this person was not even a Christian before the crime was committed. He simply took refuge in the church. And now because of a new 'convert', all of us have been excommunicated. It is very frustrating ... But we continue praying to God for a resolution of the matter." She made a sign of the cross as she ended the explanation.

Oby asked if her mother had seen Fr Damian over the matter. It was still unclear what Mama Ijeoma's role in it was.

"Of course, I have gone to see him several times to explain these things. But he would not listen. I have also gone to see him in the company of other senior members of the church from Ishi-ugwu. All we get from him are insults on how we are weak Christians. He is very intransigent on this issue. If you heard him pour insults on us, you would never believe that it is the same Reverend Father you knew. He treats us like we were born yesterday. As far as he is concerned, Mama Ijeoma and Obeta now are the only Catholics in Ishi-ugwu. By the way, Obeta has been baptised. He is now Michael Nwaeze. He nearly beat to death a young boy who called him Obeta the other day. Mama Ijeoma has been Fr Damian's dedicated emissary. He passes all the instructions and warnings through her and she cherishes playing the role. In spite of his warnings, we have stuck to our guns and refused to have anything to do with Obeta. He gets constant briefing from Mama Ijeoma. I wish them luck. You know Mama Ijeoma: She is an opportunist."

Oby was thoroughly incensed.

"Mama, this is terrible. I can't imagine F. Damian insulting you and treating you like you were his househelp." She reached out to her mother to offer consolation.

Her mother said Fr Damian treated her worse than a househelp. She added, "I would not have been perturbed but for the excommunication. We are all entitled to our religious rights."

Oby was keen to find out what led to the excommunication.

"Because of this problem," her mother explained, "we were always having crisis meetings on the issue instead of the regular Christian Association meetings and Obeta – now Michael – never had the courage to attend any of them. In effect, we were not associating with him in any way, contrary to Fr Damian's injunctions. Yet it wasn't easy to prove anyone's guilt because you could not force anyone to visit him. To test our resolve, Fr Damian instructed all of us, through Mama Ijeoma, to pass through Obeta's house on our way to church every Sunday. That was his only way of confirming that we had, indeed, contravened the ostracision decree. Except for Mama Ijeoma, no Catholic in Ishi-ugwu obeyed the instruction. Two months ago, he announced to the entire church that we had been excommunicated. We are not allowed to participate in any church functions or meetings of the Christian Mothers and Fathers. In spite of this, we are still together. Right now, we conduct our own mass at the Ishi-ugwu square with a catechist instead of a Reverend Father and we believe that God hears our prayers. Our children are not being baptised and no one can be wedded in church under the current circumstances. We have already petitioned the bishop and we hope that he will solve the problem."

Oby wondered how Mama Ijeoma would get away with all that.

"So far, she has got away with it. But not for too long. You know that she is an outlaw and she likes to dare the elders. When they finally descend on her, she will not be ostracised; she will be banished from this village. You remember the saying that many days for the thief and one day for the owner. I have never seen someone so manipulative. She took over this matter from Fr Damian as if she was being paid for it. It is terrible and unfortunate. You know that her husband, Papa Ijeoma, is very ill, almost bed-ridden. But she is not bothered by this. She spends all her time on this."

Oby was surprised that Mama Ijeoma was that close to Fr Damian. "I thought he didn't like her ways," Oby said.

"Well, anything is possible. Anything is possible. Sometimes, I think that this punishment on the community by Fr Damian is because of me," Mama Oby said.

Oby let out a shocked "Why?"

"Just a thought. Never mind. Never mind," her mother laboured, trying to avoid her daughter's eyes. For a moment, she had a flashback of the day Fr Damian made a pass at her.

"I am going to see Fr Damian myself. This whole thing doesn't make sense. One of the things you admire about Catholic Reverend Fathers is that they are well educated and should therefore be able to place religion in its proper perspective. Our Reverend Father at the university teaches religious studies to Year One and Two students. He is a specialist on traditional African religion. He would never condone what Fr Damian is doing. It shows a lot of ignorance and disrespect for a community that you are supposed to be serving. I will certainly confront him with the facts."

Mama Oby looked at her daughter in the face. "Just be careful. Very careful. I don't trust that man any more."

As soon as her mother had uttered those words, Oby's mind flashed back to Chike's story on his encounter with Fr Damian and the Reverend Sisters. She had decided to keep it secret. Now, she asked her mother what she meant.

"Just a thought. I was just saying that you should be alert at all times. I also wanted you to know that the whole of Isiakpu is outraged by his behaviour and is plotting to get him transferred from here. There are all kinds of allegations against him."

"Allegations?" Oby asked with curiosity.

"Well. You know ... occasional excessive drinking ... our church building is not progressing ... always in the company of women and that sort of thing ... Nothing proven of course."

Mama Oby did not want Oby to place weight on any of these

allegations because she was always protective of her daughter's faith in the Catholic Church.

"Where was the chief when all this was happening?" asked Oby.

"Which chief?"

"The Agaba Idu I of Isiakpu."

"Oh, the chief. The chief and Pa Okolo are busy plotting how to marry you off," Mama Oby said.

"Marry me off ... To the chief?" Oby asked, thoroughly disgusted.

"No, to his son, Ndubisi, who is in the US."

Oby asked how her mother had got to know about it.

"Pa Okolo came to me with the proposal. You should have seen him that day: most excited. You would have thought he had won a lottery."

Oby became sarcastic. "When is the wedding?"

"Don't joke," the mother warned. "This is very serious and it has not been settled yet."

"Why was Pa Okolo excited? Excited about Ndubisi or the chief?"

"I don't know. Is he not your father? When you see him you should ask him. All I know is that I have never seen him so excited and enthusiastic about something."

"Ndubisi?" Oby said, wondering who had told them she was looking for a husband. "I have to talk to Pa Okolo to stop all this marriage nonsense."

"Don't you like Ndubisi?" Mama Oby said, testing the waters. "I am told you young women of these days are fascinated by the boys studying in America."

"Is Ndubisi studying in America? If he was, he would have obtained his doctoral degree by now. If I recollect correctly, you once told me that he went to America when I was still in primary school, some ten years ago. He has since been home only once. I have never seen him. Mom, it is not everyone who is in America that is studying. Some of them live there doing all kinds of odd jobs."

"Oh, what do I know," her mother said, trying to avoid influencing Oby's views. "You know your mother is illiterate," she added.

"Pa Okolo thinks it would be a blessing if we had Chief Ugwueze as our in-law. All our problems – maybe he meant all his problems – would be solved. Besides, Ndubisi is likely to be the next Igwe and you would automatically become the queen. And I, of course, would become the queen mother!"

"How interesting!" Oby said. "But mom, I don't know what is wrong with Pa Okolo these days. I thought you told me that the chief is from a certain lineage." Oby lowered her voice and looked at her mother, goading her to give the right word but she didn't.

"What lineage?"

"You told me that he is an *osu*. Doesn't that matter any more?"

"Pa Okolo insists that since the man is now the Igwe, it doesn't matter any more. I was telling you that values in Isiakpu are shifting faster than I can cope with the changes."

"I am not for maintaining some of the outdated traditions. But this one stigmatises one and one's offspring forever. Who is going to bell the cat?"

"That is the million naira question," the mother said.

"I expected Pa Okolo not to be blinded by his own ambition when it comes to matters like this," said Oby.

"You must be joking. It shows you don't know him well. Your uncle is a first-class schemer who knows how to do ugly things without leaving his footprints. If you are dealing with him, you must be sharp. If he tells you to stand, you had better run. If he does you any favour, expect him to milk you dry moments later. That has been my experience with him even when your father was alive. I know him very well and he knows it. That I am able to read his moves every inch of the way makes him most uncomfortable. I told him quite a bit the day he brought this proposal. That is why I told you the issue is not yet settled."

Oby was listening and wondering why her mother was telling her all this about Pa Okolo. She guessed it could still be part of the woman-to-woman discussion she promised her at the beginning. Or she could be expecting a certain reaction from her.

"Mom. Please don't get worked up about Pa Okolo. He cannot force me to marry anyone. You know that."

"That doesn't worry me. It is the sort of nonsense that he says along the way that really infuriates me."

"Like what?" Oby asked.

"I don't think that we should get into it."

"Get into what, mom? You promised to have a woman-to-woman talk with me. Have you forgotten?"

"Children of these days. Why do you have to insist?"

Oby stared at her as if to say "Come on, mom."

Her mother obliged. "All right! But this conversation is strictly between you and I."

Oby gave her word.

"Pa Okolo knows that you are not circumcised and he thinks that men, suitable partners, would run away from you once they discover this. That is why he thinks that Ndubisi is your best bet. Because of his being in America, he would not have a clue." Mama Oby repeated this because she was also worried about this part of her conversation with Pa Okolo. In her days, men would not marry an uncircumcised woman because it was generally believed she would be promiscuous.

Oby burst into loud laughter. "Oh no!"

"What is it that is so amusing?" her mother asked.

"Is this the taboo subject? Mom, you are talking about my body."

"This is a serious matter, Oby."

Oby thought about her uncle and began to laugh again.

"Please tell me why you are laughing?"

"I am laughing because he has never been so wrong. These days, if you are circumcised, your options are quite limited. Boys ask you point blank whether you have been cut or not. They are not eager to relate with women who have been cut."

"That's a lie!" Mama Oby said, surprised at her vehemence.

"Okoro, Chike's friend, said that a woman who has been cut is like a bird whose wings have been clipped or fish whose fins have been cut. That they can never fly or swim into paradise, that promised land of endless happiness." Both women were laughing.

"Who is this Okoro? He must be a very naughty boy."

"Yes indeed, yes indeed," Oby replied between bouts of laughter.

"Just be very careful, my daughter. These things are very confusing these days."

"Is it confusing for you, too, mom?" Oby asked.

"Oh yes. You know that in this society, in Isiakpu for example, it is the women that are insisting on the circumcision of girls."

"Is the practice still alive?" Oby asked.

"It is very much alive. In some communities like the Amankwo, where it represents a rite of passage from childhood to adulthood, it has remained a most divisive issue, with the older women insisting on it while some younger ones want to do away with it. It is a terrible thing."

"So what do they do in Isiakpu?"

"Here, girls are circumcised at birth. Here, it doesn't really represent any rite of passage. But this is a very conservative society and the practice has persisted because there are men, diehard traditionalists, supported by a handful of women who insist that it has virtue. We tried to pressurise the late chief to outlaw the practice. I know we could have won. But by the time we had two meetings, we had lost momentum as some of the women lost courage. With this new chief, one has to be very careful. He doesn't cut straight."

"Mom, have you been cut?"

"Shut up! *Tufia*, you spoilt brat. How dare you ask your mother such a question?"

"Curiosity, mom. I wanted to know if you ever swam into paradise ..."

"I said shut up! That's it. This is the end of our conversation."

"I am sorry, mom. No more personal questions. I simply wanted to learn as much as possible about this thing. I am, after all, studying sociology."

"So this is what you have gone to the university to study?" Mama Oby asked.

"No, no, no. I mean, one needs to know these things to supplement what one is learning at the university."

"I don't know that there is anything to learn."

"But have you ever witnessed this female circumcision, especially the teenage type?"

"Not really, but my very close friend from Amankwo did. She almost died from it."

204

"How?" Oby asked.

"The way she told the story, it was very bad. Each time she remembers it, she cries and cries — even today when she is almost a grandmother."

"Mom, what happened? I want to know."

"Each time I remember the story myself, I have goose bumps," Mama Oby said, shaking her shoulders as if to ward off real goose bumps.

Oby said: "Please tell it to me."

"My friend's parents were not very keen on the circumcision," Mama Oby said. "She is their first daughter. But as you know, you are not always able to do what you like in a village. Her parents encouraged her to participate in the entire rite: dancing and singing at *otobo*, playing with her agemates, visiting uncles and receiving gifts, among other things. As you know, circumcision is a group activity. But her parents wanted her to disappear from the group as they were being led to the circumciser. She did exactly that. But the old women in the village often anticipated that one or two individuals would chicken out when the time for the real initiation came. The women would be seen dangling their sharpened knives before the girls as they did their final dance. It was a frightening experience."

Oby sat with both palms under her jaw. She was taking in the details of the story with a mixture of horror and disgust.

"As the girls were being led to three small huts which had been prepared for the operation, my friend put the family plan in action. She had all along lagged behind the group. When she thought the time was right, she took off. The plan was that she runs to an aunt who had had a terrible experience in the hands of the old women. But she did not go far. The old women saw her speeding off and made a high-pitched war cry. Lo! Before she knew it, she was between two huge men who dragged her back as she kicked and struggled. She was humiliated before her peers who burst into a song reserved for teasing cowards who thought they would become women without facing the knife. It did not stop there. To discourage such acts in the future, she was dragged to the two knife-wielding old women by the men. What is usually a sacrosanct affair between women was witnessed by men. It is they who held her legs apart as the old women sliced off a piece of her private parts. As she kicked and fought for her dignity, she splashed blood all over the men. It was a small reward but she was happy that those who had persisted on dishing out her humiliation looked like butchers when they left the hut. She nearly bled to death. Years after this incident, she still avoids sex because it is often a very painful experience for her."

"That is enough mom," Oby said. "What barbarism."

Oby still sat in the same position, tears rolling down her cheeks. Mama Oby's eyes were also swollen with tears but she did not shed any.

Said her mother, "That is the story of our lives. I have sworn that no relative of mine will undergo this terrible ordeal."

"Does it have to be this way?" Oby asked, wiping away tears with one end of her dress. The two women were quiet for a while to regain their composure.

"Mom, it is 3.30 in the morning." Oby said as she glanced at her watch. She stood up to stretch her legs. What she had heard that evening disturbed her greatly.

"Are you sure?" It was indeed 3.30 am.

Mama Oby rushed into her bedroom for her Bible. The two said a prayer and read Psalm 23, before going to bed.

CHAPTER TWENTY-ONE

Between the end of July and mid-August each year, the people of Isiakpu celebrated the the new yam festival. It was a thanksgiving festival for the gift of life.

Everyone took part in it because they each had something to be grateful to God for. Although the actual event lasted only two days, the festival would run on for two weeks.

The events of the first days were dominated by a special type of masquerade, the *Akatakpa*, whose activities reminded people of the impending festival. They also formed an integral part of the festivities. The masquerades had unique costumes made from sisal dyed in different colours and knitted so tightly that they would not reveal the identity of the wearer. Each *Akatakpa* carried several long whips, as part of the costume, with which it administered instant justice on the undisciplined and on any others whom it deemed disrespectful. As expected, even the masquerades understood and respected people's position in society and therefore only bullied, but would not flog, people capable of making trouble. Occasionally, they stepped out of line and disciplinary measures were taken against them.

Legend has it that the masquerades, which symbolise the spirits of the forefathers of Isiakpu, came with messages from the spirit world and accepted offerings in the name of all those who had lived and died on the land. From that time, the *Akatakpa* masquerade was supposed to be respected by all, especially young women and men. Old men could converse with a masquerade but older women, sixty and above, would simply step aside, as a sign of respect if both happened to be on the same path. The masquerade would in return behave in a manner that was not offensive to them. The masquerades often moved in bands of three or four, but there would be lone rangers among them.

The masquerades' treatment of women was markedly different. The *Akatakpa* could be vicious, particularly if they detected signs of insubordination, and even when the perceived disrespect had nothing to do with the symbol they represented. As the society and its values evolved, the symbolic importance of the *Akatakpa* began to wane. It became an instrument for revenge, for settling rejected amorous advances, and for teaching some people a lesson.

Thus during the festival, women would be found in small groups plotting what safe routes to take to the market. When they were lucky, they would go and return in peace. But if they were unlucky, many would return with bruises and there would be complaints of lost market wares. Some ended up in hospital. Since the identity of the masquerades was not a matter for public discussion, the bullying was often not punished. The *Akatakpa* was now known to occasionally hide in the bush, off a footpath leading to the market and would spring on unsuspecting market women who would attempt to flee, screaming and yelling as it lashed at them. During this period, the *eke* market and all the other subsidiary markets would be held in the morning only.

By 1.00 pm most women would have returned home unless they had travelled to markets outside Isiakpu, a major risk on their part. Returning safely from those markets required gathering a lot of intelligence on the activities of the *Akatakpa,* their number and movements. Occasionally, the women got assistance from older men who would escort them up to a point.

Mama Oby had only been to her shop at the *eke* market twice since the *Akatakpa* festivities began. She had instead sent Amechi, her eldest son, to the shop every day for the brisk morning business. And he had done very well. Business at the shop had picked up a few months back after Uncle Amechi advanced Mama Oby additional money to stock the shop.

Mama Oby knew she and her daughter would be easy targets for the *Akatakpa* because of the envy for their relative success. She would not let her enemies on her by venturing out. She liked to fight, but tactfully avoiding humiliation at the hands of those out to oppress her. When she came back to settle in the village after the civil war, she had teamed up with Mama Ijeoma and a few other women to organise a demonstration against the *Akatakpa* masquerades. Their activities at that time were excessively reckless and brutal.

208

The civil war had contributed to the increased brutality. Many young men, ex-soldiers who were unemployed and had become hardened from their experience in the war, used the *Akatakpa* as an outlet for pent-up anger. Rather than direct their anger at the larger society, they focused it on young women.

Mama Oby and Mama Ijeoma's protest was nipped in the bud. Their third meeting, held at Mama Oby's house, attracted a lot of young women, most of them married and victims of the male exuberance. They were ranting, beating their chests and vowing at the top of their voices to crush the brutal tradition. It was agreed that the next meeting would work out the strategy to demonstrate their anger. That meeting was never held.

Every woman was warned by her husband to dissociate from the meeting and the protest. The men had met and resolved that if there was anything wrong with the tradition, they themselves would deal with it. They would not allow women to dictate to them what to do, to stampede or force them to act as if they were a bunch of spineless men.

Every man was asked to exert control over his wife. Mama Ijeoma and Mama Oby received serious threats over their role in bringing the women together for the proposed protest. In spite of their courage, they knew that they could not go it alone. On the day of their fourth meeting, only the two of them met. Later, they were joined by a third woman who had not attended any of the previous meetings. They were certain that she had been sent to spy on the meeting. The women's voice had been silenced, but not before Mama Ijeoma and Mama Oby used the presence of the spy, who was most uncomfortable throughout, to send a clear warning to the men that the fight was not over. They were certain the message would be received.

When she left, the two women settled down to a bottle of palm wine, a very rare thing for Mama Oby. As they drank, they wondered when women would organise themselves to fight for their rights. They did not lose sight of the fact that their partial liberation came from the exposure of living in a city.

The women's attempt to organise a protest against the brutality of the *Akatakpa,* coupled with complaints from neighbouring towns and churches had forced the previous chief and his council of elders to partially suspend their activities. They had reported that young men (in *Akatakpa*) had also started using the festivities to extort money and punish their enemies. To maintain respect for tradition, a few masquerades, whose identities were known to the elders, were allowed as part of the new yam festival during the last week of the festivities.

When the chief died, the traditionalists fought to have the ban lifted. The new chief, Igwe Ugwueze, who claimed to have aligned himself with the traditionalists, lifted the ban. But it was no longer business as usual. The brutality had declined, though still evident, and the number of masquerades had also gone down. Many young men were busy pursuing other interests.

In spite of this, young and middle-aged women continued to exercise extreme caution throughout the period. In fact, the last two days of the festivities often saw a sudden increase in brutality, a weird sort of climax to the eating and drinking. All complaints had fallen on deaf ears.

The new yam festival coincided with what was popularly referred to as the August break. The heavy rains stopped around this time. Three days to the end of the festival, the sun shone brightly and the air was soft and dry. It usually was a busy day because it was also the day married daughters who could afford it made food and sent it to their fathers from their homes. Mama Oby's father had died before the civil war and as a gesture of generosity and allegiance to the family, she prepared a delicious meal of pounded yam with okra soup for Pa Okolo every year. Before noon on the day of the festival, the food would be delivered in a big basket by her son Amechi. Although the food was primarily meant for him, she knew he would eat it with all of his brothers. Pa Okolo always returned Mama Oby's gesture by sending back the emissary with two tubers of new yam from his farm. This year was no exception.

As soon as Amechi came back, the family settled down to a very delicious meal. As had become customary for her, she would invite two or three other women from the village who had no regular income or support to join them. She had a lot to be thankful for: Oby's university education which had gone very well in the first year, Amechi's secondary education which was over, and her business which had picked up. This was all mentioned in a long prayer before the meal.

Later in the day, as the family sat in the living room chatting to while away the time, they had the most unexpected visitors — Mama Ijeoma and Fr Damian. Mama Ijeoma had not been to the house for some time because of her strained relationship with Mama Oby. A few days before Oby returned from the university, however, she had sauntered into Mama Oby's house. All she had come to report was that the chief was interested in Ijeoma for his son. Her excitement dimmed when she realised that Mama Oby was not interested in the talk. The reception was extremely cold and her visit short.

Something tragic had happened this time and Mama Ijeoma had heard of it but did not have the courage to break the news to Mama Oby alone. She had gone to Fr Damian's house and persuaded him to accompany her.

Fire had razed Mama Oby's shop at the *eke* market and nothing had been saved. No one knew who had done it.

There was pandemonium when the news was broken. Fr Damian held Mama Oby as she raised her voice in a high-pitched cry, the sort that unmistakably sends the signal to the neigbourhood that something tragic has happened. She wrestled herself free from Fr Damian and fell on the floor. Everyone else joined in the yelling and crying. Within minutes, the entire compound was filled with sympathisers. Every woman who came wanted to out-wail the last one. Some fell on the floor, not minding whether they were falling on other sympathisers. In these matters, effect was important. Many women jostled to be as close to Mama Oby as possible. For some, the wailing stopped as suddenly as it had started, their agony, being largely contrived, lacked depth.

When Mama Oby had recollected herself, Fr Damian drove her to the *eke* market to look over the situation for herself. She was a courageous woman, but she could not control her emotion at the sight of what used to be her mini-supermarket. Nor could Oby.

They stood at the steps of the shop with misty eyes. Mama Oby stood staring at the sky, dotted with little stars, begging for an answers from the Almighty.

You did not have to be a fire expert to know that this was not an accident. It was the work of an arsonist. She knew immediately that this must be the handiwork of close relatives or friends. After all, some had openly threatened to teach her a lesson.

Yes, they had hit her where it hurt most, but she believed God was on her side. "Those on the side of devil will be consumed by the fire of hell," she muttered to herself. "My hands are clean. With God, my enemies shall never triumph over me," she kept saying as they drove back home.

Later that evening, Pa Okolo called on Mama Oby. Quite unlike him, he sat in a corner of the house, exchanging greetings with other visitors. This was just like his house, and it seemed strange that he would behave like a guest. All who came to sympathise with Mama Oby were obliged to acknowledge his presence and extend a word of sympathy to him as well. He sat speechless and barely nodded in acknowledgment. He kept tapping his feet on the floor, with intermittent hissing.

Looking at him, you would think that he was staring at Mama Oby but he was actually staring into space. He had a lot on his mind. Try as much as he could to conceal this, it was obvious that he was not himself. He had guilt written all over his face. He alone had a clue to what had happened. But for how long this would be, he had no idea. He was not one to cry over spilt milk. But this was different; the spilt milk had his fingerprints all over. What had happened was *alu*, whichever way one looked at it. Dogs are forbidden to eat the bones hung on their necks. Only a stupid man would steal that which he was asked to watch over. Pa Okolo was already weighing the consequences of what had happened.

Just when he was straightening his wrapper in readiness to leave, an eyewitness walked in. In spite of the mood, he made his way to Mama Oby yelling that he had seen it all. "Yes, the *Akatakpa* masquerades did it."

212

Most people sat up to listen to him.

"Are you sure?" someone asked.

"Absolutely, I was right there. If I am lying, let thunder strike now and finish me."

The fellow could not be the best eyewitness, but only he had the courage to relate what he had seen. Others would wait until everything was almost forgotten to volunteer any information, in bits and pieces, as if to suggest that they did not have the details. He was known to have psychiatric problems and many people were inclined to ask him to shut up lest he implicated innocent people. But he was insistent and with Mama Oby listening patiently, he told a credible story.

Apparently, about five *Akatakpa* masquerades had arrived at the *eke* market, acting drunk. The people who had gathered at the market to while away the evening were sent scampering to safety. One masquerade was acting very strangely. He first ran around the shop.

"At first, I thought that he was urinating because some liquid was dropping from beneath him as he did the lap around the shop. I later realised that the liquid was coming from a bottle concealed in a brown paper bag. I was very close. I don't know anyone else who saw this in detail. When they decided to leave, they dashed again in various directions chasing people further away from the shop. A few minutes after, the entire shop was engulfed in flames. The fire was so intense that no one dared to come close to it. I was so terrified that I continued to run until I got to my house. In fact, the truth is that I ran past my house. I have never seen anything like it before. The contents of the store were fuelling a ball of fire. The fire was so intense and yet so contained that it did not spread. It was a miracle. It simply lit the sky. People like me who would have liked to help put out the fire were scared stiff. Other less brave ones were simply urinating in their pants. It was very serious. It was very serious indeed. I am very sorry, Mama Oby. What they did is evil. Unfortunately, it is very difficult to identify those masquerades. One is not even supposed to talk about their identity."

By the time he finished, everybody was hissing, exchanging glances and adjusting their sitting positions. Many close friends of Mama Oby's, who sat still as the story was told, started crying again. Mama Oby was now the one consoling them.

In the midst of all the yelling and cursing, Pa Okolo sneaked out. He first headed towards his house but halfway there, turned and used a circuitous route to Uncle Ben's house. Although it was dark, he took care that no one could track his movements that night. Uncle Ben was alone outside his house, watching the moon setting. He had just come back from where he had returned the *Akatakpa* costume he had used to accomplish the task assigned to him. He was generally satisfied with the way it had gone and felt certain no one would trace it back to him. No one, of course, except Pa Okolo and Chief Ugwueze.

When Pa Okolo cleared his throat, he sat up beaming with a smile.

"Are you alone?" Pa Okolo asked.

Uncle Ben was still beaming contendedly. He expected congratulations. "Yes, I am alone. My wife went to visit her father."

"We said that you should teach her a little lesson. We didn't want you to drown her, to finish her. I thought that you understood the instruction."

Uncle Ben wanted to yell in anger at Pa Okolo's audacity. He asked him to do something which he had done to the best of his ability, and all he would get was another rebuke.

"What do you mean, Pa Okolo? It is either a full dose of the lesson or no lesson at all. Don't you understand?" Uncle Ben asked.

"Lower you voice. You have messed up the message as usual. I should never have relied on you."

"Oh yeah! Have you heard of how I executed this plan? If you don't give me credit, I will give myself some. No one can trace what happened this evening at the *eke* market to either of us. The plan and its execution smacks of genius," Uncle Ben said as he beat his chest to emphasise this point.

"You don't get it, do you? If you go to the doctor and he asks you to take two tablets of aspirin three times a day, you don't go home and take six tablets at once because you want your ailment to go fast, do you? The doctor's prescription will cure you but taking six tablets at once is suicidal. That is what it is, suicidal."

214

"Pa Okolo, I don't think that you know what happened. I am a genius. You should ask me to tell you what happened."

"Genius? How did you buy the fuel you used?"

"How did you know that I used fuel? Have you gone to the scene to sniff around?"

"Never mind. I have God-given instincts. Please answer the question. Where did you buy the fuel and through whom?"

"I sent the twins, the sons of Uncle Ezeh to buy the petrol from the dealer, Mr Okeke," Uncle Ben answered.

"Why Ezeh's sons? You couldn't find someone else to run this errand for you? Can't you see that it will point fingures at you?" Pa Okolo asked.

"You know, I am really getting tired of you treating me as a fool. I have concluded that I can never do anything that satisfies you. Never! As far as you are concerned, I am simply incapable of accomplishing even basic tasks."

"Don't put words into my mouth. You pretty much know how I feel about you. You are right. I was hoping that this assignment would redeem your image. No, you didn't want to disappoint me and you messed it up again," Pa Okolo said angrily.

"Is that you Pa Okolo?" someone passing by asked. "Good evening, sir," the strange voice continued. In a moment of fury, Pa Okolo had raised his voice, momentarily forgetting he was on a secret mission. The stranger had stumbled on them as they were discussing the use of petrol and decided to listen for a while. He did not get the entire story but got enough to link Pa Okolo to the market fire that evening.

Pa Okolo was startled but he stood motionless and gestured to Uncle Ben not to respond. The inquirer did not wait for a reply as he paced off down the road that led to Pa Okolo's house. As soon as he was sure that whoever it was had moved on, he began walking towards Uncle Ben's house. If anyone put two of them together tonight, it would spell trouble for Pa Okolo, who wanted to distance himself from the ugly incident.

"It is better that we finish this discussion inside your house. I don't know what people are doing outside their homesteads at this hour of the night. That voice sounded like that of Ezigwe, that good-for-nothing man. He is a notorious gossip. But then again, Ezigwe is not known for his politeness, he would not have addressed me as 'sir'. Who could this be?"

Pa Okolo knew that this little encounter could cause him trouble. But without the person's identity, there was nothing he could do. If he went out of his way to seek him, he would be exposing himself.

Said Uncle Ben, "Not to worry, Pa Okolo. I know what my role was supposed to be in this whole thing. I have done my best but if this affair is uncovered, both you and the chief will see my ugly side." He had become visibly angry.

"What?" Pa Okolo insisted. "What has the chief got to do with any of this, you mad man?"

"You are raising your voice again. We shall see who is mad. You think that I don't know what this whole thing is about. You and your little ambitions and the chief who wants a way to finish you. He's got it. You cannot swear that the chief doesn't know of our little secret, can you?" Uncle Ben asked, pacing around the room.

Pa Okolo got extremely agitated. "I have said it before that you are totally insane. Your madness is now manifesting itself fully. I should have left you to rot in the city rather than incur huge expenses to bring you home. Now you want to bring shame to this noble house, the house of my father Onyia. I will never allow you to do so. Please, whatever you do, leave the name of the chief out of it. If he descends on you, crocodiles would be feasting on your body within hours. Don't play with Agaba Idu I. I know a lot about him that you don't."

"I don't care what you know about him," the other said. "You may think that you know me well. But just wait and see. All these insults will come to an end. We are now engaged in an unfriendly race: there is no friend or brother. You simply have to run as fast as you can. If in the process, you trample the others to death, so be it."

The conversation was going nowhere. Pa Okolo had come to intimidate Uncle Ben into accepting that he had miscarried the assignment and therefore agree to be the scapegoat in the event that he was identified as the culprit. He had been almost certain that it would happen. But Uncle Ben was expecting congratulations on a job well done. At worst, he thought that Pa Okolo would come up with suggestions on how to avert their being linked to the crime. He was not a fool. He was simply stirring the hornet's nest in the hope that Pa Okolo would take the cue and discuss with him the crime as an accomplice. But Pa Okolo was too stubborn to make such a concession and Uncle Ben was more than willing to keep him guessing on what his next move would be.

Uncle Ben knew that he would be sacrificed if the matter was exposed. But he vowed not to make it easy for Pa Okolo.

The older man stood up. He felt cornered, and by the wrong person. "I see that we are not getting anywhere in this. I have seen a side of you that I had never known before. Whatever you do, just remember who saved your skin before. Remember the name of this family, and above all, leave the name of Agaba Idu out of it." Then he stormed out of the house.

For a moment, he thought of going to the chief's house. It was not only too late but the chief would be most upset with visits that might link him to the arson. He headed home absent-mindedly. He heard and imagined he was hearing voices. As a thick cloud passed, momentarily shielding the moon, there was a brief moment of darkness. At one point Pa Okolo stumbled and almost fell into a ditch on what had always been a familiar path.

A very worried Pa Okolo lay on his bed contemplating what he would do if Uncle Ben decided to humiliate him or the family. His thoughts had no boundaries: they wandered from the possibility of eliminating Uncle Ben – with the help of the chief – to committing suicide. It was a troubling night for him, as he lay sleepless on the bed.

Oby woke up very early the next day, brushed her teeth, washed her face and left the house without a word to anyone. She had also had a sleepless night, weighing her options and the consequences of the action she planned to take. If they simply prayed, she thought, a lot of women would continue to suffer. Yes, the Lord avenged evil. But He often worked through others. She thought the incident required a police investigation. But the police would not do anything unless the victim reported the matter. Even then, there was no guarantee of justice. It could be frustrating and, in a society where money could buy justice, what she wanted to do was as good as taking a gamble. Moreover, too many people could be implicated in the crime to the extent where the victim would become isolated. In Isiakpu, that would have serious consequences. Her mother would be the last person to allow anything of the sort to happen. She had prayed but also made up her mind that she would take the case to the police even without discussing it with her mother. It was a risk worth taking.

By 7.00 am, Oby was at the Central Police Station at Nsukka. She had always seen this compound, enclosed in barbed wire, from a distance. As a child, she had often wondered what took place in there where uniformed and non-uniformed people often interacted as if all was well. At the centre of the compound stood an old colonial redbrick house with rusty zinc roofing. The building was older than Mama Oby. This was the main police station. It had a couple of holding cells for suspects awaiting trial. There were several other buildings in the compound. These were residential quarters for junior police officers.

There was nothing remarkable about the quarters except that there appeared to be some competition among the different households as to whose clothes-line would be longest: ugly and torn underwears, singlets, baby nappies, wrappers, among others were spread for several metres in front of, and around, the houses.

As Oby approached the concrete desk at the entrance of the main building a pungent stench filled her nostrils. This odour must have been from the cells where people were held for days, sometimes weeks, with no bathing facilities.

"What brought you to us this early in the morning, young girl?" one of the officers behind the desk asked laughing. "Your boyfriend kicked you out? Ha ha ha." His colleague joined in the laughter.

"Good morning, sirs. I am here to see the inspector," Oby said calmly.

"Which Inspector?"

"The inspector on duty, sir," Oby said.

"But you have not told us what the problem is. You are a fine girl.

We also have money, mind you. If the problem is your boyfriend, you can forget him. We are also available for, you know ..." He reached out and rubbed Oby's arm. She pulled away gently. The men began to laugh again. Oby knew that getting upset would get her nowhere. The officers were still enjoying themselves with their lurid jokes when Oby asked again: "Is there an inspector on duty or do I have to travel to Enugu to get your attention?" Enugu was the seat of the regional police headquarters.

"Oh yeah! Our skinny, no-butt little girl is getting feisty."

While the officers spoke in Igbo, she responded only in English. It was a deliberate tactic aimed at creating some barrier between them. Oby had asked for an inspector because they were often better educated and she might be lucky to get one who could reason and take the matter seriously.

"*Oga no dey,*" the police officer continued. Before he could finish whatever he was saying, a tall, pot-bellied man in his late forties walked towards the desk from an inner office. Apparently, he had heard the two policemen laughing and got curious.

"What is going on here?"

"Nothing, sir," one of the policemen said. The two officers stood at attention and gave a sharp salute.

"Sir, this young girl wants to see you. She has refused to tell us what the problem is, sir," one of the officers said.

"Because you were behaving like clowns," the inspector said. Oby felt delighted.

"No, sir. Yes, sir." The officers were still standing at attention.

"Please come in, young lady."

"Yes, sir. Good morning, sir," Oby said as she walked past the two policemen.

The inspector was more than sympathetic. By the time Oby was through with making her report, other policemen had reported for duty. The inspector detailed a sergeant and two constables to accompany her to Isiakpu to investigate the suspected arson. The sergeant, a veteran of many years, knew what was required of him.

As they drove to Isiakpu, he wanted to know everything about

Oby, her family and their relationships. This was part of the investigation, he assured Oby. He talked a lot, and during twenty-minute drive he had talked of the many awards he had won because of his investigative skills. He had not attained the rank of inspector because he had a godfather, he told Oby.

They drove straight to the scene where the ruins from the fire stared everybody in the face. As soon as the villagers saw a police vehicle, they quickly disappeared.

"This is arson. There is no doubt about it," the sergeant said. "It was neatly executed otherwise, how do you explain the fact that only this shop was affected in an area where there are so many buildings around?"

As he went around, he collected three bottles from the ground, and sniffed them. He wanted to know who the petrol dealers in Isiakpu were. There were only two. As they drove to the house of one of them, Oby pointed out her mother's house on the left side of the road. The sergeant ordered the driver to stop. He wanted to talk to Mama Oby but she did not think it a good idea and persuaded the sergeant to interview her at the end of the investigation.

The petrol dealer, Mr Okeke, was notified of the presence of a police van at their home by his wife.

"Police van?" he wondered aloud. "Doing what in front of my house?"

"Are you Mr Okeke?" the sergeant asked. Oby did not get out of the police vehicle. She took cover in the van.

"Yes, sir."

"Do you sell petrol?"

"Yes sir, officer."

"Do you sell petrol in bottles?"

"Officer, I have to feed all these my children."

"Mr Okeke, that was not my question. Do you sell petrol in bottles?"

"I have sold sometimes, but as I said ..."

"Do you know that it is against the law to sell petrol in bottles?"

"Against the law? I only know that some police officers did not like the idea. But sometimes we find something for them and they don't

bother us again. You know, we give them something for cold water,"
he giggled.

"I see. You better be serious with me."

"Like how much, sir? You know that this is a dry period for us."

"Shut up or you will be arrested, foolish old man."

"Yes, sir."

"Have you sold petrol in a bottle in the last one week?"

"Yes, sir."

"Can you identify the bottles if I showed them to you?"

"I will try, officer," Okeke said. "Is everything okay?"

The sergeant asked one of the policemen to show Mr Okeke the
three bottles he had picked up from the fire site.

"Which of these bottles do you recognise?"

"It is definitely this one. I am very sure," Mr Okeke said as he
pointed to an old lucozade drink bottle which had lost its label.

"Are you sure, Mr Okeke?" the sergeant asked again.

"I am very sure. Two young twins, the children of Mr Ezeh, came
here with that bottle and said that their Uncle Ben had sent them to
buy petrol for him. I initially wondered what he could possibly do with
fuel since he did not even own a spoke of a bicycle, not to talk of a
motorcycle. But there are people like that. People use fuel for all
kinds of things."

"Who is Ben?"

"Ben Onyia, a loafer. Everybody knows him," Mr Okeke replied.

"Are you sure about all this?" the sergeant asked yet again.

"I swear. I will not lie to an officer."

"Very good, thank you very much." The officer shook Mr Okeke's
hand and for the first time since he started questioning him. He smiled
as he walked back to the police van.

"Please officer, let me look for a kola nut."

"That won't be necessary," said the sergeant. He waved to Mr
Okeke as he stepped into the van and banged the door excitedly.

"We've got the son-of-a-bitch," he announced.

Mr Okeke watched the police van turn and speed out of his
compound.

"Some police officers are children of God. Not even an ordinary kola nut. No money for cold water? God bless you. We may yet get to the promised land in my lifetime," he said.

When she discovered Uncle Ben was a prime suspect, Oby pleaded that they should drop her off anywhere along the way. The sergeant agreed but said that he still would have liked to talk to Mama Oby after the arrest.

The presence of the police van in Isiakpu had already sparked speculation and word was quickly spreading. The chief had been alerted by his *ndi oti nkpu,* noise-bearers and sycophants, with details of where the policemen had stopped and what they appeared to be doing. They picked up Uncle Ben, who had been asleep, without incident and did not interrogate him. He was simply asked to identify himself and to accompany them to Nsukka as part of the investigation into the fire incident at the *eke* market the previous evening. He showed no emotion and calmly walked into the van. As they were driving off, the chief's driver appeared with a note for the sergeant. The chief wanted them to stop by his palace before going to Nsukka. A few minutes after the sergeant was ushered into the palace, the chief walked in.

"Igwe! Igwe! Good morning, sir!" the sergeant bowed to greet the chief. The other policemen stayed in the van with Uncle Ben.

The chief said, "Yes. What were you doing in my town without first reporting to me? Quite frankly, I am not amused by it. I was tempted to call the Police Commissioner in Enugu to alert him of the insults that you give a first class traditional ruler like myself. Protocol is protocol. You cannot go sniffing around my compound without letting me know. It is not the way things are done."

"Sorry, sir. Sorry, Igwe," the sergeant said. "We meant to report to you when we have the facts. Right now, we are only investigating."

"Well, it doesn't occur to you that we can handle some of these cases the traditional way? Some of these things may be simple traditional disputes and the police are not well equipped to understand them or resolve them successfully. Don't you understand?" the chief asked.

"I understand you perfectly well. But chief, this is arson. This is

222

not petty robbery or wife abuse. It is a serious crime. It is a criminal offence under the Penal Code. I have strict instructions from my inspector," the Sergeant said.

"My friend," the chief said, "OC (officer in charge), are you listening to me? When a bus carries a message. *Ka anayo chukwu*, let's plead with God, it does not imply that the bus does not intend to complete the journey. If you keep interpreting the slogans and messages written on some of these buses and lorries that ferry people over long distances, you will never board any. You have been told to ignore these messages and simply board the vehicle if you want to travel. That is my message to you. My friend, Penal Code or no code, I am telling you that I, Agaba Idu I of Isiakpu, am capable of handling any crime in my town. We have our own legal system here. Are we clear now?"

"Chief. Eh ... I have to report to my superior officer."

"You can even report to the Police Commissioner at Enugu. I am saying that you cannot take anybody from this village without my permission. Of course, you can always disobey my orders then be ready to face the consequences."

The chief stood up, went into another room and came back with three brown envelopes.

"Here is something small for all your troubles," he announced. "You can give the smaller envelopes to your colleagues sitting in the van. A wise person never forgets where his fingers got oiled, sergeant. We are here to make you happy but you have to cooperate with us. That will be all. Ask Ben to come in here to see me."

The chief left the living room as the police officer returned to the van very confused and unhappy. He released Uncle Ben to the chief, and without saying much, asked the police driver to take him back to Nsukka. Halfway through the journey, he handed over the two envelopes to his colleagues.

"Oga, this morning is good, oo!" the driver said with excitement as he tried to guess the amount in the envelope by shaking and tossing it. This was not some petty bribe like the one he had been used to at their many, sometimes illegal, road-blocks. He had just received something almost the equivalent of his monthly salary.

"Shut up and drive." The sergeant was worried that the inspector would eat him raw.

Later that day, Chief Ugwueze drove into Mama Oby's compound apparently to offer his condolences. Before his arrival, Mama Oby and Oby had heard that his intervention had won the release of Uncle Ben. Mama Oby, who surprisingly supported Oby's decision to report the matter to the police, was very upset with the chief. She had always considered him evil and his intervention confirmed her belief.

When his limousine pulled up at her home, Mama Oby and her daughter were busy reviewing the developments, wondering whether Amechi had reached Onitsha to tell his uncle on the destruction of their shop. When they heard the car outside, Mama Oby went to welcome the visitor. Oby drew a curtain to peep out of the window. As her mother turned the doorknob, the chief's driver honked his horn.

"It is the chief, mom," Oby said.

"What is that devil doing in my compound?" Mama Oby hissed.

"Tell him to get lost. He has sold his integrity at the market. Mom, let me deal with him."

"Please, let me handle him. Stay inside, please."

The chief had no intention of getting out of his car. He wound down the tinted window, extended his hands to Mama Oby and muttered something that ended with how sorry he was at what had happened to her shop. Mama Oby simply nodded. She was totally disgusted with the farce.

The chief brought out a large brown envelope full of money. "Mama Oby, please have this as a token of my sympathy."

"That won't be necessary, chief," she told him. "Everything is under control. Thank you for your kind gesture."

"Please take this from me. I know that everything is under control but that shouldn't stop you from receiving something from your chief." He tried to shove the brown envelope into Mama Oby's palm but the parcel landed at her feet.

The chief asked his driver to move. Mama Oby quickly picked up the parcel and threw it into the car as it sped off with the chief cursing and vowing to teach her a bitter lesson. Oby was watching the drama from the house but thoroughly enjoyed the chief's humiliation.

Oby lay sleepless all that night. Uncle Ben was still free, roaming the village. He had been heard boasting about the people he had in high places, that even if he killed someone there was nothing anyone could do about it. He would be a big threat to Mama Oby and her family if he went free and unpunished.

Mama Oby had been praying for God's intervention in the matter. Oby still had a little hope in the law and decided to go back to the police station early the following morning, again without telling her mother.

It was the usual shenanigans at the police station. She could not recognise any of the policemen on duty, and she knew that this would make her case difficult. There was likely to be no file on the case, and initiating fresh investigations into a criminal act committed three days before would be difficult. Besides, whatever evidence there was would have disappeared. But she was determined.

"Good morning, sirs," Oby greeted the policemen across the counter.

"*Sisi, wetin we go do for you this morning?*"

"If you don't mind. I would like to see the officer on duty."

Oby was hoping it would be the same officer who assisted her the previous day.

"*Sisi, E bi like say we no reach to help you. Abi?*"

"I said that I would like to see the officer on duty," Oby shouted. "Is that a crime?"

"*Madam lawyer a beg you o!*" one of them said.

She knew that if there was a reasonable officer inside the office he would soon come out, if only to find out who the mad woman was. The trick worked. Luckily, it was the same officer. He had forgotten about the case and had not followed it up. He had had a lot on his mind lately.

Oby brought him up to speed on what had happened. He was very furious with the chief for having meddled in the investigation, and with his men for having succumbed to his machinations. He apologised to Oby and sent one of the policemen to fetch the sergeant who had investigated the incident. When the sergeant arrived at the police station, half-awake, the officer gave him an earful, then ordered him to go and bring in Uncle Ben. He was to book him and hand over all the evidence in the case in two hours. Luckly, the sergent had not destroyed the evidence from the investigation. He had kept it in his house, willing to let the matter die if no one resurrected it. But he was not willing to lose his job and his pension on account of it.

Uncle Ben was picked up without incident. This time, the sergeant used an unmarked police vehicle. Before noon, everyone in the village knew that Ben had been picked up and locked up at the Nsukka Police Station. No one in the village, except Oby's mother, knew that Oby had a hand in the matter. For the moment, Oby and her mother wanted it to remain that way. They were still part of this society, and they wanted to remain part of it.

The chief tried to bail out Uncle Ben without success. The Officer-in-Charge could not be compromised. The chief's intelligence warned him that if he pushed the matter further, the skeletons in his closet could all come tumbling out. No one could be sure where it would all end. When he realised this, he got Uncle Ben to confess to the crime. It was a very difficult conversation full of promises peppered with mild threats. He promised to look after his family while he was in prison and to set him up in business after his release. The chief was not prepared for a prolonged trial that could expose his role in the affair.

Pa Okolo and the chief had deliberately avoided meeting to discuss the unfolding events. Before Uncle Ben was re-arrested, Pa Okolo had sent his eldest wife to thank the chief for his kind intervention on behalf of his brother and to let him know that he fully appreciated the fact that the gesture was in recognition of his personal relationship with him. Even though she did not understand why, she was also asked to convey to the chief Pa Okolo's feeling that it was in their interest that the two be not seen together for a while.

Chief Ugwueze knew exactly what that message meant. Unfortunately as his efforts to secure the release of Uncle Ben on bail had failed, he knew a personal meeting with Pa Okolo was inevitable. He wanted him to be prepared for the fallout, and to let him know he would be away from Isiakpu for a long time. In a way, the chief also wanted Pa Okolo to prepare to be sacrificed without implicating him.

On the evening he made up his mind he was going to ask Uncle Ben to plead guilty, he sent his driver to pick up Pa Okolo from his residence as discreetly as possible.

The driver pulled up at Pa Okolo's residence at about 11.00 pm. Pa Okolo was surprised to see Bitrus, the chief's driver, but he was more surprised when the driver said he had been instructed not to return without him.

Pa Okolo had been down with malaria in the past week. An attack of malaria usually lasted two days at the longest. He had always kept a bottle of chloroquine tablets in his bedroom, and he always fully recovered after two days of self-treatment. This time, he had been down for a week and the fever, loss of appetite and general malaise were still with him. With the events of the previous week and in particular Uncle Ben's re-arrest, his anxiety was extremely high.

He struggled out of bed and, without much argument, followed Bitrus.

It was a sombre Chief Ugwueze that Pa Okolo saw as he entered his living room. He was sitting on his customary high chair, head bowed. He wore a T-shirt and a thick wrapper with one half of it flowing on to the floor. When the visitor entered the room, the host did not raise his head to acknowledge his arrival. In his bowed position, he extended a muted welcome to his guest. This was meant to convey the gravity of the situation. Pa Okolo sat down and unconsciously assumed a similar posture. The guest started tapping the floor with his toes.

He startled the chief with one heavy sigh. "Chief, I am here."

"I know that you are here."

"Well, eh?"

"Well, what? Am I supposed to jump because you are here?"

"Chief, I know that you sent for me because something serious has happened. What is it?" Pa Okolo asked, throwing caution to the wind.

"Pa Okolo, I will ignore the tone of these questions. I know that you have been under some stress lately."

"Stress-and-a-half chief. And now I think that I am hallucinating from terrible, high-powered malaria. Can't you see how I am sweating?

The only reason I am still alive today is that I know you are there for me — the wind beneath my wing."

"Pa Okolo, *aku akaligo oka*. There is not enough maize to chew with the available palm kernel. Okolo, we have run out of maize and there is no willing seller. No willing seller in spite of the price that I am offering."

"*Chinekem ooh*. Chief, what are you saying?"

"Pa Okolo, you are not a baby. When the quantity of palm kernel is more than that of maize, the recipe is no good. The taste is awful. You know that, don't you?"

"I know that, chief. What are we faced with?"

"There you go again with your questions."

"It is just that the suspense is killing me," Pa Okolo said. He was looking like a trapped rat.

"Pa Okolo. I plan to ask your brother, Ben, to confess to burning down Mama Oby's store."

Pa Okolo almost jumped in spite of his weak condition. "*Mba!* No. Chief, you cannot be serious. Confess to what?"

"What do you mean, 'confess to what?' I will see him tomorrow and I hope that he will not make life difficult for anyone else."

"But chief, we promised to protect him."

"No. You promised to protect him. Listen to me. I warned you that I don't get involved in amateur acts. After playing high-powered poker games all over the world and having dined with all sorts of devils, you and your useless brother now want to expose my naked butt to the world. I can't accept that. No. I have rejected the devil and his temptations."

He collected the flowing end of his wrapper and wiped his face, a sign of the seriousness of the matter.

"But chief, don't you see the danger this places us in?"

Pa Okolo was now sweating profusely. There was no way of guessing how Uncle Ben would react to being asked to confess. There was no way he, Pa Okolo, would accept public ridicule and go to jail. That would be playing too much into the hands of his enemies. It was a terrible situation to be in. It was like aiming for the sky and suddenly discovering that the take-off point on earth was no longer there. That was the situation facing Pa Okolo.

Said the chief, "I am not in any danger. I am only sorry for you, Okolo. I did everything possible to get that good-for-nothing brother of yours out of detention for your sake. Quite frankly, I think that a few years in jail would teach him a few useful lessons."

"But how can Igwe, a whole Agaba Idu I, give up over such a small matter? Is there anyone that is somebody in the army or police force that you have not socialised with?" Pa Okolo switched to flattery to soften the chief.

"Leave those things alone. This case is small but knotty. I felt like I was hitting my head against a wall. I don't want to believe that Mama Oby has anything to do with it. You know that when you underestimate the significance of a small boiling pot of water, it will put out a huge fire. That's the nature of this case."

"So what do I do now, chief?"

"Nothing. Just pray that your brother agrees to confess and does not implicate you in this.

"Pray?" Pa Okolo said. "In this prayer, I will need your assistance, chief. Are you going to lead the way?"

"As you know," the chief continued, "this is an *alu* and the gods will not spare any of you. I will try to protect you from the society but that will be all."

The chief wanted to emphasise that Pa Okolo was the lone criminal here. In any event, all he did was to provide advice to a friend who needed some. The chief would not accept any responsibility. Yet, he would have been quick to boast of his wisdom if his advice had not backfired. As it were, the wind was blowing and exposing the butt of the fowl.

"There is no guarantee that he will accept to do this. He had already hinted that he would not fall alone when I confronted him to tell him he had not concealed his tracks. He was very upset. I am not sure that he would agree to confess."

"We shall see. I plan to sweeten the deal for him by offering to help his family and to settle him when he gets out. But you know your brother better than I do. Someone with a skull will accept the offer but you should expect the worst from him. In the last few days that I have been to see him, he has been acting like a mad dog. He was very impatient. He did not understand why he was still being locked up."

"You now understand what I mean, chief. Ben is crazy. Very unpredictable."

"We shall see, we shall see," the chief said, recognising that everything could go wrong.

"Chief, I have washed my hands, split and served palm kernel nuts on a platter to the fowls. If you decide to fetch firewood bedevilled with termites, you should be willing to welcome lizards to your house. There is a natural consequence for all our actions. I have always fought my enemies fairly and squarely. I don't want to be served to my enemies with my hands bound together and my legs in shackles. No. Chief, Igwe, the one that will reign forever, I salute you. I salute you for your courage; for the courage of your father before you. I throw salute to you for what you wanted to do for my family and me. For me, the die is cast. There is no chance that this darkened cloud will not give birth to rain, a heavy downpour. Perhaps, that is the way it was supposed to be. Let us not sit here and question that which has been ordained. If we had succeeded, we would have taught the widow a lesson. Now that we ... I mean ... I did not succeed, what I did was to aid and abet an *alu*. Pure and simple.

"Chief, are your people still awake?" Pa Okolo thought that he saw a figure, a moving shadow, by the door leading to the chief's bedroom.

"That is my second wife. You know how it is. It is her turn tonight and she is becoming impatient. Just ignore her. She does not even know that I have no energy for it. She has no clue of what I am currently faced with. She can pace up and down as much as she wants."

"I know how it is. Women are women. They think very differently from us."

"Pa Okolo, let's get back to our discussion. Before you reach these conclusions, let me talk to your brother, Ben, tomorrow and hear what

230

he says. If you hear from me tomorrow, you know that I will have succeeded. If you don't, you should know that I have gone to Lagos to cool it off and that you should seek refuge and take care of yourself."

"Igwe, the result is the same for me. If my brother goes to prison, it would be said that I bought my freedom by mortgaging the freedom of my helpless brother. Already, tongues are wagging and fingers are being pointed in my direction. If he implicates me and I go to prison at this age, what would the society think of me? I would still not be accepted by the council of elders even if the prison term was one week. If he were to be set free, we would all claim that this whole thing was a plot by our enemies, and that further investigations were continuing in order to apprehend the real culprits. Chief, I will take care of myself. Don't worry."

"It is late, Okolo. Let us retire now."

"I have one last request, chief, if you don't mind."

"What is it?"

"The usual, my friend, that which sent the Russians to the moon."

"Vodka? I will check my stock."

"Vodu-kaa. Vodu-kaa, chief. It kills one when life is sweetest."

"Ok, you may take whatever is left with you. I have to go and sleep." The chief handed a half-bottle of vodka to Pa Okolo, reached out and patted him on the shoulder to bade him goodbye, all the while avoiding his eyes.

Pa Okolo was dropped off home by Bitrus who had all along been waiting in the car.

Once inside, Pa Okolo bolted the door to his house firmly. He was sweating again. This time not from malaria but from what he had on his mind. He paced up and down the length of his bedroom. His mind was made up. He fished out a red cap he had bought and kept for his initiation into the *Ozo* titled fraternity. Red cap chiefs were men of honour and power. Pa Okolo had been consumed by his quest for membership into this select group of respected men. He put it on and got a small mirror to examine how well it fit. He pulled it slightly to the left until it had a perfect fit. "Yes, this is Chief Okolo, the Osuofia I of Isiakpu," he said aloud.

For a moment he was filled with emotion, the kind of emotion that betrayed his anger against himself. It was no use at this point.

His mind was wandering and weaving through memories. He sat on his bed, tense. He poured himself half a glass of vodka and downed it in one gulp, spilling some of it in the process. "Vodu-kaa, *Odi chi egbu*, the great drink that kills slowly," he said with a heavy brooding sound. Then he reached out for the bottle of chloroquine, counted ten, paused, and then fifteen tablets into his left palm. That will be enough, he seemed to say to himself. On second thoughts, he poured all of its contents into his palm, all twenty-two. He grabbed the bottle of vodka, poured a bit into his mouth and emptied the chlroquine tablets into his mouth, and washed them down with the rest of the Vodu-kaa in quick gulps. When the bottle was empty, he shook his head vigorously and lay down on his bed.

Uncle Ben was arraigned at the Magistrate's Court and sentenced to twelve months in prison, with hard labour. Soon afterwards, the chief left Isiakpu for what was purpotedly an extended business trip abroad. This trip was an escape strategy, designed to let matters cool down. If he was implicated, he needed the time to deal with the matter at the highest level. He was not seen in the village for close to six months.

Pa Okolo did not wake up the next day. When his eldest wife came at around 10 am to check on how he was doing since he had malaria, she found the door firmly locked. There was no answer from inside. Two hours later, she came back. There was no sign that anyone was in there. She began to panic and ran to Uncle Eze's house.

Uncle Eze, Pa Okolo's junior brother, accompanied her to Pa Okolo's house. He broke down the door and found Pa Okolo lying peacefully on his bed. But he was dead. He pulled up his blanket and turned to look at Pa Okolo's wife, who was muttering some incoherent words and questions, as if to confirm what both of them were thinking.

The only clue to what could have happened was the empty bottle of chloroquine, lying by the bed. Postmortem examinations were not part of the culture in Isiakpu. The dead were supposed to be left alone. It was the white man's unnecessary curiosity that gave birth to postmortems, and this society frowned on them. By mutilating the dead, the belief was that you would alter their form and their destiny in the next life.

Pa Okolo's family knew that he had committed suicide but the word that was put out was that he had died of malaria. If the people knew he had committed suicide he would have been buried like a chicken.

With no proof of suicide, Pa Okolo was given a befitting burial. But even in death, he was denied the dignity of an *Ozo* man. Pa Okolo would have loved to be buried with his red cap but the society could not even honour his unwritten wish. It was not up to his family. Celebration of death as of birth was a societal affair. You have to have been initiated into the *Ozo* fraternity to be buried with a red cap. Pa Okolo went to his grave without it.

Part V

The Moon Finally Sets

CHAPTER TWENTY-TWO

Professor Akpanu Akpabio, MSc, PhD, ACIB, JP, was professor of social statistics at the University of Embakassi. He had just returned from one year's sabbatical leave at Cairo University in Egypt.

Upon his return, he added JP to the list of his credentials, and many people thought that he had become a Justice of the Peace while teaching in Cairo. He himself later explained that JP meant he was a Jerusalem Pilgrim. While in Cairo, he had the opportunity to visit Jerusalem on a Christian Pilgrimage. Since status meant everything, the various competition for title was fought in arenas. It was a serious contest. If Muslim pilgrims could be Alhaji or Alhaja, who in his right mind would deny Christian pilgrims the mere addition of JP to their names. In Nigeria, no one wanted to be an ordinary mortal. Not many people, however, knew what JP stood for in this part of the world. Prof Akpanu was certainly the first known JP in Embakassi.

In Nigeria, it was almost criminal for one to be an ordinary Mr. It felt like you were not one of them. You had to be "born again" to be Engineer Somebody, Architect so-and-so, Lawyer this and that, Reverend such-and-such, you had to be Chief this, Doctor something, Apostle that.

It was therefore not surprising to find Christian pilgrims adding JP to their names. What was somewhat unexpected was that someone like Prof Akpanu, who already had a distinguished title, would want to join in the charade.

Prof Akpanu, 46, was a short, pot-bellied, balding man who spoke with a very thick Ibibio accent. He had become an associate professor four years before his papers were sent out for external assessment for full professorship, but the vice-chancellor had several complaints about his behaviour and he simply sat on the documents. He had obtained his PhD in social statistics from Moscow University and taught there for two and half years. When he returned, he was highly respected in his field. He was full of ideas and applied his statistical knowledge to researching and publishing on social issues in Nigeria. He had returned home with three children and a beautiful Russian wife, who had trained as a nurse. Later he became hooked to wine and women — the latter mostly young students. He would sneak women into the house at night when his wife was on night duty at a nearby hospital. As would be expected, the quality of his teaching and research deteriorated and his wife, out of frustration at his shameless womanising and physical abuse, left him and returned to Russia with their three children.

He was, ironically, out one night when a family friend helped his wife and the children to flee. Everything had been well planned in collaboration with this family friend and with the cooperation of the Russian Embassy in Lagos. It was a very wet day, with intermittent rains and drizzle. The roads had mostly been deserted as the rains forced most people to remain indoors, and because there was an unusual chill. In the course of the day, Mrs Akpanu and the family friend had thought of abandoning the plan. It had been kept as simple as possible to avoid any suspicion from either Prof Akpanu or the children. They didn't think that Prof Akpanu would leave the house in such miserable weather but he did, playing right into their hands.

In spite of the inclement weather, Prof Akpanu went to his usual joint for pepper soup and beer. The beer parlour, noted chiefly for its cheap beer and idle girls, was uncharacteristically empty. Located in the high-density area of Embakassi, the "Pepper Soup Joint," or "Beer Parlour" as it was referred to, was a poorly constructed four-bedroom house whose faded green colour gave it an ugly look. To a first time visitor, the window and door curtains looked like they had been used as napkins on oily hands. This was more evident on the curtain at the main entrance. A mosaic of oil, water, beer and pepper soup deposits had created a harmonious pattern on the original design. If you stared intensely at the pattern, as many newcomers did, it was likely to create a dialogue as you imagined the many images emerging from a combination of subdued and vibrant colours. With time, the curtains had shredded at all their weak corners. But who cared? Customers knew what they were getting: cheap beer, tasty pepper soup and everything else that Cash Madam threw in as part of the entertainment. Because of space constraints, a makeshift structure made of used aluminium zinc had been put up in the space at the back of the house in order to accommodate more customers. Many, like Prof Akpanu, were hooked to the place and were Cash Madam's efficient advertising agents. Their reward was free beer or pepper soup from time to time.

One of the rooms served as both a store and an office for Cash Madam. No one, not even Cash Madam's children who occasionally came to help out, was allowed into the office alone. This room doubled up as a temporary bank.Whenever she emerged from the room, one would always feel her presence. She often animated all her patrons, except those who had debt arrears. Her strides left no one in doubt as to who was in charge. She was physically well endowed. A typical middle-aged Embakassi woman, average height, plump, light skinned with a generous, well padded derriére and a disarming smile.

Professor Akpanu wanted to leave for home earlier, but Cash Madam kept him busy with exaggerated second-hand gossip and a steady supply of beer, hoping more patrons would come. This was an unusual night at the beer parlour. At the peak of activity, usually around 8 pm each day, it would be difficult to get a seat unless you were known for your generosity to other patrons or to Cash Madam's girls. They were aggressive girls who made sure the tables were always full of bottles of beer and patrons had plenty of pepper soup and bush-meat to go with it.

As they walked between tables, carrying trays filled with chilled bottles of beer and plates of steaming pepper soup carefully balanced in their hands, serving and joking with patrons, the girls' bottoms would be pinched, fondled and patted. It was said Cash Madam only employed girls with big bottoms to meet her customers' taste. If a girl complained of being harassed, she was immediately labelled rude. Playing with, and teasing the girls was a side attraction, but part of the business. It was seen as part of the total entertainment package the patrons were paying for. For them, if you couldn't take the heat, you had to get out of the kitchen.

This was also the place for armchair politicians, government critics and the marketplace for various ideas on government policy, international affairs and football. In this marketplace, the educated, the enlightened and the highly placed mixed with pedestrians and the blue-collar workers. Everyone was an intellectual here. Everyone was a philosopher. After all, one did not have to be cerebral to have an opinion or to enjoy Cash Madam's pepper soup.

The place had a certain democratic culture that was fascinating. It also had unwritten rules: everyone was entitled to his opinion. Shout but don't shove. If an argument got out of hand, Cash Madam would emerge from her office and stride matronly to the troubled spot to sort things out. She would afterwards dispatch one of her more experienced girls to create a distraction, cool things down, massage egos, and, of course, make sure beer was kept flowing.

Arguing was good for business provided it did not get out of control. But today was different. All-day rain with a cold breeze was not good for business. In Embakassi, the tropical heat and humidity went well with chilled beer. The more beer the patrons had, the more vociferous would be their arguments, and the more drinks would be required to cool down tempers.

At about 11 pm, having downed his fifth big bottle of beer and a second plate of pepper soup that Cash Madam offered to keep him warm, Prof Akpanu got into his car and headed home. His house was a lovely bungalow located in the senior staff quarters of the university, about five kilometres from the Pepper Soup Joint. Halfway to his house, the rain intensified. Lightning flashed across the sky and thunder cracked as if to warn him of what lay ahead for him. Partly because of the weather and partly because of his drunken state, he could hardly see the potholes on the road. He kept driving in and out of them. Owing to his lack of coordination, he kept switching off his lights whenever he wanted to increase the speed of the wipers, which were already at full speed anyway. He cursed and hissed, but kept making the mistake over and over again. The fifteen-minute drive to his house took him almost an hour. But he was lucky that he got home alive. Negotiating the way around on ordinary days was tricky enough. It was a lot worse when it was dark, rainy and the driver not entirely sane.

As he pulled up in front of his house there were no unusual signs; the lights were all on except in the children's bedrooms. The children were supposed to be asleep at that time of night anyway. He sat in the car waiting for the rain to subside, and fell asleep.

He woke up two hours later and staggered up to the house. He knocked on the door but there was no response. That was unusual. His wife was usually up waiting for him.

A slight twist of the knob and the door opened. He was startled and immediately stepped backwards. He regained composure quickly. His sleep deserted him. As he stepped into the house the lightning struck and the lights went out. He ran back to his car to turn on the headlights.

Just then, the light in the house was restored. He thought his wife was playing tricks on him. That would not have been uncharacteristic of her. Upset and anxious, he walked gingerly back to the house. He realised that his wife was not sitting up waiting for him as usual. He thought everyone was asleep. But after moving from one room to the next, he realised that the house was deserted. He called out his wife's name: but there was no answer. At first, he thought the house had been burgled. But all the electronic gadgets were in their places and they were usually every burglar's first prize. The children's bedroom did not initially show that much had been taken out of it.

Elena had wanted to travel light with the children. He concluded that his wife must have gone to put up in a friend's house as a way of punishing him, a common way of sending the message home to an errant husband in Nigeria. He locked up the house and went to bed.

He was up very early in the morning to call his friends and relatives. But when he went to the kitchen for coffee he saw a short note on the dining table. He wiped his eyes, red from lack of sleep. Absently, he did as if to pick up his glasses from the table but realised he had left them in the bedroom.

The note said: "By the time you will be reading this note, I will be on my way to Moscow with the children. We shall be okay and we hope that you will be okay, too. I have forgiven you for all the emotional and physical abuse you have meted out on me, but I had to bring this misery to an end for our children's sake. We love you. Elena."

His hands trembled as he read the note. His coffee spilled all over the table when he tried to drink it. He got so agitated that he began pacing up and down the house. The sweat that had formed on his forehead turned into droplets. On the coffee table, by the corner of the dining area, stood a small portrait of the family: Elena with her beautiful smile holding six-month-old Uduak, handsome four-year-old Akpan dressed in a blue suit with a red bow-tie standing between his parents, and Akpanu himself holding Enya the goddess, — as her father fondly called her, — who had a beautiful flowery dress and was two and a half years old. The picture had been taken five years back.

He stared intensely at the picture, picked it up, placed it on top of the dining table and began hitting his head rhythmically against it. He picked up the portrait again, looked at it, his vision blurred by tears flowing down to his cheeks. In a rush of emotion, he smashed the family portrait against the floor. Yes, he no longer had a family.

And just as he had been unable to pick himself up and mend his ways to keep his family, he was unable to pick up the pieces of the glass scattered all over the dining area for weeks.

Elena and the children settled into the Soviet society and occasionally called him to find out how he was doing. All his attempts to obtain a visa to visit them in Moscow failed.

Prof Akpanu continued to drink and womanise. He continued teaching Sociology 210, a social statistics course which Oby had to take in her second year. It was usually from the students taking this difficult course that Prof Akpanu picked the girls he would enjoy. It was an annual ritual for him and no one denied him the privilege.

Oby returned to the university after a traumatic holiday in Isiapku. When she left the village, her mother was still trying to put her business back on its feet, with assistance from Uncle Amechi. He had also provided most of the money Oby needed to return to college.

Oby had learnt to separate the two worlds not just as a survival tactic but because they really were distinct for her in many ways.

240

Men dominated both, but the form their treachery took was different. In the village, her mother was the expert and Oby could only offer support. Costly as it was, her mother, seemed able to manage the village treachery. But she had serious doubts about her mother coping on her own. Most women looked up to her but she had no one to lean on. Even the church could not give her refuge.

In the university, Oby was on her own in spite of Chike. She had everything to lose if she as much as blinked. Things could get complicated, and there were no easy answers. Problems in the university were like treacherous antipodes: thorny, slippery and without a grip. In a short one year, she had already gone through a lot, but the real test was yet to come.

Oby had an average result of Grade B for her first year and was determined to do better. She knew it was not going to be easy, but with her eyes set on graduate studies and a scholarship award, she knew that she had to improve. With a stable, friendly and loving relationship, she would have little to worry about in that department. Besides, Chike would also be very busy with his final examinations.

Two evenings earlier, after a late dinner, they had walked to the garden in front of the main office block towards a concrete chair under an acacia tree not very far from where Chike, Chris and Okoro often sat to assess events and people. Oby had not yet told Chike what had transpired at home, not because she didn't want to but because she wanted to do so at her own time and place. She had some unresolved emotions about the events in her family during the holidays. She felt she would rather put them behind her in the interest of sanity.

She inched close to him on the seat until her head was buried in his chest. She locked her palm into his. Chike knew something terrible had happened at home but he had not anticipated the terrible details that Oby was to give him. He held her tightly as she fought to stem the flow of tears rolling down her cheeks. Chike was shaken.

The whole narrative sounded bizarre, and he did not know how to respond hearing about it as he was many weeks after the event. He kept saying: "That son of a bitch, that son of a bitch," almost absent-mindedly until Oby nudged him with her elbow. Oby was not worried about Chike's profanity. She was not sure whether the profanity was directed at Pa Okolo or Uncle Ben. It did not matter, either way.

"I am sorry sweetheart," he told her. "I am simply lost for words. If someone else told me this story, I would have thought that it was pulled out of a famous storyteller's hat. But this is real. I am sorry that this happened to you and your family. I knew from what you have often told me of your family that Pa Okolo was scheming but I did not think that he was capable of such evil."

Oby wiped her teary eyes with the back of her palm. "I have always thought that every family needs a strong personality like Pa Okolo to protect its members. I had no idea that his ambition, his quest for a certain status in the society would drive him to destroy that which he was supposed to protect, and ultimately lead him to self-destruction," she said.

"A dog does not eat the bones that have been hung around its neck. Not even if the dog is mad!"

"He was very treacherous," Oby continued. "But I naively thought that when the chips were down, he would stand up for us. I am really sorry that he died the way he did. It saddens me to think that I contributed to it. I feel as if the umbrella protecting my extended family has been destroyed and that I supplied the machete."

Three small birds chirped from a nearby tree. Their pitch increased as Oby spoke.

"Contributed?" Chike asked, surprised. "You did nothing wrong, my dear. Sometimes when a hunter is busy aiming at an animal with all his concentration, he often forgets that there is also a tick nearby scheming to suck life out of his balls."

"Where did you get that one from?" Oby asked.

"It is true. If you pursue a certain ambition single-mindedly it is very likely that the same ambition will consume you. It is ironic, but history is replete with accounts of many great men who got consumed in the flame of their own ambition or who forgot that like all humans, no one is perfect. Remember Brutus in William Shakespeare's *Julius Caesar* and Okonkwo in Chinua Achebe's *Things Fall Apart*? As with Pa Okolo, they would be led to take a false step and trust that

242

their messenger would interpret their message correctly, or that their act would bring respect to them. Pa Okolo is as guilty as Uncle Ben and the chief. I know he is your uncle but you had to protect your mom and your family."

"Chike, you don't understand," she said. "Who will protect my mother? She is a widow in a society that thinks such women are fair game for anyone who is interested. They have no right to their husbands' property. Sometimes their children are taken away from them. Now that the only strong male member of my family, the one that may have kept all the wolves at bay has died, my mom is exposed. It is quite an irony. Her vulnerability also increases because of my absence. Do you understand?"

She had stopped sobbing, and now wiped her nose with the back of her palm. She stared at him as if silently pleading that her thoughts be wrong and God speak through Chike saying so.

"Don't be ridiculous," he said. "I don't understand this reverse guilt. Don't forget that you and your mom are the victims here. Your mom will never be in any greater danger. You know your mother better than I do. But from what you have told me, she looks like a woman who can hold her own. Wicked acts from relatives and friends are very often deeper and more dangerous than anything that you would expect from strangers."

"But she is alone, Chike."

"And so? If Pa Okolo and Uncle Ben did not succeed, I would be surprised if someone from that village tried any tricks on her."

"Not even the chief?" Oby asked in a childlike voice.

She was yearning for reassurance, and Chike rose to the occasion. He acted like one of those fortune-tellers in Isiakpu who made a living from forecasting the future.

"Not even the chief. He is not a fool. Mark my words tonight. Yours was an act of courage and I have never been more proud of being your boyfriend. You are turning out to be everything that I hope my woman would be and more, a fighter for justice."

As he made that utterance, he lowered his lips towards hers. He paused momentarily to stare at her beautiful face, her ruffled dress and moistened lips. All this together with the bewitching scent of her perfume stirred his blood.

They were soon locked in a passionate kiss that was only interrupted by the chirping of the three birds now perched on the acacia branches above. Chike and Oby, somewhat startled but laughing, looked up the tree, and saw the birds flap their wings and fly away. It was time for the lovers to leave. The campus was tranquil and the security lights cast long shadows. Oby held to Chike tightly as they walked in silence, out of the park, towards his hostel.

Chike sat up that night and wrote a poem for Oby, praising her courage.

Oby was going down the stairs of her hostel on her way to a lecture the next day when she looked up and saw a passing cloud darkening. Streaks of sunshine cut through the dark patches of the cloud moving through the sky. Having grown up in Isiakpu, she did not need weather forecasters to feed her with their uncertainties, usually characterised by "scattered showers" or "intermittent drizzling" without any specific time when the weather change would occur and how long it would last.

In Isiakpu, one was trained to look at the sky, analyse the wind patterns by raising a moistened finger in the air, and determine whether it was going to rain or not with an accuracy that would shame the world's best weather forecasters.

She walked back to her room and picked up her red umbrella. It was not the short, sleek type most girls carried on the campus. She also put on her sweater to keep out the chill. Her roommates had learnt to trust her native instincts without openly acknowledging her talents. When Oby left, they exchanged knowing glances with raised eyebrows and a subdued giggle. They changed their dressing and fitted their sleek umbrellas into their handbags.

Oby had struggled to put the events of the holidays in Isiakpu behind her. She had given Chike strict instructions not to discuss what she had told him with anyone else. She hoped to find an opportune time to share the events with Chris, and get another perspective from him. Chris had continued to earn her respect and admiration. She had, of course, continued to worry about her mother. And it took at least a month to get a letter from Isiakpu. All she could do was to pray for her to remain strong and brave. If only she could read English, she would send her the poem that Chike had written on courage. It would have to wait for the next holiday when she would translate it for her.

When she left her hostel that morning, however, uppermost on her mind were her studies. All her second year courses required that she submit a term paper on a topic approved by the lecturer. Oby had gone through a few old term papers for style and methodology but none had helped her choose a topic. The worst of all was Prof Akpanu's course, social statistics. He had introduced a term paper for this course only the previous year. She was almost sure as she set out that morning for Prof Akpanu's class that he would start asking questions on how far each student had gone with the term paper. Fortunately, he did not, and Oby felt relieved when the lesson ended without event.

Outside the classroom, she waited with other students for the rain to subside. She was free for an hour between two lectures and was also contemplating spending the free time in the library to work on the term paper. She hoped to zero in on a topic. She also had thought of approaching Prof Akpanu for assistance. Ordinarily she would not have hesitated. Oby was sufficiently self-assured that she would seek help wherever necessary to improve her academic performance. But she had heard enough rumours about Prof Akpanu's womanising and felt that approaching him would be tantamount to giving a hungry lion a goat to watch over.

Her umbrella was unfurled as she walked in the rain. Then she felt a light touch on her shoulder. When she looked back, she came face to face with Prof Akpanu. He was asking her to escort him to his office with her umbrella. Oby's umbrella was big enough to shield two people. Besides, there were not too many students with umbrellas; the rains had caught many of them unawares.

Oby smiled and nodded agreement as Prof Akpanu, books in one hand, placed the other hand on Oby's shoulder. As soon as they stepped out, the male students started whistling. Prof Akpanu could not be bothered but Oby's discomfort was immeasurable.

At the door of his office, just as Oby was about to turn around and flee, he introduced the subject of the term paper.

"Why are we discussing this outside," he continued. "Please come in." He ushered Oby into his office and closed the door after him.

"Thank you, sir," she muttered. "Yes, sir. I have been trying to think of a good topic. But you know, sir, it is very difficult to choose a topic in your course, especially with the sort of guidelines you gave."

Oby was visibly nervous.

"Very difficult?" Prof Akpanu asked. Oby had unwittingly uttered the magic word. If the subject was difficult for her, she must have been prepared to pay any price to get through it. Exactly the sort of situation Prof Akpanu preferred.

"Yes, sir. Very difficult," she repeated the words in her innocence.

"Nothing is difficult, my daughter. It depends on you. Students of these days are very lazy. They want a degree but are not willing to pay the price to get it. The boys are worried about their girlfriends and the girls are worried about these useless, good-for-nothing boys."

"Not all of us, sir." She was looking at the floor, clutching her bag to her chest.

"Not all of you, eh? Why are you still standing? That chair is not good enough for you, eh?" he said as he motioned her to a chair.

"No sir, it is just that I have to run."

"There you go. You are a serious student but you have to run when the subject of your term paper is mentioned. You are all the same."

"Don't take it like that, sir," Oby pleaded.

"Sit down or walk out of my office," he said, raising his voice. It was an intimidating tactic he had perfected. He knocked his victims into submission with heavy doses of guilt from the outset.

Oby sat down quickly. "I am sorry, sir."

"You don't need to be sorry. I am here to help you if you are willing to help yourself and, of course, if you are willing to cooperate. The university is a great institution. It forces a child to grow up and the weak to become strong. Life out there is not a bed of roses. This place prepares you to face the real world out there. Make no mistake about it."

246

"It is true, sir."

"So you agree with me?" asked Prof Akpanu. He was smiling mockingly at her.

"Yes, sir," Oby said, not knowing what she was agreeing with.

"Your name is Oby Onyia, isn't it?"

"Yes, sir."

"Oby is a beautiful name. You look like an intelligent student also. I will help you. Yes, if you remain good."

"Thank you, sir," an uncomfortable Oby responded.

"On the term paper: I would like you to do a paper on the oil spillage and the livelihood of the fishing communities in Embakassi. This is an important subject. I will help you with the data and teach you how to manipulate the data, which is really the essence of the term paper in this course."

Oby relaxed, somewhat. "I like the topic, sir. I have been to the beach and seen the destruction. It is really terrible."

"This is not a question of going to the beach for a picnic. This is a serious matter. We are talking serious statistical analysis here."

He had thrown her back into discomfort. "Yes, Prof."

"I thought you didn't know that I am a professor. If it were not for these jokers that call themselves vice-chancellors, I would by now be the first full professor of environmental statistics in Nigeria. They are very jealous. But I usually laugh last. I do! Mark my words."

"Yes, Prof." Oby began to wonder where this would end. What was this specialty called environmental statistics all about? Is this part of the craze to be Number One?

Prof Akpanu continued, "All these 'quota professors' that have been made VCs think that they can sit in judgement over me. We shall see. They need to know that I survived Russia under Brezhnev. In Russia at the time, if you were too serious or looked unhappy, you were punished for frowning at the system. If you were so happy it meant that you were harbouring some capitalist ideas. Either way you were punished. People quickly learnt to wear a neutral look that did not betray their thoughts."

He giggled at his own exaggeration, took off his glasses and cupped his face in his palms to succour his tired eyes.

There was something contradictory about Prof Akpanu. He liked to exude an air of academic excellence but also preached that you had to use what you had to get what you needed. When he was womanising, academic excellence took a back seat. If a girl he was after spoke his language, so to say, she could get an A in his course. If you had the boldness to deny him sexual favours he would make sure that you begged for a plain C.

"Thank you, Prof," Oby said, adjusting her bag, ready to leave.

"Okay, Oby. You can go and think over this topic. Come back to my office next week and I will give you some of the materials you will need. Try and read whatever you can on this subject before then."

"Yes, sir. Thank you very much, sir." She stood up and left hurriedly. She was already 15 minutes late for her next class.

As she turned around to walk out, Prof Akpanu slid back his pair of glasses onto his fat face. "*Ete mi!*" he exclaimed in admiration.

Okoro, Chike and Chris had not had time to chat as they had often done in the past. This was their final year and they were preoccupied with their theses. Okoro, who ordinarily initiated their meetings, had been having a difficult time with his supervisor, Prof Oyot. He was a diehard Marxist whose only framework of analysis was dialectical materialism. Poor Okoro, the only materialism that he understood was buying and selling at the Aba market. The only dialectic that he knew was from his semiliterate father. Try as he may, the professor would return the draft chapters of his thesis with 'nonsense' scribbled all over it in red ink. He would have lots of references for further reading, all of which would point to the Marxist literature, and most of which Okoro did not understand. Given his background, he did not think that the real world was explained in those terms. But he needed to submit an acceptable thesis to earn his degree and it was not possible to change his supervisor.

When they met at the Freedom Park after an early dinner, it was natural that the conversation should start with everyone wanting to find out how the other was faring with their thesis.

"Don't remind me of this thesis," Okoro was quick to say when Chris asked the question. "I spent the last holidays on it, gathering all the data, and now everything that I have written so far is 'nonsense' as far as Prof Oyot is concerned."

"Prof Oyot is your supervisor? Oh boy!" Chris exclaimed. "You have to be very, very careful. We have heard how strict he is. He wants to see all the i's dotted as he meticulously reads the thesis," Chris continued.

"That is not my problem," Okoro replied. "My problem is this thing called dialectical materialism, which is the framework he has asked all of us under his supervision to use. It is driving me crazy."

"Okoro, I know the only materialism you understand is how to cheat innocent shoppers at the Aba market and pocket the loot. The trick your daddy taught you," Chike said sarcastically.

"Have you heard of capitalist accumulation, you knuckle-head?" Okoro asked, returning Chike's sarcasm. "The term was invented at Aba Market," Okoro continued. "You are talking about cheating and pocketing the loot? That is by those who are doing *boy-boy* apprenticeship. If you insist on your rights, if you think that you are a wise shopper at the Aba market, your clean-shaven head would be on offer for sale by the *ogas* before you could say Jack Robinson."

"It is a jungle, the heart of primitive accumulation. Don't you agree?" Chris interjected.

"But that is what I am telling you, it is a capitalist jungle. *Ike kete oori ee.* It is survival of the fittest and we like it that way, primitive or not." Okoro had burst into laughter.

For Okoro, the degree he was pursuing was to fulfill a family dream. His career path was not in doubt. Were it possible to do the compulsory national youth service at his father's trading company in Aba market, that was exactly what he would have done. Perhaps he would return to the company soon after his service. Because of his intelligence, his father had designated him to lead the company after him. His father had reasoned that with his degree, no one would call his son *money miss road* as they often referred to him for his lack of formal education. He was classless, with strange tastes. He was stingy to the core but always gave Okoro whatever he wanted. Okoro also had a way with him.

"It is true that we have been very busy and we have not seen each other as often as we should," Okoro said. "But there is another reason why I have asked that we all meet today." He quickly changed the subject as he surveyed their faces.

"What is it, Okoro," Chike asked. "You sound very serious."

"But you know Okoro. He wants to dramatise everything," said Chris.

"If I sound or look serious it is because what I am about to tell you is serious."

"Well, tell us," Chris said impatiently.

"I have information that the next issue of *The Bee* will focus on Oby and Chike and our different roles at the Economics Association dinner. I understand that they have timed the release of the magazine to coincide with this year's dinner," Okoro said, his tone hinting he knew more. Okoro's nose for information at the university was usually good. He was well connected to both the high and the low in the student community. He might be boisterous but he was also generous and kind. He easily associated with those who mattered and tried not to take relationships for granted. His reward came in many forms, including being able to delegate some dirty jobs, and in this case getting confidential information concerning the next edition of *The Bee,* a student magazine that could have left a permanent scar on anyone.

"What are you guys staring at?" Okoro asked. "Don't you understand what I am saying?"

"We understand, Okoro," Chris volunteered. "But I am surprised and stung. How did what happened to Oby get out?"

"Wake up, Chris. This is a small community."

"Okoro, have you checked that your information is right? This is very serious."

"I would not bother to let you guys know this if I had not checked and confirmed that what I am telling you is the truth. They have all the details right from what happened in the hall to what happened in Chike's room. Everything!"

250

"How did they get hold of that?" Chris asked.

"My brother, nothing under the sun is hidden. Someone must have seen us leave the hall with Oby, and someone did see us at Chike's hostel running around like the Three Blind Mice. They will fill in the blanks and exaggerate as usual," said Okoro.

"So what should we do?" asked Chris.

"What can we do? Should we do anything?" Chike asked.

"I am surprised at you, Chike. You know that this will devastate Oby, and you are asking whether we should do anything?" Chris asked angrily.

"Calm down, brother. I know that you mean well. But appearing in *The Bee* is a rite of passage," Chike said. "I am asking whether we shouldn't let Oby go through this rite."

"A philosophical question," said Okoro.

"What is philosophical about it? Philosophy my ass!" Chris cried. "Oby is going to be hurt, and we should not sit here debating whether or not this is a rite of passage. Whether or not this is a philosophical question. If we can, let us help."

"How do you know that Oby will not be able to handle it? I know my girlfriend and I know the stuff she is made of."

"I don't think that you know her," Chris shot back.

"If you mean biblically ..." Okoro put in. "True, Chike has not told us anything." He could not pass up the opening to crack a dirty joke. But no one was interested.

"What is your problem, Chris?" Chike followed it up. "If I don't know my girlfriend, do you?"

"How I wish that you did not ask that question," Chris responded. "If you knew her so well, you would do something to protect her. That is all."

"I think that you are way out of line, Chris."

"I am not," Chris retorted.

"I am telling you that Oby can handle this. She has handled tougher situations."

"You don't know her."

"Hey guys," Okoro called them to attention, "is there something that I need to know which you are not telling me?"

"Ask your *oyibo* brother. He is poking his nose where it does not belong."

"Chike, I think that Chris is right. We should do something if we can to stop *The Bee* from hurting Oby. But Chris, if you go to a funeral and start wailing louder than the bereaved, they will think you had a hand in the death of their relative."

"Tell him, Okoro," Chike said. "He does not understand. He thinks that he is being sensitive."

Chris said he was human and therefore cared.

"Stop it, both of you. I have already said that we should do something if we are in agreement. I have a plan.

Chris asked that they hear it.

"I want us to steal the master copy of the magazine from their office," Okoro continued.

Chike asked if that was the beginning and end of the plan.

"That is it. Without the master copy, they will be back to square one. They will simply abandon the effort."

"Well, we shall send Chris to do the job. He has been very vocal this evening," Chike suggested sarcastically.

"I don't mind. It will be for a good cause. At least someone is trying to be responsible here," Chris replied.

"I will ignore that comment," said Chike.

"I am not going to risk anything," Okoro said. "This will be professionally executed. I will get the security men on duty to look the other way. I know what they eat. I will use my new catch, my girlfriend from the Nursing School to pinch the master copy. Since she is not a student of this university, the university authorities cannot discipline her if she is caught. But who is going to catch her? Those who are supposed to watch over the building will be settled. They will be busy using the restroom at the appropriate time. They will have had a sudden diarrhoeal attack."

Chris asked him what made him think his girlfriend would agree to do the job.

"She will do anything for me right now," he said. "She is trying to convince me that she loves me. I am trying to convince her that I don't have love in my dictionary. It is a tug-of-war. Give it to women real good and they start crying love. Is good sex love? She knows that if she does this, it will raise her stakes. As for love, I will be home, free, in Aba before I can discuss that subject on my own terms."

"Okoro, you look like you have thought this through. When did you get this information?" Chike asked.

"I knew I had to have a plan before bringing the matter to you or we would not make any headway."

Chris then asked what role they were expected to play.

"To keep this to yourselves. Not even Oby should know. If you wish to contribute to the operation, that will also be appreciated."

"Okoro, this is really beyond the call of duty. Let us be very careful, though." He reminded them they all were in their final year and could not risk losing four years of university education.

"Don't worry. The university authorities will not do anything to anyone that tames *The Bee*. You know how the magazine has been dealing with them. It spares no one," Okoro said.

"Thanks, Okoro. You are a friend indeed," said Chris.

"Well, it is the least I can do for a good friend. I hope that our sister is delivering. I don't believe in people who drink a lot of Fanta. Chike, I am asking whether this is all worth it?"

"Okoro, my relationship with Oby is now at an intellectual level," Chike answered.

"That is the problem," Okoro said. "While you are busy intellectualising, someone might be busy taking care of the real business, if you know what I mean," Okoro laughed and winked at Chike.

"This is rubbish, Okoro," Chris said. "Are we going to be entertained with your roadside paternalistic jokes? How I wish that you guys would leave Oby out of this innuendo."

"Look me trouble, o!" Okoro said. "My brother, I have told you not to cry much louder than the bereaved. Wetin be your own? Chike, who is servicing the babe has not talked, but you ..."

"Servicing!" Chris cried interrupting him. "Listen to yourself. What sort of language is this? This is not your bush-meat, you know."

"I think that something has happened to you, Chris. But I know that in this matter, you are simply a back-bencher, a silent on-looker, and quite frankly you are becoming an irritating impostor," Okoro snapped.

"Okoro, I am not sure what to make of this. But Chris is, seriously speaking, behaving very strangely this evening. First, it was a question of who knows Oby better and who has her interests at heart. And now we are receiving lessons on etiquette, on what to say and how to say it," said Chike.

"Strange things happen," Okoro offered. "My father once told me that you should never pursue any matter to its logical conclusion on the first day. You should give room to second thoughts. Fresh ideas creep in gradually. So let us not dwell on this too much. Even our usual jokes are now off limits."

CHAPTER TWENTY-THREE

Oby stared at the bold inscription of Prof Akpanu's name on his office door. It was about 7.30 am.

Not many students on the campus would have been up at this time. Not on a Saturday. But Prof Akpanu had insisted that Oby should see him in his office at that time over her term paper. She did not like the time but he was the professor and she, the student.

Not going too well, was the impression Prof Akpanu had given her on her paper. A mere term paper. It was part of his psychological warfare. If her work was below average, if the grade in this course depended on this term paper the student would do everything, yes everything, to ameliorate the situation.

It had worked before, and it should not be different now. Oby was not the type to be indifferent to what appeared to be a genuine and passionate critique of her work. Her grades must not be allowed to slip. Not if she wanted to win a scholarship for her graduate studies.

When he opened the door, he looked dazed and unkempt, the effects of a hangover too visible to be ignored. He had been at Cash Madam's parlour all night until morning. That he had kept the appointment showed how important it was to him. In fact he had kept waking up between episodes of sleep to check the time, and he had barely slept. What a price to pay!

When his wife was around, nothing on earth would make him pick her up from work on a Saturday morning. Earlier than 10 am? You must be joking! His wife learnt not to ask. But today, half asleep, he got up, barely brushed his teeth and was on his way to help a student with her term paper. In his haste, he forgot the term paper at home. He could be excused because of his sleepy state. Perhaps part of it was his plan to get Oby to his house. After all, he now lived alone.

"Good morning, Prof," Oby said with a facial expression that summarised what she thought of the lecturer's state.

"Good morning, my dear," he replied trying to bouy up his energy level.

"It is kind of you, sir, to be making this sacrifice for my sake," Oby said.

"Not at all. In any relationships, there is always a give-and-take."

Give and take? Relationships? Of course! He was her professor. And she, his student. That was a very serious relationship. But Oby's antenna was inching up a bit. Buyer beware! This level of dedication by a professor was unheard of these days. What for? For the peanuts he was paid? For lack of recognition in society?

"I have to apologise, Oby," Prof Akpanu said boyishly as he inched towards Oby, who moved to a chair to avoid his foul breath.

"Apologise for what?" Oby was curious.

"I forgot your term paper at home."

"At home!" Oby snapped, but quickly recollected herself. You mean that I woke up this early for nothing, was her thought, but she could not say it. She could have said something else as well but she was too disciplined to even think about a nasty four-letter word.

"In that case, we can meet on Monday," Oby added quickly.

"Oh, no. I want to deal with it this morning." His voice was firm and his tone commanding. Oby bowed her head and waited for the next instruction.

"We will drive to my house and sort it out there. It is only a few minutes' drive."

"Oh, no!" was Oby's quick reaction as she looked up into Prof Akpanu's face. What would people think? What if, we are seen driving together? All of this raced through her mind, but the stern look on Prof Akpanu's face did not give her room for her thoughts.

"I mean ... ehm. How can you sacrifice your time like this for me, Prof?"

"Never mind. Let's go. If something is important, you would always make time for it, wouldn't you?"

"Yes, sir."

It was a short and long drive to Prof Akpanu's house. His house was some three kilometres away but for Oby, sitting in that car driving

256

through the campus and town even for a minute seemed like ages. She sat clutching her books and her handbag, holding them firmly against her chest, hardly looking up, and barely acknowledging Prof Akpanu's conversation. She was like a typical housegirl accompanying her boss to the market when the Madam was away. The truth was that she was not paying any attention to what he was saying. She was simply praying that no one would see them.

The university was quite a place. People had a way of seeing what they were not supposed to, and knowing what you thought they had no way of knowing. You always felt like you were playing in a field with floodlights roving the arena twenty-four hours a day. As she peered from the corners of her eyes, she saw a few people moving up and down. She did not look long enough to know whether they were students or workers reporting to work. Whoever they were, she did not want to be seen in Prof Akpanu's car.

When Prof Akpanu pulled up in front of his house, she quickly scrambled out and headed for the door. She could feel all eyes peering from his neighbours' windows. Prof Akpanu took his time searching for his house key. In the meantime his latest catch was on display, being advertised. He was sure to receive a phone call later to congratulate him on his latest conquest. A few male university lecturers saw this as a game. The younger the victim, the more the kudos you received.

The house was in a mess. Papers were strewn all over the place. Prof Akpanu had not done his dishes in days, and there was a bad stench coming from the kitchen. She picked up a few papers and books and put them together to create space on the sofaset. She sat with her full weight and sank into the seat. The springs were worn-out, but that was the least of Prof Akpanu's worries. Since his wife left, he had been living dangerously for long.

"Can I get you something, young lady?"

"No, sir. I am just fine."

"Just fine?"

"Yes, sir."

"Don't 'yes-sir' me. I will get you a cup of tea."

The thought of the tea coming from that kitchen did strange things to her stomach. But there had to be a limit to her objections. Her first instinct was to tidy up the house, including the kitchen. That was what her up bringing demanded. That was what her mother would have expected her to do. In fact, she should have gone to the kitchen to make the tea for both of them. But under the circumstances, she counselled herself otherwise. This was the university, and Prof Akpanu was not behaving exactly like an uncle. It was in her interest to limit the extent of their personal relationship. Even then, she still found herself dusting the chair and arranging a few of the books while Prof Akpanu went into the kitchen to heat the water.

"Here is your paper," Prof. Akpanu threw Oby's term paper at her as if to suggest it was rubbish.

"Thank you, sir," Prof Akpanu was already halfway to the kitchen to check on the water.

The paper was full of red marks. As far as Prof Akpanu was concerned, this was a substandard paper. Substandard at what level? For what purpose? This was merely a term paper, not a thesis.

As Oby flipped through the paper she could not control her emotion. Tears flowed down her cheeks ... This was a revised version of the paper and therefore the professor's second reading. What was she supposed to do now? When she heard him approaching, she quickly wiped her eyes with the back of her hand. It was still difficult to hide her state.

"A cup of tea for you, young lady. I have already added sugar and milk," Prof Akpanu said as he handed over the cup.

"Thank you, sir." Oby took a sip and quickly put the tea down on a stool. It was very hot.

"Everything okay? I hope that it is not too sweet for you?"

"Oh, no. It is just a bit hot."

"For a sweet little thing like you, I wasn't sure whether you needed further sweetening," he giggled.

"What, sir?"

"You know, too much of a sweet thing is not good for an old man like me," he said as he stooped, held and caressed Oby's jaw with his left hand. She gently broke free from his hold, but his hand landed on her right breast. He gently tapped on it with his fingers as if checking it out for firmness.

"What of this term paper, sir?" Oby attempted to refocus attention on why they had met.

"What about it?"

"It looks like I have no clue as to what you wanted me to do."

"Who said so?"

"Sir, it has more red marks, more comments now than when I gave in my first draft."

"Well, that happens. It is possible you misunderstood my instructions."

"What more can I do, sir?"

Prof Akpanu began to unbutton his shirt. He was scratching his head at the same time. He behaved like someone who had lost something but had no idea where to begin looking for it.

"Go through the paper, I am going to have a quick shower. When I come back you can repeat your question."

What more can I do? It was an innocent question, but not so innocent in Prof Akpanu's vocabulary. If you cannot write a term a paper, perhaps you can do other things. They would have the same result: a good grade. But who would judge the quality of this paper? It was obvious the term paper could never be improved.

Oby was buried in the paper trying to decipher the professor's handwriting and comments. This was too much for her. It was becoming clear that she would never make it in this class. She began to sob again. She looked at her watch. It was almost midday. What would she be doing there up till now? With him out of sight, she contemplated bolting out of the house. Suicide! In fact, instant death. She should know better. Besides, what would she say was the problem? Even her mother would blame her for insulting a teacher who was trying to help her. But Oby was no fool! As her mind wandered wildly, Prof Akpanu reappeared in dark green shorts and a half-buttoned short-sleeved shirt which exposed the scanty hair on his chest. His hair was barely combed.

He came over and sat next to Oby. "So what was the question again?" he asked.

"Which question, sir?"

"Naughty girl. Why are you playing games with me?"

"Games?"

"Yes, 'what more can I do?' I will tell you." He inched closer and forced a hard kiss on Oby as he fondled her left breast. Oby tried to wrestle her way out but in vain. The more she tried, the deeper she sank into the seat. Weak springs! He also used his right elbow to restrain her. She thought of screaming, but couldn't. Prof Akpanu had no finesse. Not that finesse was important in such circumstances. But that might have created room for Oby to manoeuvre. He did not beat about the bush. With him, you could not pretend that the message was scrambled. His was not a love affair. It was raw desire for sex.

"You see, young lady," he said. "You are such a beautiful girl, and you don't have to struggle for anything. Degree or no degree, you will get a rich man to marry you and all your problems will be solved. Prof Akpanu wants a little bit of the action before you can give everything to the rich man. That is the only thing a poor lecturer gets. For Prof Akpanu, his reward is here on earth! I desire good things like everybody else."

"What are you talking about, sir?" she was faking naivety, using this to buy time and to think of how to get out of the situation.

"If you give me what I want, I will give you what you want. Term paper or no term paper."

Again, he tried to force a kiss on her, this time squeezing every part of her body without pause, as if in a frenzy. He wanted to get to the skin. But her smooth, slim body had no folds or contours to hold onto. It seemed almost slippery. Her nylon long-sleeve blouse, well tucked into blue jeans, was of no assistance to him. Luckily, he was dressed for the occasion. A long spoon is useful when dining with the devil. She struggled, kicking in the air, and managed to wriggle free of him. She was almost choking at the thought of his thick lips and foul breath.

"Sir, I'm not that kind of a girl. I am willing to work," Oby said, trying to catch her breath.

260

"What kind of a girl? Eh! What kind of a girl? The sort that does not play with her professor ...? I don't like pretenders. Don't you have someone you are already messing around with on the campus? Don't you? Answer me? What are you going to gain from him after all? Answer me. Prof Akpanu was agitated and visibly angry. As he ranted and raved at her, she began to move back and keeping a watchful eye on his next move. Rather than cry, Oby became courageous. She kept stepping backwards, pushing a corner display stand a small portrait of Akpanu's family fell on the floor. She picked it up, eyes still on him, and tried to dust it.

"Is this your family? Eeh ya, what a lovely family."

Without uttering a word, Prof Akpanu retreated to the sofa. It was a picture of his family, all right. A family he had not seen for over a year. A family that he could no longer claim as his. The weight of it all suddenly weighed on him. But he did not say a thing. He sat up, holding his cheeks in both palms while his elbows rested on his thighs. He was almost drooling.

For a moment, Oby was not important. A man without a family, how much was he worth? What was one game missed for a lion who has lost his family? Once a brilliant professor now destroyed by alcohol and women. That would be an appropriate caption for an artist's impression of his current look.

That was the breather Oby needed. She went down on one knee. She quickly searched for, and found, one of her shoes which had fallen off while she was kicking. She knew that she had to change tactics if she wanted to get out of the house unharmed. She would have to show she was cooperative. Her mind flashed back to her mother's advice: Beware of the lecturers and the boys. She had not heeded her advice on the boys, why should she now? Her roommates had warned her to take care of herself and to ignore the advice of those who had never been to the university, her mother included.

Do all girls have to go through this? Was this what being a female university graduate implied? Selling your body for certificates?

She was determined not to allow this course to destroy her, come what may. In Isiakpu, they would say, "This matter get long scarf." It was not lost on Oby that this matter was not only tying a long scarf, it also had a tight skirt and a blouse. That was how delicate and complicated it was. That was how difficult it would be to extricate herself from the problem.

Oby approached him gently but carefully. She remembered a song they used to sing in Isiakpu in her youth. "No one should ever play with the tail of a lion whether dead or alive." You can never be sure. Lions can pretend. Could feminine instincts work? She gently patted his shoulders. He did not move. He showed no emotion.

"I am sorry, sir. I didn't mean to upset you," Oby said as gently as possible.

"I see. You will be sorry, all right. I can assure you of that. No one plays with Prof Akpanu and gets away with it. Go and ask questions. This is the University of Embakassi, don't forget. You cannot graduate in this department without this course."

"I know that, sir, but Prof ..."

"You know that I am the Alpha and the Omega on this subject. No other person in that department can teach the course. As far as this course is concerned, I hold both the yam and the knife. If it pleases me, I will cut you a piece. I can also postpone this piece when I confront a stubborn one like you. It can be very expensive. You will have to return for a re-sit exam during your long vacation. But then again, you can only pass by my grace. Go and ask questions: girls like you who think that they are smart later crawl on their knees asking Prof Akpanu to have them even on the bare floor. The real smart ones don't waste my time. *Ete mi! Igwem!* "

He was fully awake, and had a smirk on his face. He was now taunting Oby and enjoying her discomfort.

"I have no intentions of playing with you, sir. It is just that I did not tune my mind to this sort of thing. You know how the female body is. Besides ..."

"Besides what?" Prof Akpanu asked somewhat surprised.

"Never mind sir ... it is personal."

"Personal?" Prof Akpanu raised his eyes to stare at Oby.

"I mean ... It is that time of the month."

"What time of the month? Wahala don get double K-leg!"

"You know sir ... it is that time of the month for me."

"Oh," he said, disappointed. "I am going to trust you. But don't think of playing games with me."

"No, sir."

"I will be away for a conference in Lagos next week. Let us meet in my office early on Saturday, in two weeks' time. If I understand you correctly, it will not be that time of the month again. If it is, I will let you know that Prof Akpanu is not afraid of any woman's monthly."

"What of the term paper, sir."

"Do whatever you want to do with that rubbish. You don't seem to understand anything, do you?"

"No, sir." She understood everything but wasn't ready to play along.

The drive back to the campus was solemn. Oby persuaded Prof Akpanu to drop her at a supermarket to buy things she needed. It was her way of making sure he did not drive her to the university gate. Campus gossip should be avoided at all costs. When you thought nobody saw anything, everybody saw everything. Or they would soon be told everything by *The Bee*.

There was immorality everywhere but everyone tried to enforce their own moral code. The Pirates fraternity was trying to do it. Christian associations were trying to do it. *The Bee* was trying to bully everyone to behave. Behave in what way? No one had an answer.

As Oby approached her hostel, she felt as if all eyes were on her. She was right. *The Bee*, that notorious campus gossip magazine, had hit the campus. The big story in that edition was about Oby and the events on the evening of the Economics Department's dinner party. The closer she got to the hostel, the rowdier it became. Female students sat, in groups, buried in the magazine trying to figure out who had been covered in that edition. It was easy to see that Oby and Chike were the focus.

The magazine was fun to read if you were not the object of its sting. Stylistically, it always tried to alter the identity of the "victims". It was an attempt to avoid law suits. But who would sue whom? In this edition, Oby's name was spelt as Obee and Onyia was Oyiiaa.

Room 146, was shown as Room 641. There was no room 641 in any of the hostels on the campus. Besides, everyone had the code. They were sufficient details to help one decipher who was being humiliated.

When Oby stepped into the hostel, hell broke loose. Students began hitting pans and using sticks to hit at the metal poles of the building. Anything that made noise was employed. Some were shouting Chike! Chike! Omo Ewere! Crook, or some equivalent term. The noise was synchronised and rose with Oby's approach. You would have thought it was choreographed and rehearsed. The higher she climbed, the louder it became. It appeared to have ended as soon as Oby was safely inside her room. Safe? Lying on her bed was a copy of *The Bee* placed on her pillow with a long-stemmed red rose. Her roommates had bought a copy of the magazine and a rose to wish her well through this ordeal! Not really an ordeal in their eyes. It was a rite of passage. Once you survived the sting of *The Bee*, you became an initiated lady of the campus. You became a fully licensed bus with identified particulars and your boyfriend, if not already initiated, would become a full-fledged driver. A bus that carried only one passenger. The driver was hailed as a hero and the bus vilified, humiliated and driven to tears in the so-called initiation.

In the quiet of her dark room, Oby went through events of the night she lost her virginity. Surprisingly, there was so much detail, so much accuracy with lots of exaggeration, of course, that she wasn't sure whether Chike had not confided in someone and thus started the rumour that reached *The Bee*. There was a cartoon of her being carried to Chike's room. That much was true. But the cartoon portrayed her in a stupor, with legs strewn apart, with alcohol and food oozing from her mouth and nose. That was not true. She did throw up, but that was inside Chike's room. The cartoon also had a statement attributed to her. What she thought was a sacred moment between her and Chike was trivialised and laid bare for all in the most disgusting language. It hurt.

In spite of her determination to accept the ordeal, she burst out crying. This was too much. There was no respect for privacy. An academic community with non-academic manners!

With no one to talk to, she sobbed quietly in her room. What would Chike think of all of this? Of course, Chike was more prepared than she was to absorb the sting of *The Bee*. He knew of Okoro's failed attempt to stop the publication. Besides, this was not Chike's first appearance in *The Bee*. The "Kubwa" episode with a previous girlfriend had been published in *The Bee*. More importantly, Chike was a man and Oby a woman. Each was viewed through a different lens. Chike was a hero for deflowering Oby. But she was portrayed as immoral for allowing it to happen. It did not matter that she had given herself to him out of love. What love? Who cared?

That night, she skipped dinner. The drumming, whistling and cries would be too much for her to bear. Tomorrow, she reasoned, the temperature would have dropped. She would then venture out into the public light. At about 9.00 pm, still holed up in her room, she heard a similar commotion that had followed her return to the hostel. Two minutes later, there was a knock on her door. When she opened the door, Chike was standing nervously outside.

Chike knew that there was no place to hide on the campus. The best thing to do was to confront the "enemy". It was not easy persuading Oby that hiding in her room would not help matters. But he did. As soon as they stepped out, they were accorded a different reception. Instead of the pans and plates and buckets rattling, the ladies were clapping and cheering them. This was odd. One minute you were humiliated, in another minute you were feted. The women students liked the idea of Chike coming to take Oby out that evening. It was this bold and courageous action which they were cheering. In any case, a number of the girls had suffered at the hands of *The Bee* before. They could empathise. Experiences were varied, however. Some boys who had found themselves in a similar situation hid for weeks. They would avoid their girlfriends as if the women had suddenly developed some communicable disease.

Chike took Oby straight to the students' canteen. About a dozen students were still there. Chike was a popular final year student. Many people knew him.

"Hi Chikoo!" one student greeted him. The others were not sure how to react. A couple of those standing by the counter having beer were from *The Bee* and Chike knew that.

The light in the canteen was dim. That was the way the students wanted it. The boys chose their seats and corners depending on why they were there. If one was toasting a new girl, he would choose a corner where his conversation would not be audible. If he came to declare a surplus, he would sit where he could show off. If he wanted to launch new and particularly beautiful bush meat, the boy would, of course, choose a prominent position where everyone would be able to see who was with whom.

"Don't mind them," another shouted from a dark corner. "Nothing on earth will force the eye to shed blood. No, sir!" the student continued.

"Tell them, my brother," another student quipped. "There are those who own this campus. Come what may! *The Bee* or not *ama ndi ana eze*! We know who is who in this campus."

Even though the mode in which Chike was greeted by the first student who spoke and the subsequent conversations alluded to *The Bee*, it was the half-drunk student who mentioned *The Bee* explicitly. Chike understood everything but was not prepared to be dragged into the discussion. Oby was subdued but cheerful.

He held tightly to Oby with his left arm and simply acknowledged their greetings by waving back. Chike ordered a bottle of Fanta and a quarter chicken for Oby, plus a big bottle of Guinness Stout for himself. He had already had his dinner. Chike was not particular about where they sat. There was no particular motive except to let Oby shake off the effects of the sting. By the time they had settled down, the boys from *The Bee* quietly left the canteen. They were concerned about Chike's audacity. Did he have something up his sleeve?

When Chike was about to finish the second glass of his stout, Okoro walked in. He was a regular at the canteen, but was in alone, surprisingly. Okoro had so many hangers-on who benefitted from his generosity that he hardly came to the canteen alone. He just wanted to have a bottle of Guinness to enable him to sleep. That had been his father's prescription and it had always worked for him. The thesis was still a big headache. He wanted to sleep well tonight in order to devote the next day to the many corrections on the thesis.

"Okoro," Chike called out.

"Chike!" Okoro could recognise Chike's voice anywhere.

"Where have you been? You son of a b...That you have been stung by *The Bee* does not mean you should hide from your family. Not a veteran like you? You wey don get immunity," Okoro said before he realised who Chike was with.

"My sister, you are here, too? Congratulations! Oby the great!"

"Okoro, good evening," Oby said, her tone subdued.

"What is the matter with you? Don't you know that you are now a senior girl?" Okoro said.

"Senior girl?" Oby replied with a look of contempt for what she took to be a rubbish title.

"Yes, you are now officially a fully-licensed bus. And my brother here has regained his suspended driver's licence."

"Okoro, stop shouting," said Chike.

"Why? This calls for celebrations. Where is the waiter?"

"Which waiter? This is the students' canteen. Besides there is nothing to celebrate," said Chike.

"Oby, don't mind this *yeye* man. You and I can celebrate."

"Thank you, Okoro. But what is there to celebrate? This university is useless. People will not mind their own business," Oby was finally opening up.

"But where on earth do people mind their own business? America dey mind Soviet Union business, Soviet Union dey mind American business. China dey poke in nose for wetin dey happen for Russia. Wetin you think say journalism be? No be training on how to mind other people business? You spend four years and come get degree for how to mind other people business. CIA *nko*? Their lenses, their Onyokometer, they reach everywhere. No be other people's business they dey look into?"

"But Okoro, they don't look into your bedroom and splash it on the pages of the newspaper. There is a certain decency and code of conduct in journalism," Oby said.

"Oby, where have you been? Which code of conduct? Go and ask JFK of blessed memory in America. The American press followed

267

him and was reporting on what happened in his bedroom. What of the American Congress? They go probe you until thy kingdom come. The land of freedom is not that free, O! Let me tell you, O."

"Okoro, why all these American examples? Have you been there?" Chike asked teasingly.

"Do you have to go to Israel or Jerusalem to know that Jesus Christ was crucified by Pontius Pilate and his people? Do you need to go to America to know that the White House is white? Answer me? Besides, I am using American examples because you wannabees call it God's own country."

Oby was laughing at Okoro's jibes. You couldn't help it. He had the capacity to turn any situation around. When you thought that a situation was hopeless or grave, you simply needed a little dose of Okoro's tonic. He would lighten the burden. Nothing was a crisis for him. Not after growing up in Aba. A true son of his father. He had control over his destiny. His motto: Success is not by chance.

"No, Okoro. This university is a jungle. How can a magazine like *The Bee* exist here? You call this place an Ivory Tower? Ivory Tower my foot!" Oby said without inhibition. She wasn't reacting to *The Bee* alone. It was really a reflection of what she felt about what was happening around her at the University of Embakassi.

"My sister, we have all been victims of *The Bee*."

"Even you, Okoro?" she asked.

"Oh, yes! I have been called all kinds of names in *The Bee*: the Master of Bush Meat, Chief Importer; Chief Adviser to Mr Kubwa here.'

"Watch it, Okoro. Basket mouth," Chike said as Oby cackled.

"Oby, it is not that I condone *The Bee*. But it is part of the culture of this university. We all belong here. He who fetches ant-infested firewood should expect the lizards to visit his home. You pass through the university, the university must pass through you. Believe it or not, *The Bee* is useful in controlling certain excesses in this university. *Mpu na alu akana eme na* this university," Okoro said.

"What do you mean," Oby asked.

"Do you know what *mpu na alu* means? You speak Igbo, don't

you? The students in this university are capable of all kinds of sacrilege. If you study late, as I do these days, thanks to Prof Oyot, and see what I see, you will become a born-again Christian overnight. In fact, you will be speaking in tongues, in many languages, known and unknown. You know that field around the Chemistry Lab I call it the fornication field. Okoro Ohulo, what my eyes have seen, my mouth no fit talk am. If you pass there around midnight on any given day, you will be stepping on young couples screaming with reckless abandon. These are mostly first and second year students. You were talking about the jungle. If you did not have *The Bee*, this place would be Sodom and Gomorrah."

"Don't listen to Okoro," Chike said. "He is exaggerating as usual" This was to push Okoro to tell them more.

"This is no joke. The other day, I perched behind a tree in one corner of the field as a pair approached. Not knowing that they were not alone, the lady quickly undressed. It was going to be a quickie, I guessed. But she had a pair of pants on. Dumbo! Come and see the backyard. Real fat bom bom. Then, I suddenly jumped down and screamed just as the guy was unzipping. The skinny guy did not look back. He ran as fast as his legs could carry him. By the time the girl picked up all the pieces of her clothing, girdle and all, to run after him, I was not far behind. Run, run, I shouted. I was tempted to give her a push from behind. It was quite a sight. As she ran, her backyard was pumping up and down in one huge bumpy mass, pulling her downwards. It was the force of gravity. At least I remembered that bit of my physics. Her thighs were rubbing against each other. That na additional friction. How can you move with such a mass behind and heading southward when you want to run northwards. *Oku di* over! *Egbami* O! I was tempted to kick the buttocks to teach her a lesson but the Christian in me took over and I simply walked away. I wish I could speak in tongues."

"Praise the Lord!" Oby said as their laughter resounded in the canteen.

Okoro could embellish a story. Even if you didn't agree with what he said, you had to be careful not to crack your ribs from the laughter he caused. It was a good dose for the sombre mood Oby was in.

"You are lucky Chris is not here. He would have taken you to task for not minding your own business. Why didn't you go after the guy?" Chike asked.

"I was minding my own business. I was going to my room after a busy evening using my usual shortcut. Chris can go to hell."

"Watch it," Oby said, coughing. It was not a real cough. It was meant to muffle her intervention. She had been caught out defending Chris.

"Go after him?" Okoro continued. *"Tufia! Nwa eze ada efu na mmba!* A prince can never get lost in a foreign land! That guy ran faster than an antelope that had sensed the presence of a lion. He was not a real man in my view. How could he leave the girl unprotected? Which is precisely my point. These kids have no idea the commitment involved in what they are doing."

"Okoro, this na you? You are now talking commitment? This was not exactly what your father taught you?" Chike was surprised at Okoro's seemingly new language.

"My father taught me a lot of things. And commitment, especially to a friend, is one of them. He did not teach me to get knuckle-kneed for a woman if that is what you mean."

"But Okoro, were you telling all these tales to justify the obnoxiousness of *The Bee*?" Oby asked.

"No, not all. I was underscoring some of its usefulness. I tell you, people fear *The Bee* more than the VC of this university. It is better you are caught by the VC than the eye of *The Bee* if you are involved in some questionable act. Having said that, I don't agree with some of the humiliation and the exaggeration. You should ask Chike. I tried my best to see that you didn't get victimised."

"What do you mean?" Oby was curious.

"I will explain later," Chike interjected. He looked at his watch. It was past 11 pm. They were the only ones left in the canteen. It would be closing at midnight. Chike had finished an additional small bottle of Guinness which Okoro had forced on him. Okoro did not want to go beyond the small Guinness. The thesis work was weighing heavily on him.

"Let me leave the two of you to continue the celebrations," Okoro said as he made for the door. He did not wait for an answer. Chike stood up, stretched himself and adjusted his jacket. Oby followed suit and stepped out of the canteen first. She was feeling a lot more relaxed than when she first walked in. When Chike suggested that they go to his room, she hesitated. Not today of all days. This would be daring the devil. But Chike was persuasive. Take the fight to the devil's backyard and he will either become a born-again Christian or he will take to his heels. Chike's room was empty. As on all such occasions, the roommate was not expected. As a final year student, he only had one roommate who was so happy to be in Chike's company. He did whatever his roommate asked of him.

Chike wanted to get romantic but Oby interrupted him.

"No kissing, buddy boy, until you tell me something."

"I love you! That is what you want to hear, isn't it?"

"No, Mr Kubwa! I know that you love me. I have it on paper."

"What is it you called me?" Chike was surprised. He went teasingly after Oby.

"What was it you were supposed to explain to me?"

"What?"

"What was it Okoro said he did or was supposed to do about *The Bee*?"

"Oh that. Yes, he had a hint that *The Bee* was going to feature us. You know Okoro and his many connections. He had an elaborate plan to steal the artwork of *The Bee* before its publication. He executed his plan but it was too late. There was another copy of the artwork with the editor."

"So how come you all kept this from me?" Oby asked, quite surprised that Okoro would go to such lengths for her. But it could only be Okoro! Neither Chris nor Chike had the backbone to articulate or execute such a plan. It was a pleasant surprise.

"Well, Okoro and all of us felt that we should not stress you. We wanted to spare you the worry. What if he failed, as in fact happened?"

"So who else knew of this plan?"

"Chris, of course! And his new girlfriend."

"Whose new girlfriend? Chris got a new woman now?" It was not just an innocent question. There was a hint of jealousy in her eyes and tone.

"Oh, you don't want Chris to have a girlfriend?"

"Why not. Wetin be my own."

"No, Okoro's new girlfriend was a major part of the plot. She was actually used to steal the artwork from the offices of *The Bee*."

"Oh Chike, you and your friends are so considerate. Going to this extent for my sake. I am very touched."

"I have solid friends. And for you, Oby, my primary responsibility is to protect you in this jungle."

"Now are you ready?" Oby asked from the blue.

"Ready for what?"

"You too dey ask questions. Shut up and kiss me! Is that door locked?"

They made passionate love for a long, long time. They were comfortable with each other and this comfort grew by the day.

Afterwards, they sat on the bed, not saying much. Oby was staring at the floor while Chike was staring at her and rubbing her shoulders.

"Today has been a Black Saturday for me," Oby said suddenly as she looked up.

"I know what you mean," Chike tried to hold her close in a comforting embrace.

"No. You don't know what I mean," Oby said.

"So what do you mean?"

"You know I have been telling you about Prof Akpanu in my department but you have not taken it seriously."

"What happened?" Chike was anxious.

"He asked me to go to his office this morning to review my term paper and I ended up in his house."

"His house? Oby, you shouldn't have."

"What do you mean I shouldn't have?"

"Just that you need to be a little careful with that bastard."

"Chike, do you think that I would go to his house out of my own volition?"

272

"He forced you?"

"Don't be so naive. He did not throw me into his car, if that is what you mean."

"I am sorry. So what happened?"

"He forgot my term paper at home and he wanted us to go and get it. This was before 8 am."

"That is an old trick. He wanted to get you to his house."

"Whatever it was, I ended up in his house and he tried to force himself on me," Oby said as she shook her head, as if shaking off the memory.

"What! That ugly toad laid his hands on you?"

"Chike, I got out of the situation using a combination of lies, feminine charm and tact. God was on my side. You have just made love to a woman in her monthly."

"Oh, he fell for that too! I thought he was smarter."

"What would you have done? Asked for a laboratory test? You crook!" Oby hit Chike on the head lovingly with a pillow.

"Don't ask me. But I have my formula."

"On a serious note, though, what should I do with this man?"

"You just have to be careful," Chike said while avoiding Oby's eyes.

"Be careful? That doesn't help me."

"I know. Prof Akpanu is notoriously dangerous."

"I know that. But I need help. He is prepared to fail me. That much he said today."

"Oby, I wish I had the formula on this one. This is something the other girls may be in a better position to advise you on."

"Which girls? Nobody has the answers. Everybody wants you to use your senses. It is almost like you have to do what you have to do. What that means, nobody is willing to say."

"I know what I don't want you to do. I don't want you to sleep with the professor. But what you should do in order to pass the course, I don't know. This is one of those issues that wears a long headscarf."

"That is the dilemma," Oby was quick to add. "The man is clear about what he wants," she continued.

"Oby, what can I say? This is a difficult one. I wish we could trust the system and take the risk. This man has been getting away with his lechery for years. No student has had the courage to bring this up. I guess they fear that the system will not protect them. They may be victims twice. In fact, some have suffered more than twice."

"Well, I guess that I have to do what I have to do. What else can I say?" Oby said resignedly.

"Just be careful," Chike put in timidly. It was all bone without flesh. She needed more than that. If her mother had been here, her injunction would be firm: "Fail the course, if you have to. But avoid the man like a leper." She would not blink over it. But her mother was not a university graduate. It may not be the smartest thing to do in the circumstances, but then what was?

That Saturday, as she lay in bed at night going over the events of the day in her mind, Oby reached out for her Bible. She turned to Psalm 120 and read from the top:

> When I was in trouble, I called to the Lord,
> and he answered me.
> Lord, save me from liars and from those who plan
> evil.
> You who plan evil, what will God do to you?
> How will he punish you?
> He will punish you with the sharp arrows of a warrior
> and with burning coals of wood.

274

CHAPTER TWENTY-FOUR

Chris had not seen Oby since the Black Saturday. Partly because he was studiously avoiding her, and partly because he was very busy with his thesis. He had a deadline to meet.

He thought Oby was too pained by the magazine to want to see him. He, too, did not want to see her in her pained state. The day after *The Bee* came out, he had stepped out of his hostel, flicked his lighter with his right hand while holding up the magazine with his left. It took time lighting up, but when it did, it was all ashes in a few minutes. He stood there in the full view of students returning from church as he watched the magazine burn up.

Everyone paused, stunned. Suddenly, the silence was broken. Some cheered. Others jeered. It was a one-man protest. A dance with the deaf.

There had never been an agreement on the role of *The Bee* among students. Not now. Nor ever. It was fun when others were being humiliated. The larger question of moderation and decency could wait. Until it hit home. The naked aggression against women was part of campus entertainment. Powerless and disorganised, they were used against each other. No one asked why. You simply endured or watched other people's pain and anguish.

That day, Chris got ready to go to see Oby. But on the way, his courage failed him. No. It was his emotions that failed him. He didn't know how to react if Oby was not holding up well. He turned and headed back to his hostel.

A week was what he needed to pull himself together. Why couldn't they do more to protect her? Could he have done something beyond following Okoro's plan? These questions bothered him.

Oby had come out of her class and was walking towards the Administration Block when she felt a soft hand on her shoulders. She sniffed in the air like a blind dog guessing at who it was. She did not have to sniff. She placed her hands on his hand without looking back.

"Chris, where have you been?" She turned and hugged him heartily. Chris held her tightly as he pecked at her cheek.

"Oby, how now?" was all he could say, not answering the question directly. He understood the question: Why were you not there to share in my pain?

"You are one person I have wanted to see for days. Chris, this university na wa, oo!" Oby said as she held his hands and led him towards the park, to one of those familiar concrete seats. She was anxious to talk to Chris. She had even thought of going to his hostel. Her enthusiasm was only checked by the thought that she might be opening herself up to another *Bee* attack. It was too much to risk so soon.

"Chris, I asked where you have been. Your sister has been fried several times over," she said as they sat down.

"I know what you mean. Oby, I am very sorry. To tell you the truth, I was hiding. I could not bring myself to see you after *The Bee* came out. Knowing you, I thought you would be devastated. I just couldn't."

"You just couldn't do what?"

"See you in such a state." He was avoiding her gaze.

"Oh Chris! Your sister is learning fast. In the jungle, you learn to adapt. Man-eat-man or is it man-eat-woman? If you are bitten, you get immunity. No be so?"

"Oby, you never cease to amaze me. I just wished that we ... I mean, I could have done something to prevent all this. I felt so helpless."

"Don't get me wrong. I cried like a baby after reading *The Bee*. But thanks to Chike, I quickly got over it. He was so wonderful. He came that day and took me out. It was a very courageous thing to do."

"That was nice of him. I just wish that I could have ..."

"Well, Chike told me of the plans you all had to prevent the publication of *The Bee*. That was really sweet of you."

"That was basically Okoro's plan," said Chris.

"But you all supported it and gave ideas."

"Well, I guess we did."

'Don't be so hard on yourself. I have put *The Bee* behind me. I

276

have even a greater burden than *The Bee*. This one will make or break me."

"What are you talking about?" Chris asked anxiously.

"My brother, as I said, the jungle is full of traps. You skip one, you are caught in the other. You can never be immunised against all the attacks. Never! You have to learn to hop, skip and jump."

"Oby! What is it? Do I look like a mind reader?"

"You know Prof Akpanu, don't you?"

"Oh my God!" The man was a snake. Every animal in the jungle fears the snake. Especially those with poisonous fangs. It was better not to encounter him.

"What is it, Chris?"

"No. Please go on. I am sorry."

"Don't interrupt me," Oby said without even a flicker of smile.

"I am sorry."

"The Prof has been hitting on me. I have mentioned this to you guys before but nobody paid attention. Now the man wants to fail me. That much he has told me. Unless ..."

"Unless what? That toad! Over my dead body."

"Chris, this is very serious. The same day *The Bee* came out, I was in his house."

"In his house? You must be joking! In whose house?"

"In Prof Akpanu's house. I went there to review my term paper."

"You don't dine with a snake. Not in his own lair. And then ..."

"Yes, I am not that naive. I went to his office early that morning as we had agreed. He had forgotten the term paper in his haste, and so on and so forth."

"Yeah right! I hope that he forgot his ugly, short dude at home as well!"

"Chris!"

"I am sorry. Then what happened?"

"Oh! To cut the story short, he came after me like a sex-starved gorilla."

"Gorilla indeed. That man is ugly."

"That is besides the point. I thank God that I got out okay. It could have been worse."

"Yes, it could have been worse," his head and legs were shaking.

"So how did you get out?"

"A combination of charm, lies and promises."

"Promises?" Chris stood up.

"Yes, I told him that next Saturday he will have his way."

"I will kill him first."

"Stop saying that. You would soon be dead. And please sit down and lower your voice."

"Oby, look. This bastard has got away with this for years. Not this time. Not with you. Over my ...." He didn't quite complete that as his eyes caught Oby's.

"What can we do?" Tears were rolling down her cheeks. Chris offered his handkerchief.

"Don't worry," he said at length.

"Don't worry? I have a date with the man next Saturday. What should I do?"

"If he lays his hands on you again, kick him as hard as you can between his legs," Chris suggested rather helplessly.

"Do what?"

"Kick him. Whatever he says, don't agree to go to his house."

"Chris are you out of your mind? Do you know what that means? I will fail his course and I will never graduate. This is not an elective course, you know."

Again, Oby began to cry. She used the handkerchief to muffle her sobs and wipe her tears. Chris, helpless, had his arms around her and was tapping his feet on the ground. He was struggling to control his own tears. He must not expose his weakness. He was going to do whatever it took to assist her. This was the defining moment.

"Oby, this is the end of the road for Prof Akpanu. As they say, many days for the thief, but one day for the owner. This is the limit. His cup is full! Take it from me."

"I have often wondered, why me? Of all the girls in his class, why me?"

"Because you are special. Very special. The type men go to war for. Prof Akpanu likes the taste of special things. But not this time."

278

"But why have all these girls not done anything to stop him before?"

"Because it takes a special and courageous person like you to do something."

"Me?"

"Yes. Oby, do you remember the civil rights movement in the US?"

"Yes, I know a little bit of that US history."

"Well, it was basically started by a young woman who refused to move to a back seat in a bus to allow a white man take her front-row seat. Remember this was mandated by law. Her refusal not only ignited a massive public bus-boycott, but it led to civil disobedience. The United States has never been the same since."

"Chris, I am not Rosa Parks, and you are not Martin Luther King Jnr." She had a deep sense of humility and an awareness of the historical and circumstantial differences of the two events and the key players. "I am Oby Onyia, a simple village girl from Isiakpu. The first member of my family to go to university. I cannot afford to blow this chance. It will devastate my mom. Who will fight for me?"

"Oby, you have missed the point. It takes one person to start a revolution. Perhaps God wants to use you." She thought about that for a while: "Perhaps God wants to use you."

"Maybe God will fight for me?" she said. For a moment, her faith uplifted her. But only for a moment.

"Maybe," Chris answered. "Maybe." He wanted to say that it would be divine intervention with a human hand but didn't. He wouldn't be able to explain it. Not yet!

"I am scared, Chris. I am very scared." She looked at her watch. She still had a few minutes to get to her next lecture.

"Everything will be okay," Chris reassured her as he stood up. He held her and kissed her lips. It was the first time that this had happened. Its significance was, however, lost in the debris of her greater burden.

"I will let you know what happens on Saturday," she said. "Please pray for me." She ran towards the classroom.

They had been together for close to an hour, but the time had passed easily. It was that time of the year when students were busy with term papers, and the mid-term examinations were still on. Students crisscrossed the compound, preoccupied with their thoughts. No one paid them any attention. Sitting where they did, in the middle of the garden, they were out of normal eyes' range.

As Chris walked towards the library, he remembered one of Martin Luther King's quotations: "True peace is not merely the absence of tension, it is the presence of justice." Justice for all.

The following day, it was business as usual for Oby. She got back to her hostel at about 3 pm. A letter lay on her bed. It was from her mother. It had all the usual characteristics: Her brother's handwriting and a short khaki envelope with five two-naira stamps pasted across the envelope from the top right hand corner downwards. Although her mother read the Bible in Igbo she could not write in English. The sender's name and address were often obscured by these stamps.

She picked up the envelope with the Nsukka postmark, stamped over a month back. It sometimes took two months for a letter to get to Embakassi from Nsukka. She placed her books on the desk and threw herself on her bed. She was very eager to hear what Mama had to say.

She wanted to know how Oby was faring. There were no telephones in Isiakpu. To post the letter, her mother had had to send one of the children to Nsukka Post Office near the police station. Despite her problems on campus, Oby was equally concerned about her mother and wanted to know all that had happened in Isiakpu.

She tore the envelope eagerly. In her haste, she almost tore a part of the letter. Finally, there it was:

My dear Oby,

How are you, my daughter? I have been thinking about you a lot recently. I hope that you are fine. I am relying on our good Lord to protect you. Each night, before we go to bed, we thank God for our lives and for your life in particular, and we ask God to protect you in that strange land where there is no father, no mother or relation.

I am slowly rebuilding my shop. Business has picked up. Everybody wants to buy from Mama Oby. I don't know whether it is just good fortune, sympathy or curiosity. But business has never been better. I want to expand the shop a little but I am waiting for you to come back and give me advice. Please don't forget to write to your uncle in Onitsha to thank him for everything.

I don't want you to worry about anything. God is on our side. Your uncles and their wives have become closer and friendlier as if the deceased Papa (may his soul rest in peace) was responsible for the cold reception we received from the family. I know that he was revered, but I did not know that he was feared. It is said that it had to be this way, but we take it that it is the way God wanted it. Nothing surprises God.

Fr Damian has left Isiakpu. Did you know that? You people, the educated ones, have a way of knowing things even before they happen. We heard that he was given a scholarship to go to Rome for further studies. We thank God for his life and pray for him. Let God forgive all of us our trespasses. Amen. We have a new priest, Fr Michael Anayo. He is much older. We are still observing him. But in his few months in Isiakpu, he has taken steps to have everybody reconciled. The Catholic Church is back again. We are one family. It is a miracle. Please praise God for that.

Now, how are you, my daughter? How is school? I hope that you are studying hard. Don't let anything distract you. I have not gone to university but I know that the eyes of many wolves in men's clothing will be on a young beautiful woman like you. Even your lecturers! You must resist all temptations. You must refuse the devil and all his machinations. Prayers will conquer everything. Don't sell your dignity for the sake of a degree. In a strange land, the stranger must always be on full alert. We want you to graduate and you will graduate by the grace of God. Cow wey no get tail, na God dey drive am flies!

All your brothers and sisters are fine. They send their warm greetings. We are hoping that God will answer our prayers this year with respect to Amechi's university admission. He is also getting restless. He is not discussing anything but business. After this year, we will let him go. You should write him a letter to tell him not to give me hypertension in this house. All will be well. Our Father in Heaven has already ordained it. We just have to do our best.

Finally, I hope that you have been reading your Bible. Knowing the word of the Lord, is the beginning of wisdom. When you are in difficulty, run to Him. When you are happy, rejoice with Him. Every occasion is reflected in the Psalms. That is what you were brought up on, that is what I hope you are living on. Praise be to Him for He has bestowed His blessings on us.

Take very good care of yourself. God bless you, my daughter. And don't do anything silly!

Your loving mother,

Madam Onyia.

Oby held the letter to her chest as she lay on her back with her eyes closed. She was relieved that her mother was happy. Even if she wasn't, she would not say so. But the letter was written from the heart. As always!

How she wished her mother was here. If only she knew what she was going through. "Who will fight for me? Where are you, mom?" Immersed in these thoughts and questions without answers, Oby fell asleep.

"No! No, no! Stop it, Prof! Stop it!" Oby shouted. She kicked her bedcover away and sat up on her bed, supporting herself on both hands. She was sweating. There was no one else in the room, thank God. She did not have to explain her dream to anyone.

She had lain partially naked on the couch in the professor's office, but her legs were tightly locked together. Prof Akpanu was about to enter her, by force. He had had enough of her teasing. Her mind was not made up. As he came down on her with his full weight, she started to yell and kick.

She stood up and, just to reassure it was a dream, checked that she still wore her pants. She was visibly shaken even as she walked to the bathroom.

She remembered her mother's advice: "Prayer will conquer all." She remembered Jesus Christ in the final hours before he was betrayed by Judas, and his arrest by the chief priest and scribes on the orders of Pontius Pilate. She remembered his prayer at the Garden of

Gethsemane: "Lord, if it were possible, the hour might pass me by. Abba! Father! All things are possible for Thee; Remove this cup from me; yet not what I will but what Thou wilt. My Father, if it cannot pass away unless I drink it, Thy will be done." She took her Bible from a bedside drawer and read the entire chapter."Keep watching and praying, that you may not enter into temptation; the spirit is willing, but the flesh is weak." She knew what she didn't want to do. But she didn't know how to get out of her quagmire. Her spirit was willing to fight Prof Akpanu but her instincts warned her of the consequences of such a fight. When she shut her Bible, she was still alone in her room fighting the mist in her eyes. Unfortunately, the eyes that cry are also the eyes one sees with. The Bible was a great source of courage and inspiration for her. But her immediate worry remained: "Who will fight for me?"

It had rained all night on Friday and Oby lay awake, tossing and turning in her bed. Her appointment with Prof Akpanu was the next day. It was still a toss-up. She didn't know whether to go or not. If she did go, she wasn't sure what she should do. She had looked for divine guidance; none was forthcoming. Only a deadly bolt of lightning could save her. For sure, that was the only thing that would prevent Prof Akpanu from keeping the appointment. She did not want to wish him ill, but she still hoped some *dens ex machina* would step in and save her.

She stepped out of the hostel in a dark-blue flowery dress and carrying her college handbag. It had some books in it. Some camouflage! After all she was going to consult her professor. She also carried a short, ladies umbrella. She had thought all night about what to wear. A pair of blue jeans was always a tough one to crack. At least, it would make the struggle labour-intensive. But what was the point? By keeping the appointment, was she not more than halfway there? If she wore her flowery dress, it would be easy to get it over with.

The sky was deep blue and overcast. There was hardly anyone walking around the university that cold morning. To walk out of view of the watching eyes, the binoculars, and the birds, she took a long route to Prof Akpanu's office. She walked as if going off the campus, stopped shortly before the gate and made a dramatic and quick left turn. She was now hidden between blocks of offices and lecture rooms. On her way, she encountered two campus workers, but did not look up. They, too, were in a hurry. They were going home after night duty. But what was there to raise their curiosity? They had seen worse things, the kind of things that Okoro had described, and some more.

Once away from the blocks of lecture rooms, she quickened her pace. As Prof Akpanu's office came into sight, his old jalopy was parked in front of his office. He had nothing to hide. He was ready for the appointment.

The door was open. "Come in," he said when he heard the timid knock. He smiled, stood up from his desk and went to receive Oby. He locked the door after her. His victim was firmly in the cage.

"Good morning, Prof."

"Good morning, my dear," he smiled and placed his hands on her shoulders. He was wearing a rumpled T-shirt and loose khaki trousers, which were not ironed either.

"How was your conference, sir?"

"Hectic. Very hectic," he rambled on for a few minutes, saying how he had mesmerised everybody with his statistical ingenuity. Oby maintained a mock smile, listening, but hearing nothing. He seemed unusually gay so early in the morning. A bottle of Johnnie Walker whisky stood on his desk. He went for the bottle and poured himself a third drink. He was already celebrating his conquest in advance. Oby sat meekly, hands folded across her chest. She was deep in thought, cold but sweating.

"Want a drink, my young lady?"

"No, sir."

"It is good for this cold weather."

"Thank you, sir."

"You have something for me young lady, don't you?"

"What?" Oby asked with sudden alertness.

"I have something for you," said Prof Akpan. He pulled out his drawer and took out a wrapped gift. A cheap, make-believe, gold-coated bangle almost as expensive as the wrapper.

284

He sat on the couch and invited Oby over to receive her gift. He did not give Oby a chance to unwrap the gift, he did it himself. His breath reeked of alcohol not minding her discomfort since entering his office, he bent over and kissed her on the lips. She did not respond. More importantly, she did not object. So he squeezed her breast. Oby cried out in pain. He was momentarily startled, and apologised. He laid her on the couch gently like a mother puts her baby to sleep. He began to tell her how nice she looked but all his words were flying by her ears. She lay stiff, uncommunicating, her hands across her chest. He slowly began to take off her clothes. First the shoes. He paused after each item to gauge her reaction. Not that he cared, but it was important in informing his next move and his temperament. He went for a fourth drink. A quick gulp. He slid his right hand under her dress. Oby moved and changed position without any apparent serious objection.

"Relax, my dear," he said. "I am not going to hurt you. Akpanu just wants a small *buttei*. It keeps the professor happy, and the student gets what she wants." He was drunk and smiling all by himself. He tried again.

First, he pulled the elastic band of her pants. It snapped and Oby jerked up. She was still stiff and had her teeth clenched. He skillfully manoeuvred the pants down her legs. He had certainly done this many times before. Once the pants were past the knee, the rest was always easy. He stood up, unzipped his trousers and pulled them down, leaving them unfolded on the floor. He hesitated for a moment. Then he dropped his pants. He bent over and finally removed Oby's pants. He did not drop them on the floor. He flung them on his desk.

It was now time for action. He bent over to kiss her while trying to hold her legs apart.

Oby had a sudden surge of energy. She had suddenly sat up and, with both hands resting firmly on the couch, kicked Prof Akpanu between the legs. The kick was packed with such strength the force of it sent the man rolling back, clutching his groin and writhing in pain.

Oby got up, did not even look at him, took her pants, and put them back on quickly. She grabbed her bag and made for the door. He tried to get up but couldn't. He was in serious pain.

As she dashed out of the door, she collided with a man wearing a bowler hat and dark glasses. It was Chris. He dashed into Prof Akpanu's office and started clicking away with his camera. He took a dozen pictures of the professor lying naked on the floor with both hands between his legs. He twisted and turned in an effort to avoid the camera, like a rat avoiding a torch light. But Chris followed him. He wanted his face on all the pictures. This was the end of the road for Prof Akpanu. His final chapter was being written in an unanticipated and undignified manner. He would have preferred to be the author but no, a village girl was rewriting the rules of the game in which he had become the villain.

"That bitch set me up. That bitch set me up. I am going to get her. That bitch set me up," he muttered in between cries of pain and anguish. Chris felt like kicking his ass but thought better of it. Chris walked away, quietly shutting the door behind him.

Oby was sobbing in one of the empty classrooms. What had she done? What would become of her? Her university education? Would the professor be okay?

Chris knew that she would not have gone far. He looked for her in the empty classrooms. When he found her, she shot up and fell into his arms with teary eyes and a running nose. He used his handkerchief, a regular part of his dressing, to wipe her eyes and nose.

"Will he be okay?" Oby asked.

"Why are you worried about him?"

"Chris, will he be okay?"

"The s.o.b. will be okay. It hurts, that is all. And he deserves the pain."

"I am sorry. I didn't mean to hurt him."

"Let's get out of here before you start your guilt-tripping. Who is the victim here?"

"And you, what brought you here?" Oby asked with a flash of a smile.

"I know where we can get a warm breakfast. We can talk when we get there."

Oby took out a comb from her bag, patted her hair backwards and held it with a hair band. She smoothed the edges with her comb.

In less than ten minutes, they were in a restaurant in one of the obscure parts of Embakassi town. It had been a silent taxi ride from the campus gate. They had both sat at the back, Oby's head resting on his shoulder. Her heart was pounding. Chris had his arms around her. She was very worried about the future, her future at the university. Was this the end of the road? Chris was not sure how to translate his emotions to Oby. What he wanted, he couldn't get. What he had was not good enough.

The restaurant was a familiar setting for Chris. He had been there on two other occasions. It was Ifeoma, his bush meat from the Nursing School, who had introduced him to the place. This was not Hotel Metropol, Okoro's favourite spot. But it wasn't infested with prostitutes either. This was not Cash Madam's beer parlour where armchair politicians and critics drowned each other's voices. This was a very neat *buka*, simple, clean. For some reason only religious pictures adorned the light-blue wall, as if they were intended to send a message of sobriety. The single but large-roomed *buka* was hardly illuminated by its single window. Its tasty and reasonably priced food was its only advertisement. Chris chose a secluded corner where they could talk privately.

"What am I going to do?" Oby asked as soon as they had placed their orders.

"Your troubles are over," Chris told her, confidently.

"What do you mean?"

"The man is finished. We have finished him."

"How do you mean?" Oby asked.

"First, you humiliate the man. Then I capture everything on my camera. Wait till he sees his naked butt in print," Chris said triumphantly.

"You are going to send the pictures to him?" Oby asked agitatedly.

"Of course. That is the idea. The pictures will silence him. Forever! There are no two ways about it."

"Silence him, eh?"

"Yes. We now have strong evidence in the photos. That's powerful evidence."

"What if he ignores the evidence? Who cares in this university?" Oby was trying to close all the loopholes. She did not want to cling onto false hope.

"The man is not a fool. He is a professor. I will send him one or two copies of the picture, and that will do it. He has his enemies in this university as well. Such people will want to lay their hands on these pictures."

"Really?"

"Trust me. It will be a silent truce. He will never bother you again. He will even think twice before he bothers another female student."

"We have to pray that your camera does not play tricks on us," Oby said as she looked over Chris' shoulder to make sure that the camera was still hanging firmly from the seat.

"You bet. This is not one of those two-for-a-penny cameras. Straight from London where quality work is done. Even though I said it casually, I felt that somehow, you would remember to kick the man between his legs."

The two laughed and Oby tried to cover her face.

"No. I didn't take you seriously. Quite frankly, I wasn't thinking about kicking him until it happened. I cannot explain it. It just happened. I think it was the Holy Spirit."

"Whatever it was, it worked according to plan. Even if you didn't kick the man, I was going to break that door and still catch him red-handed."

"You, break the door?"

"Yes, I had assembled the stones. Huge chunks. The ones left over from the new building," Chris said.

"Chris. Is this you?"

"There is an Okoro in all of us. If something is important to you, you will find a way of accomplishing it."

"I am very grateful," she said as she looked up at the young Embakassi girl who placed a plate of hot *akamu* maize porridge and hot *akara* fried beanballs before her. It was everyone's morning delicacy in that part of Nigeria.

"You are welcome," the waitress said, unaware Oby was responding to Chris. He looked at her and the two laughed.

288

"You know, Oby, I did not sleep last night. I went around Prof Akpanu's office to survey the environment. It was then that I discovered that the peeping hole on his door was not working well. You can actually see someone inside his office even though it would be somewhat fuzzy. At least you can see movements. So I knew that I would be able to time my entry."

"So, Chris. What did you see?" Oby asked excitedly. "I hope you didn't see what you were not supposed to see?"

"I will tell you some other day."

"No, tell me now," Oby said as she gave him a spoonful of *akamu*.

"Oh, you want me to tell you the colour of your pants?"

"Hey Chris! Was that what you were supposed to be looking at?"

"Well ..."

"So what colour was it?"

"Let us just say that it has some flowers on it," Chris guessed.

"Thief!"

"Do you want me to tell you the size?"

"No."

"I even saw your foggy bottom."

"Foggy what?"

"Never mind. It is just an American expression."

"So did you see me enter Prof Akpanu's office."

"Of course. I took my position at around 6.00 am. I saw him drive up to his office and I saw you walk in like you were entering a funeral parlour." They burst out laughing again.

"Chris, I can't thank you enough. I mean, seriously. I had no idea that you could do all that you did."

"*Enenia nwa ite, ogbonyua oku.* Never underrate the capacity of a small pot, it too, has the potency to put off a huge fire."

"Chris! It is not like that. It is just that ... you know."

"You know what?"

"You are such a gentleman. You know ... polished, sweet and all that."

"But Oby, look at you, beautiful, intelligent, warm, cultured and very considerate. *Ibu Nwanyi eji eje mba.* You are the sort of lady that a man proudly takes to foreign places. An ambassador!" Chris was shaking his head to indicate that it was too late for him. His friend was way ahead of him in the queue. Oby was spoken for. It was his loss.

As their plates were cleared, Oby reached across the table and held his hands. Her palm was sweaty and his heart was racing again.

"Chris. You are my friend and you will continue to be my friend. I will never forget what you did for me today."

"It is not like that, Oby. I simply wish it could be otherwise. Why is today not yesterday? Why? I wish I could turn the hand of the clock backwards. How I wish I was the one who volunteered to take you to your hostel that fateful afternoon when you arrived at the campus for the first time. I guess we will never know. What if?"

"What are you talking about, Chris? You are making me nervous."

"Oby, have you ever thought of us ... You know as ..."

"As what?" Oby wanted to take back the question as soon as she asked it. She understood the question but did not want to answer it. She tried to place her hands on his mouth to prevent him from answering the question. It was too late.

"... As a couple. Have you, ever?" He tightened his grip on her hand as if to squeeze out an answer.

She simply nodded in the affirmative, her lips pursed tight. Her eyes were becoming misty again. She took the handkerchief from her bag and dabbed at her eyes.

"Chris, please!"

"I have often wondered what we could be. I have even dreamt, several times, of what life would be like with you. I guess we will never know."

"Chris, please! Why are you doing this to me?" she pleaded as she wiped her eyes again.

Chris excused himself and went to the bathroom. He had to straighten himself up.

When he came back, Oby was standing up. She handed the camera over to him with a look that said her life depended on it.

"I think we should head back to the campus," Oby said.

"I think so, too." He paid the bill and hailed a taxi.

A week later, Chris sent two copies of the pictures to Prof Akpanu. They were the ugliest of the lot. He enclosed a note that simply read: "There is more from where these came. Do the right thing or else ... You have been warned."

Oby revised her term paper and turned it in. She had no contact whatsoever with Prof Akpanu except in the lecture hall. He missed half of the lectures anyway. In the end, she got a B in the course, which she thought was the grade she deserved.

CHAPTER TWENTY-FIVE

A woman's period one week late, when she is used to having it regularly, is a source of concern. Two weeks late is alarming.

In the midst of Oby's troubles she did not even notice that she was past her due time. It is not unusual for anxiety and sleeplessness to alter the clock. Given what she had gone through lately, a week's delay would not be unusual. But two weeks was quite unusual. There were no other indications that anything was wrong.

She had always been very careful about her relationship with Chike. She had insisted on Chike using a condom. He, in turn, was trying to persuade her to go on the pill. She had consulted with a physician, Dr Ema Inyang, on the possibility of going on the pill. The regime was extremely rigid, and the side effects unclear.

"It varies from person to person," she was advised. Dr Inyang was very conservative. She was a sturdy little woman who had divorced and was a staunch defender of women's rights. She wanted to know why an unmarried woman would take the pill. Her advice was that if one wanted to have sex, one should ask her partner to use a condom. Oby had agreed, and that was the way it had been with Chike for the most part. On one occasion, however, they got carried away in the flood of passion and when they thought of what they had not done, it was too late. Nothing happened. This time, the timing may have been off and the consequences dire.

She brought out a calendar and tried to figure out her unsafe days. Bingo! While she was not a master on this, it appeared that the day on which *The Bee* stung Oby, was her most fertile hour. Nature had a way of playing tricks on women. You are most vulnerable when you are most unsafe. As she stared at the calendar, her breathing became audible and her heart raced. What if? What if she was pregnant? She didn't want to think about it. But she could not escape to fantasy island.

Her mind was now focused on the problem at hand. There was only one option. She would have to marry Chike, give birth to the baby and request her mother to look after the child. Her education would go on uninterrupted. It would be the best option. Abortion? That was out of the question. Oby remembered with terror her mother's dream which she had shared with her during the holidays. In the dream, her mother was shown how Oby would die if ever she had an abortion.

She had taken it as a divine message and passed it on to Oby. At every opportunity, her mother tried to reinforce the message. Sometimes subtly, sometimes not so subtly. It was a very serious message passed in a light tone. It was a message Oby would not want to put to test. The consequences for a "doubting Oby" might be too great to contemplate. Death! In spite of her religion, she was not ready to pass on to glorious heaven yet. But she was racing ahead of herself. Nothing was known for sure. There were girls who skipped their period for months and there were others who never had it at all.

That evening, as she was having her bath, she examined her body, looking for tell-tale signs. She pressed her breasts to check for unusual tenderness, for any change in the shape of the nipples. Nope! Everything was the same. No increase in size either. Her abdomen was as flat as it could be. There was nothing to suggest that anything was amiss. But the only way of confirming whether she was pregnant or not was to take a preganancy test. Or should she wait a little longer?

She was scared. What would her mother say? Would this bring shame to the Onyia family? Would this interrupt her education? Would this cause a celebration for the likes of Mama Ijeoma? What would her fellow university students say? A naive village girl had succumbed to the pressures of university life. Where was her common sense? Where was all that her mother had taught her?

At the University of Embakassi, this was not one of the stories that made the rounds. It was a non-issue. The answer was simple. If you were pregnant, you got rid of the pregnancy. Simple! It was between you and your boyfriend. God would understand the necessity. God would forgive you. There was no moral quagmire. There was no right to life movement. No anti-abortion movement. On paper, it was illegal.

In practice, everyone did it and no one got prosecuted. Doctors only reminded the patient of the illegality in order to underscore the risks and justify the high charges. It was an expensive affair. But that was no deterrent.

Oby knew only too well that the road that was well travelled was not necessarily the road to salvation. She knew that on this issue many students voted with their feet. On this issue, a key democratic principle breaks down: the majority does not carry the day. The gap between truth and reality was wider. Is there absoluteness in truth? Is truth universal? Are truth and morality one and the same thing? Isn't reality used to check the truth? Do moral standards vary across space and time? What of the cultural context? Perhaps the moral standards of a university are more complicated than those of a simple village like Isiakpu?

She tossed and turned over these questions. There were no answers. She must resolve everything herself. She was exhausted, but sleep was not taking advantage of her weakened body. Her brain was still fully alert.

Oby was at the doctor's clinic first thing in the morning. It was easy to see that she had not slept well. She was very anxious. As a matter of routine, all non-expectant patients to this gynaecological clinic submitted their urine sample for laboratory tests. One of the key tests was the pregnancy test. This was often conducted before the patient saw the doctor.

The doctor was late in coming to the clinic. Oby was pacing back and forth, and the nurses were murmuring and giggling at her apparent discomfort. They had seen her kind of agitation many times before.

"Yes, Miss Onyia. What brought you here today?" Dr Inyang asked as she ushered Oby into her consulting room.

"I don't know. I came to have a test and ... ehm ..." Oby said, trying to avoid the doctor's eyes.

"The pregnancy test? I can see that it is confirmed positive."

"Positive?" Oby cried in anguish.

"Is that not what you wanted?" Dr Inyang asked with a touch of sarcasm.

"Of course not!" Oby tried to conceal her emotion.

"Well, I advised you earlier to insist that your partner uses the condom. Didn't I?"

"Yes, you know how it is. This was a mistake."

"Well, it is a costly mistake. But you don't have to worry. You can register with us for ante-natal care. We have a discount for students."

"Students?" Oby asked curiously.

"Yes, students. Some of whom are married, of course."

"How common is this?"

"Why are you worried about others. Come over here," the doctor gestured towards the examination couch. Oby lay stretched on the couch and the doctor passed her hands under her blouse and examined her abdomen, chest and pulse.

"When was your last period?"

"October 10."

"It looks like your EDD is July 17 next year."

"What is EDD, doctor?"

"Sorry. Expected Date of Delivery."

"So doctor, what do I do now?"

"What do you do? Have you discussed this with the father of the baby?"

"No."

"Well, that is the starting point. Do you know how he is going to react?"

"I have no idea. We have never discussed this scenario before. But he has been a very kind and generous guy."

"That is good. But I have seen men change, do a complete turn, once their girlfriends unexpectedly becomes pregnant. Men are something else. I think that they are from Jupiter. Let's hope this one is different."

"Well, I hope he is ready for it because I am going to have this baby."

"Good for you and good luck," said the doctor as she saw Oby to the door.

That evening, Oby went to Chike's room to seek him out, but he was not there. His roommate was just waking up from an afternoon nap. He had no idea where Chike was. Oby decided to wait. She must get this over with today. She tried to distract herself with an old *Time* magazine, but her mind would not be deceived. Chike's roommate got ready and excused himself. Poor boy, he had been sent into exile quite a number of times, not necessarily on the account of Oby. Chike's other friends sometimes found it convenient to use his room as their rendezvous.

An hour later, Chike burst into the room. He had no idea that Oby was there, and her presence quite surprised him. This was a first. Chike always knew when Oby was expected in his room. Every detail of their romantic encounter was often planned well in advance. Even ordinary visits attracted the same detailed communication and plans. Today's was different. Oby was alone in the room, lying comfortably on his bed reading an old magazine.

"Oby, what a surprise!? Is everything okay or you are just missing your darling?" Chike sat on the bed and gave Oby a peck on the cheek.

"Everything is okay. Where have you been? I have been waiting for you for over an hour."

"I had no idea you were here," Chike said apologetically.

"Chike, you and I have been dating now for almost two years. You have been very loving and understanding. I can say the same for myself. Is that not right?"

"Yes, that is correct."

"I have also shared my aspirations, my ambition and all my future plans with you, haven't I?"

"Yes, you have. But where are all these questions leading to?"

"Please don't raise your voice. Is that door locked?" Oby asked a visibly anxious Chike. He stood up and went to lock the door.

He came back to the bed and sat down.

"Now Chike, you wouldn't do anything to hurt me, would you?"
"No."

"And you wouldn't do anything to humiliate me, would you?"

"Of course not. Now Oby, what are these questions all about? Did

296

you hear that I was going after another girl? Are my enemies at work again?"

"No! No! No! Chike. When you and I started this relationship, we promised to trust each other. I trust you."

"So what is the problem?" Chike asked somewhat confused.

"Chike, you know you are my first and my only one. It means a lot to me."

"That means a lot to me, too."

"Good. When we started this relationship you said that you would be in it for the whole hog. Is that not right?"

"Have I ever disappointed you?" Chike asked helplessly. He could not guess where this was leading to. Oby did not answer the question.

Said Chike, "I know that I did not protect you from *The Bee*. Not because we did not try. I know that I wasn't of much assistance with the Prof Akpanu problem. But I am happy that my good friend had a better plan. All of this is behind us now. You know, Oby, that I love you. So what is the problem?"

"Chike, I am pregnant."

"Pregnant?" His tone expressed his incredulity.

"Yes. EDD is July 17, next year."

"What is EDD for crying out loud?"

"Expected Date of Delivery, Chike. I went to see my doctor this morning."

"Delivery?" he said. "Who is talking about delivery? Are we not jumping too fast?"

"Well, if you are pregnant, don't you have to deliver?" Oby asked.

"Well, it depends."

"Depends on what?"

"It depends on the circumstances," Chike said as he stood up from the bed. He brushed his hair backwards with his left hand and walked towards his wardrobe. He was not looking for anything in particular. He was distressed.

"I can see that you are not happy," Oby said.

"I am not unhappy. How do you expect me to react to such news? It is not as if you were inviting me to a Christmas party."

"So what do you want us to do?" Oby asked as she sat up on the bed. She was ready for the worst.

"Oby, what options do we have? We are not married. We are both students. This might disrupt your education. I am confused."

"But who said that students can't get married. My mother will look after the child and my education will go on uninterrupted. Thank God, I will deliver during the long vacation."

"What are you talking about, Oby?"

"You heard me? Let's get married and have the child."

"Are you crazy? I love you and all that. But we are not ready. Period."

"We are not ready. Why don't you say that you are not ready, because I am." Oby's firm resolve was as a result of her mother's dream. At the back of her mind she truly believed that something terrible would happen to her if she had an abortion. But she did not want to tell Chike this. He would simply see it as superstition.

"Oby, you don't understand. I have planned that when I finish from here in a few months' time, I will go off for the youth service and be settled into a nice banking job by the time you are graduating. I have planned it, every inch of the way."

"So what do you want us to do?" Oby repeated, this time in a voice that demanded an answer.

"This news is trying to put a spanner in the works. Everything has been planned."

Chike was hoping that Oby would volunteer the answer herself. He had only one option in mind.

"Well, Chike you are not answering the question. For the umpteenth time, what do you want us to do?"

"Well, you have to have an abortion. I think that is our only option."

"Oh, really? Well, that is not an option for me," she said.

She had known it would come to this. But she did not know that the word abortion coming out of Chike's mouth would bruise her so much. She began to sob silently. Tears rolled down her cheeks. Chike reached into his wardrobe for a box of tissue. He handed it over to her, sat by her and placed his arm around her. Oby slowly threw his hand. She

298

wanted to be left alone. What was the point in being together if you always ended up alone when there was a problem? In this case a problem that was jointly created.

"I thought that I was loved," she said. "I thought that I could count on you. What hollow emptiness you leave in me. What was the meaning of those reassuring words, the poetic phrases? Chike, I thought that you loved me unconditionally. I gave myself to you freely and lovingly. What can I say? Now I know that words mean different things to different people."

Chike sat motionless like a stone. Oby straightened herself up and left the room without a word.

That evening, Chike sought the company of Okoro and Chris. He asked them to delay going to the cafeteria till much later when the crowd would be smaller and they could have some privacy. Because of the work on their theses and preparations for the final year examinations, they had tended to meet less often.

They arrived at the cafeteria at about the agreed time. The hall had only a handful of students. There was a risk of feeding on the crumbs if one arrived this late. But they were lucky. There was still a lot of food. The kitchen staff may have overestimated the number of students coming in for dinner. This happened from time to time, especially when the kitchen staff wanted doggy packs for their families. Chris, Chike and Okoro filled their plates with white rice, plantain, and beef stew. They went to a corner of the hall. Okoro was dying to know why Chike had asked to meet them.

"So Chike, what's on your mind?" Okoro asked, his mouth full of plantain.

"Oh well, why don't we finish eating first?"

"Finish our food?" Chris said. "Is that the new rule? You know we are all very busy, Chike."

"As you know, when a goat is able to eat the palm frond that a man is carrying on his head, it is basically belittling that man," Chike said as the others munched away.

"What is the essence of these half-baked proverbs? Please get to the point," said Okoro.

299

"Chike, for a minute I thought that it was Okoro speaking. He has really infected you. Very soon you will join the chorus of 'according to my father'. You guys are perfecting the art of suspense," Chris said.

"Oby is pregnant," Chike said, surveying their expressions.

"What?" Chris blurted out.

"Control yourself, young man," Okoro said. Chris appeared to be shattered by the news. "This discussion is for the initiated."

"What are you talking about?" Chris asked.

"Congratulations, my friend. Welcome to the club," Okoro said as he extended his hands to Chike, ignoring Chris' query. Almost as a reflex, he accepted the handshake but immediately raised questions.

"Congratulations on what, Okoro? Let us be serious, please. I have called you guys here because I need your advice." Chike was visibly disturbed.

"I can tell you that congratulations are in order," said Okoro.

"How?" asked Chike.

"At least now we can call you a man. Do you know how many men would want to trade places with you? Do you know? Thousands. It means that you are not shooting empty shells. From where I come, congratulations would be in order."

Both Chike and Chris were looking at Okoro with amazement. His capacity to make light of serious matters was amazing.

"Chike, how do you know this for sure?" Chris asked with a sombre voice.

"Oby has done all the tests and the doctor has already given an EDD of July 17."

"What is EDD?" Okoro asked.

"Expected date of delivery," Chike sighed.

"So what does Oby think about all of this?" Chris asked.

"Oby wants to have the baby, and that is the trouble."

"Wants to have the baby? Ha! That's serious," Chris remarked.

"Of course, it is serious. Who told her that everyone who gets pregnant must have a baby? By now I would be having God-knows-how-many children," Okoro said.

"She is very adamant about this," Chike said.

"Adamant? Well, you have to consider what she thinks. There is no other way." Chris was trying to conceal his ambivalence on the issue. If Oby had a baby with Chike, that would seal his fate as far as his hopes on her were concerned. Yet, he would not want Oby to be hurt. It was a very difficult situation to be in.

"So you guys have discussed the abortion option," Okoro asked.

"She does not want to hear the word."

"Now I know why you are in trouble, Chike. Very soon, you will become Papa Emeka," Okoro started laughing.

"This is not a laughing matter," Chris admonished.

"What do you want me to do?" Okoro asked. "If our hands are tied, let us accept the inevitable. Either you are moving or you step aside. You cannot simply block the way."

"And what do you think, Chike?" Chris asked.

"What kind of a question is that? I told her that we should terminate the pregnancy and that I am not prepared for marriage now."

Okoro got more serious. "I see a slight problem. But I also think that Oby is posturing. My advice, and take it from an expert, is that you should go back to her and try to persuade her. Only you can do this. You know how women are. She was testing the waters. Besides, she is so emotional right now that she needs a little push to see reality. This will be your plan A."

Chris said he thought Okoro's was a good idea. "But knowing Oby, I wouldn't be surprised if her mind is already made up. In that case, you will be stuck. I would suggest that you handle this with utmost care."

"Oh no," Okoro protested. "That is not what I am saying. No one will be stuck with anything. It must be by mutual consent. One person cannot constitute the parents of a child. If persuasion fails, we shall try something else. I am from Aba, don't you guys forget. That will be plan B. It has never failed."

Chris wanted to know what Okoro had in mind. "What is plan B? You and your crude ideas! Make sure that you don't experiment with Oby. You will not find the consequences funny."

"You don't know what it is and you are already jumping," Chike said.

"Chike, I have been telling you that lately Chris has been crying more than the bereaved. Perhaps he knows the cause of death. You cannot use the hands of a baboon to steal meat from your friend's pot of soup because they resemble those of a human. You can hardly conceal it. That's all I have to say for now."

"What are you talking about?" Chris asked.

"He is talking about standing firm with a friend come what may!" Chike answered.

"I think we should get going," Chris suggested. The cafeteria was empty and theirs was the only table that was yet to be cleared.

A week later, Chike was in Okoro's room to activate plan B. Oby could not be persuaded. She was firm and resolved, buried deep in her religion and concerned about what her mother would say.

Chris felt intimidated. His conscience was torturing him because of the remarks made by both Chike and Okoro. A traitor? A traitor with a cause. He avoided making contact with Oby and could not forewarn her of plan B. He did not have any clue what it was. Besides, he did not want to embarrass Oby with his knowledge of her condition. She had not dared to confide in him either. Why risk his friendship with Okoro and Chike when it wasn't clear that he would be the natural beneficiary? Given Chris' position on issues, he was excluded from the execution of plan B.

Okoro travelled to Aba that Friday afternoon and returned the next day. Further delays would complicate matters. The more advanced the pregnancy the more the risks involved. Okoro and Chike were pleased with the outcome of Okoro's trip to Aba. He got to Aba late in the evening but was still able to commission the production of touch-and-go, as this abortion-inducing concoction was known. He paid slightly more for the urgent service. The concoction, in a powder form, was usually already ready. But it would be prepared in different ways depending on the size of the pregnancy. Okoro did not want to take chances. He asked for a potent one.

Touch-and-go dissolved completely in water or any other drink and was therefore especially appropriate in this case. Okoro had employed it before under similar circumstances and it had worked perfectly well.

Up till today, the girl still thought she had had a miscarriage. Girls who did not have money to pay the doctor for a D&C also used this method. With all its anguish and pain, it was effective in most cases and began working within hours. This was how it had got its name. It was an illegal drug, sold under strict confidential rules. It would be difficult to walk into the street and buy it but Okoro was not a newcomer to the game.

The plan involved convincing Oby that Chike had changed his mind and that he wanted them to have the baby and that they would marry. This would ease her tension and bring her closer to Chike and his friends. Touch-and-go would be mixed with a new flavoured punch bought specifically from Aba for the purpose of concealing any lingering tastes from the powder. Plan B would be executed without a hitch.

Oby spent that evening with Chike in his room. He was his usual self — romantic and very apologetic for what he called his childishness the past fortnight. Oby in turn reassured him that all would be well.

"What made you change your mind?" Oby asked.

"Well, you see, I prayed about it. I also realised what a wonderful wife and mother you were going to be."

"Have you told anyone?" Oby asked.

"Why?"

"It is possible that they put pressure on you," Oby asked.

"Pressure on me? You don't know me well."

"I know you very well. You succumb easily to pressure and quite frankly, that worries me about you."

"You have nothing to worry about."

"But seriously, have you told anyone?"

Chike hesitated before answering the question. "Yes, I have told my two friends on campus."

"Chris and Okoro?"

"Yes."

"What did they say?"

"They wanted me to handle it my way. They would support any decision we reached."

"That is interesting. Even Okoro? He had no wacko ideas?" Oby sounded very curious.

Chike responded nervously: "Okoro is so tied up with his thesis that his other ideas are drying up."

Oby asked for a drink. These days she often had a dry mouth and throat. Chike took a sip of the punch already mixed with the touch-and-go and offered it to Oby. She was thirsty and gulped down the entire drink.

"What sort of flavour is this?"

"This is punchy peach. Here is the packet." He showed her the sachet Okoro had bought at Aba.

"You and your exotic punch drinks. This one tastes unusual but I like it."

"I'm glad you do. Oby, I told you that I have a meeting with my thesis professor in a few minutes. If you like, you can stay here, but I have to run."

"Oh no. I have some assignments I must complete this evening in my room," Oby said.

All night, Oby could not sleep. She experienced pains that started like menstrual cramps, intensifying as each minute went by. Initially, she thought of enduring it all in silence. She sat up and went to use the restroom. That was when she noticed the first blood spots. She came back to the room and searched for her sanitary towels. She found one, but the spots were becoming heavier by the minute.

What was happening? She could not tell. Perhaps this was normal in pregnancy. Perhaps it was what they called a miscarriage. She had no idea. But she was in pain and was passing thick clots of blood. She started praying and silently chanting Psalm 23. Her two roommates were fast asleep.

She thought of waking them up. Perhaps they would know what was happening to her. When she stood up, her sanitary towel dropped with a huge lump of clotted blood besides her bed. She knew then that something was seriously wrong. She woke her roommates. It was now almost 6 am.

She explained to them what she had been going through all night. For the first time she told them that she was pregnant. It did not shock them. They were much older. They had seen it all. They knew that she was having a miscarriage. They asked her whether she had taken anything to induce an abortion and she, of course, innocently denied any knowledge of what they were talking about.

Oby, supported by her roommates, walked slowly up to the campus gate. She did not want anyone else to know what was happening. She wanted to go to her gynaecologist, the same tough doctor she saw whenever she had a problem. One of her roommates went with her to the clinic while the other went in search of Chike, Chris or Okoro. Oby gave the three room numbers in case Chike was not in his room. Chris' hostel was the closest to the gate.

Ada got to him first and asked him to let Chike know Oby had been taken to the hospital in serious condition. She provided no further details since she did not know how much they knew. Besides, this was not the sort of ailment that you talked too much about.

The doctor was summoned from her house, a few minutes' drive away. She was furious at having her early morning sleep interrupted. But when she saw Oby, she knew there was an emergency. Oby was still passing blood and was feverish. Before the doctor could finish asking her questions on what could have happened to her, Oby passed out. She knew that this was not normal. The nurses readied the small theatre attached to the clinic for a D&C and the doctor tried to revive Oby. She controlled the flow of blood and immediately set out to perform the D&C. Chris arrived at the clinic after sending a note to Chike. He suspected foul play immediately but had no way of proving anything. This must be plan B, he thought. He waited outside while the doctor and the nurses did their best to save Oby's life. He was soon joined by Chike, who was sweating even that early in the morning. On his way to the clinic he had branched off to Okoro's room to tell him what was happening. He dismissed it as not unusual and went back to sleep. But not for too long. His better senses caught up with him and he thought it best to make a quick emergency trip to Aba, just in case.

The doctor finished the D&C and as she waited for Oby to come to, she called the police. Then she set about interrogating Chike and Chris. Chris revealed that there was a plan B which he knew nothing about. Chike denied it initially but buckled under pressure. The doctor pretended that this was a matter between them and that only the truth would save Oby. With such assurance, he revealed the details.

"I was only doing it because I was afraid that it would hurt our future," Chike said as the doctor listened to the story of touch-and-go. Chris listened in disbelief.

"You wanted to kill her for your own future. You did not have her in mind."

"That is not true. I love her."

"You guys make me sick. You abuse the word love," the doctor said furiously.

"Chike, I warned you about Okoro and his crude ways."

"Who is Okoro?" the doctor asked.

"Please leave Okoro out of this. I am responsible for everything."

"Good. Because you will be going to jail. Alone," the doctor said.

"I thought that we were discussing this just between us."

"Oh no. I am compelled by law to report attempted murder. That was what you were trying to do. You wanted to kill an innocent girl who loved you unconditionally," the doctor said.

"Doctor, you don't mean ..."

"I don't mean what?"

"Are you going to turn this into a police case? I am the first son of my mother to go to the university. All hopes hinge on me, doctor. The university will expel me in my final year. This will ruin my life. Please help me, doctor," Chike cried.

"You should have thought about all of this before embarking on the mission to kill your girlfriend," the doctor said.

"That was not my intention. Chris, please plead with her. Beg her for me, please," Chike was sobbing like a baby. Chris sat motionless. He did not respond.

When the doctor stood up to check on Oby, there was a knock on the door.

A police sergeant in full uniform walked into the clinic.

"Good morning, doctor," the sergeant said.

"Good morning, officer. How are you?"

"I am fine. Did you call the station?"

"Yes, officer. Take this bastard away and charge him with procuring an illegal abortion. Better still, charge him with attempted murder," Dr Inyang gestured towards Chike.

"No, doctor. No, officer. It was only a mistake."

"Officer. Expect my report on this tomorrow. I will make sure that he rots in jail."

"Jail? Doctor what are you talking about. Have you asked Oby what she wants to do?"

"This is between you and the law. It is now out of Oby's hands."

"No. She loves me and I love her," Chike said tearfully.

"Officer! What are you waiting for?"

Chike was led away in handcuffs towards a police van parked across the street.

Dr Inyang walked into one of the rooms to check on Oby. She was recovering. She checked her pulse. It was normal. Oby stirred but did not turn.

"Oby, can you hear me?" the doctor asked. Oby did not reply.

"Oby, I said can you hear me?" Still there was no reply.

"Oby, there is a young man who is here to see you. His name is Chris."

Oby turned and smiled. Like someone who was in a happy dream.

Dr Inyang was surprised. "Oby, Chris is here." She wanted to use Chris' name since it seemed to work. Oby smiled again and opened her eyes.

"Chris, come in here," Dr Inyang called from the room.

It was now a wide smile as Chris took Oby's hands and stroked them.

"Oby, it is me. Chris."

Oby nodded as Dr Inyang, somewhat confused, left the room. He leaned over and kissed her gently on the lips. She responded with a broad approving smile. She was weak and tired. But she was sending enough signs to acknowledge Chris' affection.

"Oby, I am very sorry. I will never leave you again. I love you very much," Chris said as he leaned over her bed.

"I love you, too," Oby spoke for the first time since her surgery. It was a whisper. She did not have to say anything more.

Later that night, they sat looking out of the clinic window at the full moon and the passing clouds. They held each other and said very little for most of the time. Oby looked up at the sky and remembered the mad man at the beach who reminded Chike and her that the moon also sets. But she also remembered Psalm 121: "The sun cannot hurt you during the day, and the moon cannot hurt you at night. The Lord will protect you from all dangers. He will guide your life."